Cherish The Dream

He tread water next to her. "You're a quick learner, princess."

"Why do you call me that?" she demanded in mock irritation.

Amusement flickered over his rugged features. "The first time I laid eyes on you, I thought you looked like a princess from a fairy tale."

He grinned at her with wicked glee. Theodora pounded both hands against the surface, sending geysers of water spraying over his head and shoulders. Before he could grab her, she screamed in mock terror, dove under the water, and headed toward shore.

In two strokes he caught up with her. He grasped her waist and pulled her to him. Even under the dark water, his mouth found hers, and he kissed her roughly, passionately, possessively. . . .

Cherish the Dream

KATHLEEN HARRINGTON

AVON BOOKS ◆ NEW YORK

CHERISH THE DREAM is an original publication of Avon Books. This work has never before appeared in book form. This work is a novel. Any similarity to actual persons or events is purely coincidental.

AVON BOOKS
A division of
The Hearst Corporation
105 Madison Avenue
New York, New York 10016

Copyright © 1990 by Kathleen Harrington
Inside cover author photograph by Roy Daniels
Published by arrangement with the author
Library of Congress Catalog Card Number: 90-92993
ISBN: 0-380-76123-8

First Avon Books Printing: September 1990

AVON TRADEMARK REG. U.S. PAT. OFF. AND IN OTHER COUNTRIES, MARCA REGISTRADA, HECHO EN U.S.A.

Printed in the U.S.A.

RA 10 9 8 7 6 5 4 3 2 1

To my husband, Ed,
and my son, Rick,
with all my love

Chapter 1

June 1836
Fort Leavenworth
Kansas Territory

"**T**he Gordons have arrived, sir."

Carefully trimming his thick mustache in front of a mirror, Captain Blade Roberts snorted in disdain at the news. "It's about time those damn New England tenderfeet showed up. If they can't get to Leavenworth on time, how the hell do they think they can keep up with us crossing the mountains?"

Scowling, Blade strode over to his aide-de-camp, who remained at attention just inside the door. Taking the vellum paper extended to him, Blade turned it to catch the late-afternoon light streaming through the westerly window. The words were brief and penned in fancy calligraphy, as befitted the skilled mapmaker who had written them.

Have arrived. Delay unavoidable. We are at your service.
Theo. & Thos. Gordon

Blade crushed the paper and tossed it into a basket across the room. His orders snapped like a flag in a crisp wind. "Convey my compliments to the Gordon brothers, Lieutenant Haintzelman, and instruct them that their appearance at the ball tonight is mandatory."

At his junior officer's crisp salute, the scowling features on the captain's face softened, and he reached for a cheroot from inside his dress tunic. "That goes for you, too, Peter. If I have to attend this blasted, mealymouthed affair to honor our departure, by God, I'll not be the only martyr enduring the boredom. Half the ladies in Fort Leavenworth will expect a dance with at least one member of our expedition." He grinned, knowing Haintzelman was looking forward to the fete in their honor. More than once that week he'd spoken of waltzing with the commandant's lovely niece. "I'll expect you not to disappoint them."

Lieutenant Haintzelman returned the grin. "Yes, sir!"

As he watched the young man leave the room, Blade Roberts absently lit a Havana cheroot. He opened the door that led to the second-story balcony and walked out onto the portico that ran the entire length of the bachelor officers' quarters. Preoccupied, he gazed down at the bustling, late-afternoon traffic.

Protected by four sturdy log blockhouses, the square of the cantonment was filled with the equipment and supplies that would be required to undertake the arduous journey ahead of them. Tents, tools, small barrels of water, stout double canvas sacks of flour, coffee, and bacon stood in neat rows on the packed earth. Alongside these were tin canisters of butter oil and India-rubber sacks of sugar. Packages of dried vegetables, tea, and pemmican were stacked in mounds and carefully covered with tarpaulins. In the nearby stables, horses and pack mules were being readied. Their braying and bawling filled the still air. The sharp clang-clang of the blacksmith's hammer added to the cacophony, denoting the final touches being given to the harness equipment.

Blade knew that the members of the United States government's geological team would need everything they could carry. The real trick had been to pack only what was absolutely essential. During the months to come, there would be no luxuries that would slow down their progress. A distance of two thousand miles lay before them, and for most of those miles they would have to live as abstemiously as possible. They were taking only one wagon to transport the scientific equipment; all other supplies would be carried by animals, which could negotiate the treacherous, unmapped mountain passes.

Captain Roberts looked out over the walls of the stockade to the rolling sea of grass in the distance. Westward, beyond

Fort Leavenworth, toward the setting sun, stretched those unexplored miles of rivers, prairies, and deserts. Blade knew that the lives of forty men would be solely in his care once they left the protection of the outpost, and the consciousness of that responsibility spread into his reverie like a wildfire burning across the open country. He was determined to avoid the terrible casualties that had plagued Colonel Henry Dodge's campaign through Comanche territory only two years before. Needless casualties, resulting from ignorance and poor hygiene. As an ignored subordinate officer on that nightmare journey, Blade had watched in frustration while a third of the men fell, and had sworn to himself that no one placed under his command would ever suffer such a useless and unnecessary death. He knew what lay out there on the plains, where he had been raised.

A hawk, its wings spread wide, drifted on the downward current of a breeze as it sighted its prey, bringing to Blade images of the childhood he'd spent in a Cheyenne village—playing mock war games with his Indian cousins, learning to ride like the wind blowing across the prairie, proudly shooting his first bow and arrow with his noble grandfather beside him.

Suddenly and irresistibly, Blade's dark eyes were pulled from their survey of the hawk to follow the progress of a figure crossing the cantonment's wide square. The form was slim and curvaceous, the small back straight and proud. There was an arrogant tilt to the head, crowned by a magnificent mass of blond curls that seemed almost too thick and heavy for the long, slender white neck. Magically, the hair caught the fading sunlight and threw it back in sparks of gold. Straining to catch a glimpse of the woman's face, he placed his hands on the wooden railing and leaned out over the edge of the parapet.

Below, the company's blacksmith looked up from his work in the open doorway of his shop and, spotting the captain, nodded. "Afternoon, Captain Roberts," the sergeant called in his deep, booming bass.

Hearing the greeting, the young woman turned and looked upward, catching Blade's frank, open appraisal of her.

At the sight of her straight on, Blade sucked in his breath. She was exquisite. Wide, arching brows framed luminous eyes, a delicate nose, and a pair of soft, finely molded lips partially

opened in a half-smile. Her diaphanous yellow dress molded
firm breasts and a tiny waist, then fell in unpleated folds to
her fancy slippers. She was a fairy creature, as out of place in
the frontier world of an army post as an enchanted princess
stepping off the pages of a child's nursery tale.

She must have just arrived on the steamboat *Liberator* that
afternoon, Blade decided, or he would have heard about the
Beauty by now. He surmised she must be the spouse of a newly
arrived officer and wondered, in spite of himself, just how
faithful a wife she might be. No doubt, she would be at the
festivities that evening.

Unbidden, an image of her, soft and naked, surrendering in
his arms, filled his senses. Feeling a tightness in his loins, he
watched her salute him with a brief, tentative wave before
continuing on her way. Puffing on his cigar, he admired her
graceful carriage, hoping she'd look back at him so that he
could return her salutation. She didn't. Disappointed, he
stepped back into his spartan room.

Theodora Gordon knew he was watching her as she walked
toward the commandant's home, and it took all of her self-
control not to look back at the magnificent male creature standing on the balcony above the square. So that was Captain Blade
Roberts! Not at all what she'd expected.

He seemed far too young to be in charge of such an important
campaign. His powerful shoulders and muscular chest had been
evident even under the blue uniform jacket, and his long, well-
formed legs encased in tight buff pants and shiny black riding
boots were those of an athlete. Although she knew she had
little experience to draw from when appraising the physique
of the opposite sex, she realized instinctively that here was a
superb example. Her lips turned up in a smile as she anticipated
their meeting that evening with pleasure.

Did Captain Roberts realize who she was? she wondered,
crossing the wide lawn that led up to the colonel's house. Did
he know they would be spending the next six months together
on the trail? In her excitement, she could scarcely keep from
skipping over the grass and up the steps.

Theodora stood on the veranda and looked out across the
fort's square. How very different it was from her own New

England countryside, with its precise stone fences and charming covered bridges.

For the past eight years, she'd dreamed of coming to the frontier with her brother.

Even before they had begun their formal education, the Gordon children had spent hours together pouring over botanical and geophysical plates in the tomes of their father's library. Secretly, they had planned just such an expedition, delighting in the few written reports they read of the natural wonders of the world out beyond civilization.

In time, the twins' family had come to share that dream with them, for their father and uncles, all university professors, prized scientific research above all other considerations. Thomas and Theodora had been accompanied by their father and grandmother all the way to Philadelphia, where they said a tearful farewell. From the city of William Penn, the twins traveled by bumpy stagecoach to Pittsburgh.

With a smile, Theodora remembered their excitement as they boarded the riverboat *Boston* that took them down the Ohio River to the great Mississippi. Riding the packet down that rolling, muddy current, with its power to toss whole trees in its waves, Theodora felt the love of the land tug at her heart. She watched in awe the great river that was the lifeline of the frontier, carrying keelboats loaded with furs and hides, and paddlewheelers crowded with emigrants, drummers with goods to sell, and rough frontiersmen returning to the backcountry.

Twelve hundred miles from Cincinnati, they reached the bustling waterfront of St. Louis. Tom and Theodora, laughing in exhilaration, had to elbow their way along the crowded sidewalks piled high with produce and merchandise. They stayed at Jefferson Barracks, where they watched in mingled fear and curiosity the arrival of almost a hundred Sauk Indians, painted and dressed in their finest regalia, who were negotiating a treaty for the sale of their land. Eagerly, they began the last leg of their westward journey and boarded the steamboat that would take them up the Missouri River to Fort Leavenworth. They had arrived at the fort that afternoon, and now, as she watched the hustle and bustle of the fort, Theodora felt her ever-present excitement flare up like a torch. They were here at last!

* * *

The windows of the commandant's fine two-story brick home were thrown open to the balmy spring evening. Streams of guests crowded through the main salon into all the rooms, flowed onto the wide second-floor veranda, up and down the staircase, and finally spilled out onto the carefully tended lawn, their noisy chattering reaching up toward the starlit sky. Lanterns placed strategically along the gravel walkway enticed romantically inclined young belles. They strolled with handsome officers of the First Dragoons, who zealously attempted to woo them, for members of the fairer sex were a rare commodity on the frontier.

Inside the large salon, which had been emptied of all furniture to create a ballroom, an army band played waltzes. Flashes of dress blue uniforms with their yellow facings, orange sashes, and black riding boots contrasted boldly with the whirling pastels of the ladies, as their dainty feet flew across the oak-planked floor.

Captain Blade Roberts was holding the commandant's niece in his arms, and he twirled her lightly around the ballroom. Irritated by her nonsensical chatter, but striving to hide his mounting frustration, he looked over the top of her brown curls and searched in vain for the gorgeous blonde.

"Oh, Captain!" Nell Henderson sighed and rolled her blue eyes up at him dramatically. "I think you are just too, too brave, going out into the wilderness with all those wild savages!"

"You forget, Miss Henderson, I grew up in that wilderness." Ignoring her look of shock that he would state in plain words what was only whispered behind spread fans, Blade guided her off the dance floor as the music came to a momentary pause.

They were met by Lieutenant Haintzelman, who bowed to the brunette hanging so persistently on the captain's sleeve. He peered at the petite debutante from behind his spectacles.

"My compliments, Miss Henderson," the lieutenant said. "I believe this is my dance coming up."

Firmly taking her arm, Haintzelman turned to his commanding officer. His nearsighted eyes twinkled unaccountably, and he appeared to be smothering a grin as he delivered a message to the man beside him. "By the way, sir, the Gordons are here. They're with Colonel Kearny in his office. He'd like you to join them immediately."

Not stopping to explain further, Haintzelman pulled the reluctant girl onto the dance floor. Blade was left to find his own way to the commandant's study.

As he entered the cluttered office, Blade felt a surge of satisfaction. There, in the center of the room, deep in conversation with three admiring gentlemen, stood the mysterious beauty he'd seen earlier in the square. She was dressed in an emerald-green satin gown that barely covered the firm, white globes of her breasts. When she turned from the civilian with whom she was talking to greet the new arrival, he saw that her green eyes exactly matched her gown. Her eyebrows were dark, surprisingly so for one of such fair complexion, for her flawless skin was the color of cream. Long, thick, luxurious lashes swept down, casting shadows on her rosy cheeks. With her was a young man dressed in a black tuxedo that set off his blond hair like a flag on Independence Day. A wide smile lit up his face and his clear hazel eyes reflected his bubbling excitement.

So the mysterious lady was one of the Gordon brothers' wives.

Blade noted Lieutenant Wesley Fletcher, an idiotic grin on his pretty-boy Southern face, hovering beside her, practically drooling all over her bare shoulders. He was doggedly elbowing Corporal Overbury out of the circle, which was not easy to do given Overbury's girth, while keeping up a nonstop flow of Dixie flatteries into her dainty ear.

Leaning over the huge map spread out on his desk, Colonel Kearny looked up and smiled. "Ah, you're here, Blade. Thomas and Theodora Gordon, may I present Captain Roberts of the renowned Corps of Topographical Engineers."

Bending from the waist in his best West Point bow, Roberts took her small white-gloved hand in his large white-gloved hand and lifted it to his lips. "Mrs. Gordon, the pleasure is all mine."

As she stood in front of him, her fingers resting lightly in his strong ones, Theodora tilted her head back and looked up into his dark eyes.

He was very tall. And very handsome. Thick black hair came down to the top of his collar and a mustache framed his strong mouth. High cheekbones rose above a straight, aquiline nose. His chin was square and determined. Shockingly, a small gold hoop hung from one earlobe, adding a barbaric splendor to his appearance. Yet despite the shiny bangle, he exuded sheer, raw, male power.

A knowledge of that effect upon her was evident in his confident gaze. It seemed obvious that he was used to women staring at him. Yet, despite his nonchalant acceptance of her open admiration, the attraction she'd felt toward him earlier that afternoon became even stronger and more compelling. His smile awoke within her a stirring of some unknown emotion. She suddenly felt awkward and defensive.

With a slight frown, she snatched her hand from his grasp. "You have the wrong title, Captain Roberts," she answered, determined to remain unruffled. "It's *Miss* Gordon."

Not a wife, but an unmarried sister! *How lucky can I get?* Blade Roberts asked himself.

Without comment, he turned to the golden-haired man standing beside her and addressed him with annoyance. "Good to make your acquaintance at last, Gordon. I was afraid we'd have to leave you and your brother behind. Once the new grass covers the prairie, the journey can't be put off, or we'd risk being stranded in the mountains in an early snow. You can understand my concern over your tardy arrival."

Gordon blushed and hastened to apologize. "I'm sorry, sir. We were regrettably detained on the last stage of our journey."

Blade's disgust at the excuse was undisguised. "Being sorry doesn't get us over the mountains, Gordon. I suggest that in the future you keep it in mind."

Stepping closer, Theodora reached out and clasped her brother's hand. Her voice shook with humiliation at the public dressing-down. "The delay wasn't our fault, Captain Roberts. The steamship hit a sandbar and had to be pried off with long poles by the passengers and crew. It was two days before we could continue our journey."

Recognizing her distress on her brother's behalf, Blade bent his head and spoke to her as though she were a foolish child. "Such delays are not uncommon, Miss Gordon, and should be planned for accordingly. On a journey of this importance, no possibility should be overlooked. However, now that your brothers are here, we need put off our departure no longer.''

"No need t' be so harsh with them, Captain,'' Lieutenant Fletcher interjected with a sneer. "Remember, they're Easterners. How could they be expected t' know when the buffalo grass ripens on the plains?''

Blade met Fletcher's pale blue eyes with open hostility. "They'd better know it. According to their dossier they are well schooled in the natural sciences. Between the two of them, the Gordon brothers are supposed to have studied topography, cartography, botany, and ornithology. Therefore, I assumed I wasn't taking totally green, inexperienced scientists on this trip, but men who had participated in at least a few limited excursions into the uncivilized world beyond Manhattan Island.''

Theodora Gordon's jade eyes glittered. "I can assure you, Captain Roberts, that we are neither green nor inexperienced. We've studied under Thomas Nuttall, John Townsend, and Asa Gray, and have accompanied our tutors on several botanical excursions. We were well aware of the need to be ready to leave as soon as the grasses ripened. Even you must admit that spring has come early this year, and only a soothsayer could have predicted the need to leave before the first of June!''

Blade heard only one word of this outraged admonishment. "*We? You* studied under Nuttall? Since when do women study botany, Miss Gordon? Has the learned world lost its senses since I've been on the frontier? Are women now allowed to enter Harvard?''

Her pointed chin lifted in defiance to his open sarcasm. "Women will never be allowed to enter Harvard, Captain Roberts, as well you know. My formal schooling was at Mount Holyoke in Massachusetts. But my family provided me with private tutors from the Harvard faculty during the summer months, several of whom hold national reputations. You'll find that I am quite capable of the duties assigned to me on this surveying expedition and I intend to carry them out with distinction.''

"Well said, my dear,'' Fletcher exclaimed.

Blade Roberts stared in amazement at the lovely young

woman. "Is it actually your preposterous belief, Miss Gordon, that you'll be allowed to accompany my troop of forty men into the wilderness?"

The blond-haired brother squeezed Theodora's hand and replied with the brashness of a gamboling puppy. "My sister and I are looking forward to our exploration of the wilderness territories with you, Captain. This trip will be the fulfillment of both our dreams."

Slowly, a suspicion arose in Blade's mind. "Just where *is* your brother, Mr. Gordon? It was my understanding there were two of you. A cartographer and a naturalist."

"That's correct, sir. I'm an experienced mapmaker. I've studied under some of the best topologists at Harvard. Theodora, my sister, is the naturalist and has studied botany. I'm sure you'll find we're well qualified for our positions on this campaign."

Colonel Kearny left the map-laden table over which he'd been leaning and came to stand beside the young lady. "Miss Gordon has been employed by the Linnean Society of Massachusetts to study and complete detailed drawings of the flora and fauna to be found in the unexplored West. Her work will extend and supplement the studies of Nuttall, Audubon, and Townsend. Work for which she is well qualified, I might add."

Kearny turned a glare on the captain that defied any possible thought of insubordination. "She will accompany you on this mission, Captain Roberts."

"The hell she will!" Blade growled. He jammed an unlit cheroot into his mouth and rocked back on the heels of his highly polished cavalry boots. His jaw jutted out pugnaciously and his narrowed eyes seemed to dare the foolish New Englanders to protest.

It was Kearny who broke the awkward silence. He turned to the shocked group, standing wide-eyed and self-conscious in the center of the room, and swept his hand toward the door in a polite wave of dismissal. "If you'll be kind enough to leave us, Miss Gordon? Mr. Gordon? Gentlemen? I'd like to have a few words with my *junior* officer alone, please."

In his early forties and well known for his strong, intelligent leadership, Lieutenant Colonel Stephen Watts Kearny was a hot-tempered frontier veteran. Admired by the men under his authority and by the hierarchy in Washington alike, he had been sent to administrate the westernmost army outpost of the frontier, a command which, in effect, covered millions of acres of uncivilized Indian country known as the Great American Desert. A slight man of medium height, with large round eyes over a prominent nose, he maintained firm control of the soldiers under him by his personal strength and charisma. He now turned this combination on the captain who stood so contentiously before him.

Pointing to a chair piled high with books, he spoke in a calm manner. "Get rid of that seegar, Captain Roberts, and sit down. There are a few things we'd better discuss before you return to your socializing."

Blade threw the unlit cheroot on the desk. "I'd rather stand, sir." Determination showed in the belligerent set of his shoulders and the clenched fists at his sides. His black eyes were as hard as obsidian.

"Very well. As you will." Kearny sat down in the chair behind his desk and leaned back, his chin cupped in one hand.

"You seem to object to Miss Gordon's participation in this survey, Captain Roberts," Kearny said quietly. "Do you doubt her qualifications? I can assure you, her credentials are all in order."

Blade stepped forward and leaned both hands on the desk. "My God, Colonel, how can you even consider this ridiculous plan? No white woman has ever crossed the plains! Taking a female out there would be exposing her to horrible risks." He straightened and hooked his thumbs in his belt. "Dammit, she'll be dead within a month."

"Nonsense, Blade. The plains are home to countless women who survive out there quite well."

"Hell, yes! Indian women! Females born and raised in the broiling heat and freezing winds and the day-to-day uncertainty of raiding war parties. What do you think would happen to Theodora Gordon should she fall into the hands of the Blackfoot or the Gros Ventres?"

Kearny jumped up. His words were sharp. "It's your responsibility, Captain Roberts, to see that Miss Gordon doesn't fall into the hands of savages."

Kearny strode to the center of the room's braided rag rug. Turning, he faced the captain. Concern edged his even words. "Keep that girl close to you, Blade. And keep one shot reserved."

Blade's large fist slammed down on the colonel's desk, rebellion written on his hawklike features. "No, by God! I refuse to take her! I'll not bring any woman into hostile country. It's insane and I'll have no part of it."

"I'm afraid you have no choice, Captain Roberts. The Gordons are going on this mission."

Blade rubbed the muscles in the back of his neck and faced Kearny with a gesture of resignation. "All right! All right! I'll take Tom Gordon, as young and green as he is. I'll wipe his nose and smack his butt when he needs it. But I won't take the woman."

Coming back to his desk, Kearny lifted the map spread across its top and sat down on the edge of it, slowly rolling the paper into a tight cylinder. "You know, Blade, one of the purposes of this mission is to encourage people to settle in the Far West. There are many members of Congress who believe it's our country's destiny to spread from one coast to the other. They are the men who've supported this campaign against all the nay-sayers. At the very least, we owe them our full cooperation."

"Do the Gordons realize that our final destination is California?"

"Yes." Kearny stood, laid down the map, and moved around to the front of his desk. Pulling out the right-hand drawer, he removed a packet and tossed it to Blade. "Here are your secret orders from the Secretary of War instructing you to discover an overland route through the Sierras. And your visa from the Mexican consul in Washington. These papers cover not only you and the Gordons but the men under your command as well. They'll allow you to enter California legally as a brigade of fur trappers." The colonel shrugged philosophically. "The presence of a beautiful woman is never hard to explain."

"Great," Blade said sarcastically as he shoved the papers inside his dark blue tunic. "Who else knows about this *secret* mission? If word gets out that half a company of mounted U.S.

dragoons is heading for the Pacific Ocean, the *Californios* will meet us at the border with an armed patrol and charge us with illegal entry. We'll end up cooling our heels in a calaboose in Monterey for the next couple of years.''

Kearny spoke in a soothing voice. "No one else is aware of your ultimate goal, Roberts, outside of your guide and the three French Canadian voyageurs, whom you yourself told. Of course, Lieutenant Fletcher, as your second-in-command, will also be apprised of your orders.''

At Blade's snort of disdain, Kearny continued in his most authoritative voice, emphasizing each word. "When you reach South Pass, you'll report to Captain Bonniville. He's fully aware that there will be a woman on the expedition, and he recognizes her importance. If we're to wrest Oregon from British hands and California from the Mexicans, we'll need large numbers of families to settle there as quickly as possible. That means we must show the people of this country that women and children can reach the Pacific coast safely. The fact that a female is a part of this pilgrimage will prove it can be done.''

"Fine,'' Blade replied. "But first let me map a safe route over the Sierras.''

"Damnation, Roberts, you have no choice. Either Theodora Gordon leaves with this expedition, or it doesn't leave at all.''

Blade crossed his arms. Scorn laced his words. "Just what idiot is responsible for this madness?''

"The orders come straight from Washington, Blade. The Gordons are a very wealthy and influential Massachusetts family. One of Miss Gordon's uncles is a state senator. Her grandmother is on the governing board of the Linnean Society of that same state, which has donated most generously to the cost of this very expensive project. A donation which I am afraid comes with some definite strings attached. Matching funds have also been promised by a New York entrepreneur, who is, I'm told, Miss Gordon's fiancé. The total amount of these promised monies is nearly twice the appropriation ordered by Congress—an appropriation which, of itself, would have gotten you barely halfway to South Pass. You can't go without their dollars, Blade. And she comes with the money.''

Blade's square jaw was set in granite. "Someone needs to

sit down with Miss Gordon and make her face reality. This expedition isn't going to be a Sunday school picnic. The risks will be almost insurmountable for the men, let alone a woman. Surely someone can make her see reason.''

Kearny sighed. ''Theodora wants to go on this trip to learn more about the wilderness. No one outside her family takes her so-called studies seriously. But certain members of Congress want her to go because she's a woman. I'm sure some of the dangers have been mentioned to her. I don't want you upsetting her, Blade, about things that might not happen.'' He retrieved the rolled-up map and pointed it at the captain like a marshal's baton. ''You're under orders not to bring up this subject with her. The decision has been made at the highest level. It's completely out of your hands.''

''Why wasn't I told all this before?''

''Dammit, Blade, because I knew you'd react exactly the way you are now.''

''And if I refuse to take Miss Gordon?''

Shaking his head in exasperation, Colonel Kearny walked over to the window. As he looked out at the guests on his trampled lawn, their gay party costumes highlighted by the colored lanterns, he shrugged his shoulders in a gesture of complete indifference and made his bluff. ''Then I'll be forced to replace you with Wesley Fletcher.''

The smack of a fist hitting the wall brought the colonel around.

Swearing savagely, Blade turned and opened the door, then stopped, his hand on the knob. He looked back over his shoulder. ''And what if Miss Gordon changes her mind and decides not to go with us?''

''If Miss Gordon decides of her own volition not to participate in this history-making junket, then of course, you may leave without her.''

''That's all I need to know,'' Blade said, and exited the room, slamming the door behind him.

Chapter 2

Theodora Gordon realized with embarrassment that she danced the waltz with the agility and precision of a twelve-year-old child. Parties and flirtations had never interested her, not even in her adolescence. During the summer of her fifteenth year she had invested exactly six hours to the study of the dance as a special surprise for her father's birthday celebration. She'd waltzed with him that night and he'd declared her a wonderful dancer. Since that time, no other partner had ever paid her a single compliment on her dancing skills; had anyone done so she would have called him a liar.

Now, eight years after those few short lessons, she dearly regretted their brevity. Held tightly in the arms of Lieutenant Wesley Fletcher, the strains of the waltz floating around them in three-quarter time, Theodora trod on his previously immaculate cavalry boots on every second beat. Had she been able to listen to the music, she reasoned to herself, she might have had a chance. But inside her head, drowning out the lovely melody, echoed the sarcastic words of devastatingly handsome Captain Blade Roberts: *Since when do women study botany?*

She smiled apologetically at the tall, fair-haired Lieutenant Fletcher and shook her head. "Perhaps we should sit down, Lieutenant. I seem to be dancing more on your toes than on my own."

Undaunted, Fletcher tightened his grip around her waist and gazed into her eyes. "You're doin' fine, Miz Gordon. Just relax and follow my lead. You're upset, and understandably so. But don't let anythin' that Captain Roberts said bother you.

15

It's common knowledge the fellow's manners are atrocious. Come on now, smile and enjoy the party. It's in our honor, after all.''

Why *had* Roberts taken such an extreme dislike to her? she wondered miserably, recalling how attracted she'd felt when she'd seen him standing on the balcony above her that afternoon. And why should she care so much? After all, she'd never been successful at flirtations or particularly at ease with small talk. Lines of beaux had never stood on her doorstep, for when it came to talking with women, most men seemed to prefer empty-headed nonsense to discussions of science or politics or even business. Usually, when they realized she was bookish, they reacted with polite indifference or boredom. None had shown such outright anger at her as the captain, but then, he was like no man she'd ever met.

Thankfully, Theodora heard the band strike up "The Girl I Left Behind Me," signaling that dinner was about to be served. She accepted with gratitude Fletcher's escort onto the wide portico that stretched across the back of the house.

Outside on the lawn, borrowed tables were piled high with hams, roasts, and game birds. Mounds of corn biscuits, butter and honey, platters of fresh greens and wild spring onions were crowded between plates of chocolate cakes, berry pies, and syllabubs. In honor of the evening's special guests, there were bottles of champagne, and the *pop-pop-pop* of the corks as the bottles were broached brought squeals of laughter from the ladies putting the final touches on the sumptuous meal.

At one long table in the center of the yard, Theodora could see Colonel and Mrs. Kearny just sitting down. Throughout the crowd, amongst the tailored blue uniforms of the First Regiment of Dragoons and the pastel chiffon finery of their wives and daughters, stood out the homemade buckskin outfits of the Creole and French Canadian voyageurs who were also members of the expedition. These veteran trailblazers appeared ill at ease among the citified population of Fort Leavenworth, but the presence of the ladies seemed to act as a powerful inducement to socialize despite their rusty manners.

"I believe this table is reserved for the rankin' members of the expedition, Miz Gordon," Fletcher said, leading her to a long table and pulling out a chair for her with a flamboyant gesture.

Apprehensively, Theodora sank down, for directly across from her sat Captain Blade Roberts, who impolitely remained seated at her appearance. Roberts watched her take her place without a word, his black stare raking insolently over her, but when Lieutenant Fletcher sat down beside her, Roberts broke his self-imposed silence. "Don't get too comfortable there, Fletcher. Your place is somewhere at the other end of the table."

With mute disbelief Fletcher read the name on the place card. He'd exchanged that very card for his own not thirty minutes before and it didn't take the wisdom of Solomon to know who had switched it back again.

Ignoring Blade, he turned to Theodora. "I'm sorry, Miz Gordon. I seem t' have taken your brother's chair. May I have the pleasure of another dance with you after dinner?"

Pleased by his chivalry, Theodora smiled. "You're very brave, Lieutenant Fletcher, to ask for more after the terrible punishment I meted out to you on the dance floor already tonight. Another waltz with me and you might not be able to walk tomorrow."

Without compunction, Blade interrupted this private exchange. "Yes, I saw you dancing with Miss Gordon earlier, Fletcher. No doubt, the lady's heavy regimen of studies never allowed her time for the practice of the finer arts in which the fairer sex are generally educated. You're to be commended on your fortitude."

Fletcher kept his eyes on Theodora as he lifted her hand to his lips. He seemed to be holding himself on a tight rein. "If it's brave t' hold an angel in one's arms under the guise of waltzin', I hope I may always be considered so courageous. Till after dinner, Miz Gordon, when we shall resume our dance."

He departed with a bow, leaving Theodora to wonder again what had set the captain against her. It was a tragedy that the man with whom she would be working so closely in the weeks ahead had taken such an intense and immediate dislike to her.

The need for conversation between them was forestalled by the arrival of three other guests.

"There you are, Teddy," Thomas called to his twin, his eyes twinkling. "I looked for you in the ballroom, but somehow I missed you. Sis, this is Miss Ellen Henderson, the commandant's niece. She's from Atlanta and is visiting her aunt and uncle for the summer. And this is Second Lieutenant Peter Haintzelman, who's going to be the clerk on our journey."

Blade, who had stood politely upon the arrival of Nell Henderson, placed his hand on the shoulder of the man next to him, who had also risen, and interjected, "While we are having introductions, Mr. and Miss Gordon, this is Ezekiel Conyers, our scout. Zeke was employed by the American Fur Company when he was a nineteen-year-old Kentucky runaway and has been roaming the Rocky Mountains for the past forty years."

Zeke was a venerable mountain man. A full gray beard came down to the middle of his chest and he wore buckskins with fringe hanging from his sleeves and leggings. His leather hat was banded in fox fur with an eagle's feather pushed rakishly through the wide brim, and a huge flintlock pistol hung by a wide strap across his chest, its shiny, smoothbore barrel reflecting the orange-colored light of a nearby paper lantern.

Zeke grinned in fascination at the Gordons. "Jumpin' Jehoshaphat, would you look at that blond hair on the two of them! What a twin prize you'd be to some varmint that collected scalps!"

The skin on the back of Theodora's neck prickled at his words. Not once had she ever considered her brother's or her own hair as a "prize," and she reached nervously for her champagne glass.

After helping Nell Henderson to be seated, Thomas slipped into the seat beside his sister. Roberts and Conyers regained their chairs. Doggedly, Peter Haintzelman sat down on the other side of the commandant's niece and shoved the place card beneath his plate, ignoring the twinkle in the captain's black eyes.

For a time all talk ceased as the dishes of food were passed up and down the table. Once that task was completed, the guests were free to continue their interrupted conversation.

"Thank you for including me at your table, Captain Roberts, even though I'm not really a member of your exploring party,"

Nell Henderson said sweetly, staring across the board at him with her heart in her cornflower-blue eyes.

Blade smiled back at her, his teeth shining white beneath his dark mustache, the warmth never quite reaching his eyes. "I thought that Miss Gordon, being the only female member of the team, would enjoy your companionship, Miss Henderson, rather than sitting here with an all-male group. I thought you two might want to swap recipes or quilting patterns."

Her eyes narrowed, Theodora smiled at the captain. Her voice dripped honey. "Why how kind of you, Captain Roberts. I wouldn't have suspected you capable of such thoughtfulness," she cooed, inwardly seething at the patronizing statement. "But I'm afraid I'll be far too busy on this trip to do any quilting. However, if you consider the subject of patterns so interesting, perhaps you should ask Miss Henderson for one yourself."

Anger replaced the smug expression on his face, bringing a feeling of triumph to Theodora. If he thought she would meekly take every insult he dished out, he would soon discover the error of his thinking.

Nell looked in puzzlement from one to the other and addressed the mountain man turned scout. "Have you fought with the Indians many times, Mr. Conyers?"

Arrested by her question just as he was about to fork in a mouthful of ham, Zeke scoffed. "More times than I'd care to remember, Miss Nellie. Once I had to outrun a group of eight Blackfoot braves on their Indian ponies. And I was afoot."

Thomas Gordon looked up from his plate and whistled softly. "Gosh! However did you manage to escape, Zeke?"

"Hid out by day and traveled by night. Lost my powder swimmin' a river and my boots as well. When I finally arrived at a fur-tradin' stockade, I was near naked and nigh starved to death. But anythin' was better than lettin' 'em catch me alive."

"Would it have been so awful?" Nell asked, her eyes wide with dreadful fascination.

Zeke chewed his food thoughtfully. "Awful enough, I guess. I once saw the body of a friend of mine that'd been tortured by them heathens. They'd staked him to the ground and—"

"That'll be enough talk about torture for now, Zeke," the

captain interrupted. "I'm sure Miss Gordon has already studied the creative ways that Indians deal with their unfortunate captives. That came between bird-watching and plant-pressing, didn't it, Miss Gordon?"

Somberly, Theodora turned her eyes on the mocking ones watching her and hid her shaking hands under the tablecloth. No mention of Indian torture had been made in the correspondence coming from the capital, and the thought made the food sit like a lump in her stomach. She'd assumed the travelers would be safe, since they were to be escorted by mounted dragoons. She had accepted that there would be many inconveniences, but not the possibility of capture and mutilation at the hands of savages.

Still, it wasn't her intention to amuse the captain by showing just how frightened she was. "Quite honestly, Captain Roberts, I know very little about the natives of the plains. But I have studied ancient civilizations, and human beings are all pretty much alike, I believe. We all seem to be driven by the same basic needs and desires; only the outward cultural trappings are different."

After lighting a cheroot from the candle in the center of the table, Blade leaned back in his chair and blew a puff of smoke into the air, a sardonic smile on his lips. His dark eyes seemed to glint evilly in the candlelight. "And have you studied much about man's basic needs, Miss Gordon?"

Clearly disturbed by the sudden turn in the conversation, Tom looked questioningly at his sister and then at Roberts. "Would you like to go inside now, Teddy? It's starting to get a little cool out here."

"No, I'm fine, Tom. You go on and enjoy the party. I'm sure Miss Henderson would love to waltz with you."

Nell looked at Tom and smiled. "Why I declare, Mr. Gordon, I think that would be a marvelous idea."

Watching them depart, Theodora wondered nervously what the captain's next move would be.

Unfolding his powerful legs, Blade stood and tossed his napkin on the white tablecloth. His eyes taunted her. "Perhaps you'd care to take a stroll with me, Miss Gordon. I can show you around the fort, since you don't seem to relish the dancing."

"I would enjoy that, Captain," Theodora replied, standing and shaking out the folds of her green satin dress. Not for the world would she shirk from a head-to-head confrontation with the pompous oaf. She was ready to show the intimidating officer that, if he was determined to be her enemy, she was unafraid of him.

They left the table, Theodora allowing the captain to steer her around the commandant's noisy house and into the quiet square of Fort Leavenworth. Behind them she could hear the muffled tones of the festivities as the band resumed its playing in the ballroom. The strains of "Fare Thee Well, You Sweethearts" carried through the soft spring evening, and the plaintive melody tugged at Theodora's heart, reminding her that she would soon be leaving.

Except for the few men on sentinel duty, the square was deserted. Walking beside the tall officer, Theodora discovered to her annoyance that the top of her head barely reached his shoulder. He was even larger than she'd first realized. Peeking up at him from the corner of her eye, she noted again his sharp features, almost hawkish with their high cheekbones and strong chin. Lowering her eyes, she took in his muscled legs stretching the cloth of his blue uniform tautly over his thighs. She had never been near a man so masculine, so self-assured, so certain of his own ability to manipulate those around her. She was convinced that he was about to try to control her, and that thought sent a quiver of nervous energy through her body.

If she's jumpy now, Blade mused, she'll be terrified in just a few minutes. After she's been attacked by a real, live Cheyenne Indian, she'll run back to Massachusetts so fast she won't even stop to say good-bye.

He bent his head. His tone was soft and reassuring. "You seem a little high-strung tonight, Miss Gordon. I hope you weren't frightened by Conyers's story of Indian torture?"

Determined to hide her misgivings, Theodora came to a halt, turning to face him in the lantern light shining from a nearby window. "Now that, Captain Roberts, is an outright lie. We'd deal much better together, sir, if you wouldn't mince words with me. What you really hope is that I was frightened to death by his ghoulish tale. Pooh, it will take more than some fireside ghost story to scare me away from this trip."

He looked down at her upturned face. The scent of wild-flowers drifted up from her golden hair and assailed his senses, causing him to doubt for a moment the wisdom of his plan. He'd never mistreated a female in his life, no matter what the provocation. And she was so damn lovely. Under any other circumstances he'd be competing with Wesley Fletcher in playing the besotted fool.

"What an intrepid little adventuress you are!" he goaded, refusing to listen to his conscience. "Were you always so fearless, Miss Gordon?"

The notion that she was a fearless adventuress made her laugh. If the captain only knew how her legs were shaking under the folds of her satin skirt, he'd have a different opinion of her courage. "Being raised in Cambridge, I didn't have much of which to be afraid, Captain. All my life I've been surrounded by gentle scholars and educators. My father and my uncle are both members of the Harvard faculty."

"A regular little bluenose," Blade replied, but his tone didn't match his sarcastic words. "And a Puritan too, no doubt, if I remember my history lesson about Massachusetts."

Slipping his hand under her elbow, he resumed their walk, leading her past the darkened stone storehouse that served both the quartermaster and the commissary department.

"Yes, some of my ancestors were Puritans, though my family is now more freethinking than in the past. But my mother's people belong to the Society of Friends. The Gordons have always placed a great emphasis on the use of the intellect rather than on brute force. What about you, Captain Roberts? Do you have some pilgrim roots?"

A wide grin split his face, and a deep chuckle arose from his chest. She couldn't have been wider from the mark if she'd shot with a warped arrow. "No, Miss Gordon, I'm afraid my ancestors have always believed quite strongly in the idea that might makes right."

Baffled by his laughter, Theodora wished she could see his eyes, but the darkness prevented it. She wondered if he was teasing her. His rapid changes of mood confused her, but she couldn't deny to herself that he was a stunningly attractive man. If only they could be friends, the journey would be the realization of all she'd dreamed. She didn't want to prove anything—not to him, not to anyone. She simply wanted to gather all the information she could about the flora and fauna of the western territory, catalogue her discoveries, and bring home the specimens. She'd gladly leave the dangerous work to the men.

"I thought you might like to inspect some of the horses we'll be taking," Blade said, guiding her into a long stable as he'd planned. In a way, he hated to frighten her so, but if it meant saving her life in the long run, they would both benefit from his scheme.

Inside the steeply roofed building, a scattering of lanterns along the walls gave a soft glow to the piles of golden hay stacked along one side. Except for the horses, whose soft whickers at the couple's sudden appearance told the intruders that they'd disturbed the animals' rest, the barn was deserted.

Theodora, curious to see them, started to move toward the stall of a magnificent gray stallion.

Kicking the door shut with his boot, Blade seized her elbow and pulled her to him. With one swift movement he had his arms around her and was kissing her savagely. It was a bruising, violent kiss.

The suddenness of his actions caught Theodora by surprise and she tried to pull away from him. Frightened by the barely leashed power she felt in his muscular arms, she struggled, attempting to break free. Escape was impossible. His firm, demanding lips boldly covered hers, his tongue probing her mouth and touching her intimately. She felt his strong hand slide up from her waist and cover her breast, and the shock of his warm touch penetrating the thinness of her gown ignited a fire inside her.

Frantically, she tried to pull free of his demanding lips, but he held her head effortlessly in one hand. She felt the power of fingers that could easily crush her skull.

Drawn to him by an attraction that seemed stronger than her own will, she was frightened, not only of him but also of the strange new sensation she felt leap inside herself.

When she had first seen him, she had felt that same compulsion surge through her and had turned away lest he read the longing in her eyes. Now, despite his rudeness, that need to be close to him, to touch him and be touched by him, enveloped her, and she swayed, her knees nearly buckling beneath her.

Blade felt her passionate response and a thrill went through him. He changed his kiss as she clung to him, no longer punishing her but persuading and appealing. He moved his tongue rhythmically in and out of her mouth, urging her to follow his seductive lead, and felt her return his kiss without reservation.

As she yielded to his touch, Blade slipped his fingers inside the bodice of her gown, caressing a silken breast and gently touching its rosy peak.

Desire shot through Theodora. Suddenly frantic with fear of the unknown, she pushed with both hands against his chest. The sound of her dress ripping brought them both to a standstill. Her breath came in ragged gasps.

Deliberately, Blade released her and stepped back. He quickly regained control, despite the rushing of blood in his veins. His voice was calm and detached. "That wasn't half bad for a prudish New England spinster whose only knowledge of life has come from between the covers of a book."

The crack of her hand across his cheek rang out in the quiet stable, and the force of the blow jerked his head, causing a lock of his straight black hair to fall across his forehead.

"You animal," Theodora hissed, as she tried to repair her rent gown with shaking fingers and pull the torn satin cloth over her white breasts. Tears of mortification rolled down her cheeks. Her voice broke on a sob. "Don't . . . don't you ever touch me again."

From the door of the stables came a slow drawl. "I should kill y' for that, Roberts."

Wesley Fletcher stood just inside the building, his hand resting on his sidearm.

"And I should have known you'd follow us, Fletcher," Blade replied in disgust, turning and blocking the shaking girl from the lieutenant's sight. "Since when did Miss Gordon's virtue become your responsibility?"

"Any woman you manhandle is my concern, Roberts. You're nothin' but a filthy breed. You're not fit t' touch the hem of a white woman's dress. If y' weren't a senior officer, I'd call y' out right now."

Blade walked over to the lieutenant and pulled a glove from

the pair tucked in his belt. "Here, let me make it easy for you, Fletcher." He struck the man lightly across the face.

"You'll pay for that, Roberts!" Fletcher cried, enraged, his hand going to his cheek.

"I am at your service," came the scornful reply.

Blade departed, not once looking back at the girl standing so still and solemn, the tears not yet dried upon her cheeks and her emerald eyes blazing with fury and humiliation.

But Blade knew he was far from detached. What had begun as a cold, calculated move to frighten her away had turned into the most impassioned kiss he'd ever experienced. Had she realized the effect she'd had upon him, all his planning would have been in vain.

"Miz Gordon," Lieutenant Fletcher said as he went over to her, "is there anythin' I can do?" His pale gaze dropped to the torn gown and lingered there.

"Yes, Lieutenant, there is," she snapped, refusing to show just how shaken she really was. "Kindly escort me to Colonel Kearny at once."

Chapter 3

Blade was already out of bed and stropping his razor when the pounding on the door began. Expecting to find Fletcher's seconds come to deliver the cartel, he opened the door and stood back in an unspoken invitation for the men to enter. But it wasn't for a duel that the five soldiers had arrived at the captain's quarters before dawn.

An embarrassed Sergeant Michael O'Fallon, his three gold stripes shining on his dark blue shell jacket, was flanked by four privates, who listened in amazement to the orders barked in his gravelly voice.

"Captain Roberts, sir," O'Fallon said, clearing his throat in apprehension. "If you don't mind, sir, I'll be taking you to the guardhouse now, under Colonel Kearny's orders. And you'd best be coming along with no fight, now, for I wouldn't want to hurt you, sir, you being a West Point man and all." The threat was a halfhearted attempt at humor, for everyone present knew he would never lay a hand on a senior officer.

"What the hell's going on here, Sergeant?" Blade demanded. He walked across the room and jerked a clean shirt out of his bureau drawer. "This is totally against regulations. Have you lost your senses or has Colonel Kearny?"

"Now, I'm only following my orders, Captain. Naturally, I'd like to take you peaceful like. But if it comes to a fight, well, then I'd have to say I don't mind mixing it up with you. I've always wondered how you'd do in a real donnybrook. Why, I only brought these four along in case I bit off more than I could chew.'' Determined to make a joke of the entire proceedings, O'Fallon rubbed his palms together in mock anticipation.

Sitting down on the lumpy mattress filled with the dry grass the occupants of Fort Leavenworth euphemistically called prairie feathers, Blade reached for his boots. As he pulled them on, he questioned the enlisted man with dawning suspicion. "Are you telling me, Sergeant, that I'm being placed under arrest?''

"Why, I never said no such thing, Captain. Me and the boys are merely here to escort you to the guardhouse. I said nothing about arresting you, mind you, so don't go holding a grudge against a man who's merely obeying orders."

Blade stood and grabbed his blue tunic jacket, slipping into it and buckling his sword belt over his tasseled sash. "Any objections, O'Fallon?" he asked, placing a hand on the ornate sword hilt.

"Sure and no one mentioned disarming you, Captain. Those weren't my orders, sir.''

Blade sighed in resignation. "Lead on, Sergeant. I haven't had my breakfast yet and I've got a lot of things to do today.''

Inside its thick walls the stone guardhouse was dark and cool. From his desk a corporal looked up over his coffee mug when the escorted prisoner entered. He jumped to his feet and saluted. "I have orders to place you in a cell, Captain Roberts, until the colonel sends for you.''

"Just what the hell is going on here, Steen?" Blade snapped, irritated by the soldier's undue formality.

Coughing nervously and brushing biscuit crumbs off his tunic, Corporal Steen came around to stand in front of the irate captain. "I'm not sure myself, Captain. I just received orders to keep you under surveillance until further advised. Would you mind following me, please?" His brown eyes issued an unspoken plea for cooperation.

A glimmer of light dawned. So Kearny had found out about the proposed duel. And to prevent his meeting with Lieutenant Fletcher, the colonel was detaining both of them until it'd be too late for Fletcher's seconds to call and arrange a time and place. Since the survey team was leaving the next day, they'd have to fight that morning or not at all, for as Fletcher's commanding officer on the expedition, Blade could never ethically meet him in a duel once they left Leavenworth.

Shrugging, Blade acceded. "Very well, Corporal. But send word to Colonel Kearny that I await his pleasure. I need to make some last-minute preparations for our departure tomorrow, and I don't have time to spare cooling my heels in jail."

Blade left his escort of guards and followed Steen down the narrow passageway and into a small cell. Although Corporal Steen eyed the long saber that hung at his prisoner's side speculatively, he made no mention of the weapon and, retreating quietly, left the iron-barred door ajar.

As he turned around his small prison, Blade vented his frustration with an oath. Then he unhooked his saber, tossed it on the narrow cot, and lay down beside it, hoping to catch a little more sleep before he had to face the duties of the day. An hour later, his rest was disturbed.

"Colonel Kearny's ready to see you now, sir," Sergeant O'Fallon barked. "I'm to hold your sword for you." He stretched out a huge hand.

Grabbing his long saber, Blade threw it handle-first to the sergeant and rose from the narrow bed in one fluid motion. "It's about time! What the devil is Kearny thinking of? I've wasted half the morning in this farce."

Stoically prepared for a violent tongue-lashing from the hot-tempered commandant, Blade followed the sergeant down the hall and into the main room of the guardhouse. He surveyed the assembled company in surprise.

Seated behind a long wooden table sat Lieutenant Colonel Kearny. On either side of him were the fort's quartermaster, Captain Lewis Harris, and the post surgeon, Major Langdon Sprague. The morning light from the nearby window winked on the gold lace slashes of the officers' cuffs and the gold stripes along the outer seams of their dark blue trousers. Every man in the room, with the exception of the insouciant prisoner, had a long dragoon saber hanging by his side. The chamber itself had been cleared of all other personnel, except for Second Lieutenant Haintzelman, who sat at the end of the long table with a tablet for recording the notes of the proceedings.

Kearny nodded briefly in acknowledgment to Blade, his face

set in stern disapproval of Blade's nonchalant stance. "Captain Roberts, you've been called before me to face a very serious accusation. This is not a formal hearing and you're not under arrest at this time. But a charge has been lodged against you which cannot be ignored. I'm using this informal inquiry to ascertain the facts surrounding the events of last evening. I've asked Major Sprague and Captain Harris to attend and offer the wisdom of their combined experience to the matter."

Without allowing Blade to reply, Kearny addressed the enlisted man standing at attention just beside the door. "Sergeant O'Fallon, please bring in Miss Gordon."

The door to a side room was opened, and Theodora entered with her brother at her side. Dressed in a lavender riding outfit, its high, military-style collar and cuffs trimmed in black velvet, and a matching pillbox hat perched atop her brilliant curls, she marched into the room. Her features were hazy behind a lavender veil, the netting just covering her eyes and sweeping across the top of her pert nose. She refused the assistance of Thomas Gordon, who solicitously tried to hold her elbow. Not once did she glance at Blade, who stood in the middle of the room, less than four feet from the chair in which she sat down.

His freckles standing out on his white face like sprinkles of cinnamon, Tom eased down beside Theodora and adjusted the vest beneath his brown frock coat with restless fingers. The angry look in his hazel eyes questioned why such a horrible thing had to happen on the eve of their grand adventure.

Kearny spoke evenly, his voice clear in the quiet room. "Some very serious charges have been brought against you by Miss Gordon, Captain Roberts. You stand accused of conduct unbecoming an officer and a gentleman. Theodora came to me late last night in an extremely distraught state and charged that you attempted to molest her. She states that if it were not for the timely arrival on the scene of Lieutenant Wesley Fletcher, you would have forced yourself upon her. Do you deny these accusations, Captain?"

No longer indifferent to the proceedings, Blade glared at Theodora, and his fists clenched and unclenched as he attempted to control his raging temper. He'd never dreamed she would have the audacity to press charges against him.

Involuntarily, Theodora squirmed against the back of her

chair and swallowed her fear. Her heart pounded against her ribs. She'd never seen any man so furious, and she wondered what would happen if he didn't manage to gain the control he so valiantly sought.

Suddenly, Blade snorted in disdain and swung his gaze back to the three officers seated in front of him. "It was never my intention to force anything upon Miss Gordon against her will, sir. When she agreed to inspect the deserted stables with me, I assumed she was as anxious for a roll in the hay as I was. I'm sorry that I misread her intentions."

A choking gasp came from Theodora's dry throat. She started to rise, but Tom was already on his feet with a roar.

"You malign my sister!" His face was red, his eyes round with indignation. Shaking a fist at the tall prisoner, he rushed toward him. "I demand satisfaction for those lies!"

He reminded Theodora of a foolhardy puppy yipping furiously at an enraged bear. Her heart sank. She couldn't allow her brother to attempt to defend her honor against this monster. He would smash Tom without even exerting himself.

Intercepting the brash young man, O'Fallon pinned Tom's arms to his sides and glanced at Kearny.

"That will be all from you, Mr. Gordon," Kearny declared. "Any future disruption on your part, and I'll have you removed from the room. Now, sit down. And stay there."

In the ensuing silence, papers rustled uneasily at the end of the table, where Lieutenant Haintzelman was taking down the details of the litigation with pen and ink.

Major Sprague leaned forward, his middle-age paunch spreading over the edge of the table. "And just what did you think her intentions were, Captain?"

"I'm only a mere male, sir." Blade spread his hands in a fatalistic gesture. "How can any man divine the intentions of the subtle female mind? Women are ruled by their emotions. Perhaps it was her gown, displaying all her feminine endowments, or perhaps it was the romantic walk in the empty square in the moonlight that misled me, but I thought she was expecting a kiss and a little squeeze."

Horrified, Theodora could stand no more. She leaped from her chair and took a step toward him, shaking with indignation. "How dare you place the blame on me, Captain! 'Twas you who grabbed me, and you who kissed me! You're not such a dolt as to think I invited that!''

Blade turned from the tribunal and faced the trembling young woman with a look of scorn. ''Funny, but I thought you were enjoying it, Miss Gordon. Until Lieutenant Fletcher arrived on the scene and your belated sense of modesty compelled you to slap my face.''

The two combatants squared off like fighting cocks, oblivious to their fascinated audience.

''And I suppose I tore my own gown, too!'' she cried, determined to maintain her righteous indignation. But shame for her response to him the night before burned her cheeks, and she wished desperately that she had never insisted on lodging the charge against him. She should have heeded Kearny's advice and allowed the matter to be forgotten.

''Ah, the torn dress. Please accept my apologies on that score, Miss Gordon, for that truly was an accident. I'll be happy to make complete restitution. But next time, try to get one that leaves a little more to the imagination. It may save you from a similar incident in the future.''

The smack of a heavy oak ruler on the table brought their mutual accusations to a halt. ''That is quite enough, Captain Roberts. Since it appears that there's just one person's word against another, we're lucky to have an eyewitness to the event. Sergeant O'Fallon, bring in Lieutenant Fletcher.''

Wesley Fletcher entered, pristine in his immaculate blue-and-gold uniform, and stood beside the disheveled prisoner in the center of the room. He could barely contain a satisfied smile as he saluted sharply and stood at attention before the council.

''At ease, Lieutenant,'' Kearny addressed him. ''It's our understanding, sir, that you were present last evening when the contretemps between Captain Roberts and Miss Gordon took place. Is this true?''

Fletcher's manicured fingers deftly smoothed the ends of his tawny mustache. ''It is, sir.''

''Please tell us, then, exactly what you saw last night.''

''I'd just stepped inside the stables when I saw Miz Gordon slap the captain's face, sir. She was cryin'.''

Tapping his fingers on the table top, Captain Harris interrupted. "Did you see him tear her dress?"

"No, sir. Captain Roberts blocked my view."

"Then how did you know she was crying, Lieutenant Fletcher, if you couldn't see her?" Major Sprague inquired.

Fletcher looked at Theodora, encouragement in his pale blue eyes. "I heard her sobs. And I distinctly heard her call him an animal."

"And did you see what happened prior to the slap, Fletcher?" asked the post surgeon.

His lip curled in disdain, Lieutenant Fletcher turned back to the three seated officers. "I didn't have t' see it, sir. I knew what was goin' t' happen before they even went int' that barn. That's why I followed them. Captain Roberts's reputation at West Point has preceded him. He was nearly dismissed from the academy over a scandal involvin' a woman."

Colonel Kearny waved his hand in a gesture of impatience. "We're not here to pass judgment on what happened during Captain Roberts's undergraduate years, Lieutenant Fletcher. Since, by your own admission, you didn't see the captain actually attack Miss Gordon, the rest of your testimony can only be considered speculation on your part. You're dismissed for now. But please remain in the building."

"But I object, sir!" Fletcher exclaimed as he stepped forward. "The blame lies squarely on Roberts's shoulders!"

"That will be all, Lieutenant," Kearny declared, motioning for Sergeant O'Fallon to escort Fletcher from the room.

The commandant turned to Blade. "Now, Captain Roberts, let's get this straight. You say you believed that Miss Gordon was inviting your attentions. If this were so, why then did she react in such anger? Why label you an animal?"

Blade smiled and shrugged his shoulders, hiding his anger. "I believe the expression goes 'Hell hath no fury like a woman scorned.' Miss Gordon was apparently disappointed because there was to be no more than an innocent kiss and a little fondling. I prefer my women to have more experience and I told her so."

Enraged, Thomas Gordon again shot to his feet, his fists clenched. "You swine!" he cried, advancing toward the obdurate officer. "I'll shove those words down your throat!"

Once again the oak ruler was pounded on the table. "That will be enough from you, Mr. Gordon. I won't warn you again. Sit down!"

Rising, Kearny came around the long table and stood near Theodora. He addressed the distraught woman in a soft, kindly voice. "Is this true, Miss Gordon? Did Captain Roberts say at the time that he declined further involvement with you because of your inexperience; in effect, attempting to protect your virtue in spite of yourself?"

Tears welled up in the magnificent emerald eyes and sparkled on the thick lashes. "Who do you believe, Colonel Kearny? Me or this man who has distorted everything that was said and done last night?"

Kearny sighed. "I believe you both, Miss Gordon. I think that you very unwisely entered a deserted building in the company of an unmarried officer and then became upset when he misinterpreted your flirtatious behavior. In the future, young lady, I'd advise you not to allow yourself to be placed in such questionable circumstances."

Then the colonel turned his attention on Blade. "As for you, Captain Roberts, I place the bulk of the blame for this unfortunate incident squarely on your shoulders. You realized Miss Gordon's youth and innocence, and yet accompanied her into the empty stables and attempted to steal a kiss. The two of you are about to embark on a journey of uncounted miles in each other's company. I'm placing Miss Gordon's well-being in your hands, Captain. Forthwith, you are solely responsible for her in every way, and that includes the protection of her virtue—even from yourself if need be."

"Yes, sir," Blade answered grimly. The muscles in his cheek twitched with the strain of maintaining his self-control.

Colonel Kearny turned back to Theodora and gently took her hand. "My dear, don't think for a minute that I doubt your virtue, only that I question the wisdom of your actions last night. But I know you've learned a bitter lesson from this experience. Rather than jeopardize the expedition by ordering a formal inquiry, I would like all of you to leave tomorrow as planned. On your trip with Captain Roberts I want you to keep a journal of everything that takes place between you. If, on the advent of your return, you still wish to place charges against him, I promise that I'll personally hold the court-martial and will accept the contents of your diary as testimony. In the meantime, I'm asking you to forgive and forget. Please accept the captain's deepest and most abject apology for all the unpleasantness he has caused you."

Expectantly, Kearny looked at Blade.

Blade bowed his head slightly to Theodora and, without the slightest hint of sincerity, said, "My deepest and most abject apology, Miss Gordon."

She returned his gaze with freezing politeness. Her words were strained as she nodded. "Very well. For the sake of the expedition, I accept."

"Now," Kearny continued, turning to Tom, "I want you and Captain Roberts to shake hands and put this unfortunate business behind you."

His hazel eyes filled with confusion, Gordon hesitated, then stood and reached out his hand to Blade. "For the time being, Captain, and for the sake of the expedition, I'm willing to set this aside. But if in the future you should manhandle my sister again, I shall be forced to call you out."

Shaking the young man's hand, Blade felt the first hint of guilt. "It won't happen again, Gordon. You have my word on it."

"Fine," Kearny said. "Now, Miss Gordon, I suggest you let your brother take you to my house, where Mrs. Kearny is waiting to serve you breakfast. I understand that my niece has invited you on a strawberry-picking foray this morning. It's my wish that you go with her and let the men here see to the final inspection of the supplies. Your brother can check your equipment one final time, while you have the last fling of socializing before you take on your scientific responsibilities. And I shall look forward to seeing you at dinner this evening."

"Thank you, Colonel," Theodora replied stiffly. She cast one last look of animosity at Blade and left on her brother's arm.

"Now, sir," Kearny continued, turning to Blade, "we have one more problem to deal with."

He dismissed Harris, Sprague, and Haintzelman with a nod, then glanced over at Sergeant O'Fallon. "Bring Fletcher back in here."

At the appearance of Lieutenant Fletcher, Blade squared his shoulders and stood with feet spread apart. The contempt between the two men was palpable.

The commandant looked from one man to the other. "Now then, gentlemen, let's deal with this proposed duel. You are hereby ordered to refrain from any such idiotic and illegal plan to protect your so-called honor. By God, I'll not have such nonsense under my jurisdiction. Is that understood, gentlemen? There'll be no duel, if I have to place you both under house arrest until you leave tomorrow morning. I want your word as officers that you'll not attempt to meet one another. Is that clear? If it isn't, you'll be confined to your quarters for the remainder of the day. Do I have your word, Captain?"

Blade's voice betrayed no emotion. "Yes, sir."

"And yours, Fletcher?"

"Y' have my word as a gentleman, Colonel," came the drawled, bored response.

"Good. We'll hope that the proposed duel will be accepted as the reason for these irregular proceedings, gentlemen. You're under orders not to discuss the affair involving Miss Gordon with anyone. I've already spoken to the others present. I want it to appear that you were brought here strictly because of the personal quarrel between you." Kearny turned to go. "You men are dismissed. Now, let's get this expedition on its way."

Chapter 4

～～☞⚬⚬☜～～

True to Colonel Kearny's wishes, Theodora breakfasted later that morning on flapjacks and maple syrup with Mary Kearny and her niece. Soon after, she found herself, to her dismay, mounted on a gentle mare with an oddly syncopated gait, for all the horses to be used on the journey west were resting for the long trek. With Nell Henderson she left the stable and headed for the stockade gate where their escort of soldiers awaited them. Picking her way slowly through the mounds of provisions in the cantonment's wide yard, she politely followed Nell's lead. In the square, men bustled about, some tallying cartons and boxes of cartridges, others carefully packing a small Yankee spring wagon with scientific equipment individually wrapped in canvas coverings. Unabashed, Nell rode directly up to Blade Roberts, who with Lieutenant Haintzelman was reviewing everything on the long list of provisions to be packed on the mules the next morning.

"Oh, Captain Roberts!" she trilled, affecting surprise at finding him. "How are you this morning?" Her large blue eyes studied the handsome man with open admiration.

Distracted, Blade scarcely glanced up at them, while Peter Haintzelman gazed in spellbound awe at their beauty, his share of the work completely forgotten.

Both women were demurely mounted sidesaddle. Theodora was resplendent in her lavender riding habit and Nell wore a pale blue outfit with a matching top hat that set off her curls.

Blade nodded brusquely. "Busy, Miss Henderson. Good morning."

37

Not to be brushed off so easily, Nell leaned over and lightly touched the braid on his shoulder. "I do hope you'll come for dinner tonight, Captain. Theodora and I are going strawberry picking and my aunt has promised a marvelous dessert. Do say you won't be too busy to come?"

Blade's eyes were fixed upon the list in his hand, from which he had been checking items as Haintzelman called them off. "I'll be there, Miss Henderson. Colonel Kearny has already ordered me to make my appearance."

Satisfied, Nell tugged on the reins of her bay and turned toward the open gates of the fort. She smiled brightly and waved good-bye. "Then I'll talk to you tonight, Captain Roberts."

Behind her, Theodora sat stiffly on her borrowed mount. Without a hint of recognition, she turned her back on Blade Roberts and followed Nell toward their escorts, who were patiently waiting at the gate.

It had been no surprise to anyone under his command that Blade was in a black temper that morning. So far, he hadn't been timid about showing it either. He scowled furiously as he watched the women ride off, then turned to a trooper who had the temerity to walk up and ask a question.

"I don't care how many times you've checked them, Belknap, unpack the blasted tents and check them again!" Blade exploded. "We're not going on a church picnic and it's about time everyone started realizing it."

Stomping off, Blade left the men scurrying around, trying their best to avoid his notice. Already that morning he had blistered two men with his withering tongue, and no one wanted to be the third.

His sharp words carried across the square. Theodora jumped in spite of herself and accidentally struck her horse with her short riding crop. Taking offense at this shabby treatment, the roan reacted with unexpected energy and took off past the waiting escort and out through the stockade gate at an erratic gallop, her rider barely hanging on. The lavender netting of Theodora's veil billowed behind her.

The mounted dragoons chased after the startled mare, trying to offer assistance.

Nell's laughter indicated just what a clumsy picture she

presented, and Theodora gritted her teeth and pulled back sharply on the reins. She finally brought the horse under control before the would-be rescuers caught up with her. By then, unfortunately for Theodora's self-esteem, they were out of sight of the fort and its critical inhabitants.

Theodora and Nell were accompanied by a patrol of four men led by Corporal Overbury. Surrounded by the high-spirited dragoons, who were delighted to have pulled such plush duty on that beautiful June day, the ladies galloped over the grass-covered prairie. The deep-blue sky was dotted by puffy clouds that cast shadows on the sun-warmed land. The air was so clear they could see for miles across the limitless expanse of plain surrounding them.

The group reached a small stand of cottonwoods along Bee Creek and dismounted. Under the trees the dappled light played on the nearby stream and provided a cool haven from the sun. Wildflowers bloomed in abundance along the creek banks, and Theodora's educated eye picked out the scarlet flowers of the mallow, small white primroses, and tall lilac flowers as large as foxgloves. Recognizing them from her studies, though she had only seen them in books, she planned to pick samples of the native flora that she would later press and carefully label with their scientific names.

The trip up the Missouri on the *Liberator* had shown her plants and scenery as alien to her native Massachusetts as the mountain man, Ezekiel Conyers, would have been in the somber halls of Harvard, and Theodora was overwhelmed by the size and diversity of the untamed lands she had seen. At times, the fear of the unknown rose like a specter within her, but she ruthlessly quelled it, refusing to admit even to herself the perils that awaited them. She'd studied too long and too hard to give up her dream at the first hint of danger.

Now, incredibly, Theodora thought, here she was at the edge of the vast, rolling plains of the Great American Desert, frolicking on the bank of Bee Creek with four dragoons of the First Regiment of the U.S. Army and a belle from Atlanta, Georgia.

"There are the wild strawberries," Nell pointed out. "Let's see who can fill their pail the fastest. If I'm in a contest, I'll be sure not to eat every other one I pick."

Nell's suggestion proved an excellent idea, and so enjoyable was the berry picking and the picnic, that it was late afternoon before they arrived back at the fort to find the members of the expedition still hard at work in the square.

Theodora made a beeline for the room she shared with Nell in the commandant's home. Tearing up the stairs and into the bedroom, she snatched off her hat and tossed it on a bureau. She wanted to change quickly and return to the square to check over her things one last time before their departure in the morning. Turning to glance at herself in the mirror over the chest of drawers, Theodora came to a halt. There by the wall stood both her trunks; they must have been overlooked in the confusion of the final preparations. On closer inspection, however, Theodora discovered that the locks on both trunks had been opened. She lifted the lid of each and found that the contents had been rifled. In the larger trunk, her books had been stacked on top of her elegant green satin gown, and in the other her finest lingerie was scattered carelessly over her rose velvet evening dress.

Theodora tore out of the room and down the stairs to the first floor and into the kitchen. "Delilah," she called to the woman busily kneading dough on the countertop, "please send Abner up for my trunks. They've been forgotten! They need to be loaded in the wagon this afternoon. And someone has opened my luggage and gone through my things."

The tall Negress smiled at her. "No, chile, dey didn't fo'get. Dey b'ought dose trunks down and den took dem back up ag'in. De Cap'an, he say dere's no mo' room in de wagon. Yo' trunks are goin' to be shipped back to Massachoo on de next steamboat goin' east."

"They are not!" Theodora blurted out, and made a dash for the door. She wouldn't let him do this to her. He was a bully, but he wasn't going to ride roughshod over her.

As she ran across the gravel path and into the busy square, Theodora spotted the overbearing captain standing with Zeke Conyers behind the wagon that should have contained her two trunks. In seconds she stood directly in front of him.

Seeing her expression, Zeke silently touched the brim of his hat and ambled off.

"I want my baggage brought down and loaded on this wagon," she said without preamble, forcing herself to remain calm despite the slamming of her heart against her ribs. She gulped in a quick breath of air and raced on. "All the things I need for the journey are in those trunks."

Blade's black gaze bored into her. "All the things you need, Miss Gordon, are packed and ready to be loaded on mules in the morning. We don't have room in the wagon for personal effects. I sent your trunks back up earlier today."

"*You* sent them back?" came her indignant reply.

Blade took a step toward her. "You had way too much in those trunks, Miss Gordon. You must've had twenty books. I picked out four of them for you. The rest must remain behind."

Hands on her hips, Theodora demanded in a shrill voice, "I need those books for my work! And what about my dresses? All my evening gowns are still in the trunks! What am I supposed to wear when I get to California?"

Moving so close that his gleaming black cavalry boots touched the hem of her lavender riding habit, Blade spoke in a quiet voice through clenched teeth. "Let's not announce our destination to the world, Miss Gordon. I'll buy you some new gowns when we get there."

"And what about my lingerie? Am I expected to go without undergarments until we reach the Pacific Coast as well?" she cried, her voice quivering.

There was no immediate reply. Aware, all too late, of the unnatural quiet that had descended on the busy cantonment, Theodora looked around to find all of the men standing and waiting in gleeful fascination for the captain's answer.

Blade's words came crisp and clear. His attempt to remain calm was clearly nearing the breaking point. "You packed far too much, Miss Gordon. So I went through your things and picked out everything you'd need for the trip."

"You dare? You dare to go through my personal belongings with your dirty hands and your evil thoughts? You should be horsewhipped for that!"

Turning abruptly, Blade strode to the front of the wagon and reached under the seat. He jerked out a large mule skinner's whip, its rawhide strip cutting through the air with a crack. He returned and threw it at her feet. His dark eyes glittered with rage. "There's the whip to do it with, miss."

She reached down and snatched it from the dirt. With one frustrated sob, Theodora hurled the whip at his broad chest. It hit with a thud and fell to the ground. "You beast!" she cried. Tears welling up in her eyes, she turned and ran back to the house.

Blade pulled his gaze from her departing figure and looked at the mountain men and soldiers, who struggled in vain to hide their grins.

"What the devil are you gawking at?" he shouted. "If you've got nothing better to do than stand around here, we can always drill for two hours when we're done packing!"

As she sat down to dinner in the Kearnys' cheerful dining room, Theodora had the uneasy feeling that it might have been wiser if she'd skipped the meal entirely. At the belated appearance of Captain Roberts, who came in after everyone else was seated and casually nodded to Mary Kearny before hanging his long dragoon sword on the back of his chair, the food began to stick in Theodora's throat. Mere swallowing turned into an act of sheer determination. To her relief, Lieutenant Fletcher was seated directly across from her, and his gentle smile reassured her that he, for one, understood her predicament.

That evening nothing could have kept the conversation away from the next morning's departure, however, and Theodora's excitement, despite her uneasiness in Roberts's presence, mounted with the discussion of routes that could be taken to the Platte River.

After dinner, the ladies retired to Mrs. Kearny's drawing room, promising the gentlemen strawberry tarts as soon as they rejoined them. In short order, the men appeared, and Theodora smiled at her brother as he sat beside her on the sofa. The understanding between them had never required words, but tonight they could barely contain their joy and wished to share it with each other, just as they had been doing every evening since leaving home.

Before they could begin their conversation, however, a large form stood directly in front of them, and they looked up into the scowling face of Blade Roberts.

"May I speak to both of you privately, please?" he asked.

Glancing at each other, they nodded agreement and stood as one.

Blade forced a polite smile and motioned toward the door. "After you," he said. "We'll use the colonel's study."

The room was empty and dark when they entered, and brother and sister waited silently while Blade lit a lamp on the large desk.

"Sit down, please," he said, indicating two tall ladder-back chairs.

"What can we do for you, sir?" Tom asked as he took a seat.

Defiantly, Theodora walked around the chair reserved for her and gripped its back with tight fingers. What was he up to? she wondered. He'd tried frightening her away with a seduction attempt that she doubted was even genuine. He'd ordered that most of her personal belongings be left behind. Now it seemed he was going to try charm where brute strength hadn't worked. She set her lips in a thin, straight line and regarded him with defiance. "Yes, Captain Roberts, just what do you have to say to us that you didn't say already this morning at the inquiry?"

Unprovoked by her attack, Blade leaned one hip on the edge of the colonel's desk and crossed his arms. "I'd like to reason calmly with you both," he replied. "Perhaps that's something I should have tried from the very beginning. Neither of you can have the slightest notion of what you're getting into. It'll be hard enough for you, Tom, to endure the hardships that face us. Thirst, heat, hunger, physical pain, and suffering. All inevitable on a trip like this. It will be impossible for Miss Gordon. No woman has ever crossed the plains because no woman can survive the journey. Tom, I'm asking you to stop your sister from going. If you value her life—if you love her—you'll do that."

Wide-eyed and grave, Tom stared back at the captain, trying to be wise beyond his twenty-three years. "You're certain Teddy can't survive the trip?"

"Wait a minute," Theodora interrupted. "Whether I can survive or not has never been proven because no female has ever tried to cross the plains before. At least no white one. But we all know that Lewis and Clark had a woman with them.

She led them across the wilderness. If she could survive the journey, then so can I. I'm strong and healthy. I can make it!''

"Sacajawea was an Indian squaw, Miss Gordon." Blade waved one hand in dismissal of her absurd notion. "She led them into the country in which she was born. You've no conception of the hardships that await you. You won't last two weeks."

Tom turned to his sister and placed a hand on her arm. "Teddy, he could be right. Maybe we are attempting something that can't be done. Maybe you shouldn't go on this trip."

Pulling away from her brother, Theodora came around the chair and faced the tall captain. Since the moment they'd met him, he'd behaved abominably. He was snide and rude and overbearing. But this cold, calculating man would not be allowed to snatch their dream from them.

She held her shoulders back and her head high and met his eyes with determination. "Don't let this officious, dictatorial man sway you, Tom. Our dream was to go together and we will. I'm leaving with the expedition in the morning. And nothing will change my mind!"

Theodora turned to go, then whirled back. "But before we depart, Captain Roberts," she added, glaring at him, "let me make my feelings toward you clear, lest on this journey you misread my intentions once again. Where you are concerned, I *am* ruled by my emotions. I have never disliked any human being as much as I dislike you!"

In a swirl of rose velvet, she left the room.

"And I thought gently bred young ladies were supposed to be sweet and docile!" Blade shouted.

The door closed on his words with a bang.

But a look of admiration shone on his face. Such spunkiness had to be admired in anyone—even that razor-tongued little shrew.

As he lifted his shoulders in a fatalistic gesture, Tom Gordon shook his head. "Females don't seem to come that way in my family. I'm afraid, Captain Roberts, that I have never been able to change Teddy's mind once it was made up. She's never heeded my warnings in the past and it seems unlikely that she'll start now."

Running a hand through his thick hair, Blade asked in exasperation, "Just who *can* change Miss Gordon's mind once she thinks it's made up?"

Tom shook his head and grinned ruefully. "No one I've met yet, sir!"

Chapter 5

Captain Roberts took a sheaf of papers from Colonel Kearny's outstretched hand and slipped them inside his fringed buckskin shirt. They stood on Kearny's wide portico, apart from the other members of the geographical team gathered for a solemn farewell.

"Give my regards to Bonniville when you see him, Captain," the colonel said. "And good luck." Then he turned to the group clustered on his porch. "Good luck to all of you."

The Gordon twins, themselves dressed in buckskins, stood side by side. Without speaking, Theodora felt the thrill of excitement shared between them. She turned to Mrs. Kearny. "Good-bye, Mary. Thank you for your warm hospitality. I'm sure I'll remember your strawberry tarts in the days ahead."

Mary Kearny put her arms around Theodora and hugged her tenderly. Tears filled her soft brown eyes. "Good luck, Theodora. My prayers go with you on this journey."

Theodora turned to Nell and smiled. "I hope the remainder of your visit at Fort Leavenworth is pleasant. It won't be long until you're safely back home in Atlanta with your parents."

"Oh, Theodora, I shall never forget this day!" Nell exclaimed, her blue eyes wide with admiration.

At that moment their horses were led up by five mounted dragoons. With a nod, Blade signaled that it was time to leave, and everyone moved to his horse. For a minute, as if he was about to say something to her, the captain stared thoughtfully at Theodora, watching her reach for the reins of her mare. Then without a word he moved to his own gray stallion.

It seemed to Theodora that every soul in Fort Leavenworth, young and old, was present to see the U.S. Army's Scientific Exploring Expedition depart on that historic June morning. Excitement stirred the crowd. Tiny children clung to their mothers' calico skirts, staring in wonder at the rough mountaineers clad in homemade buckskins, their long muskets shining in the first rays of the sun. Holding tightly to their fathers' callused hands, girls in pigtails gazed in romantic fascination at the dragoons in their blue-and-gold uniforms with their long cavalry sabers clanking at their sides.

A murmur of surprise ran through the onlookers when Theodora mounted. Boldly, she sat astride a high-spirited chestnut, her split doeskin skirt revealing her calves in high-top riding boots. Ignoring the ripple of disapproval that passed through the crowd, she straightened the wide-brimmed hat on her blond hair with determination. She was flaunting convention, but she'd decided on her apparel and mode of riding long before she came west.

Beside her, on his own mount, Tom shot her a look of support. Brother and sister were in complete agreement that it would be foolish for either of them to try to endure the long trek dressed in city clothes, or for Theodora to attempt to cross the continent sidesaddle.

Now, prepared for a look of censure from the officious Captain Roberts, she defiantly searched the throng for him.

Sensing her gaze upon him, Blade turned War Shield toward her and rode up. His black eyes sparkling in appreciation, he took in the curves revealed by the soft doeskin garment. "I'm happy to see you displaying such good sense, Miss Gordon. When I saw you sidesaddle on that old roan yesterday, I was afraid you'd changed your mind about riding astride."

Lowering her thick lashes under his bold regard, Theodora barely nodded her acknowledgment. Her voice was low and strained. "We Gordons are nothing if not practical, Captain Roberts. It wouldn't be sensible to dress as if this were a church picnic."

Blade didn't miss the repetition of his sarcastic words from the day before, and flashed a crooked grin. He touched his hat in silent reply, wheeled his mount around, and rode to the front of the column.

Theodora's lips turned up in a half-smile as she watched his broad back, so tall and erect in the saddle. Relief washed over her. His forthright acceptance of her shocking apparel meant more than she'd thought possible. Then she squirmed uncomfortably as the full meaning of his words sank in. The split skirt had come as no surprise to Blade Roberts this morning— he'd seen her buckskins when he'd gone through her trunks. It had been his arbitrary decision that the evening gowns would be left behind, but not her outrageous riding habits!

In the center of the square four strong mules stood hitched to the Yankee spring wagon. Pack mules, loaded with the carefully chosen provisions, waited patiently for the bell-mare to lead them away. Behind the wagon, a small herd of horses, mules, and cattle was clustered under the supervision of mounted herdsmen.

As each member of the convoy found his place in the column, Colonel Kearny strode up to Captain Roberts. He reached up and shook Blade's hand. "God go with you all." He returned to the porch steps and saluted the members of the expedition, watching them slowly pass by. Over their heads the company's pennant snapped in the crisp spring breeze.

Just before they reached the fort's open gate, a young boy in tattered overalls ran from the crowd and tried to hand Blade a small American flag. The captain shook his head and pointed back over his shoulder to Theodora. With a gap-toothed grin of understanding, the barefoot tadpole waited until Theodora rode up. Then he stretched up on his dusty toes and handed it to her. "God bless America!" he cried.

Tears misting her eyes at the look of reverence on his round, innocent face, Theodora received the miniature stars and bars. "And God bless you," she answered as she wiped her suddenly damp cheeks.

A roar of approval ascended from the cantonment square. Shouts of encouragement rose from the people of Fort Leavenworth as they wildly cheered the brave members of the expedition riding past the stockade walls. Five little boys followed them across the grassy meadow and ran behind them for as long as they could keep the riders in sight, finally quitting their chase to stand, gasping for breath and watching the gallant company disappear from view.

Captain Blade Roberts and guide Ezekiel Conyers led the column, followed by three of the French Canadians—Baptiste Lejeunesse, Basil Guion, and Louis Chardonnais. In the weeks ahead, Conyers and the mountain men would form the advance party that would scout the trail and hunt for food.

Behind them rode Lieutenant Fletcher, second-in-command, and Lieutenant Haintzelman, the captain's aide-de-camp, with the Gordons immediately following. In the center of the column, directly under the surveillance of Corporal Overbury, rode a half-company of the First Regiment of Mounted Dragoons in their dark blue uniforms, their brass buttons shining in the early-morning sunlight. After the troopers came the wagon and the livestock, guarded by the soldiers who had been designated to herd them under Sergeant O'Fallon. The four mountain men who would be the rear guard on the journey were the last to pass through the wooden palisades.

"Well, Sis," Tom said, riding beside her. "We're leaving at last."

Lieutenant Haintzelman glanced over his shoulder and grinned. "I know just how you feel, Tom. I'm fresh from the Point and a long way from my papa's farm in Pennsylvania. This is my first campaign, and I couldn't sleep last night, just thinking about it."

"Me either!" Theodora admitted, relieved to know that she and Tom weren't the only greenhorns on the trip. She turned and looked back at the steadfast walls of Fort Leavenworth, standing like a lighthouse on the edge of a sea of wilderness.

Under the cloudless blue sky, the column rode slowly and deliberately, setting the pace for the days ahead. Roberts and Conyers were seasoned veterans of the frontier, and they knew that the people and animals would have to build up their strength before they could stay on the trail for hours at a time, day after day, week after week. There was no need to push anyone that first day. Before them, the green grass of the prairie stretched ahead as far as the eye could see, broken only by clumps of willows and cottonwoods growing along the creek banks.

The convoy stopped at noon at Salt Creek, where there was ample wood, water, and grass. Theodora and Tom were surprised to learn that they'd go no farther that day. Instead, the afternoon would be spent practicing the chores of camping and getting used to the routine.

Pickets were posted on the highest points around the camp, the horses unsaddled and the mules unpacked. The mounts were tethered and side-hobbled for further safeguards, then allowed to graze under the watchful eyes of the herdsmen.

The rest of the troupe gathered in the center of the campsite under the shade of the cottonwoods, some perched on fallen logs, others sprawled informally on the thick grass, and listened to Captain Roberts explain the routine. Guard duty was assigned and the camp conductor indicated the sites for the tents, the wagon, and the cooking fires.

"Lieutenant Haintzelman," Blade said, delegating responsibilities, "I want you to help Tom learn the ropes. He can take picket duty alongside you until he's ready to be on his own. Get him one of the extra carbines and some cartridges and powder from the packs."

A frown appeared on Tom's usually carefree features, and he cleared his throat. "Ah, there's just one problem, Captain."

Blade narrowed his eyes. "And what's that, Gordon? Didn't you intend to take your turn at guard duty?"

"It's not that, sir," Tom protested. "It's just that I don't know how to use a rifle."

"Holy Moses!" muttered Ezekiel Conyers, his gray beard shaking back and forth across his thin chest. "The kid starts out across In'jun country, and he cain't even shoot a gun. It's enough to give a body the jimjams."

"Well, he won't learn any younger," Blade commented with resignation.

"I'd like to learn to use a weapon also," Theodora piped up irrepressibly from her place beside Tom on a huge tree trunk. "I've always wanted to learn to shoot."

Arms folded across his muscular chest, Blade eyed her thoughtfully. "That might not be a bad idea, Miss Gordon."

"I'll be happy t' teach them, sir," Lieutenant Fletcher drawled. "I'm an expert at the new carbines." His blue gaze rested longingly on Theodora's seductive form.

"You're in charge of the evening watch, Fletcher. I want your men checking, cleaning, and oiling their weapons under your direct supervision as of now. Get going."

Turning and gazing out over the herd of livestock, Blade spotted the bulky form of the Irish sergeant talking to one of the pickets. "O'Fallon! Get over here!" Blade hollered, a muscle in his cheek twitching, whether from irritation with Tom's incompetence, Theodora's impertinence, or Fletcher's audacity, not even he was certain. Striving to remain patient, he strode up and down in front of the quiet group until the sergeant arrived, out of breath.

Saluting, O'Fallon answered, "Yes, sir!"

"Sergeant, we've just discovered that our two young New Englanders can't shoot a gun. After camp is set up and dinner is over, I suggest you take them aside and begin teaching them the basics of loading a carbine. I'll check on their progress as soon as I can get away."

O'Fallon grinned sympathetically. "Why now, sir, I'd be right happy to."

Blade turned to Theodora. "And now, Miss Gordon, as for your responsibilities."

She sat up straight and tall, anxious to be given some part in the camping chores. "Whatever you wish, Captain Roberts."

"I want you to help Julius Twiggs with his work."

Assisting Theodora up from the log, he guided her to the wagon, where the driver stood leaning against one of the wheels. "Miss Gordon, I want you to meet our cook. Twiggs, meet Miss Theodora Gordon. She'll be your assistant on this trip."

Julius Twiggs was unlike anyone Theodora had ever met. His grizzled white hair contrasted starkly with his dark, wrinkled skin. Bushy white brows and high cheekbones accentuated the kindest brown eyes she'd ever seen. He was taller even than Blade, who until that moment was the tallest man she'd ever known. "Mr. Twiggs, how do you do?" she said at last.

Julius bowed politely. "How do you do, Miss Theo."

Blade seemed unimpressed with the cook's formality. "Twiggs will show you what to do, Miss Gordon. He's in charge of cooking for forty men and can sorely use an assistant."

As Blade started to move away, Theodora took a step toward him, then hesitated, deciding against risking further censure.

Apparently sensing her confusion, he turned back to look at her searchingly. "Is there anything wrong, Miss Gordon?" he asked.

"There's just one problem, Captain Roberts," she mumbled, and flushed in embarrassment.

"And what's that, Miss Gordon?"

"I can't cook."

"You what!" The stunned look on Blade's face betrayed his disbelief. "Every woman knows how to cook!"

"Not this one, Captain," Theodora answered, and winced beneath his glare. "I was raised in a home where there was a housekeeper who took care of all the cooking, cleaning, and laundering."

Blade shook his head in amazement. "What do you think, Twiggs? Can she be of any help to you?"

A front tooth flashed with gold as Twiggs smiled and nodded his grizzled head. "You bet! I teach Miss Theo. We get along fine. Don't you fret none, Miss Theo. Old Twiggs will teach you just what you need to know. I don't cook for fancy. I cook for surviving. Been on plenty of campaigns. You go on, Captain. Miss Theo and Twiggs will fix us all up some dinner."

Together, Theodora and Twiggs watched Blade return to the rest of the party. Twiggs smiled down at her. "Ever milked a cow?"

Deflated at this further evidence of a lack of a practical education, Theodora could only shake her head.

Twiggs was moved to compassion. "Not to worry, Miss Theo. Milking is one thing you learn real quick. Grab that tin bucket. I'll give you your first lesson in camp chores."

Relieved at his easy acceptance of her predicament, Theodora snatched up the pail and skipped along beside him. "Mr. Twiggs, I'm sorry if I stared at you, but I've never seen anyone quite like you before."

The gold tooth flashed again. "Not many like me in the world. My daddy was a runaway slave. Mama was a Seminole Indian. Grew up in the Everglades hunting 'gators."

Theodora soon found that Julius had exaggerated the ease of learning to milk a cow, but they finally returned, each carrying a pail of sweet milk. Under Julius's direction, Theodora helped mix corn bread batter and poured it carefully into a huge mess pan. Fascinated, she watched as he deftly moved about his kitchen under the trees, frying up great slices of ham in an enormous iron skillet.

Soon the meal was ready and Julius raised a little trumpet to his lips. Three short dissonant blasts brought the men hustling over to the fire.

After helping Julius serve the hungry crew, Theodora joined Peter and Tom on their favorite tree trunk.

His plate heaped with ham and beans and corn bread, Lieutenant Fletcher sat down beside them. "I understand the two of y' are goin' t' be trained in weaponry later this afternoon," he began, blithely ignoring the presence of the other lieutenant. He carefully wiped his blond mustache with a white handkerchief. "I'd be happy t' give y' any help y' might need."

Realizing just whom Fletcher would like to help, Tom grinned. "Thanks, Fletcher, but Sergeant O'Fallon told me he would instruct us later. Right after we finish eating Lieutenant Haintzelman is going to show us how to set up our tent. Teddy's going to work with us, so she and I can learn to put up our tent without anyone else's assistance. We want to become as independent as possible."

But the much-sought-after independence came slowly. Their first attempt to raise the tent ended in the collapse of the shelter on top of their heads, and the twins had to crawl ignominiously from beneath the canvas to the roar of good-hearted laughter from the others. Louis Chardonnais came over and helped raise it with professional expertise.

"There, little cabbages," Louis said, his brown eyes twinkling. "At least tonight you will sleep in comfort."

Their studies for the day were far from over, for Sergeant O'Fallon appeared with an armful of bedding. "Well now," he said, "you'll be getting the hang of it before too long, I'm thinking. Put these blankets inside and come with me. It's time for your first lesson in weapons."

"Great!" Tom exclaimed as he heaved the blankets into the tent.

"Fine," Theodora added, and forced a smile. If learning to shoot a rifle was as difficult as learning to pitch a tent or milk a cow, maybe she should have kept her mouth closed for once. But it was too late now.

Obediently, she followed in Tom's and O'Fallon's wake; behind them came Peter Haintzelman. The small group walked to the outskirts of camp, beyond the thicket of cottonwoods, and up to a grassy knoll, where Corporal Overbury joined them with two brand-new carbines cradled in the crook of his plump arm.

"Now, children," Sergeant O'Fallon lectured in his thick brogue, taking one of the carbines and holding it so that the sunlight flashed against its barrel, "this is a weapon you've not seen before. What we're looking at here is a breech-loading, smooth-bore sixty-nine-caliber carbine made at Harpers Ferry especially for the First Regiment of Dragoons. This rifle will shoot straighter and faster than any weapon known to man. And you're about to learn to use it." His grin indicated the rare privilege he was bestowing.

Delight shown in Tom's hazel eyes. "I've heard about these new percussion rifles."

"These are real beauties," Peter added, as he took the other one from Overbury. "We've only had them a few weeks ourselves and haven't had that much extra time to practice with them."

Deftly, O'Fallon showed them how to load the firearm, identifying the various parts and explaining how the hammer hitting the plunger would set off the cap that contained the priming charge. He reminded Theodora of a tutor she'd once had who took much the same inordinate pride in explaining the parts of a flower.

Blade Roberts joined them just as the actual practice was about to begin. He stood quietly beside Theodora while the sergeant helped her brother assume the correct stance. She was vibrantly aware of the captain's magnetic presence; he was so close his muscular thigh brushed against her skirt. Refusing to acknowledge the effect of his nearness on her, she peeked at him from beneath lowered lashes. He watched the lesson intently, seemingly unconscious that they were almost touching.

Tom placed the butt of the rifle against his shoulder and squeezed the trigger gently, as O'Fallon directed, aiming at a designated tree trunk. His first shot was wide of the mark.

"You've got to remember to sight, boyo." O'Fallon chuckled, and patted Tom's shoulder.

It was Theodora's turn next, and Blade swung the full force of his black eyes upon her. She caught her breath at their intensity. "Now, Miss Gordon, you try it. And remember to squeeze gently."

Surely the sensual quality in his deep voice was just in her imagination?

Helping her raise the weapon to her shoulder, Blade eased the rifle into place. Then he stepped back and nodded.

Her hands shook from the sheer weight of the carbine as she sighted down the barrel. She closed her eyes and pulled the trigger. The muzzle kicked up wildly and the blast knocked her backward. Tripping over the hem of her skirt, she landed on her bottom with a soft plop, her feet stuck out in front of her. Miraculously, she had retained her grip on the heavy carbine.

Blade's strong hands encircled her waist and lifted her to her feet. "Not too bad for the first try," he commented, as he pried the weapon from her rigid fingers and tossed it to Overbury to reload. "But you need to hold the butt firmly against your shoulder so it won't kick up on you."

Retrieving the carbine from the corporal, he put it back in Theodora's hands. "Here, let me help you." Blade's sinewy arms encircled her as he raised the rifle and guided it to her shoulder. "Hold it firm, Miss Gordon, and sight right down the barrel. That's it. Keep your eyes open. Now squeeze the trigger."

The kick of the rifle knocked her against him, and she felt his powerful chest and thighs absorb the jolt effortlessly. Feeling his hard body next to hers, Theodora knew a sudden, intense longing to turn in his arms and raise her lips to his. The memory of those demanding lips covering her own erased all thoughts of cartridges, powder, and priming pans. Flushed with desire, she wondered if he knew from the quickened rise and fall of her breasts that her heart was pounding wildly.

Blade chuckled softly in her ear and inhaled the sweet fragrance of wildflowers that drifted from her hair. "Are you sure you really want to learn to shoot a gun, Miss Gordon? The carbine's almost as long as you are tall."

"Yes, I'm sure, Captain Roberts," she snapped, afraid he'd suspect her true feelings. "You never know when some vicious reature might attack you. Next time I'll be ready.''

She pulled away from him, averted her eyes, and began to
eload the weapon just as O'Fallon had taught her.

Why did she feel so confused every time she was near the
brutish captain? Hadn't he tried to seduce her, then told vicious
ies about her at the hearing? This physical reaction to him
ould be controlled. All she needed to do was listen to her
intellect and not her erratic feelings. No other man had made
 her behave like a romantic schoolgirl, and she wasn't going
o let this lecher be the first.

Just then O'Fallon came over to Blade. ''Was there some-
hing wrong now, sir?''

Blade's voice was detached and professional. ''No, Sergeant, I was just helping Miss Gordon. Carry on.'' He turned
and left without another word.

They spent the afternoon drilling on the loading and firing
of the carbine, during which time various members of the
camping party wandered out to the grassy knoll to watch their
progress. The mountain men were intrigued by the new percussion rifles, but professed their faith in their own reliable
muzzle-loading muskets. O'Fallon was a thorough drill instructor and insisted that they practice reloading the rifle over and
over, until the twins felt they could have done it blindfolded.

''Do we get to keep these, Sergeant?'' Tom asked.

''That's what the Captain told me.'' O'Fallon turned to
Theodora. ''But a little colleen like yourself had better keep
t in her saddle holster except in an emergency.''

''If there's an emergency,'' Lieutenant Fletcher drawled as
he joined them, ''I'll look out for Miz Gordon. There'll be no
need for her t' worry her pretty head about usin' firearms.''

''Sure and we all know we can count on you in a crisis,
Fletcher,'' the sergeant said cryptically before he turned and
departed.

Fletcher stretched and yawned. ''This conversation's much
too tedious for a sweet thing like you, Miz Gordon,'' he admonished. He took her elbow. ''Let's excuse ourselves and
take a walk together before supper time.''

''Supper?'' Theodora cried in concern and pulled away from
him. ''Is it that late already? I've got to help Mr. Twiggs
prepare the meal.''

"I think it's disgustin' that you've been given the humiliatin' task of helpin' that nigra half-breed t' cook," Fletcher complained in annoyance. "A gently bred lady isn't asked t' do the menial chores of servants."

Tom regarded his sister with genuine concern. "Does it upset you to help with the cooking, Teddy? I could speak to Roberts about it."

"I don't mind, truly." She reached for his arm, as if afraid he'd leave to seek out the captain at once. "I want to be a real part of this trip. I told Captain Roberts I would do my share of the chores and I will."

Hooking his fingers in his sword belt, Fletcher tossed his blond head and sneered in disdain. "Roberts doesn't have the slightest idea what a real lady should do. He'll expect y' t' work like a squaw. He's as primitive as a half-naked savage. And even less perceptive."

"Nevertheless, Lieutenant," Theodora replied, as she felt a flush spread across her cheeks at his comparison, "I promised Julius I would help gather firewood for supper, and I intend to do it." She glanced at her brother. "Gentlemen, if you'll excuse me?"

The supper was delicious. Twiggs had a flair for cooking over an open fire, and the venison that the hunters had brought in that afternoon was served in juicy steaks, accompanied by carrots and potatoes.

After the cleanup, Theodora sat on a fallen log in the fading sunlight, a small pair of scissors in her hand. During the day she had broken three fingernails, and with resignation she began snipping off the rest.

Blade paused to watch her pare them down with ruthless determination. "That's too bad about your lovely nails, Miss Gordon. Life on the trail can be rather harsh."

Theodora thrust out her chin and gazed defiantly into his black eyes. His solicitude didn't fool her. He was only trying to point out one more reason why she should have remained at Fort Leavenworth. "I don't mind, Captain Roberts. I'll gladly sacrifice my long fingernails to be on this trip. I'll chop off my hair, if I have to."

"That won't be necessary," he quickly replied. A look of concern crossed his rugged features. "Don't even think of cutting it, Miss Gordon. If it becomes too much of a bother on the trail, you can always braid it."

She regarded him with curiosity. It seemed strange for him to be so concerned about such a personal decision as the length of her hair, considering all the serious problems facing him in the weeks ahead. She remembered Fletcher's scornful remark that Blade wouldn't even know how to treat a lady. Was he really the barbarian that Fletcher painted?

"Is there some problem, Miss Gordon? Is it that you don't know how to braid hair?"

Theodora jumped up and shook the folds of her skirt. She didn't need to be reminded that, so far, she'd been a complete failure. "As a matter of fact, Captain," she replied defensively, "you finally hit upon something I *can* do." Stung by his patronizing words, she turned to go. "Good night."

Blade caught her elbow and held her effortlessly to the spot as he tried to read her thoughts. He didn't regret the phony seduction attempt in the stable; he'd done it to save her life, and he'd do it again if he thought it would work. But since her participation in the expedition was now a fact, he wanted to set the bad feelings aside. Instead of indifference on her face each time she looked at him, he yearned to see her bewitching smile—the one she bestowed so frequently on Fletcher. "I'm sorry I upset you the night we met, Miss Gordon. My intentions were honorable, even if my actions were not."

"Your actions were despicable, Captain." She looked away from his frank gaze, apparently determined to hold on to her righteous anger.

"Perhaps. But what happened that evening went far beyond what I had planned, believe me. Surely you can feel that there is something special between us?"

"Oh, there's something between us all right!" she spat out. "There's a memory of being assaulted for me and a possible court-martial for you!"

Blade gripped her shoulders with his strong fingers and pulled her to him. "Is the memory of my kiss so unpleasant, Miss Gordon? Or is it that the feelings I aroused in you were deeper than you'd ever felt before? Did your fiancé ever kiss you like that?" Jealousy of the unknown suitor flamed up inside him. "Did you respond to his kiss the way you did to mine?"

His touch burned through her shirt, and she trembled at the passion in his ebony eyes. She felt as if she were splitting in two. One part of her wanted to treat him with the cold disdain he deserved; the other longed to put her arms around him and renew that soul-wrenching kiss.

"Martin Van Vliet is a gentleman—something you'd know nothing about. He gave me a chaste betrothal kiss on the night of our engagement, with the approval of my father and grandmother. Now, let go of me, Captain Roberts," she hissed through clenched teeth. "The entire camp is watching!"

Inexplicably, his deep voice softened. "Be thankful they are, *vehoka*, or I'd be tempted to prove my point."

Releasing her, Blade watched as she stalked over to her tent. Relief at her words quenched his jealous fears. Despite her passionate response to his kiss, no man had ever known her intimately. Of that he was certain. Although why that thought brought such a feeling of satisfaction, he couldn't begin to fathom.

Chapter 6

That night a fine, steady rain came out of the north, bringing with it a lingering touch of winter. The first drops hitting the roof of the tent woke Theodora, and she burrowed under the blankets as she listened in trepidation to the sound of the wind shaking the canvas. But despite her concern, the shelter proved a snug haven, and it stood firm against the buffets.

"Tom, are you awake?" she whispered into the darkness, trying in vain to see her brother asleep on the other side. His only answer was a light snore. He'd always been a sound sleeper.

Restless, she stretched and rolled onto her back. She pulled the covers up to her chin, stared at the canvas ceiling, and thought about Blade Roberts. The handsome captain continued to baffle her. His charming efforts to befriend her, starting from the first day on the trail, seemed so contradictory to his wanton attempt to seduce her the night they met. Not once since they'd left Fort Leavenworth had he given her any reason to suspect he would repeat his lecherous actions. But what did she want from him? A warm flush crept over her as she remembered the feel of his tongue touching hers so intimately. Somehow the more she thought of it, the less shocking it seemed, though she certainly hadn't known that a man would want to do that. What else would a man want to do? she wondered. She wished she had spent less time memorizing phyla and more time listening to the chatter of the other young ladies at Mount Holyoke.

The camp came alive to the call of reveille. Yawning, Theo-

dora quickly pulled on her buckskins and rain poncho, jammed
on her boots, and stumbled outside. The rain continued, and
in the darkness she could barely make out the shapes of the
men as they scurried about, repacking the supplies and checking the animals. Behind her, Tom groped for his breeches.

"Ye gads, what time do you think it is?" he moaned, his
hazel eyes heavy-lidded with sleep.

"I'm not sure." Theodora glanced over her shoulder and
laughed at his expression of horror. "But I don't think either
of us has ever been awake at this hour before. Hurry up, or
we'll be left behind!"

Quickly they repacked their bedrolls and dismantled the tent.
Following her brother's lead, Theodora walked into the cluster
of nearby cottonwoods. Tom waited a short distance away
while she attended to her needs. The evening before, Roberts
had explained the forthcoming routine to them, adamant that
Theodora never be left alone beyond calling distance. Her
cheeks had flushed when he phlegmatically explained the rules
for her daily toilette, no more perturbed than if he had been
addressing a child who might have to get up in the middle of
the night. She had been unable to meet the disinterested eyes
that glittered like black jets in the firelight. For once at a loss
for words, she had nodded to indicate her understanding, grateful to Tom, who confidently assured the captain that he would
be responsible for his sister's personal needs.

They left the grove and walked to the edge of the creek.
Kneeling, they splashed water on their hands and faces and
shared a bar of soap. Then they hurried to catch their hobbled
mounts and grab a handful of corn bread and sliced ham from
Twiggs on their way past the wagon.

The rain came down in a steady stream that first full day on
the trail, and by evening, when they made camp, an exhausted
Theodora climbed down from the saddle on shaky legs. Her
hair was plastered to her head; her hat and gloves were cold
and soggy. She pulled at her leather skirt; it was soaking wet
and clammy against her legs. Every muscle ached, and despite
her best efforts she groaned, realizing that she would have no
rest for a long time to come. The animals had to be tended,
the tent erected, and the evening meal prepared before she
could even consider relaxing. Yet she yearned to crawl ignobly

into her tent (after someone else raised it for her) and fall sound asleep.

So far she hadn't made a single entry in her journal, or gathered one botanical specimen, or sketched a solitary example of the many birds she'd seen during the last two days. Holding Athena's reins, she sat on the drenched ground, her elbows on her upraised knees, her head lowered to her forearms, and wondered how she would ever get the energy to stand up again.

Blade appeared out of the pouring rain and stood before her. With an effort she raised her head and looked up at him. His deep blue cape accentuated his broad shoulders. From her ground-level vantage point, he resembled a small mountain. Even through the downpour she could see the glint of triumph in his mocking eyes.

"Tired, Miss Gordon? It's still not too late to change your mind. I could easily send you back under escort, and the men could catch up with us in a few days."

The strength she had despaired of only moments before surged through her. Theodora jumped to her feet. "I was simply waiting for orders, Captain," she snapped as she drew on all the resources of her willpower to remain standing.

His devilish grin made his sharp, clear-cut features appear almost boyish. "In that case, just report to Twiggs. He'll keep you busy."

The routine of the trail was established in the next few days, despite the foul weather. The troupe rose long before dawn, ate a quick breakfast beside the spring wagon, packed the mules, saddled the horses, and moved out while it was still dark. Ezekiel Conyers, accompanied by the three French Canadians, formed the advance scouting party; they rode well ahead, marking the trail and hunting, as well as finding the next campsite with the three necessary qualifications—plenty of grass, wood, and water. In addition, each site was chosen for its defensive attributes: high ground with ample water. The caravan traveled until mid-afternoon, set up camp, picketed the animals, took turns standing watch, and ate an early meal. And each time they came to a creek or a spring, they crossed before making camp, lest the rains increase and hamper the fording.

The men grew increasingly worried about the weather, for as they covered the miles, they seemed to be riding into the worst of it. At last, on the eighth morning out, the rain stopped, the air grew still and heavy, and the sun shone for several hours.

"Hallelujah!" Twiggs called to Theodora from his wagon seat, his gold tooth flashing. A huge, dilapidated Mexican sombrero covered his grizzled head. "Sunshine at last!"

Cold and miserable, she lifted her face to the warming rays. "Oh, doesn't it feel good, Julius?"

She never heard his answer, for ahead she saw Conyers, the French Canadians at his heels, racing his horse toward the front of the column. He gestured to Roberts as he came at a ground-devouring gallop. At a call from Blade, Sergeant O'Fallon wheeled his horse around and shouted to Corporal Overbury. The orders came down through the ranks: Make camp. At once.

Leading the way, Roberts and Conyers headed for the highest ground available—a small, treeless rise, well above the banks of Vermilion Creek. The animals, nervous and skittish despite the calm, sultry air, tried to break through the cordon of herdsmen, who methodically lassoed and side-hobbled them one by one. Theodora watched in puzzlement as even the two dairy cows were lashed and hobbled. Together, soldiers and mountain men worked at a breakneck pace raising the shelters and picketing the livestock, but even as they labored, the storm appeared on the flat horizon.

The tempest moved with incredible speed, its black clouds flying across the darkening sky. Far off, tremendous bolts of lightning sliced through the clouds, followed by boom after boom of crashing thunder. Terrified, the horses whinnied and the mules brayed, as they tried to shake off their bonds and flee.

Watching helplessly, Theodora turned and spotted Conyers close by. The mounting wind whipped his gray beard into snarls and threatened the eagle's feather on the slouch hat he clutched to his head. She ran to him. "What is it, Zeke? What's happening?"

He placed his hands on her trembling shoulders. "Don't you

worry yore pretty head, Miss Gordon. We'll be all right. But it's gonna be a real prairie waterspout, yesiree. Yore saddle and bedroll in the tent?''

She nodded as the first sprinkles hit her face.

"Good. Now find yore brother. Then pull yore personal belongin's inside the tent and sit tight.''

With tremendous velocity the storm approached. Peeking out from the flap of their tent, Theodora and Tom watched. It didn't just pour. The rain came down in sheets as though rushing headlong over a falls. Cascades of it were beaten by the high winds and tossed in every direction. Across the plains the water rushed, filling depressions on the ground and turning them into ravines of raging torrents. The angry wind smashed the downpour against their refuge, and they looked at each other with awe.

Outside in the deluge they could see dim shapes trying to calm the frightened livestock. With the rain came huge, rounded chunks of ice. The hail pounded on the men and cattle. It bounced off the taut canvas until all they could hear was the sound of it beating on their fragile shelter.

Despite her fear Theodora tried in vain to discern the shape of her beautiful chestnut. "Athena will be terrified! I've got to go to her!''

Before Tom could answer, she crawled through the small opening, holding her hands over her head and face to protect herself. Her brother was right behind her, and together they raced toward the horses, nearly blinded by the downpour that blew directly in their faces. Large chunks of hail pounded on them, making it almost impossible to continue.

At last they reached the others, who held the restraints of the rearing, plunging animals.

"Athena!'' Theodora screamed into the wind. "Athena!''

All the horses had been tied securely to a long rope, and the twins raced along it, each searching blindly for his own. Tom nearly stumbled by High Flight, only to recognize the gelding at the last minute. He grabbed the lead line and reached up to pat its neck.

At last Theodora found Athena, safely lashed beside the captain's gray stallion. With both the horses' fetters held tightly in his hand, Blade was stroking their necks and talking to them continuously.

Theodora reached up, pulled on Athena's rope, and patted the mare's nose. "It's all right, girl," she cried over the roar as she tried to keep her face protected from the hail. "I'm with you now!"

"What the hell are you doing out here?" Blade shouted. "I gave orders for you to stay in your tent!"

She moved closer to him and screamed in his ear. "I had to come. I couldn't leave Athena out here alone."

"Dammit, she's not alone!" he hollered back, and pulled Theodora closer to him with one hand.

To Theodora's amazement, War Shield was not plunging wildly about. Although nervous and frightened, the well-trained animal was listening to Blade. He seemed to sense his master's composure. Gradually, the high-strung mare, influenced by the powerful stallion, calmed as well, and their owners stood side by side in the torrent, soothing them.

Ducking her head, Theodora tried unsuccessfully to bury herself under her rubber poncho. She had dashed out without her hat, although it was so sodden and limp it would have offered little protection anyway. In contrast, Blade's wide hat kept the hail off his face, and the rain ran in rivulets down its brim.

Shaking his head at her predicament, Blade opened his rainproof cape and pulled her under its shelter. She fit under his arm like a doll, protected from the driving rain and the stinging chunks of ice.

Theodora put her arms around his waist and buried her wet head on his chest. She was trembling. She wanted to believe it was only from the cold and not from fear of the storm, but she knew better. Roll after roll of thunder crashed above their heads, and she was grateful she couldn't see the jagged bolts of lightning striking the prairie. The feel of his muscles, firm and taut under his soft buckskin shirt, promised security, and like Athena, her fear dissolved under his steadying influence. Strangely though, beneath the ear she pressed to his muscular chest, his heartbeat steadily increased. She wondered with misgiving if the storm could possibly get any worse. He'd always seemed so supremely self-confident, so unruffled.

Theodora, not the raging tempest, was the reason for Blade's quickened pulse. But it was not an excitement that he was in any hurry to end. With her slim arms clasped tightly around him, her rounded breasts pressed firmly against his rib cage, and her head laid so trustingly on his chest, he felt desire leap up within him. Not for the first time, he recalled with pleasure the feeling of her soft lips under his own, the satin smoothness of her skin beneath his touch. Since their initial evening on the trail she had treated him with polite indifference, preferring the company of Wesley Fletcher and Peter Haintzelman. But he knew she had responded to his kiss, to his caress, and he was certain he could bring her to that passionate response again. A longing washed over him to hold her silken body next to his, to feel her arch with pleasure at his touch, to ignite within her a throbbing, relentless need, and then guide her to its fulfillment.

Like a warning bell, his promise to Kearny intruded on his lustful fantasies. *You are solely responsible for her in every way, and that includes the protection of her virtue—even from yourself.*

Bit by bit, the awareness of his tense muscles rippling under her hands replaced Theodora's thoughts of the storm. The spicy, aromatic scent of the cheroots in his pocket mingled with the masculine smell of leather and filled her senses. Memories of his kiss intruded on her brief feeling of security and she peeked out from under his cape. The hail, much smaller, was falling less frequently now, and the sheets of driving rain had diminished to the status of an ordinary Massachusetts rainstorm. She smiled tentatively up at him, hoping he had no inkling of her thoughts, then stepped out from under the shelter of his arm.

"Thank you, Captain," she said, suddenly shy as she turned and patted Athena on her velvet nose. "You certainly have a way of quieting down distraught females," she added with a nervous laugh, indicating the mare.

"You're no longer frightened, I hope," Blade said gently.

Theodora turned to stare at him, searching for the reason for the tenderness in his voice. "Oh, pooh! I wasn't frightened. I was speaking of my horse, Captain."

"Were you?"

A bashful smile played at the corners of her mouth, and she

shrugged. "I guess I was a little worried. And when I heard your heart pounding, I thought you were frightened too."

His boyish smile was devastating. "It wasn't the storm that caused my pulse to race, *vehoka*." His ebony eyes caught and held her gaze, telling her without words what had sent the blood pounding through his veins.

With supreme effort, she pulled her own gaze away. "I'd better look for Tom," she murmured, and turned to go.

As she hurried away a strange ache spiraled through her body, causing the oddest wish to return to the shelter of his cape and cling once again to those firm, rippling muscles. The dratted man brought on the strangest feelings. If he could do that to her, even after what had happened back at Fort Leavenworth, he was twice as dangerous as any thunderstorm!

Tom was inside their tent when she entered.

"There you are, Teddy. I looked for you after the hail stopped, but I missed you in the rain." The relief in his voice made her feel guilty.

Theodora hesitated. She wondered how to tell him why he hadn't been able to find her. "I was sheltering under Captain Roberts's cape," she blurted out, opting for the brutal truth.

Tom's cheery smile creased his freckled face as he pulled off his soaking boots. "That was very generous of Roberts to give up his rain gear. He must be soaked to the skin." The mischievous look in his greenish brown eyes teased her.

Gratefully, Theodora returned her brother's smile. "Wasn't it?" She grinned, pulling off her poncho and wringing out her dripping hair.

"And it's a good thing you're so much shorter than the captain. Otherwise you'd never have fitted so snugly under his arm."

Theodora laughed out loud at Tom's words. "Well, you wouldn't have wanted the poor captain to come down with influenza, standing out there without his rain gear, would you?"

The storm receded as quickly as it had appeared, and by early evening the sky was clear and filled with stars. Wandering to the edge of the camp, Theodora saw the silhouettes of the sentries in a semicircle around them. She spotted a young

private, his back to her, seated on the grass with his carbine
resting across his knees. She had learned that at night the guards
remained on the ground, a position that enabled them to see
an intruder's outline against the sky. No one from the expedition was allowed past the picket line after dark, so anyone
beyond its perimeter would be assumed to be an enemy.

With a sense of wonder, Theodora looked out at the treeless
horizon and black velvet sky. Only the faint glow from the
campfires competed with the brilliance of the countless stars.
The air was so clear, so crisp, Theodora felt as though, if she
really stretched, she could reach up and touch a nearer star.

"It's truly magnificent, isn't it?" a soft voice drawled at
her shoulder. "But not nearly as lovely as you."

Startled, she swung around to find Lieutenant Fletcher standing nearby. He had followed her from the campfire. She sighed
as she looked upward again. "Marvelous! What makes them
seem so close?"

Fletcher moved to her side. "Out here, Miz Gordon, everythin' seems bigger than life. The storms, the stars, the
people. But it's only a mirage. A trick of nature. Things are
the same size as they are back home, but on the plains there's
nothin' with which t' compare them. No handy yardstick t'
measure them by. The same men on the frontier, whisked back
t' your hometown in New England, would seem quite ordinary,
really."

Instinctively, Theodora knew he was hinting about Blade.
She wondered if he'd seen her sheltering under the captain's
arm. But if Tom hadn't spotted her in the pouring rain, it was
unlikely that the lieutenant had.

"I can't imagine Captain Roberts being ordinary in any
setting," she replied with irony as she smoothed the lace at
her throat. Earlier she had changed from her soggy buckskins
to a simple cotton frock, delighted to find it still dry inside her
pack. Although Blade had left behind her fancy evening gowns,
she'd discovered several daytime dresses.

Fletcher placed his hand on her arm. "He's not only ordinary, but also common. Cheap and tawdry. Roberts's veneer
of civilization is as thin as the gold finish on a gypsy's trinket.
Why do you think he discarded his uniform before he even
left the fort? That alone should give you some indication of

where his true loyalty lies. I've had the misfortune of knowing Roberts since we were in the academy t'gether, where his very presence was proof that enough family money will buy acceptance anywhere, even int' West Point.''

"Captain Roberts's family is wealthy?" she asked in surprise.

"How else do y' think he could buy his way int' polite society? Some people would allow the devil himself int' their homes, if he were backed by enough gold." Fletcher dropped her elbow and stepped away, a sneer marring his good looks. "But don't let that genteel New Orleans background fool y', Miz Gordon. Scholars claim that a man's character is formed by the time he is five years old. Roberts lived with the savages until he was twelve. Doesn't that tell y' somethin'?"

"Knowing almost nothing about the Plains Indians, Lieutenant Fletcher, I'm clearly unable to make an informed judgment on Captain Roberts's character. But I find it very hard to think of him as unpatriotic."

Fletcher smiled and traced the edge of his blond mustache with a thumbnail. "I've no need to lie about him t' you. You've experienced his savagery personally."

His reference to Roberts's attack on her person startled her, and she looked away, toward the center of camp. There she saw Tom and Lieutenant Haintzelman beside a large telescope mounted on a tripod. Blade was gazing through the instrument, sighting the stars.

"Oh look!" she interrupted, pointing to the small group. "Captain Roberts has set up the telescope. Let's go see if we can look through it."

Blade stepped back from the instrument and glanced surreptitiously at the approaching young woman. He smiled to himself at the success of his plan. There'd been no reason to get the telescope out of the wagon, for they were only a week's journey away from Fort Leavenworth and had no need to take astronomical readings so soon. But he'd known that the telescope would draw Theodora away from that blasted, slicktongued Southerner quicker than anything else he had at hand.

"Sis," Tom called with enthusiasm. "Come over here. The captain's telescope is excellent."

"May I, Captain?" she asked politely, barely able to suppress her eagerness. To her chagrin, she sounded like a little girl asking for a treat.

"Certainly, Miss Gordon," he replied, guiding her up to the instrument and putting his hands on her shoulders as she bent to look through the lens. "We've sighted Jupiter. You can easily see its satellites."

Tom was right. The telescope was a superbly made instrument, and the heavens swept down toward her through the glass. "Yes, I can see it," she whispered in awe. "How beautiful!"

Blade knelt down on one knee beside her and reached up to steady the scope. "Look closely. The dark streaks are its belts and the bright spaces between are called zones. Can you find them?"

"Yes," she answered softly.

"Peter wants a turn, Sis," Tom interrupted. "He hasn't had a chance to look yet."

Tearing herself away from the telescope, Theodora reluctantly stepped aside. "Go ahead, Peter. It's your turn," she offered.

Blade stood up. "You can look again when he's finished, Miss Gordon. I'll help you find Saturn with its rings."

A pleased smile lit her face and her green eyes shone like jewels. "I'd enjoy that, Captain Roberts," she said brightly.

No one paid the least attention to Lieutenant Fletcher, who stood on the far side of the firelight, his long fingers clenched on his sidearm.

Chapter 7

The next morning Theodora awoke to the sound of rushing water. The rains had swollen Vermilion Creek to a fast-moving stream, and now she realized why they had stopped so far above the banks. Had they encamped near the water's edge, their site would have been flooded while they slept.

The thought of the steadily rising waters pushed the travelers along, for they were to cross the Big Blue River that day. But their efforts to race to the upper crossing were in vain, for coming upon the river they found it swollen and dangerous, not only from the recent storm but also from the runoff water from melting snowpacks in the high plains and distant mountains. A swift current turned the normally peaceful river into a frothing, bubbling caldron of freezing water. At the sight of its turmoil, Theodora's heart lurched.

Wesley Fletcher, riding next to her, saw her terrified eyes. "Y'all right, Miz Gordon?" he questioned as he reined in his sorrel on the banks above the river.

Theodora stared down at the turgid waters and gulped. "It's just that I . . . I can't swim, Lieutenant."

"You're probably not the only one who can't. Don't worry. We'll get y' over safely." Fletcher studied her for a moment, sympathy on his handsome features. "Y' know, y' can still return t' Leavenworth," he pointed out. "It's not too late. I'd be happy t' escort y' back t' the fort and then catch up with the expedition."

Tempted beyond belief to accept his kind offer, Theodora swallowed her fears. "That's very generous of you, Lieutenant, but I can't give up so soon. I may not be able to swim, but I'm sure Athena can. And a Gordon never cries off.'' Touching the ends of the reins to her mare's side, she turned her mount and started toward the riverbank.

When she reached the others, Theodora found Twiggs busy unloading the Yankee spring wagon.

"Can I help?" she offered, puzzled that he would be taking out the tin plates, the frying pans, the coffeepot, and the kettles so early in the day.

"Yes, Miss Theo. Sure can. Got to take everything out of this wagon." Twiggs jumped up inside and started to hand things down to her.

Theodora set the milking buckets on the grass, then turned and reached up for the ax, hatchet, and spade. "Why do we need to unload the wagon?"

Twiggs grinned and shook his white, grizzled head. His soft brown eyes glowed with pleasure. He always seemed to delight in explaining the wonders of the journey to her. "Going to turn this wagon into a boat. Yes'm. A boat. Float it right 'cross that river.''

"How can we do that, Julius?" Intrigued, Theodora lifted down the medicine chest with its supply of quinine, opium, and cathartics.

"*How* be the captain's problem. He said unload, so he can make a boat. Old Twiggs unloads. Captain makes the boat.''

He handed down the barometer, chronometer, thermometer, sextant, and telescope, each carefully wrapped in its own canvas bag.

Theodora watched the men work while she helped unload the supplies. The packs were removed from the horses, and the four mules were unhitched from the wagon. Two dragoons came over and assisted with the rest of the supplies, and soon the wagon was emptied. Then Sergeant O'Fallon and two privates released the axles and tongue from the wagon bed, and it was lifted up off its wheels and set on the ground.

Next water casks were emptied, stoppered tight, placed inside the wagon bed and secured with ropes. On the outside of the wagon, one cask was lashed to each side at the center. Finally, O'Fallon and six of the troopers turned the entire wagon bed, casks and all, upside down and carried it to the water's edge.

Seeing Tom and Lieutenant Haintzelman toting packs to the bank, Theodora followed them down to the river.

Blade, who'd been checking the ropes, walked toward them. "Okay, Gordon. It's time you started earning your keep. Calculate the distance across the river and let me know how much rope we'll need."

"You bet," Tom called. "Let's go, Teddy and Peter! You can give me a hand."

When he'd finished his computations, Tom ran to Roberts. "Sixteen hundred feet, Captain," he said, barely resisting the urge to salute. Since the beginning of the journey, Tom had grudgingly come to admire Blade for his strong, decisive leadership. He'd also seen the way the captain's features softened whenever he looked at Teddy, and knew instinctively that Blade was captivated by her. Far from mistreating her, since they'd left the fort the captain had behaved toward her with such old-fashioned courtesy that several times Tom had had to hurry away before he laughed out loud.

Blade nodded. "That's about what I'd figured. Let's measure out the line." He looked up and seemed to notice Theodora for the first time. "Sergeant O'Fallon," he hollered as he passed by her, "I'm putting you in charge of the princess."

"Aye, sir!"

Theodora glared at the captain's back. Just when she'd started to change her mind about him, he behaved like the oaf she knew him to be. Well, she certainly hadn't expected *him* to take care of her!

All of the men, except for the soldiers who tended the livestock, the sentries who guarded the perimeter, and Tom, who came to stand at her side, gathered at the edge of the Big Blue. In the center of the circle stood the captain, hatless and shirtless and holding a coil of thin cord in his hand.

Theodora put her hand on her brother's arm. "What's he going to do?"

"He's going to swim the river."

Her fingers tightened. She looked out across the roiling water. "How can he possibly make it?"

"I don't know, Sis, but he's sure going to try."

Blade walked down to the churning river and, laying the cord on the ground, sat down and yanked off his leather boots, then his socks. Standing, he stripped off his buckskin breeches and stood naked on the water's edge. The sinewy muscles of his back and thighs rippled like molten copper in the sunlight. His broad chest was covered with straight black hair that narrowed to a thin line descending across his abdomen.

Theodora knew a genteel young lady should look modestly away, but she couldn't take her eyes off him. He stood like a statue—a superb example of the male body, poised gracefully over the raging torrent. He held one end of the thin cord in his teeth. Without a backward look, he splashed into the river and dove into its roaring depths. It was heart-stopping seconds before she sighted his dark head bobbing to the surface.

Theodora gripped her brother's arm. "No one can swim that far in such a current," she said. "He'll never do it."

"He's got to, Teddy," Tom answered. "If you've never prayed hard before, now's the time to start."

Blade's powerful arms flashed through the water, taking him closer and closer to the opposite bank despite the pull of the swift current. At last he reached the shore. He staggered up the incline and bent over, his hands on his knees as he caught his breath. He held the cord in his hand and signaled with it to Conyers, who attached a lariat to the other end.

Theodora slowly expelled the breath she'd been holding. "Thank God."

"Thank Roberts!" Tom exclaimed. "What a feat!"

They watched as the rope was pulled across the river and tied to a cottonwood on the other side. Then Blade walked to the edge of the river and waited.

Spellbound, Theodora stared at him until she realized that he was looking straight at her. Even from that distance she could see his mocking grin, and she felt the heat rise on her cheeks in mortification. Well, if he'd drowned, she told herself as she turned her back, he wouldn't have thought it was so funny!

Conyers, with War Shield's reins looped around his wrist, Lejeunesse, and Guion were the first to cross, swimming behind their horses while holding on to their tails. The rope acted as a guide, and they held on to it, keeping it between themselves and the downward pull of the current. Each man dragged a rope behind him.

"Load the wagon bed!" Blade shouted across, dressed now in the dry breeches and jerkin that had ridden over on War Shield's back.

Quickly, several men under O'Fallon's direction loaded the cooking utensils onto the inverted wagon. Packs of supplies were then placed on the makeshift raft. The signal was given and the men on the far shore pulled it across with the rope, straining to hold the wagon steady against the wild current. Two more times the wagon-boat was floated across piled high with provisions.

At last, Sergeant O'Fallon called to Theodora. "Get on your horse, lass. We'll be taking those who can't swim across right after this load."

With trepidation, Theodora took Athena's reins from Lieutenant Fletcher and led the chestnut down to the water. "I thought I'd ride over on your boat, Sergeant," she said with a nervous smile. She pushed a strand of hair from her eyes and prayed that her stark terror didn't show.

Understanding lit his blue gaze and his rough, gravelly voice rang with encouragement. "No, *mavourneen*. You'll be much safer on your own sweet little filly. The wagon bed isn't all that steady. Sure and it could easily tip over, darlin', and land on top of you. Now don't you be worrying none, for we'll be tying you to your saddle so you won't be falling off."

O'Fallon lifted her into the saddle. He checked the halter and stirrup straps, tightened the girth, then took the reins and led Athena to the water's edge. There he picked up a rope made of lariats and slipped one over the mare's neck. Behind her, Theodora saw Corporal Overbury, his face pasty white with terror as the lariat was slipped over his mount's head. Directly in back of him came a young private. She wondered in distraction if she was the same moribund green as he was. With a feeling of doom she watched as the same procedure was repeated for the other three soldiers who couldn't swim, until all six horses were tied together. More than anything, she wished she didn't have to cross that rain-swollen river.

Then Louis Chardonnais tied her to her saddle.

From under his coonskin cap he grinned at her with sym-

pathy. "Don't be afraid, *ma fille*. Just hold on to her mane.
The men on the other side will guide her across with the rope.
Even if she stumbles, she won't throw you. You'll pass over
in perfect safety."

"Aye, get her tied nice and tight," O'Fallon said, coming
up to stand beside her and check Chardonnais's handiwork.

Theodora glanced at her brother, who stood nearby watching
with deep concern, then nodded her readiness. She knew her
attempted smile came out a sickly grimace. "See you on the
other side, Tom," she said.

When the horses had been strung out in a single line and
everything was prepared, Chardonnais carefully led Athena
into the water, while Roberts, Conyers, Guion, and Lejeunesse
pulled on the rope from the opposite side. One by one the
horses began to swim across, guided by the men on the far
shore.

Theodora stared at the swirling flood and clutched Athena's
mane, her heart pounding. She gasped and gritted her teeth as
the cold water came up to her waist. Beneath her, she could
feel Athena straining, stretching her legs in long, powerful
strokes. As the first person in line, Theodora was directly
behind the wagon bed loaded with the scientific instruments.
Suddenly, one of the casks broke loose and floated downstream, bobbing wildly in the white, frothy water. The raft
bounced with a jerk, and the telescope slipped out of its leash
and plopped into the water in front of her. Without thinking,
Theodora reached down to grab it when it came by.

As she stretched, her saddle came loose and slid off Athena's
back. Terrified, Theodora plunged into the icy water. Down,
down under the freezing torrent she slipped, holding desperately to the telescope in her panic to grab onto something solid.
Tied securely to the saddle, she rode the current that tossed
her about like some evil, smothering dragon from a childish
nightmare.

Theodora knew she was going to drown. She hadn't a chance
of loosening the rope around her waist. She clung to the telescope, knowing that when they found her, she'd be clutching
it in her death grip. At least her dying wouldn't be a total
waste.

On shore the men watched in horror as her blond curls

disappeared under the water. It had happened so fast, she hadn't even cried out.

"Teddy!" Tom screamed. He splashed into the river, boots and all. Peter was right behind him.

"You'll never make it, Gordon!" he cried in Tom's ear. He threw his arm around Tom's neck and pulled him off his feet. Waist-deep, the two young men fell into the water, limbs thrashing as Tom struggled to shuck off his unwanted rescuer. When they surfaced, Chardonnais and O'Fallon were at their side, and Tom was held fast by a pair of strong hands.

"You'd not be reaching her, lad, before the captain," O'Fallon said.

Lifting Peter like a matchstick in his burly arms, Chardonnais nodded in agreement. "*Oui*, if anyone can save her, the *capitaine* will."

Tom looked across the river through blurred eyes and saw that Roberts was already in action.

Blade had raced for War Shield and leaped onto his back. He guided him into the deathly cold water as he estimated rapidly the point at which he would intersect Theodora's lethal ride downstream. Urged on by his beloved master, the magnificent stallion swam with all the strength in his body.

Blade thanked *Maheo* for the strong current as he battled his way across its savage onslaught, for without it the girl and saddle would have sunk like a stone.

Desperately, he scanned the torrent and spotted her wet hair streaming out across the water. He reached down and grabbed the stirrup strap. The weight of the saddle and its unconscious rider, sucked along by the current, almost pulled the strap out of his hand. He tightened his grip and used his knees to guide War Shield along beside Theodora. His long knife flashed, freeing her from her bonds, and he lifted her up over his shoulder.

Beside him, Zeke Conyers swam his own big roan. He reached out and grabbed the telescope that fell from her numb arms. As the saddle came by, he plucked it out of the deluge as well.

Theodora lay perfectly still across Blade's shoulder, her face and limp arms hanging, her boots trailing in the water, her ivory skin turning blue. As War Shield's hooves struck bottom, her stomach was jarred and she coughed, then started choking. Blade struck her hard on her back, and she retched and gasped for breath.

Once on the bank, Blade pulled his horse to a stop and dismounted. He slid Theodora off his shoulder and held her tightly in his arms. "Get me some blankets!" he shouted as he carried her up the grassy bank with long strides. "And get a fire started. Now!"

Laying her on the grass, he stripped away her soaking clothes. In spite of his fear, he felt a surge of raw lust at the sight of the graceful arms, the perfect round breasts, the tiny waist and slim hips, the long tapering legs, the delicate hands and feet. He'd never seen a more exquisite female shape, all smooth and soft and ivory. While he worked over her, frantic to revive her, in one corner of his mind he laid her beautiful, naked body on a fur-covered bed and explored the luscious curves with slow, sensual abandon.

Ruthlessly, he shoved his errant thoughts aside. He jerked off his damp buckskin shirt and pulled it over her, then rubbed her cold arms and legs in a frantic attempt to revive her circulation, for he knew she was suffering from loss of body heat.

"Theodora! Theodora! Wake up," he called, the dread in his voice reaching through the fog that surrounded her. "Look at me, *vehona*."

Slowly, Theodora's lids fluttered, and she gazed mesmerized into his gorgeous midnight eyes, framed by their thick black lashes. Strange, she thought in confusion, I never noticed till now the silver flecks in them.

"Am I still alive?" she whispered.

He leaned over her, his hands pressed on either side of her head. "By God, don't ever scare me like that again, or I'll wring your little neck." Despite his harsh words, relief shone on his face.

In bewilderment she lifted her icy hands to his bare arms and slid her fingers across the bulging muscles of his biceps. She explored the powerful chest and wide shoulders that she had admired only a short time before on the opposite riverbank. Warmth seemed to leap from his bronze skin, to trace paths of fire up her fingers and hands. Without questioning her own motives, she raised up toward him. She slid her arms around his neck. He moved back on his knees, taking her with him, and she cradled her head against the base of his throat. "I'm so cold," she confessed, as she snuggled her cheek against the straight black hair on his chest. "And you're burning up."

He chuckled softly and wrapped his arms around her. "It's no wonder I'm hot, princess. Your touch would set a eunuch on fire. And I can guarantee you, I'm an absolutely normal male. So if you don't want me to explode like a fiery volcano, you'd better stop running those dainty fingers across my bare skin."

At his words Theodora came to her senses. Unable to meet his gaze, she held her hands perfectly still, too embarrassed even to remove them.

Basil Guion rushed to their side, and Blade reluctantly pulled her arms from his neck and wrapped the woolen blankets Guion had brought around her.

Next to her, Lejeunesse started a fire, and gradually Theodora felt the warmth return to her body. She tried unsuccessfully to get up, but the weight of the blankets seemed to hold her down.

Blade gently pushed her back onto the soft sod. "You stay right where you are, Theodora. I don't want you moving for the rest of the day. We'll build the camp around you."

"Yes, sir!" she quipped weakly. "Any more orders?"

Tenderly, he pushed the wet strands of her hair away from her forehead. "One more. The next rest day, you're learning how to swim. And I'm the one who's going to teach you."

Huddled beside the fire, Theodora watched while the fording continued. Easing their frightened mounts into the swirling water, the men drove the herd of horses, mules, and two cows across. Wide-eyed with fear, the animals swam with their necks up, their nostrils flared, and their tails flat out on the rushing torrent.

Tom and Peter came across together, side by side. They held onto the tails of their horses and shouted encouragement to each other.

After the backbreaking task of dragging the axles and wheels across with ropes, the men reassembled the wagon. Twiggs reloaded his supplies and the scientific instruments, including the priceless telescope, and then began to prepare supper, whistling joyfully.

Wrapped in her blankets, Theodora realized with dismay that she was nude under Roberts's shirt. The thought that she had been stripped while unconscious was so disconcerting that she hid in her tent as soon as it was raised. Tom came in three different times to check on her. She assured him that she was all right, just humiliated to have made a public spectacle of herself. It took all her courage to join the others for supper, but the looks turned on her told her clearly that every man there was simply thankful she had survived. Expressions of concern and kindness poured forth, even from the rough French Canadian trappers, who knew little of the niceties of society.

Wesley Fletcher, solicitous of her every whim, hovered about her. He ran his graceful white hand through his sun-bleached curls and repeated over and over, "How terrible! Y' might've been killed, Miz Gordon! Y' could have died in that river!"

Over the banging of Twiggs's pots and pans, she overheard Sergeant O'Fallon as he talked with Blade. "Faith, Captain, and I checked her saddle myself," O'Fallon declared. "Why the girth was as tight as a drum."

Blade and Zeke Conyers closeted themselves in the captain's quarters immediately after supper.

Standing in the middle of the tent, Zeke pushed up his fur-trimmed hat and shook his gray head. "Well, I reckon this hyar's purty hard to believe, Blade, but that thar strap's been cut by a knife for shore. 'Twarn't jest ordinary wear and tear that split that leather. No siree. Some sneakin' polecat cut that girth, shore as we're lookin' at it."

Blade turned the saddle strap over in his hand and slowly nodded in agreement. "Yes, but who, Zeke? Who would want to harm Theodora?"

Blade lifted the closed flap and stared at the mixed congregation spread out in front of him. Was it a mountain man, who hid a secret hatred of women? Or a lovesick trooper, angry and jealous in his unrequited love for her? Or a demented killer, who struck at Theodora merely because she was an easy prey?

Blade closed the flap and flung the strap on his bedroll. "Whoever it is, Zeke, we'll find him. He'll trip himself up, sooner or later. In the meantime, don't tell anyone about this. Except for you and Julius, Haintzelman and O'Fallon are the only men on this expedition that I can completely trust. If the bastard doesn't know he's under suspicion, he'll be a lot less careful. And that'll make him a whole lot easier to find.''

"Yer dern right, Blade. We're gonna have to smoke this skunk out, and when we do, he's gonna stink to high heaven. Meantime, I'll keep my eyes and ears open. You jest keep your eyes peeled on that li'l gal.''

Blade met his scout's piercing brown gaze with determination. "I intend to do just that.''

At the sound of footsteps approaching the tent, the two men fell silent. With a look of suspicion, Conyers lifted the flap. Theodora stood holding Blade's shirt folded carefully over her arm.

"May I speak with you, Captain?'' she asked in a soft, shy voice.

"Certainly, Miss Gordon. Come in.''

"Reckon I'll be moseyin' along, Cap'n,'' Zeke said. He touched his hat and nodded. "Miss Gordon. Glad you're still here with us, li'l gal.''

As Conyers left, Theodora stepped inside the tent. "I wanted to return your shirt, Captain. And to thank you for saving my life.'' She knew that the effort it cost her to mention the use of his garment was evident in her rosy cheeks and her lowered lashes. Each time she thought about him removing her clothing, or the way she'd run her hands over his bare chest and shoulders, she wanted to hide her face in her hands. But she also knew he'd acted solely to save her life.

"If it's any comfort to you, Miss Gordon, no one saw you undressed but me. I was between you and the others and had you covered with my shirt before Guion brought the blankets.''

Theodora lifted her lashes and met his open, unembarrassed regard. "Thank you, Captain. It helps to know that. Being the only woman on a scientific expedition has its disadvantages.''

His teeth shone white and even under his black mustache as he grinned. The gold earring winked in the candlelight. "Well, look at it this way, Miss Gordon. Earlier this afternoon, you saw me without a stitch of clothing on, so you really aren't at a disadvantage where we're concerned.''

"Well, at least I didn't parade up and down on the bank in front of you," she snapped, indignant that he would mention her previous ogling of him.

"No, miss," Blade replied, instantly solemn and penitent under her accusing glare. "You surely didn't." But the smile never left his eyes.

"You are the most provoking man!" she retorted, shoving his shirt into his hands and turning to leave.

"And you are the most enchanting woman," he replied. But she'd already departed the shelter and didn't hear him.

The smile hovering on his lips faded as he recalled the harsh reality of her near drowning. When he discovered who had tampered with her saddle girth, he'd stake the bastard out on the prairie and flay him alive. The other members of the expedition would believe it was an atrocity committed by the heathen Pawnee. Only Conyers and Twiggs would ever suspect it was the work of a vengeful Cheyenne.

Chapter 8

A fter crossing the rain-swollen Big Blue River on the tenth of June, Blade Roberts knew the scientific aspects of the expedition must begin in earnest. A major purpose of the mission was to create large-scale maps of the region backed by detailed topographical surveys. Passable trails had to be charted and grades and elevations determined with mathematical accuracy.

In the early evenings, he and Tom Gordon retired to his tent, where the oil lamp burned long after the other men had turned in for the night. Working over the collapsible map table, they charted the longitude and latitude of their daily position, the altitude above sea level, and the high and low temperature readings taken during the day. Frequently, Theodora worked with them, helping her brother draw the detailed maps. To Blade's surprise, they were an extremely professional team, collaborating as harmoniously as neighbors at a cornhusking party. Each seemed to know the other's intent before it was even expressed.

Their skills as cartographer and naturalist astounded Blade. Gone was their aura of inexperience and naïveté. With the advent of the precise technical work, they set aside their carefree, youthful exuberance and became trained experts.

Once the scientific work was in progress, Blade relieved Theodora of a large part of her camp duties. Though she still assisted Julius with the evening meal, a private was detailed to gather firewood and wash the dishes, giving her time to

organize and enter in her journal the botanical specimens she
collected during the late afternoons.

One evening when Blade saw her making an entry in her
personal diary, he stopped and watched her. He wondered with
curiosity what denunciation of his character she was penning
with such ruthless energy.

Theodora refused to be intimidated and continued writing,
ignoring the mocking half-smile on his lips. Let him worry a
little, she thought. She brushed the soft end of the quill back
and forth under her chin and watched his retreat. There was
no need to admit to him that her first entry had told in glowing
words about his rescue of her from the flooding river. But her
feelings about the bold captain were changing, and the memory
of his strong hands on her unclothed body ignited a fire inside
her.

The days became longer and hotter after they crossed the
Big Sandy River during the second week of their journey. After
the heavy rains, the prairie was blooming, mile upon mile
covered with thick grasses. Wild roses were scattered across
its endless expanse, mixed with clumps of sagebrush, the narrow leaves glittering silver in the warm wind. The fragrance
of the blossoms drifted on the breeze. At every opportunity
Theodora gathered wildflowers and compared them carefully
with the many species described in Nuttall's catalogue, one of
the few books she'd been allowed to bring.

Blade frequently rode back from the front of the column to
make sure she had seen the sights—a wild turkey proudly
spreading its feathers before its mate, or a mockingbird calling
to its fellows, or a kingbird feeding its young. One morning
he halted the caravan and called her forward. With a finger to
his lips he pointed to a mother quail dragging her wing along
the ground as though injured. He dismounted and lifted Theodora down. Quietly, he led her to a nest of bobwhites, and
together they knelt and watched the newly hatched babies
scrambling among the twigs and fluff and broken eggshells.

"They're so tiny and helpless," Theodora said softly. "How
can they possibly survive in this savage country?"

"Savage is a harsh word, Miss Gordon." Blade stood and
looked out over the open grasslands. "It's often used to de-

scribe things one doesn't understand. The plains provide a bountiful life to those who respect its power and accept its challenges. With its incredible variety of plants and animals, it has a magnificence all its own. But to the newcomer this land can be very unforgiving."

As she gazed up into his midnight eyes, Theodora read the depth of feeling behind his words. She rose and stood beside his tall form, remembering the time she'd fitted snugly under his arm. "You love this land, don't you, Captain Roberts?"

"How could a person love anything so savage?" he quipped, the barbarous hoop in his ear flashing and a devilish grin spreading across his bronzed face.

Upon reaching the Little Blue River, the atmosphere among the soldiers changed dramatically, for they knew they were entering Pawnee country. The men were constantly on the alert, for the Pawnee were known to be hostile to the white man. The camp was startled awake one night by the heart-stopping battle cry of an Indian warrior. Knowing that Tom was on picket duty, Theodora raced from her tent straight into the arms of a bare-chested Blade Roberts. Together they joined the small crowd gathered on the edge of the bivouac and watched as Baptiste Lejeunesse carried what seemed to be a body into camp. He flung it dramatically at Tom, who dropped it on the grass like a handful of burning coals. The men burst into howls of laughter when they realized that the supposed corpse was only a scarecrow: an army overcoat draped over sticks and purposely left to flutter in the night breeze and frighten the young, inexperienced picket.

With the power of a grizzly bear, Lejeunesse enveloped Tom in a headlock, his curly black beard nearly covering Tom's eyes. "You should have seen him, *Capitaine*. He offered to go with me to investigate! What a little banty rooster he is!" Lejeunesse ruffled Tom's hair.

Blade shook his head at their crazy antics. The good-natured joke had brought relief to the atmosphere of dread that had permeated the campaign since leaving the Big Sandy. Placing his hand on Theodora's elbow, Blade guided her toward her tent.

"Is Tom going to be all right out there, Captain?" she asked.

She hated to leave her brother alone after such a scare.

The concern on her upturned face touched Blade. "Your brother just proved his mettle tonight, Miss Gordon. He's earned the respect of every man in camp. He'll be fine." He stopped and took her small fingers in his. "How about a cup of coffee, since we're both wide awake now?"

Theodora smiled. His kindness was like a candle in the evening dusk, bringing a warm glow. "That sounds like a great idea. I know I couldn't go right back to sleep. I'd just lie there and worry about Tom."

He retained her hand and led her to a log that had been pulled up to the fire earlier that afternoon. He regarded her thoughtfully as she sat down. "You and your brother are very close, aren't you, Miss Gordon?"

"Yes, I guess we are." She glanced up in surprise to see an expression of sincere concern on his face. "You see, our mother died when we were born, and we were our parents' only children. Tom wasn't strong when he was young. I've always felt responsible for him, even though he's the older." She shrugged. "By three minutes, anyway."

Blade lifted the large coffeepot from the fire with a folded cloth and poured coffee into two tin cups. He handed one to Theodora and sat down beside her. Silently, they watched the others return to their tents, some still chuckling over the practical joke.

Blade regarded her over his steaming cup. "How is it that you're so well educated? You must admit, it's unusual for a young woman to receive any formal schooling."

Theodora smiled. She knew he was trying hard not to give offense. "When Tom and I were children, we were often housebound due to his frequent illnesses. So tutors came and went through the years, and I was always allowed to keep Tom company and take part in his lessons. We had a nurse, of course, but when Tom was very ill I always stayed close by."

The warm, rich aroma of coffee drifted from her cup. She leaned her elbows on her knees and gazed into the flames. "I can remember standing beside my father's desk in his study when I was no taller than his chair, as I watched him catalogue plant specimens and waited for word that I could go up and see Tom after a particularly bad spell. As I told you before, my father and uncle are both members of the Harvard faculty. What I didn't mention was my maternal grandmother, who taught me at an early age to question the dictums that the outside world considered absolutes. She's a Quaker minister. All my life she has encouraged me to question 'Why' and, even more shockingly, to ask 'Why not.' Do you find such upbringing of a female child scandalous?''

Blade admired her finely sculpted profile in the glow of the firelight. "Not considering you were born a baby bluestocking," he teased.

But he thought about his own childhood. He'd been raised in a culture that accepted the importance of women as a fact of life. If a young warrior was treated with special regard, it was because everyone knew he faced the possibility of a very short life. But in the Cheyenne camp it was the women who made the decisions regarding the tribe—when to move camp and when to follow the proscribed rituals. In the privacy of their lodges, the women spoke their minds freely and their husbands listened.

He looked at Theodora and sensed her need for reassurance. "It's always difficult when you feel different from those around you."

"Yes." Theodora smiled at his understanding words. "When Tom went to Harvard and I attended the ladies' seminary, I soon learned that the outside world didn't approve of a female scientist. Most of my teachers at Mount Holyoke were appalled that I would stay up all night poring over books. They feared it would ruin my complexion, and nothing, I was told, was more fatal to a woman's chances than that!''

"It doesn't seem to have done you any harm," Blade affirmed cryptically, for her words had reminded him of her engagement.

Surprised at the sharpness of his tone, Theodora saw the criticism in his ebony eyes. "What do you mean by that, Captain?"

"You are engaged to be married, are you not? How did you ever talk your fiancé into allowing you to come on this journey?"

"There wasn't any question of *allowing* me. I was *going* on this expedition. Besides, Martin is very interested in my scientific studies.'' At his look of surprise, she continued. ''He has agreed to publish my journal when I return. He's also promised to help me continue my research after we're married. He has a fine personal library and will be expanding it while I'm gone, so that I can do much of my work at home.''

With her answer, Blade at last found the final piece to the puzzle, a piece he'd been searching for since he first met her. What kind of man would allow his fiancée to embark on a perilous journey of unknown duration, even financing it so generously that every man jack of the expedition had one of the newly invented percussion rifles? Only a fool, desperately in love, or a shrewd businessman willing to pay the price— one measured in thousands of dollars—for her hand in marriage. Blade's anger almost choked him. He stood and poured his coffee onto the fire. That Theodora would value herself so cheaply that she'd bargain her hand for this trip merely to gain the notoriety, the so-called prestige of being the first white woman to cross the continent, enraged him. ''Then it was either that or no engagement, I take it.''

Theodora rose and set her tin cup down on a rock near the fire. ''That's putting it rather strongly, Captain Roberts. Placed in that context, it sounds as though I'm not in love with the man I plan to wed.''

''Are you?'' His dark eyes flashed. The muscles on his bare chest rippled as he hooked his thumbs into his belt and moved to stand directly in front of her.

Theodora tilted her head to stare up at him. ''I refuse to answer such a personal question, and you have no right to ask it.''

''It's hardly a complex question. Just a simple yes or no would suffice.''

With her hands on her hips she glared at him. ''Of course I love Martin. Why else would I agree to marry him? What kind of a person do you think I am, Captain Roberts?''

They were mere inches apart. His voice was low and husky. ''I think you are a very naive young woman, who doesn't have the slightest idea what it means to really love a man. To love him so much you wouldn't dream of leaving him to go traipsing off across the country with forty strangers.''

''We're hardly strangers anymore, Captain,'' Theodora said

through clenched teeth. She moved to go around him, but he forestalled her with a sideways step.

He was silent, his mouth set in a thin, compressed line. Then, as he followed her train of thought, the sudden merriment in his dark eyes glistened in the fire's glow. He grinned his slow, mocking grin. "No, we're certainly not. Are we, Miss Gordon?"

For a moment Theodora thought he was going to kiss her. It was the horrible sense of disappointment, when he turned and walked away, that made her mad enough to want to grab the coffeepot and pour its contents down the back of his neck.

Despite all their fears, they saw not a single Indian that night, and the next morning Blade declared a well-deserved rest day. Although Theodora had forgotten his promise to teach her how to swim, he had not. A short distance downriver, he'd spied a fine running stream feeding into the Little Blue the previous day, and it was there that he led her. The spot offered privacy, surrounded as it was by leafy brush and tall cotton-woods.

Dressed in a yellow cotton frock that she saved for the days when they didn't travel, Theodora followed Blade, torn between a reluctance to place herself so completely in his hands and a desire to learn the mysterious art of swimming. The close call with drowning had left her determined to learn how to stay afloat.

When he reached the protected spot, Blade turned and smiled his encouragement. He seemed to sense her apprehension. He quietly dropped the cape he was carrying to the ground. Then he stripped off his boots, socks, and shirt. He stood beside the wide stream, dressed in a pair of old buckskin breeches that had been slashed off in a jagged edge at the knees. He laid his carbine on the pile of clothing, but retained the sheathed knife strapped to his muscular thigh.

Remote and dignified, he spoke like a tutor to a young pupil. "You'll need to take off your dress and petticoat, Miss Gordon. You can't learn to swim in them. Or your shoes and stockings, either."

Theodora peered suspiciously up at him beneath her lashes

and tried to find a hint of lascivious intentions. There was none.

Blade waded out into the clear, bubbling water until it reached his waist, then dove underneath and surfaced well out in the deep stream.

Coming to the top, he spread his arms and tread water. With a smile hovering on his mouth, he flicked his black hair from his eyes. "Get undressed and get in here, Miss Gordon. You're going to have a swimming lesson, whether you want one or not."

The memory of the way they'd touched each other so intimately the day he'd rescued her from drowning rose up before her, and for a second Theodora debated walking away—just leaving him there in the water. But she knew he'd be out of the stream and beside her long before she reached camp. He seemed to read her thoughts.

"I wouldn't try running away if I were you." His voice was as sweet as treacle. "Your brother agreed that you needed to learn to swim, and that I should be the one to teach you. So even if you made it to camp before I caught you, you'd only be sent back here like a naughty child."

"I'm not a child, Captain," Theodora corrected with a wrathful glance, indignant at his mocking. Fortified by her anger, she unbuttoned the yellow dress and slipped it off. Her camisole followed. Sitting on the grassy bank, she pulled off her shoes, stockings, and garters and set them neatly by her dress. Then, standing and untying the bands at her waist, she dropped the frilly petticoat to the ground and stepped out of its circle. Dressed in lacy chemise and pantaloons, she waded into the water.

Blade caught his breath at the sight of her. Her blond hair fell in a long braid over her shoulder and lay on one firm, full breast. Above the thin batiste of her undergarments, her bosom rose and fell in her agitation, causing the shadow of her cleavage to show dark against the smooth alabaster of her skin. Her tiny waist was encased in the satin ribbons of the chemise, and a graceful ruffle trimmed with little bows followed the curve of her hips in a tantalizing, swaying motion above her long, slender legs. He didn't know where to look first, his previous determination to keep the lesson on a purely altruistic plane fleeing like a herd of frightened pronghorns before a raging prairie fire.

Her words brought him back to the task at hand.

"Oh, no! It's too cold!" She stood knee-deep in the water, her arms clutched to her chest.

He moved toward her and smiled. "You'll get used to it. Come on. All the way in." Without warning, he grabbed her fingers and gently pulled her into the water.

As she felt her feet leave the sandy bottom, Theodora reached frantically for his shoulders, and as his arms moved slowly in the water, she clung to him.

He held her up as easily as a child holds his favorite toy. "The first thing you need to learn," he said into the pink shell of her ear, "is how not to sink like a rock, the way you did the other day. You can keep yourself afloat, Miss Gordon, by moving your arms and legs the way I am."

He spanned her slender waist with his hands and started to push her away from him.

She resisted his gentle shove with determination, and clutched his shoulders, the tip of her cold nose touching his gold earring.

"You're going to have to trust me, Theodora. You do just what I do. If you start to go under, I promise I'll catch you." Gently, he pried her fingers from around his neck and slowly moved her in front of him, while he retained hold of one trembling hand.

Theodora watched his legs churning the clear water and imitated his movements.

"That's it. Now move your arms like this."

He started to release her hand, and she lunged for him, clinging desperately to his shoulders. "No, don't let me go yet."

"Try it, Theodora," he instructed. He firmly thrust her away once more and held her up with one hand on her waist. "Just move your arms and legs like me, and keep your chin above water. Go on. I won't let you drown. Trust me."

As she looked into his raven-black eyes, Theodora felt his strength of will reach out to her. She did trust him. She had, ever since he'd saved her life in the flooding river. She knew he sincerely wanted to teach her how to swim for her own protection. Her eyes never leaving his, she slowly released her desperate hold on his forearm and moved her hands in circles, following his example. "Like—like this?" she asked, as she tilted her mouth up above the water.

"You're doing great!" he exclaimed. He kept his arms on either side of her, ready to catch her if she started to go under. "Don't forget to kick your legs. That's it. You can do it."

Thrilled, Theodora looked at him, brimming with excitement. "It feels wonderful. Now show me how to swim like you."

Blade grinned. "Let's get in a little closer to the shore and I'll give you your first swimming lesson. But don't think you're going to swim like me in one session. And don't go trying anything foolish when I'm not around. Understand?"

He pulled her closer to the bank and stopped where they could stand shoulder-deep in the water. Patiently, he taught her how to swim. She was a quick and enthusiastic learner, and they spent the afternoon splashing and laughing at her mistakes until finally she was ready to try it alone.

"I'll go to the middle and you come out to me. You can do it, Theodora. Just remember everything we've practiced. And don't forget to breathe and kick."

Blade swam to the deeper part and turned to face her. "All right. Come on," he gently urged.

Trust overcame her fears. Theodora slipped into the water and paddled to him. Her hard-won goal was reached, and she gasped for breath. She was exultant. "I did it! I did it!" she cried, laughing in his arms.

Blade looked into her shining eyes with water drops sparkling on their fringe of long lashes. Entranced by her beauty, he gazed upon the upturned face, wet and glowing, the golden hair dark with water and falling in one long braid behind her back. He chuckled mischievously. Taking her with him, he dropped under the water, kicking them farther and farther below the surface.

Just when Theodora thought she could last no longer, he allowed them to begin their ascent.

Embracing him fiercely, she surfaced with her arms wrapped tightly around his neck, her bare legs entwined with his strong ones, her breasts taut against his muscled chest. She gasped for breath and panted in his ear, her cold, wet cheek pressed to his. "For God's sake, Blade, why did you do that?"

With her body clinging to his, Blade smiled. Passion lit his eyes. "I'm sorry, little scholar. I couldn't help myself."

He kissed her, his firm mouth covering hers, his tongue boldly demanding entrance to plunder its softness. They slipped under the water again, and he pulled her with him toward the shore while his hands slid up and down her back and over her slender hips.

When they surfaced once more, Theodora clung to him as though her life depended upon it. But this time she realized what he was doing and was no longer frightened. "Don't you dare let go of me," she teased, as her laughter rang out in the quiet afternoon.

"Don't worry, *vehona*," he answered, and his lips softly brushed hers. One strong hand cupped her buttocks, bringing her firmly against his lean, muscular body. "I haven't the least intention of ever letting you go."

She looked into his eyes and saw in their jet-black depths the mysterious longing she felt within herself. The world around them seemed to stand still.

The spell was broken by the sound of Tom's voice. "Okay, Teddy, I'm ready to help with the lesson now." He waded into the water, dressed only in breeches. "I'm sorry I'm so late. I started playing cards with Private Belknap and forgot the time." Sheepishly, he grinned at them and shrugged. "But I won a pair of cavalry gloves from him."

As Blade released her, Theodora stared in dismay at Tom. She'd completely forgotten that her brother had promised to join them in only a few minutes. Mortified, she avoided the captain's dark eyes as they watched her with haunting intensity. "Watch me, Tom," she called, pinning a bright smile on her face. "Wait there and I'll swim in to you."

After the swimming lesson Theodora had determined to treat Blade Roberts with complete detachment, believing that an attitude of regal indifference would deflate his presumptuous treatment of her faster than one of embarrassment or defiance. She'd stomped out of the water dripping wet and boiling mad. At herself.

She'd let him do it to her again.

After all her resolutions to keep the cheeky, brazen man at arm's length, she'd let him kiss her. And more than just kiss, she admitted. The memory of his strong fingers curving over her backside, covered only by the thin, soaking wet pantaloons, brought a hot flush to her skin. Why did she allow him to take such shameless familiarities with her? She knew there would never be anything between them. Discounting all that Lieutenant Fletcher had told her about Blade's uncivilized background—for Wesley's eagerness to spread gossip made her question his motives, if not his veracity—she and the captain were as mismatched as a Thoroughbred racer and a plow horse. There could never be any relationship between them except a light flirtation. And as inexperienced as she was, still she doubted that Blade was interested in anything more than a carefree dalliance. His promise to Colonel Kearny to the contrary, the bold captain was taking liberties he had no business even dreaming about.

So when he approached her at mess that evening, she avoided meeting his gaze. And when he asked politely for a second cup of coffee, she pretended not to hear him, letting Twiggs spring up to wait on the impertinent officer. Instead, with a flirtatious smile, she offered a second helping to Wesley Fletcher and sat down on a log beside him while he ate. This time when the handsome lieutenant criticized their commander, she was ready to listen.

Seated on the ground next to them, Ezekiel Conyers lit his pipe. When Fletcher excused himself to check on the evening pickets, Conyers's dark brown eyes watched him leave through a wreath of smoke.

"Reckon it's mighty easy to talk about a man behind his back," Conyers said to no one in particular. " 'Specially if'n yore a yeller-livered polecat."

Theodora stiffened and grasped her plate on her lap with both hands. "I'm not frightened of Captain Roberts. He's officious and overbearing. And I'm not afraid to tell him so to his face."

Conyers took the stem of his pipe out of his mouth and tamped on the tobacco in the corncob bowl. "Well, those are pow'rful big words for a li'l gal. But if by 'officious' you mean the cap'n expects his orders to be obeyed 'thout question, yore darn tootin.' Out here on the prairie you only get one mistake. But if'n it's sum'pin' else has you all riled up, I'd jest as soon stay outta it.''

Theodora looked down at the eagle feather in the scout's hatband and grew thoughtful. ''You speak Cheyenne, don't you, Zeke?''

''Yep.''

''What does *vehoka* mean?''

'' 'Little white woman.' ''

She pursed her lips and looked across the campsite at the tall captain with narrowed eyes. ''And what does *vehona* stand for?''

The Kentuckian took his time and puffed on his pipe before answering her. ''Well, now, Miss Gordon, that thar title means 'princess.' ''

Turning this information over in her mind, Theodora placed her dish on the grass by her feet. ''I can understand *vehoka*, Zeke, but why does he call me 'princess'? Is Captain Roberts making fun of me?''

''Maybe so. Cain't never tell with the cap'n. In'jun braves are taught from the time thar knee-high to a grasshopper not to show thar feelin's. One thing I've larned, though, is that under that cool mask of his the cap'n has the dog-gonedest sense of humor. But I don't rightly think Blade Stalker's laughin' at you, li'l gal. Sum'pin' tells me he takes you more seriously than any other member of this hyar whole pack train.''

''Blade Stalker?'' she repeated with curiosity.

''That thar's his Cheyenne handle. In'jun's are given names with meanin's.''

Theodora waited to hear the meaning of such a ferocious title, but the scout just sat and quietly drew on his pipe.

''Well,'' she said at last, ''what's the significance behind the captain's Indian name?''

Zeke eyed her thoughtfully. ''Reckon I'll let the cap'n tell you that, pun'kin. When he's ready to.''

The next day the nomads reached the river the French-Canadians called *La Riviere Plate*. Winding across the prairie with a monotonous beauty of its own, the river had cut a path through the tall buffalo grasses over the countless years, carrying the melting snow and silt from the faraway mountains down to the muddy Missouri.

"The Omaha and Otoes called the river *Ni bthaska*, meaning 'flat water,'" Blade explained to Theodora as they rode along its bank.

He'd ridden beside her all that day, breaking down her cool indifference bit by bit. He knew she couldn't resist the wealth of information with which he bombarded her, and he tantalized her with stories of the early French trappers who had first traversed the plains. Self-conscious and shy, she listened politely, like visiting royalty deigning to accept the homage of some minor dignitary. He knew the reason for her studied composure, but wisely refrained from mentioning their impassioned kiss.

With some discomposure of his own, Blade suspected that what he felt for her went beyond the obvious physical attraction. He wanted her more than any woman he'd ever known. The fact that she was betrothed to some wealthy New York entrepreneur named Martin Van Vliet didn't bother him in the least. If it weren't for the promise he'd made to Colonel Kearny, he'd be free to pursue her himself. The idea of seducing the golden-haired beauty conjured up pleasant images. But his word as an officer stood between him and Theodora Gordon, and Kearny couldn't have built a more impregnable barrier. Blade had given the colonel his sworn promise that he would protect the young woman—from himself, if need be. The princess was as safe as if she sat atop a glass mountain.

As she rode beside Captain Roberts, Theodora leaned forward and absently patted Athena's glossy neck with her gloved hand. Blade's near presence brought back every vivid detail of the recent swimming lesson. How could she so easily forget the man she was engaged to marry? she accused herself.

She'd first met Martin Van Vliet when she was fifteen and he was thirty-four. She'd accompanied her father to the publisher's office in Manhattan where Charles Gordon attempted to sell his book on the classification of plants. Although Martin seemed more interested in her than in her father's scholarly manual, he agreed to publish it. In the years that followed the financier kept in touch with the Gordons, and while Theodora

was at Mount Holyoke, he traveled from New York to see her.
Martin had never pursued her romantically during those first
years, though she sensed he had had more than a platonic
interest in her from the beginning. He seemed to be waiting
for her to grow up.

He proposed on her nineteenth birthday, and on every birthday thereafter, until finally, at twenty-three, she accepted on
one condition: that first she accompany the scientific expedition
on which Tom was going. Reluctantly, Martin agreed. In the
end he even contributed heavily to the cost of the journey,
saying that it was in his best interest to see that the campaign
was well planned and amply supplied. He drew up a written
betrothal contract and laughed at her astonishment when he
presented it to her.

"Waiting a whole year for an elusive female, after spending
all that money on her, is bad enough," he teased. "I've no
intention of ending up without a bride."

When she'd agreed to marry Martin, she reflected, she hadn't
felt the thrill she experienced each time Blade touched her.
With her fiancé she was comfortable, relaxed. Their worlds
were compatible, for Martin shared her interests, and her few
excursions into New York's high society had occurred under
his protection. With Martin's sophisticated guidance their relationship had evolved until marriage seemed the logical thing.
She knew her father and brother respected him. And besides,
at twenty-three she was considered a hopeless spinster by all
the young ladies with whom she'd attended school. Who else
but a publisher would ever want a bluestocking recluse with
her nose forever in a book?

Sighing, she returned from her reverie to peep under her
lashes at the broad-shouldered captain riding beside her. For
some mysterious reason she was physically drawn to him in a
way she'd never felt before, while her mind told her she should
be repulsed. Unconsciously, her gaze sought him out time and
again during the day; in the evening, she was pulled to his side
like a compass needle ever seeking north.

No woman would ever marry *him* because it was the reasonable thing to do. His very nature demanded total capitu-
lation. And surrendering to Captain Roberts, otherwise known
as Blade Stalker, was the last thing she intended to do.

She'd never met a man more totally unsuitable for her. He was brash and cocksure of himself. An aura of power, even barely leashed violence, hovered about him, from the carbine he carried with such ease to the deadly hunting knife he wore strapped to his thigh. He was a warrior. A career soldier and proud of it. More than that: he gloried in it. Since childhood, she'd been taught that differences could be solved through peaceful compromise. She doubted that *compromise* was even a part of Blade Roberts's vocabulary.

They followed the valley along the Platte, over flat country with water standing in ponds. The cottonwoods and occasional hockberries, which had grown along the river bottom, became increasingly more sparse. Off in the distance, herds of red deer gamboled, and Theodora wondered if they knew they were safe from the hunters since buffalo were all around them now and the huge creatures were so much easier to bag.

As the company rode through the high grass, it disturbed a family of jackrabbits, who hopped at amazing speed to safety, their fuzzy tails signaling their departure. Whippoorwills and marsh wrens rose from the muddy banks in a flurry of wings at their approach. The beauty of the plains thrilled Theodora, and she was always anxious to reach their evening campsite and collect more botanical samples for her journal.

The travelers still covered only eighteen to twenty miles per day, despite their hard-won expertise on the trail, and made camp by three o'clock in the afternoon. This left time for her to collect specimens, while the horses and mules grazed on the thick grass before being brought into the campsite at evening time.

On the sixth day after reaching the Platte, Theodora realized the inconvenience the lack of timber would cause her. Not just in firewood, which was now being replaced by buffalo chips, but because of her need for privacy as the only female among forty men.

After explaining their problem to Lieutenant Haintzelman, Tom and Theodora walked upriver until they reached a tributary and followed its fork. Here bushes, vines and wildflowers grew along the bank, and meadowlarks filled the air with song. The stream was cool and clear.

"Oh, Tom, I'm going to take a bath," Theodora said. The thought of washing away the day's dust and grime was too appealing to forgo.

"Me, too, Sis. I'll be right over there by those rocks." Setting the butt of his carbine on the ground and bracing it against a boulder, Tom took off his sweat-soaked hat and ran his fingers through his damp hair. He grinned mischievously. "I think I'll go in clothes and all, and do my laundry at the same time."

Theodora laughed. "I'm going to do my washing, but I don't intend to do it while it's on my body. I brought along a change of clothes. I'll hang my wet ones on those bushes. We can look for plants while they dry."

Handing her brother a bar of soap, Theodora waited until she heard his splash and wild yell of enjoyment as he hit the cold water. She stripped off her dress. The feel of the cool water on her hot skin was wonderful. She lathered her long hair and plunged under the surface to rinse it off. She swam in the shallow water, delighted to find that she hadn't forgotten the skills Blade had taught her. Then she waded out, dried herself on a linen towel, and changed into a cotton dress.

She washed her clothes and spread her wet laundry over the berry bushes on the bank. "All right, Tom," she called.

Her brother appeared carrying a handful of lavender flowers he'd picked while he was waiting for her. He was barefoot, and his dripping clothes left puddles of water on the dirt bank. "Look here, Teddy. Have you ever seen wildflowers like this before?"

It was a small *Astragalus gracillis*. "Only in books. Where did you find them?"

"Come on, I'll show you," Tom said as he grabbed her hand.

Theodora found more of the same species and then spotted another *Penstemon* she couldn't identify. It was a rare azure. "I wish I had Nuttall's catalogue with me," she complained.

"Hey, look over here!" Tom called, pointing to a bright magenta blossom. "I bet you've never seen a flower like this before either."

Together brother and sister moved from spot to spot, gathering the plants as miners would gather nuggets of gold. They scrambled up the creek bank and onto the flat plain, moving from one discovery to another in their excitement. Neither noticed the sun dropping to the horizon, as it spread its red blanket across the prairie.

It was twilight when they realized they were lost.

Chapter 9

Blade Roberts stepped back from the map table and rubbed the aching muscles in his neck. Annoyed at Tom's continued absence, he glanced over the work he'd managed to complete by himself before supper time. It wasn't nearly enough. He needed Gordon's expert skill at cartography, for the draftsman's nimble fingers could sketch the lay of the land on its grid of latitude and longitude lines at twice the speed of his own.

Where the hell was Tom? Blade had been so engrossed in his work that he didn't realize that the sun was setting until he stood and gazed through the tent's opening at the burnished plains. Leaving the shelter, he called to the burly officer standing near the picket line. "O'Fallon, find Gordon and send him to me. Check with Belknap. The two of them could be playing cards somewhere."

All around him the camp bustled with activity, but neither of the twins was in view. Blade felt an unaccountable stab of apprehension. Usually this near mealtime he could spy Theodora's blond curls alongside Twiggs's grizzled head in the camp mess. And this was the first time Tom had been late since leaving Fort Leavenworth three weeks ago.

If Belknap had talked Tom into gambling again, Blade decided, he'd have to clamp down on them both.

Fifteen minutes later, O'Fallon entered the captain's quarters with Lieutenant Haintzelman at his side. "Captain, the twins are missing," he announced. Anxiety thickened his brogue. "Aye, and we've searched every tent in the blessed camp. They're not with Belknap. He's over by the fire cleaning his rifle and swearing he hasn't seen Tom since morning.''

Blade stepped back from the map table and threw down his pen. Splotches of blue ink splashed across the white parchment, puddling in miniature lakes. ''What the hell are you talking about, Sergeant?'' The ill-defined uneasiness he'd felt earlier crystallized into alarm. By God, if this was true he'd have somebody's hide!

Peter pushed his spectacles up the bridge of his sunburnt nose and nearly choked on his own words. ''That's . . . that's right, Captain. Tom told me about four hours ago that he was taking Teddy . . . ah, Miss Gordon . . . upriver for some privacy, since there were no trees along the bank. Nobody's seen either of them since.'' As if for reassurance, he turned to O'Fallon, then faced Blade again. ''But they should be all right, sir. I've told them before that if they ever get lost they should stay put until somebody finds them.''

''Then let's pray we find them before someone else does, Lieutenant,'' Blade snapped. Grabbing his rifle, he hurried from the tent with the two men at his heels. He scanned the busy campsite. ''Has Conyers returned yet?''

O'Fallon shook his head. ''Negative, sir.''

''Then send Guion to find him.'' Blade checked his carbine as he strode toward the hobbled livestock. ''I want Conyers to follow me as quickly as possible. I'm going to pick up the Gordons' trail. Let's hope to hell I can find it before dark. If I'm not back by nightfall, start a roaring blaze for a signal. And inform Lieutenant Fletcher that I'm leaving. He'll be in charge if anything else comes up.'' He glanced at his aide-de-camp. ''Haintzelman, you come with me.''

Even in the fading light, Blade easily found their bathing spot. Theodora's laundry, dry now, waved like flags from the bushes, and he touched the lacy chemise with anxious fingers. The image of her wading into the clear stream rose before him, and the possibility that someone had discovered her swimming there sent a wrench of foreboding through his gut. He forced himself to reason calmly. If the Gordons had taken time to bathe and do their laundry, they couldn't have gone too far.

Ruthlessly, Blade smothered his growing dread as he rapidly gathered up her things, folded them, and put them in his saddlebags.

"They were here for a while, Lieutenant," he called to the young officer seated on his horse nearby. "Looks like Tom swam over by those rocks while Miss Gordon was doing her laundry. Then they both climbed up the bank. No sign of a struggle."

"Shall I get some men to fan out and search the bank, Captain?" Peter asked as he turned his mount.

"No, wait. I'll try to pick up their trail first. I don't want a bunch of damn fools stomping around in the grass, destroying all trace of them." He glanced at Peter. "Try firing your rifle again. They could be fairly close."

Haintzelman pulled his carbine from its scabbard and pointed it skyward. They waited hopefully, but the explosion brought no answering reply.

Studying the scarred turf along the stream, Blade followed their footsteps. He knew they'd started off spontaneously, for though Theodora had been fully clothed, Tom had been barefoot and dripping wet as he clambered up the ravine and then sat down on its ridge to pull on his boots. The earth was torn where they'd pulled up botanical specimens.

Blade stood with War Shield's reins held loosely in his gloved hands. He scanned the bank, which rose in a gentle slope to the rolling grassland that surrounded them. "Looks like they went flower hunting. Ever read the story of Hansel and Gretel, Lieutenant?"

Peter grinned as comprehension dawned. "Then all we have to do is follow the trail of broken plants?"

"That's all. The hard part's doing it in the dark."

By now the light was nearly gone. Blade led War Shield up the slope and onto the plain, the young officer following close behind. Blade knew the flatness was a deception, for the prairie was pocked with ridges, gullies, and ravines through which the greenhorns could wander for miles, unseen from afar even in the daylight. There was no method to their hike; they seemed to have cut back and forth across the ground at whim, looking ahead only as far as their impulsive noses.

At last they heard the crack of a rifle behind them. Haintzelman turned to face the captain. Peter's hair had been bleached to white from the sun, and in contrast to his dark blue uniform, it and his pale face were all that were visible now in the inky darkness. "It could be them, sir."

"No, that was Conyers's Kentucky rifle." Blade fired his carbine, reloaded, and sat back in the saddle, waiting impatiently for the scout to overtake them. The night was their enemy as much as the Pawnee, and he chafed at his inability to continue trailing the missing twins. He knew he had to find them fast.

Although there was no moon that night, Zeke followed the sound of the blast like a hound scenting a coon.

"Any luck, Cap'n?" he called. He was no more than a dark shape against the horizon.

Frustrated, Blade leaned forward and patted War Shield's neck. The great beast stamped his hooves and shook his head fretfully, jingling the harness in the quiet evening. "No. It took too much time following their trail in the dark. I kept losing it and had to go back over the same damn ground all over again."

"Tarnation, Blade, you'd have to be a mountain cat and follow the trail with yore nose in this light." Conyers pulled his roan alongside the gray stallion and pushed his hat back on his head. "No response a'tall to yore shots?"

Blade shook his head, trying in vain to see into the darkness. "None. They've been gone for over six hours now. No telling how far they've traveled." He fought to keep his voice detached. The thought of Theodora in the hands of hostile Indians chilled the blood in his veins.

Beside them, Peter stirred in his saddle as he compulsively shifted the stock of his carbine back and forth in its holster. "Will we go back to camp and wait till daylight, sir?"

"No, we'll stay right here, Lieutenant. No sense retracing our steps tomorrow morning." Blade dismounted and loosened War Shield's cinch, then lifted down his saddle and blanket.

"Yo're right there, Cap'n." Conyers joined him. "I've got some jerky in my bags. Leastways we won't go hungry."

Blade glanced at Peter. "Gather up some buffalo chips,

Haintzelman. We'll make a fire. There's always a chance the Gordons may see it.''

They dined on jerky washed down with water from their canteens. Then Blade sat in front of the fire and smoked a cheroot, and the sweet aroma wafted through the campsite on the clean night air. He listened to every noise that came from the wilderness around them, the image of two frightened young people, alone and unprotected, ever in his mind. Before eating, he'd checked his carbine and placed it on the ground beside him, then taken out a whetstone from his bag and sharpened the long blade of his bowie knife in an attempt to calm his tense nerves. Now he was quiet, just listening, as he rested one arm across an upraised knee and remembered the feel of Theodora's sweet young arms wrapped around him.

Theodora Gordon was like no other woman he'd ever met. And he'd known plenty of them. Before she charged into his life like a green-eyed dervish, he'd thought there were only two kinds of unattached Eastern females: those who were fascinated by the hidden savagery they suspected lay beneath the surface of his fine West Point manners, and those who looked down on him with pointed distaste, openly contemptuous of his mixed blood. The first kind bored him and the second left him indifferent. And both types, though they tried to hide it, were afraid of him, expecting him to treat them with harsh brutality.

But not the stubborn, stiff-necked Miss Gordon. She didn't seem to give a damn about his Indian heritage, and he was certain at least one person had enlightened her on that score by now. Rather than being intrigued by his ferocity, she'd made it clear that she held his brute strength in disdain. He knew very little about the Quakers, but Haintzelman came from Pennsylvania, and he'd questioned the lieutenant about the sect. Peter had told him that the Society of Friends, as they called themselves, believed in turning the other cheek, no matter what the provocation. Blade scowled at the thought of what would happen if they tried *that* philosophy on a Pawnee war party.

And although the fiery little blonde professed to believe in peaceable conciliation, he wasn't so sure she practiced it. When he'd thrown the horsewhip at her feet and dared her to teach him some manners, it wasn't the feeling of brotherly love he'd glimpsed in those sparkling green eyes. Hell, for a second he'd thought she was actually going to accept his challenge and try to use it on him.

"Don't think any Indians will bother us, do you?" Peter questioned Conyers in a half-whisper.

"If'n they do, boy, we ain't never gonna hear 'em comin'," the scout replied, as he lit his yellow pipe and drew on its stem. He stretched his thin legs with their long buckskin fringes toward the fire and propped his shoulders against his saddle.

Sitting cross-legged, Peter moved his rifle closer to him. "Are they really as sneaky as the French Canucks say?"

"Yep, maybe even better." A cloud of smoke rose on the night breeze from the corncob pipe. "Onc't I was out on the prairie by myself, I tied my hoss to my wrist 'fore I went to sleep at night. Come mornin', I woke up to find my mare gone. Some ornery varmint had crept up and cut the rope durin' the night and then skeedaddled. I hadn't heard nary a sound."

Blade glanced at the two men with irritation. He stood and wandered to the edge of the firelight. The sight of Theodora's flashing eyes as she'd handed him back his shirt, the feel of her soft little bottom in his cupped hand as he'd taught her how to swim, the smell of wildflowers drifting from her hair as she'd sheltered under his cape rose up to haunt him.

Does Tom still have his rifle? he questioned the silent prairie. It hadn't been in his scabbard back at camp, or in his tent. The inability to continue the search rankled like a fresh saddle sore. From early childhood, Blade had been taught the responsibilities of a leader. A good one didn't take out a hunting party and not bring his men back safely. At the age of twelve he'd accompanied his grandfather on a horse raid and seen the middle-aged man fearlessly risk almost certain death to rescue a wounded young brave.

"A good chief places the lives of his warriors before his own," Painted Robe had told his grandson. "To lose many men shows that you are not worthy to be a chief. And too soon you will find that you are chief only of yourself. When you go into battle, *nixa*, use your best ability. Remember that only the stones stay on the earth forever.''

Blade Stalker had known his grandfather spoke the truth, for in the winter's lodge he'd often listened with his cousins to the story of the Cheyenne chief who'd fallen asleep, only to wake up the next morning to discover the rest of the tribe had moved away in the night without him. So different from the white men, who, after a military disaster, generally sought to make some junior officer a scapegoat while protecting the incompetent general in charge.

Shaking his head to clear the images of just such a failed campaign, Blade squinted and tried to pierce the darkness. As a lovely melody plays over and over in one's mind, the memory of Theodora's exquisite form rose up to taunt him once again. The thought of her full, round breasts pressed against his chest, her slim arms draped around his neck, her graceful hands sliding across his bare skin brought renewed hunger. The heat he'd felt as she'd curled against him, seeking his warmth, roared through his loins. How could one little, insignificant female so quickly overturn his emotional detachment? What was so different about this hardheaded New England blue-stocking that he swung back and forth like a pendulum, one minute wanting to blister her backside and the next wanting to explore every inch of her smooth, ivory skin?

When he got that exasperating blond wench back, he'd hobble her in the middle of camp like the perverse, headstrong mule she was. And he vowed to *Maheo* he'd never spend another night like this again.

More than five miles away, Theodora sat beside Tom, cold, hungry, and frightened. When they'd finally realized they were lost, they'd searched for a familiar landmark until it became too dark to see. Both brother and sister suspected that everything seemed "turned around," as they'd been warned it might if they got lost. Exhausted and angry at their own stupidity, they decided at last to shelter in a hollow. Finding some brittle willow branches in the dried-up gully, they propped Teddy's white petticoat over their heads to provide some protection from the breeze—for though the days were hot the nights remained cool—and in the hope that it would be visible to their rescuers in the morning. Both refused to mention what would happen if the wrong searchers spotted it first, for the fear of being narrowly missed by the soldiers compelled them to take the chance. Then, without the cheering warmth of a fire, they sat under the makeshift tent and waited to be found.

Theodora took off her boots and rubbed her blistered toes. Her feet were swollen and sore, and her legs ached up to her knees. "We must have walked twenty miles, Tom. They'd better find us tomorrow. Honestly, I don't think I can walk a step farther." She refused to voice the fear that had been haunting her since twilight: *What if we're never found?*

Tom answered her thoughts. "They'll find us, Teddy. They won't quit searching till they do."

"I can't believe they will either, Tom. Not with Blade Roberts in charge. The man's as arrogant and self-assured as that Oxford scholar who came to visit Papa once, but he's also courageous," she admitted reluctantly. "And tenacious. He'll never give up searching until he finds us."

"And you'll be able to walk tomorrow, Sis." Tom's tone was bright and cheerful, though his irrepressible grin was absent. "You'll see. You'll feel a whole lot better in the morning." He ran a nervous hand over his gunstock. "It's darn lucky we both learned how to use this rifle," he added. "We can take turns keeping watch. You go to sleep, and I'll wake you in a couple of hours."

But Theodora was far from sleepy. She leaned against the sandy bank that rose behind them and hugged her arms over her chest for warmth. "If it takes a while for our rescuers to find us, at least we have the gun. We can shoot our breakfast tomorrow when it's light."

Tom chuckled wryly. "Now that's something I'd like to see—you shooting your own food."

Theodora couldn't help but laugh. "You're right. All the rules and regulations taught at that fancy ladies' seminary never prepared me for stalking game."

"And if we should by some miracle catch something, do you think you'll really be able to prepare and cook it?"

Theodora giggled. "Just what do you think I've been learning from Julius Twiggs for the last three weeks, Tom? Believe me, it hasn't been tatting.''

''Well, lie down and try to get some rest, Sis. I'll wake you later and you can spell me while I sleep.''

But neither of them got any rest that night. Every sound in the dark brought them both up with a start.

Stretched out on the ground in the middle of the night, Theodora turned onto her side and looked out into the darkness. ''Tom, do you think we'll ever see Papa and Grandma again?''

''Of course we'll see them! Now go to sleep and don't be so silly.''

She knew her brother was right. This was no time to get morbid and pessimistic. Yet somehow Cambridge had never seemed so far away. She closed her eyes and tried to picture the shaded, irregular streets around the university where their father would soon be walking on his way to his classroom. The image of Massachusetts Hall, with its long gabled sides, brought an aching lump to her throat, and she brushed away the tears that crept down her cheeks despite all her brave intentions. She wasn't afraid.

She was terrified.

She remembered Martin Van Vliet's angry words to her father the last night they saw him in New York. ''You allowed Theodora too much freedom when she was growing up. Thanks to you, she now has the confounded notion that she can do anything she wants. And that's just not logical for a woman! I'm going along with this absurd idea as her husband-to-be, but I guarantee you both that it'll only bring heartache in the long run. My only concern is for her welfare. Females can't handle the rigors of scientific research in the field. They're just too fragile.''

Well, there was one man on this scientific expedition who agreed wholeheartedly with Martin. And he just happened to be the only man who could bring her and Tom back home alive. Whatever would Blade say when he found them?

Gad, he was a cantankerous, mule-headed brute! He didn't hesitate to ride roughshod over her or anyone else who threatened to stand in his way. She'd never met any man who radiated such smoldering, untapped power. Were that violence unleashed, she had no doubt he'd resemble the volcano he'd compared himself to. And yet . . .

Every time she'd been near enough to touch him, she'd nearly thrown herself into his arms. Even now, the memory of his sinewy muscles under her fingers brought a delicious tingle of excitement. The thought of him holding her cuddled so close against his wide chest sent an unfamiliar, gnawing ache through her.

This kind of thinking had to stop, she scolded herself. Blade Roberts was everything she disliked in a man. Rude, overbearing, and proud. It was no wonder they couldn't get along. The gun-toting, knife-wielding army captain had absolutely nothing in common with a female botanist from Massachusetts.

Restlessly, Theodora rolled onto her back and placed her forearm across her closed eyes. *But I wish he were here right now, with his cocky self-assurance and his know-it-all grin,* she admitted to herself. *It'd be worth the ungodly scolding I know I've got coming!*

Finally, toward morning, she fell into an exhausted sleep.

Blade watched the first glimmer of light come up over the horizon. He'd taken the last watch and had been awake for two hours. Nudging the soles of his sleeping partners with his boot, he lifted his blanket and saddle and swung them up on War Shield's back. "Let's go, men. By the time we're mounted, we'll have enough light to see by."

Together he and Conyers read the signs left by the carefree pair on the previous day. Each spear of bent grass, each heel mark caught their attention. They moved so rapidly, Peter was amazed.

"How can you see the signs from such great distances?" he asked Zeke, as he watched Blade ride at a sharp trot well in front of them. "The captain doesn't even slow down long enough to look at anything close."

"Jest look ahead, thar in the grass," Conyers answered. "The blades that've been turned over show a different shade of green from the grass around it."

But as hard as Peter looked, he couldn't see a variance in

the tall buffalo grass that stretched out for miles ahead of them in the gray dawn.

They rode over hilly ground, through gullies and around buffalo wallows. Then, at sunrise, Blade spotted a patch of white cloth waving in the morning breeze. Relief flooded him. It was the Gordons, alive and well—if no one else had found them first. "There they are!" he called over his shoulder, and urged War Shield into a gallop.

Hearing the hoofbeats coming toward them, Tom jumped up, rifle in hand. When he recognized the big stallion, he ran up the shallow bank of their ravine and waved. He beamed with joy at their deliverance.

Blade dismounted, his heartbeat rapid beneath his ribs. Seeing Tom without his sister, a feeling of dread engulfed him. His words were sharp and loud. "Where's Theodora?"

"She's over there, Captain," Tom said, and pointed toward the improvised tent with a sheepish look. "Sound asleep." He shrugged in embarrassment. "We were awake all night."

Pulling off his leather gloves and tucking them in his belt, Blade strode down the incline. The petticoat awning provided shade from the morning sun. Its lacy ruffle fluttered in the breeze like a pennant atop a castle turret. Under it lay a sleeping beauty, her blond tresses spreading in waves across one arm, her boots and stockings on the ground beside her, her bare, blistered feet peeking from under the hem of her dress. At the sight of her so peaceful and safe, his apprehension dissolved. With infinite tenderness he swooped her up in his arms.

As she was lifted from under her shelter, the sunlight struck her face. Startled, Theodora stiffened and looked into Blade's eyes, then relaxed. The overwhelming security of being held in his strong arms flowed through her, and she laid her head trustingly against his shoulder. She felt him pull her even tighter against the solid wall of his chest. "What took you so long?" she questioned with relief, slipping her hands around his neck.

Blade carried her over to War Shield and set her on her feet. "I came as fast as I could," he informed her. He mounted and lifted her up in front of him. "Don't forget her plants and boots," he called to Tom, and turned his stallion homeward. "Zeke," he added over his shoulder, "stay and help these two get everything. We wouldn't want anyone to get lost again."

"That's for dern sure, Cap'n. We'll be comin' along a little ways behind you. You jest git that li'l gal safely back to camp." Conyers gave a careless wave, urging the officer onward.

With his arms firmly around Theodora, Blade pushed War Shield into a gallop.

Theodora sat up straight and rigid, prepared for a well-deserved reprimand. She ached from the sleepless night on the hard ground and hoped he'd get it over with before she felt any worse. Unwilling to begin a conversation that would end in her own chastisement, she continued to wait for him to make the first move. But he was apparently in no hurry.

At last he slowed his horse and pulled her back against him. "Get some sleep, Miss Gordon," he instructed without rancor. "We've got a ways to go before we reach camp. And you'll need your strength for the long day's ride ahead."

She pushed against his shoulders, trying to sit up. "I couldn't possibly sleep now, Captain Roberts. Not when we're alone together. It isn't decent."

He slammed her back against him. His arms encompassed her so tightly she felt the vibrations in his chest when he spoke. "It wasn't very decent of you to wander off like that yesterday, either. Everyone was worried sick. It'll be even more indecent if you fall off your horse this afternoon because you can't stay awake. We don't need to lose any more time than we already have."

Although sleep was the last thing on her mind, Theodora recognized the common sense of his suggestion. Instead of struggling against his firm hold, she leaned back and allowed him to support her weight. The silence of the morning was broken only by the warble of birds and the steady, monotonous beat of War Shield's hooves. Little by little, her eyelids dropped and her head nodded, as weariness overcame her scruples.

Blade gazed down at his precious burden. Theodora's thick, silky lashes rested on her smooth cheeks, turned to a light brown now from the long days in the sun. Her eyebrows arched above them in a faint suggestion of surprise. Her soft

ps, opened slightly in sleep, revealed the edges of even
'hite teeth.

If you only knew, princess, the scare you put me through,
e scolded her silently, you'd understand why I can't decide
hether to kiss that delectable mouth of yours or paddle your
aughty behind.

Theodora blinked in confusion. She stirred and wondered
rossly why she was being held so tightly. Then the memory
f that interminable night on the prairie brought her to full
onsciousness, and she glanced down to see a pair of muscular
rms enveloping her. Realizing just whose arms they were,
ne attempted to straighten, but Blade held her to him effort-
ssly. With her head cradled on his shoulder, she peeked
pward and recognized immediately the determined thrust of
is square chin, covered now with a night's stubble of heavy
eard.

Blade had pulled to a halt under a shady stand of trees; it
vas the sudden cessation of movement that had, no doubt,
wakened her. He dismounted and, spanning her waist with
is hands, lifted her down. As she met his gaze, she marveled
gain at the flecks of silver in his black eyes. She tore her gaze
rom his and looked around. A fresh running stream bubbled
arough a small cluster of cottonwoods.

"Are you thirsty?" His manner was relaxed, even carefree.

"Yes," she replied warily. Baffled by his offhanded ques-
on, she couldn't decide whether he was angry or amused.

Blade lifted his canteen from the saddle horn and knelt beside
ne stream. He refilled the canteen with cool water, stood, and
ffered it to her without a word.

Theodora took the metal container and gulped the water,
uenching her terrible thirst. She wiped her mouth with the
ack of her hand. "I'm sorry for the trouble Tom and I
aused," she apologized. She knew they'd be in camp soon,
nd she wanted to get the tongue-lashing over with before they
vere surrounded by a curious audience. "We were collecting
lora and lost all sense of time. We'll never do such a stupid
hing again."

"We'll talk about that later," he said as he stared at the
vater drops trickling down her chin. His low, deep voice was

a caress. "Right now I'll just take your apology." He pulle
her into his arms before she'd even guessed his intentions. Hi
eyes glowed with desire. Bending his head, he kissed her softly
his tongue licking the water off her lips with such open hunge
that Theodora felt he wanted to devour her. He raised his hea
and looked at the curls spilling over her shoulder, and th
yearning revealed in his eyes made the breath catch in he
throat. He lifted her against him, one strong hand entangle
in her hair, and gently brushed her forehead, her eyelids, he
cheeks, her wet chin with his warm lips.

"You . . . you mustn't," Theodora gasped and tried to jer
away. She still held the water-filled canteen, and its content
splashed against her dress and soaked through the cotton t
her heated skin.

With her denial, the bonds of his restrained tenderness ex
ploded and his mouth swooped down upon hers. He kissed he
passionately, his tongue probing until her lips surrendered t
his assault. Then he moved back to read the answering passio
she knew was in her eyes.

"I promised myself last night that you'd pay for the worr
you put me through," he murmured. "Not to mention the los
sleep. Now it's time for you to show your gratitude. What i
the proper reward for being rescued in the wilderness? Surel
it's worth an innocent kiss."

Theodora pushed against his chest with the open containe
and the water sloshed once again. This time she half expecte
steam to rise from their smoldering bodies. "Innocent? Yo
don't know the meaning of the word!"

His white teeth flashed beneath the thick mustache as
moved toward her. "Ah, but there's so much I do know
little bluenose. And I'm more than willing to share my know
ledge."

He kissed her again, a consuming, breathtaking kiss. Hi
hand moved over her breast, cupping its fullness through th
wet material. With unhurried expertise his long fingers un
buttoned the front of her dress and slipped inside, rubbing th
thin batiste that covered her swelling nipple. He lowered hi
dark head and kissed the pulse that fluttered at the base of he
throat. Theodora leaned back, arching against his sinewy arm
His hand slid to her other breast, and a jolt of passion swep

rough her at his feather-light touch. It seemed so right to be
eld, to be kissed, to be touched by him, as though it should
o on forever. When his mouth found her lips again, she
nswered his obvious invitation. Tentatively, she touched his
ongue with her own, following it across his lips and into the
warmth of his mouth in a dance of discovery. She could feel
is delight as he tightened his hold on her and groaned deep
a his throat.

At the faint sound of hoofbeats behind them, Blade lifted
is head and calmly redid her buttons, paying no heed to her
carlet cheeks. He pried the canteen from her tight fingers and
eplaced the lid dangling from its chain. Possessively, linger-
agly, his gaze moved over her face, her hair, her breasts. "If
ou ever wander off like that again," he said in a voice so
ow she could barely make out the words, "I'll tan you within
n inch of your life."

Chapter 10

The Gordons were welcomed back with an exuberant joy that embarrassed them both. The troopers and mountain men ran out to meet them, crowding around their horses as they approached. Everyone escorted them into camp, all the while shouting questions and offering thanks to God that they had been safely returned.

"Hallelujah!" Twiggs exclaimed, waving his battered sombrero in the air as he ran beside War Shield. His brown face was wrinkled in deep creases with an ear-splitting grin. "A sight for sore eyes! That's for sure. Knew the captain would find you. Knew it for certain."

In his excitement Sergeant O'Fallon pounded Basil Guion on the back, causing the diminutive voyageur to lurch and teeter precariously until the burly Irishman grabbed him by the shirttails and hauled him upright again. "Will you be looking at the likes of them now, you little spalpeen! Saints preserve us if they don't look as though they've been taking a Sunday stroll in the park. And us fearing we'd not be seeing hide nor hair of them again!"

"Be careful, *barbare*," Guion cried with mock indignation. "You'll knock the teeth right out of my head." But he laughed good-naturedly in quiet jubilation.

At breakfast, Private Belknap hurried to bring Theodora and Tom the plates Julius had piled high with thick slices of hot buffalo meat. Even Fletcher—who had never waited on anyone before—brought them both cups of steaming coffee. Tom drank his gratefully and asked for more.

"I thought I'd never see y' ag'in," Fletcher told Theodora. "The chances of anyone findin' y' alive were almost nil. It would've been easier t' find a needle in a haystack." The shock on his pale face made her squirm with shame at their carelessness. It was the closest Lieutenant Fletcher had ever come to praising Blade, and his quavering voice betrayed how truly overwhelmed he was with their rescue.

"It was miraculous, wasn't it?" Mortified, Theodora set down the tin cup of coffee and turned back to Twiggs and Belknap, continuing the tale of her adventure and forgetting the coffee until Fletcher reminded her to drink it up, for they'd soon be going. But by then it was cold, and she poured the entire contents on the ashes before she'd even tasted it.

Immediately, Fletcher reached across her shoulder and picked up the cup. "Wait. I'll get you some more."

"No, don't bother," she answered, uncomfortable at his obvious solicitude. "I need to pack up my gear and help Tom dismantle our tent."

The caravan made such a late start that morning that the sojourners skipped the midday rest period and continued steadily along the valley of the Platte River into the late afternoon. It was a hot, clear day, and the summer sun beat down on them until Theodora shifted uncomfortably in the saddle and recalled with nostalgia the earlier days of cool rain.

She wiped her moist brow with the back of her gloved hand and wondered if it was only the weather that caused her skin to feel as if it was on fire. Each time she thought about Blade's touch, her cheeks flamed with embarrassment. Each time he got near her, he became bolder and more insistent. It had to stop. She would make him stop. There would be no more kisses, even if she had to avoid him for the rest of the journey like a Quaker shunning a stage performance.

Cantering his horse alongside his sister's, Tom took off his leather hat and ran his yellow scarf over his wet brow and hair. He was tired and thirsty and soaked with sweat. His buckskin shirt clung to his back, and he resisted the impulse to pull it over his head, for he knew the sun would fry his white, freckled skin like trout in a pan of hot grease. The previous night awake on the plains had taken its toll. He'd been plagued with diarrhea since morning, but refused to complain to anyone, knowing he fiasco had been his own fault. He'd acted like a green girl, vandering out across open territory without even a horse, endangering Teddy and causing Roberts and the others a night of discomfort and worry. He shook his head and tried to clear his blurred vision, but the world careened wildly with a sickening lurch. Gad, he'd never be so foolish again.

Theodora came out of her own disheartened reverie and noticed Tom's slumped shoulders. She realized he was fighting exhaustion. Although she'd rested that morning, secure in Blade's arms, her brother had had no sleep for more than twenty-four hours. She urged her mare closer to High Flight and stared at Tom. "Are you all right?"

Beads of sweat rolled down his face and neck; his hair was plastered to his brow under the brim of his slouch hat. His stomach roiled within him, the nausea coming in waves. He tried to grin, but grimaced in pain instead. "As a matter of fact, no."

Theodora's green eyes revealed her worry. "You look awful, Tom. Let me tell Captain Roberts that we should stop early today so you can rest."

As she moved to go, Tom reached out and caught her arm, ignoring the dizziness brought on by the sudden action. He wouldn't cause the campaign more loss of time. Not after the botch he'd made of things. "No, Sis. Don't. Anyone who wanders away from camp and gets lost like a pea-brained school kid deserves to be exhausted the next day. I'll be all right."

Theodora gave in against her better judgment. She knew how desperately Tom wanted to save face in front of the others. But during the afternoon she watched in alarm as he grew steadily weaker. He frequently shook his head, trying to clear it, and it became obvious that it was an effort for him merely to stay upright in the saddle.

Finally she could stand it no longer. "I'm going to talk to Blade," she told her brother. "You can't go on like this."

"Wait, Teddy," Tom called weakly, and his voice cracked in his dry throat. He moved to take hold of her reins and swayed precariously. With a supreme effort, he grabbed High Flight's mane and righted himself.

Theodora had seen enough. She kicked Athena's flanks and galloped toward the head of the column.

"Captain," she cried. "Captain Roberts!"

He must have recognized the fear in her call, for he turned his stallion and raced to meet her. Alarm gave his face a stern appearance. "What's wrong, Miss Gordon?"

"It's my brother!" She pointed over her shoulder. "He's not well."

Blade looked back at the center of the column. As they both watched, Tom slipped off his horse and lay in a still heap on the ground.

All that afternoon Tom grew worse. The symptoms of acute dysentery progressed, and he began vomiting as well. Unable to keep even water in his stomach, he quickly became so dehydrated that he suffered agonizing cramps in the muscles of his legs and feet. Theodora hovered over him, wiping his face with a wet cloth, dripping water on his parched lips and over his swollen tongue. She talked incessantly to him, for he grew quiet and apathetic, a manner so unlike her high-spirited brother that she felt her heart would tear apart with fear for him.

Blade entered the Gordons' tent as soon as the camp was settled. The foul smell of disease filled its close confines. He went over to Tom, who lay motionless on his rumpled, soiled bedroll, and crouched beside him. "Tom," he called softly, "how do you feel?"

The young man opened his eyes and blinked repeatedly, as though trying to focus on the figure in front of him. His voice was the hoary whisper of an old man. "Kind'a bad, Captain."

"Did you eat or drink anything when you and Theodora were out there alone?"

Tom shook his head and stared at Blade from bleak eyes. "Nothing," he said. "We had nothing to eat the whole time."

"What about water? Did you drink any during the night?"

Again Tom shook his head. He tried to push up on his elbows, but fell back on the blankets in exhaustion. "Wait a minute," he gasped. "Yes, I did. In the morning while Teddy was still sleeping, I walked over to a nearby buffalo wallow and drank."

One word thundered through Blade's mind: *cholera*.

During the campaign of '34, Blade had seen enough of the

disease to recognize its symptoms. He squeezed Tom's hand and then laid it back on the youth's chest. "You try to rest, Tom." He rose, took Theodora by the elbow, and pulled her to the side of the tent. "I want to speak with you outside for a moment," he whispered, trying hard to keep his shock from showing on his face. "Haintzelman can sit with Tom for a few minutes."

Theodora shook her head, her eyes wide with fear. She gripped her hands in front of her, the knuckles of her delicate fingers white with the pressure. "No, I can't leave him."

Blade took no time to argue. He pushed her from the tent and motioned for Peter, who waited nearby. "Stay with Gordon while I talk with his sister."

Implacably, Blade pulled her away from the shelter and led her to his own. He hustled her inside and lowered the flap. Roughly, he yanked her to him. As his hands imprisoned her arms, part of his mind recognized that his iron grip was an unnecessary overreaction. Yet her struggle to free herself only deepened his panic. "Did you drink from that lagoon, Miss Gordon?" he demanded. Despite his efforts to remain calm, he heard his voice echo loud and harsh in the canvas-enshrouded stillness. "Did you drink that water?" he repeated and jerked her toward him.

Her head flew back at the abrupt movement.

"No, I . . . I drank from the stream we bathed in. I didn't drink again until you gave me your canteen. Why? Was the wallow tainted? Is . . . is that what . . . what you think?" Her face turned white. Her lips trembled. She gripped the front of his buckskin shirt with rigid fingers, her teeth chattering in terror. "Is Tom going to die?"

Blade ignored her questions as he forced himself to keep his relief from showing in his voice. "From now on I don't want you to eat or drink anything unless I've checked it first." He maintained his viselike grip on her while he searched her troubled eyes for acquiescence. Once, just once, couldn't she accept his commands without balking?

"Please! Stop acting like this," Theodora complained, averting her face. Tears of frustration rolled down her cheeks. "I don't understand you. My brother is over there suffering and you're talking to me about what I should eat and drink!"

Blade refused to let her go. "Theodora, I want your sworn promise that you won't drink or eat anything without my supervision."

The scorn she felt for his behavior showed on her tightly compressed lips, and she lifted her shoulders in a shrug of disgust. "If you're going to make such a scene over this— then, yes." It was clear that all she wanted was to return to Tom.

Blade read the lack of commitment in her expressive eyes. He shook her until her head flew back and forth on her slim neck and her teeth came together with a crack. Damn, he'd get her attention, one way or another. She wouldn't become a victim of cholera. Not if it was in his power to prevent it. "Say the words after me, Theodora: I swear to God . . . Say it! Repeat the words to me!"

His ferocity at last frightened her into submission. "All right!" she cried. "I swear to God . . ."

"That I will never . . ." His words were low and insistent.

"That I will never . . ."

"Never!" he roared.

"Never!"

"Eat or drink anything not approved by me." He shook her again, impatient for her words. "Say it, Theodora!"

"Eat or drink anything not approved by you." She turned her head away from him, tears flowing down her cheeks unheeded.

Satisfied at last, Blade released her and stepped back. He looked at the top of her bent head, her golden curls loosened and disheveled by his brutality. His jaw clenched as he steeled himself to hear her sobs. But she didn't break down.

Rubbing her shoulders where he had held her in his powerful grip, she glared up at him in rage. Diamondlike tears sparkled on her thick lashes. "*Now* may I have your permission to return to my brother?" she asked with bitter sarcasm.

Without a word Blade pulled back the flap of the tent and stood aside. He strove to keep his expression remote and unreadable. He couldn't tell her that the thought of losing her had turned him into a wild man. That all he wanted to do was protect her. That he'd give his own life to keep her safe. He couldn't tell her, because he knew she'd never believe him.

And because he'd seen the contempt in her eyes.

They tended the sick man through the night; Blade, Peter, and Julius all took turns helping Theodora. Because the disease was so contagious, no one else was allowed near. The entire camp was still and hushed, and the sounds of Tom's moans could be heard clearly through the canvas walls. Excruciating cramps spread into his arms, abdomen, and back, and Theodora wished in vain for something to relieve his agony.

But there was nothing they could do to stop the course of the disease. They couldn't even administer opium to relieve the pain, for no medication would stay in his stomach long enough to give him relief.

"Oh, Tom," she cried in despair as she lifted his head with trembling hands to sponge him once again. "If only there was some way I could help you."

As the hours went by with agonizing slowness, she never left his side. She sat on the ground beside his bedroll and held his hand. When she tried to pray, the words stuck in her throat, fear choking her.

This can't be happening, she told herself, looking down at Tom's tortured face. It's all a bad dream. A nightmare from which I'll awake and laugh at my foolishness. Dear God, tell me this isn't real!

She was vaguely aware that Blade sat across from her on Tom's other side. He'd helped her nurse her brother through the night, though they'd hardly spoken a word.

Near dawn Tom ceased his restless movements and lay strangely still. Theodora pressed her hand to her brother's cheek in terror. It was cold and clammy. Her heart lurched when she saw the rapid change in him. His skin was lax, his cheeks hollow, and he was blue around the mouth. She took his wrist in her shaking fingers, but could no longer feel even a faint pulse.

So weak that he was unable to move, Tom raised his lids and stared at her, his hazel eyes lackluster and sunken, his golden hair plastered to his skull with sweat, his freckles turned to rusty blotches on his sallow skin. Slowly, painfully, he turned his face to the captain. His lips moved soundlessly.

Realizing that Tom wanted to tell him something, Blade slid his arm under Tom's shoulders and lifted him up.

"Roberts," the dying man croaked in a guttural whisper. "Take care of Teddy for me."

"No, Tom," Theodora wailed. She placed her arm beneath his back and shook her head helplessly. "You're going to get well. We're going to go home together."

The compassion in his eyes unmistakable, Blade took the young man's hand. He gently squeezed the frail, sensitive fingers. His words were firm and clear. "I will, Tom. You have my promise that nothing will ever hurt Theodora as long as I'm alive."

Through his pain, Tom gave a twisted grin. "That sounds like a deal to me, Roberts," he gasped.

He collapsed in their arms.

"Tommy! Tommy!" she screamed, clutching him to her. "Tommy! Don't go! Don't go away from me! You can't die! I won't let you go!"

On the twenty-fourth day after departing Fort Leavenworth, the members of the U.S. Army's Scientific Expedition buried their cartographer, Thomas Algernon Gordon—a victim of the dreaded Asiatic cholera. His shallow grave was surrounded by forty men, hatless, with heads bowed. A steady wind, which had arisen during the night, whipped their scarves against their faces and blew the hair into their eyes as Tom's body was lowered into the earth.

Theodora watched Peter and Julius solemnly toss spadefuls of dirt on Tom's makeshift canvas shroud in the gray dawn light. Across from her stood the dragoons and the mountain men with stunned expressions on their somber faces, while beside her Sergeant O'Fallon, the veins on his thick neck standing out like ropes, read from his worn Bible in his booming Irish accent: "Yea, though I walk through the valley of the shadow of death . . ."

At the tragic words, Calvin Belknap pushed his thick brown locks out of his eyes, surreptitiously wiping his cheeks of tears at the same time. He wasn't the only man who stood blinking against the eye-watering wind, grateful for the excuse it provided. The sudden, unexpected death of the exuberant twenty-three-year-old shocked and frightened them all, reminding them of their own mortality as they stood and prayed in the middle of a vast, treeless grassland.

Theodora glanced up at Blade Roberts's compassionate face, thankful for his presence. He stood beside her, so close he almost brushed against her shoulder, and watched in quiet contemplation. Despite the previous afternoon's harsh words, which stood between them like the high, sharp palisades of an army fort, his manner was meticulously correct, and his composure lent a feeling of sanity and order to a world that had suddenly turned crazy.

Tears streamed down Theodora's cneeks as she tried to fight the aching pain in her throat. *Oh, Tommy, Tommy,* she called silently, covering her mouth with trembling fingers to hold back the sobs.

But this time Tom didn't answer her unspoken words, and the emptiness sliced through her chest.

After the passage had been read, Blade turned to Theodora. "I'm terribly sorry, Miss Gordon." His deep voice was clearly audible, even in the brisk wind. "I'd give anything not to have had this happen."

Theodora looked up at him, torn by her confused emotions. She was thankful for the help he had given her during that long, horrible night; he'd helped nurse Tom with a gentleness she'd never suspected possible in the fierce captain. Yet, irrationally, she also felt that he, as the leader of the expedition, had somehow failed in his responsibility to prevent her brother's death. His sympathetic words meant little to her now—not after the way he'd behaved the previous afternoon. He'd cowed her into submission, but at a terrible price. In her agonized and bewildered search for someone or something to blame, she turned on him. "Tom's death was needless, Captain Roberts. Had he been forewarned about the tainted wallows, he'd be alive today."

The expression on Blade's hawklike features turned to stone; not a hint of his inner feelings showed in his guarded expression. "And had I suspected he'd be alone out on the prairie, I'd have warned him."

At last the dirt filled the grave, and the men shuffled restlessly, no one quite sure what to do next. Then Julius Twiggs laid down his spade, picked up his dusty, weathered sombrero, and walked over to Theodora. He took her small hand in his gnarled one, and his grizzled white head bent over her blond curls. The compassion in his brown eyes spoke to her heart, even before his comforting words. "One sad day, Miss Theo. Tom fine boy. Miss him dreadful."

"Thank you," Theodora answered through her tears. "Tom thought so much of all of you, the way you took us under your wings and helped us learn to take care of ourselves. And no one could have been kinder to us than you, Julius."

Twiggs's brief speech seemed to free the others from their state of befuddlement, and one by one they went up to Theodora to shake her hand and murmur the age-old phrases of solace.

"I've made a cross, Miz Gordon," Fletcher said softly, after everyone had given her their condolences. "I've carved Tom's name on it for y'. I'll be right back with it." He left, heading quickly for his pack, as the rest of the men milled around waiting for the signal to leave.

"Time to mount up," Blade ordered. He nodded to Sergeant O'Fallon to assist Theodora to her horse.

"Wait!" she cried. She gestured toward the mound of fresh earth. "We can't leave before we mark Tom's grave."

Blade's mouth was drawn into a firm line; his jaw was hard and unyielding. "I'm sorry, Miss Gordon. We can't place a marker." Looking up at Haintzelman, who'd already mounted his horse, Blade continued. "Lieutenant, see that every man and animal moves across this grave. Tell Twiggs to drive the wagon over it as well. I want the earth packed firm and hard. We'll leave no trace of what's happened here today."

"No!" Theodora screamed. "How will I find Tom again if we don't mark the place?" Panic took hold of her, and she shook like a child waking from a nightmare. "I'll never find him again!"

Blade's face softened. He spoke with quiet compassion. "I won't forget this place, Miss Gordon. I'll bring you back to it one day."

Looking around her at the treeless, undulating prairie, with no visible landmark, not even a distinctive bush, Theodora shuddered. She shook her head. "I can't . . . leave Tom here without a marker to show me where he is. I can't do that, Captain."

Before Blade could answer, Fletcher returned, carrying a small wooden cross with the dead man's name scratched across it. "Here, Miz Gordon," he said as he offered it to her. "It's rough, but it'll do until y' can get somethin' more substantial."

Blade grabbed the cross from Fletcher's hand with an oath and broke it savagely over his knee. He flung the two jagged pieces of wood, and they sailed across the tall buffalo grass in a high curving arc, bouncing crazily as they hit the ground. "Dammit, Fletcher, get to your horse!" he roared, his wrath instantaneous. "Just one more word from you, and I'll place you under arrest." He doubled his fists, and for a moment it seemed as though he was going to strike the junior officer. Then, with obvious self-mastery, he turned his back. "Sergeant O'Fallon," he barked as he strode toward War Shield, "put the lady on her horse."

At first Theodora struggled and tried to pull away from the bulky sergeant's hold on her elbow. Then, realizing it was hopeless, she leaned against his solid girth and clutched his sleeve in her trembling fingers. "No, no," she sobbed against his shoulder. "I can't leave Tommy all alone out here. Please, oh please, don't make me go."

Gently, O'Fallon led her to Athena. His eyes were tormented as he looked down at her. "There, there," he crooned in his thick brogue. "Sure and we have to be going now, *macushla*. The captain has his reasons. And Tom doesn't need you now, darlin' girl. He's with God's lovely angels."

Seeing her distress, Peter jumped down from his horse and ran over to help. Together Haintzelman and O'Fallon lifted her onto the mare, then mounted and pulled their horses up on either side of her.

Behind them, the procession was strung out in a double column, waiting. At Blade's signal, the campaigners rode somberly across the grave, driving the horses and mules before them. Even the wagon wheels crossed the length of it, leaving behind the deep impression of their rims in the sandy soil. No one spoke a word, but Theodora's sobs could be heard on the morning breeze.

At the head of the column, Lieutenant Fletcher raced up to Blade, his back stiff with outrage. "Was it necessary for her t' see that?'' he shouted at the captain, and those behind them looked up to watch.

Blade turned to face the lieutenant. Rage blazed through him at Fletcher's thoughtless interference. "Better this, Lieutenant," he said in a low, angry voice that carried no farther than the two of them, "than seeing a piece of her brother's clothing—or his scalp—on some Pawnee buck."

Sick at heart, Peter rode beside the weeping girl. He knew every man in the company was deeply affected by Tom's untimely death. Peter wondered if Theodora would ever be able to accept her sudden, devastating loss. As the caravan crossed the prairie that morning, Peter knew each member kept his wordless vigil in deference to her.

By mid-morning, they reached the crest of a rise, and no one could resist turning for one last look at the far-off, deserted burial site.

Theodora gazed in stunned misery at her brother's unmarked grave; the only evidence of its location was the line of trampled grass where the entire expedition had ridden. To leave the site, never to find it again, was unthinkable. It was as though the prairie itself stood by silently, like an evil specter, waiting only for them to depart before swallowing up all evidence that Tom had ever existed. How could she possibly return to her father without being able to bring him back one day to the place where his only son lay buried?

Without thinking, Theodora spurred Athena and raced back across the empty plain. The horrified faces of the men flashed by, but no one had the heart to stop her wild flight to rejoin her brother.

No one except Blade. Reacting instantly, he galloped behind her. His stallion covered the ground between them effortlessly as they flew past the halted column of men. Within minutes, he reached out, grabbed her reins, and pulled the mare to a skidding halt. Lieutenant Haintzelman came up quickly behind them.

"Let me go," she cried, as she yanked futiley on her lines. Her hat had fallen off in the frantic ride, and her hair had come loose, curling about her shoulders and blowing in the wind. "Leave me alone. I have to go back to Tom."

"You can't go back, Miss Gordon." Blade's face was stern

and unyielding. He seemed to purposefully steel himself from showing her any sympathy. "Going back won't help Tom, and you must keep up with us. Staying here will only make the inevitable leaving harder."

"Dear God, don't you have any feelings?" she cried as she slid from Athena's saddle. She ran down the steep bank, nearly toppling as the toe of her boot caught in a thick bunch of grama grass. With her arms outstretched, she quickly regained her balance and continued her frenzied attempt to reach her brother.

Leaping from War Shield, Blade was right behind her. He grabbed her, ignoring her flailing hands, and held her tightly, pinning her arms securely to her sides. She sobbed in despair and fought him until at last she grew still, her anguished cries muffled against his broad chest.

"You're going to get back on that horse, Miss Gordon," Blade told her, "or I'm going to put you on and tie you to the saddle. You *can't* stay here, do you understand? We *have* to keep going. Help me get her back on her horse, Haintzelman," Blade ordered the lieutenant.

Together they tenderly lifted her onto Athena, but this time the captain kept the reins in his gloved hand. He led the chestnut mare over to his stallion, then remounted and rode back up the column, his features once again impassive. Behind him, Theodora sat in the saddle, stiff and unbending.

For Theodora, it was as though she were falling headfirst down a dark, spiraling tunnel. The need to block out reality, to withdraw from normal life, consumed her. She rode behind Blade Roberts, the reins of her horse securely in his hand, and tried to crawl inside herself to a haven of security. To a place where her brother was still alive. But as hard as she tried, she couldn't hear Tom's voice. And the stillness inside her was overwhelming.

When they camped that afternoon by a slough on the Platte, Theodora stood beside the spring wagon and gazed eastward in despair. Tears streamed down her cheeks, but she made no attempt to wipe them away. Moving around her, Julius set up his kitchen, his soft brown eyes turning to check on her time and again. Belknap spoke to her in a whisper, leading her with kindness to an upended wooden box that Twiggs had set down for her. She was scarcely aware of either of them, unable to discern what they said to her, for the silence within her was deafening. She stood beside the crate, disconsolate, staring eastward.

The hustle and bustle of the campground faded from her consciousness, and she sat awkwardly on the wooden box. Her throat ached with unspoken self-recriminations. If only she had stayed awake with Tom the night they were lost, had warned him not to drink from the prairie lagoon, or had drunk the water with him, they wouldn't be separated now. How would she ever explain to her gentle father that she had survived the trek, only to leave her twin brother buried and forgotten somewhere in this horrible wasteland?

"Miss Gordon. Miss Gordon," someone called to her down the bleak tunnel she inhabited. "You need to eat something. Here. Here's a plate for you. Take it."

But she pushed the dish away. How could she possibly eat when she felt so miserable?

For a while she was left in peace, and she returned to her silent vigil. *Tommy, Tommy*, she called in hopelessness. *Please, come back. Come back to me. I was supposed to take care of you. How shall I ever tell Papa?*

Time blurred for her, and she never noticed the dusk turn to dark. Someone put his hands on her shoulders and lifted her with infinite gentleness. "Time for bed, Miss Theo. Take you to your tent now."

Theodora allowed Julius to lead her into her tent, following him blindly in her tears. She sat down on the opened bedroll and stared across the shelter, waiting in the flickering flame of a lantern. Someone came in and sat down across from her, but it wasn't Tom, so she paid him no attention. In the dim light she sat patiently and waited through the endless night.

Blade felt a dull, gnawing heartache spread through him as he watched her staring with blank eyes at the canvas wall. What were the chances that she would pull out of her over-powering grief alive? The very real possibility that she would soon begin to feel the symptoms of cholera tormented him. That she might suffer the same agonizing death as her brother filled him with rage at his impotence. He had been so careful, so very careful. All of his planning, all of his knowledge about the prairie, all of his skill as a military leader had been for nothing. He could lose her in a matter of hours. His only consolation was that if she did become ill, she would go quickly, without prolonged, needless suffering, for she had no will to live. His heart turned to stone inside him. He couldn't bear to think of a future without her.

Two days later, the caravan reached the South Platte River. Blade looked around at the treeless campsite and watched Calvin Belknap carry an armful of buffalo chips to the pit that Twiggs had dug for the cook fire. Beside the Yankee spring wagon, on an upturned crate, sat Theodora Gordon. Still silent. Still weeping. Still staring eastward.

She hadn't eaten or slept since Tom's death, and dark circles shadowed her green eyes, reddened and blurred now from her endless tears. Blade knew she hadn't slept, for he'd kept vigil with her, night after night, with the help of Peter and Julius. They'd taken turns sitting up with her, afraid that if she were left alone she might try to return to Tom. They'd tried unsuccessfully to talk with her during those long, desperate hours, but she'd steadfastly ignored them. She seemed to be waiting and listening. And they all knew for whom she listened.

Through the long, silent hours Blade had wanted to enfold her in his arms and soothe her, to rock her to sleep like a frightened child. But some instinct warned him not to touch her. If he forced her to accept the physical tangibility of his comforting embrace, she would shatter like a dropped mirror, for her withdrawal from life was the dream, and the emptiness of life without Tom was the reality she was not yet ready to face.

Now, Blade walked over and stood in front of her, blocking her easterly vision of the horizon. "It's time you started your chores again, Miss Gordon," he said without preamble. His voice was loud enough to carry throughout the entire bivouac. "I've given you enough time. Now you need to pick up your share of the load."

All around them the men stopped in astonishment at his callous words. They were clearly appalled to think that he would insist that the grief-stricken lady do her share of the mess work in her present state of shock.

Through a haze of pain Theodora looked up in confusion at

Blade. She focused on him with difficulty. "What? Did you say something to me?"

"I said, Miss Gordon, that you need to get up and get to work." He enunciated the words with the precision of a drill sergeant barking orders at a new recruit. "Now stand up, Miss Gordon. I'm sure Twiggs has something you could help him with."

Slowly, Theodora rose. Without a word she walked over to Julius, took the large burlap bag of macaroni from his hands, and poured its contents into the kettle of hot water that hung suspended from an iron tripod over the fire. It was as though she were not even conscious of her behavior, but merely acting out some pathetic charade.

"Glad to have your help, Miss Theo. That's for sure." Twiggs smiled at her, his eyes warm with sympathy.

As Blade stalked through the crowd of men, he ignored their astonished looks. Inside his tent he leaned with both hands on the map table already set up for his work and stared blindly at the papers spread before him. He'd known the minute Tom Gordon died that the chances he'd lose Theodora, too, were staggering. They'd been attached by a deep bond of familial love, and her grief was as deep as that bond had been, making it nearly impossible for her to go on without her twin. But Blade was determined to do everything in his power to keep Theodora alive—even if it meant forcing her to work, to eat, to sleep. Even if she hated him for it.

The next morning saw the start of Blade's calculated attempt to bring Theodora back to the routine of everyday life. When he saw Haintzelman folding her things and replacing them in her packs, he hurried over. "From now on, Lieutenant, the lady needs to be responsible for her own belongings. We don't have time to coddle a prima donna on this trip."

Peter's jaw hardened as he bit back a scathing retort at Blade's sarcastic tone. Without a sound Theodora rose from her place on the crate beside her tent and quietly took her journal from the lieutenant's rigid fingers. Turning her back on the captain, she knelt beside her equipment and began to place it in her pack.

But Blade wasn't finished yet. "Private Belknap can help Miss Gordon with her tent, Lieutenant," he told Peter, who had started dismantling the shelter. "She can't do it entirely by herself, but she certainly doesn't need to sit by like an invalid while the two of you wait on her." He slapped his gloves against his palm. "Now I believe you have other duties, Haintzelman. See to them."

"Yes, sir," Peter snapped, his blue eyes as cold as shadows on snow. It was the first time he'd even come close to questioning his senior officer's orders, and Blade waited to see if he would make a further comment. But his commander's belligerent stance must have warned him to keep his thoughts to himself, for Peter turned abruptly on his heel and stalked away.

Blade turned to Belknap next. "When you finish helping Miss Gordon take down her tent, Private, go back to your chores with Twiggs. I expect the lady to saddle and care for her own horse as of this morning, just as she was doing three days ago."

Intimidated, the unhappy private saluted and promptly started to pull up the iron tent stakes.

Then Blade approached the kneeling woman. She was bent over her pack, one long braid falling across her shoulder. Her lashes lay against the purple shadows under her eyes, and her pale skin seemed almost translucent in the morning light. "I trust that's satisfactory with you, Miss Gordon? You certainly don't expect those men to take on your responsibilities, as well as keep up with their own duties, do you?"

Theodora looked up at the tall form and scowled. What did this man want from her? All of her thoughts were directed at the lonely grave site, now miles away, to which she could never return. She had no energy to spare for the insignificant details of camp life. Didn't he realize that without Tom she was only half alive?

"Well, Miss Gordon?" he persisted. "I asked you a question. I'd like the courtesy of a reply."

Theodora stood. She blinked and shook her head, trying to concentrate. "What are you talking about, Captain Roberts? I didn't hear your question."

Blade stepped even closer, until they were just inches apart. His black eyes riveted her to the spot. His words were precise, pronounced with caustic exaggeration. "Do you think the men should have to do your work, Miss Gordon? Or are you capable of handling your own chores?''

''I can handle my own chores, Captain,'' she repeated in a monotone, as though by rote. ''The men don't have to do my work for me.''

''Good. Fine. Then I'd like to see you get busy.''

Her glance drifted away from the dark eyes watching her with such heartless intensity. Without another word she joined Private Belknap, who was lifting down her canvas tent.

That afternoon, as the others made camp, Blade sought her out once again. Dressed in a green broadcloth blouse and buckskin skirt, she stood leaning against Twiggs's wagon, as though she'd paused in the middle of a chore and had completely forgotten what she was doing. Her eyes were glued on the eastern horizon.

''Have you collected any botanical specimens today, Miss Gordon?'' Blade inquired in a sharp tone.

She jumped with a start at the suddenness of his question. Though he'd made no attempt to approach quietly, she hadn't even heard him draw near.

Her voice was faint and disinterested. She never met his eyes. ''No, I didn't look for any this afternoon, Captain Roberts. I just didn't find the time.''

He hovered over her, blocking any view except his own shirt front. ''Then I'll take you. I want you to collect at least a few samples every day, Theodora. You came out here to learn about the flora and fauna of the prairies, and I intend to see that you do just that.''

She shook her head. ''I should really help Julius right now.'' She tried to step around him, but he forestalled her.

''That won't be necessary. I've already told him you'd be with me for a while. Now let's pick up your carbine from your tent and get going.''

''My carbine?'' At last she looked up and met his gaze. ''Why, I haven't used my rifle since the day Sergeant O'Fallon showed Tom . . .'' She gulped and swallowed, blinking back tears. ''. . . Tom and me how to shoot it.''

Taking her elbow, Blade directed her toward her shelter. She was forced to skip to keep up with his long strides. ''From now on, I want you to carry your weapon with you everywhere you go. Right now, I'm going to have you take some target practice with me. Then we'll find a few plants for your collection.''

''Not today, Captain,'' she demurred, ineffectually tugging against his firm grip. ''I really don't feel up to it.''

''I don't remember asking you if you did, Miss Gordon. I'm in charge of this expedition. I give the orders. You take them. Now come on.''

At her tent Blade picked up her carbine from its saddle scabbard and handed it to her. He guided her to the edge of camp, where a target had been tacked to a cottonwood. They spent thirty minutes reviewing the loading and shooting of the rifle, then searched together for botanical specimens.

For five days Blade hounded Theodora, waking her early in the morning to give her extra time to dismantle her tent with Belknap's help, pack her belongings, and saddle Athena. In the afternoons, he saw that she had time to bathe in a nearby stream, then took her searching for new specimens for her collection, followed by thirty minutes of rigorous target practice. After that she was expected to help Twiggs with the mess and spend at least an hour on her journal. Roberts goaded her into writing in her diary daily, as well. But nothing seemed to pierce the curtain of grief that separated her from the world around her. She rarely spoke, ate almost nothing set in front of her, took no interest in her surroundings. Like a mechanical doll wound by a spring, she performed the functions required of her, then sat down on the crate, spent, useless, and unmoving.

A full week after Tom Gordon's death, Blade could see no improvement. In addition, he worried constantly that someone might once again try to take her life. She would make an easy prey, for she'd offer no resistance in her present state. Finally, in frustration, he ordered that a target in the shape of a man be set up.

When Theodora saw the human silhouette, she lowered her rifle and glared at him. ''I can't shoot at that!'' she protested. A flush stained her pale cheeks.

Blade was surprised by the vehemence in her voice. She'd spoken in a monotone since they'd left the grave site. He hardened himself to answer with mocking derision. "You're a slow learner, Miss Gordon. I give the orders, remember?" Without waiting for her reply, he encircled her with his arms and forced her to raise the heavy carbine, guiding it into place. "Should you ever find yourself separated from the group again, I want you to know how to use this."

Theodora found herself sighting down the barrel, despite her lack of interest in the procedure. "Very well, Captain," she said, her lips pursed tight. She closed her eyes and squeezed the trigger. The shot didn't even come close.

Blade absorbed the shock of the kickback and tried to ignore the marvelous feel of her curves pressed against him. He reloaded and, like a man enjoying his own self-torture, placed his arms around her once more. "Let's try it again, Theodora. You don't have the skill to merely wound or disarm a man. At least not yet. So aim for the trunk of the body, not an arm or a leg. And aim to kill."

"I could never shoot another human being, no matter what the provocation!" She gasped in horror as she turned partway around in his arms to look up at him.

"Don't be a little fool," he told her, his temper rising at the willful streak that could cost her life. "If a man is trying to hurt you, you shoot to kill."

She gritted her teeth and spoke with caustic derision. "Did it ever occur to you, Blade Roberts, that not everyone is like you? Some people believe in finding other solutions besides the application of brute force. But go ahead. Call me names. I already know *you* for what you are."

His jaw tightened and his body tensed as he prepared for some slur against his mixed blood. He'd been the recipient of prejudice in the past, but the thought that she would stoop to bigoted name-calling made him unaccountably furious. His low voice held the warning rumble of a mountain lion, though he doubted she'd heed it. "And what am I, Miss Gordon?"

Lifting her pointed chin, she met his gaze with unhesitating determination. Her green eyes sparkled with anger. "You're a ruffian, Captain Roberts!"

The unexpected, innocuous epithet, hurled with such righteous indignation, left him speechless. He quirked an eyebrow and stared at her in delighted surprise. He could feel the laughter bubbling up inside him, tugging at the corners of his mouth. He shook his head and fought to answer her with grave sobriety. "Well, I've been called some bad things in my life, Miss Theodora Gordon, but never anything as mean as that."

She knew he was laughing at her and she was furious. Color flushed her delicate features. She visibly ground her teeth and straightened like a hunting lance in his arms. Before she could get a word out, Blade turned her back around to face the target and brought the rifle in her hands up for her to sight. This time Theodora aimed with deadly accuracy. The bullet struck the human figure directly in the chest.

At last Blade had his answer. If he could stoke that fiery temper of hers high enough, she'd rejoin the world with a vengeance. He'd just have to be sure he wasn't at the wrong end of her rifle barrel when she did.

That evening it wasn't Twiggs's gentle hands, or Peter's sympathetic ones, that offered Theodora her supper. Instead Blade appeared in front of her with a dish of venison stew. "I want you to eat this, Miss Gordon," he said. "And I want you to eat *now*."

"I couldn't, Captain Roberts," she murmured, and waved away the food with a halfhearted gesture. "I couldn't get it down."

"You'll eat, Miss Gordon," he growled through clenched teeth, "if I have to force it down you."

Once again she surfaced from her cloud of misery to stare at him in anger. "I don't want any," she snapped, her lips pursed together in a thin line. At last the determination in his black ones penetrated her detachment.

He glared down at her, perched on her wooden seat. "I didn't ask if you wanted it, Miss Gordon." His tone was filled with an ominous threat. "Now, start eating this supper or I'll spoon it down your throat."

With a glare of pure frustration, she reached for the bowl of stew, took it from Blade's outstretched hand, and dumped it on the trampled grass between them. It just missed the toes of his dusty black boots.

Blade pulled his long knife from its sheath on his thigh and flung it in front of her feet. It landed with a thunk, its blade buried deep, the handle vibrating back and forth. His voice was cold and mocking. "It's the Cheyenne custom for a woman to show the depth of her grief by hacking off a finger or two. Go ahead, Miss Gordon, prove your despair. Chop one off and let's get this infernal caterwauling over with, so we can get on with the work we came out here to do."

Incensed by his heartlessness, Theodora reached down and snatched the knife from the dirt. Brandishing the razor-sharp blade, she leapt up to face him. "I hate you! I'll cut off your—"

"That's it, Theodora. Hate me!" Blade grabbed her by the shoulders and shook her, ignoring the wicked blade that danced in front of his face. "Hate me as if your life depended on it!"

He released her and turned, heading for her tent in long strides. In moments he was back, her diary in his hand. He threw it to her, and she caught it without thinking. "Here! Write it all down, Miss Gordon. Every blasted, unfeeling word I've said. And live to see me eat those words."

"I'll live!" she screamed, as she clutched the journal to her breast. "I'll live to see you court-martialed, Blade Roberts. I'll see you stripped of your rank and drummed out of the army, if it's the last thing I do!"

Chapter 11

Heartsick, Theodora stood beside Lieutenant Haintzelman on the low riverbank of the sludgy, yellow South Platte River, with its treacherous sandbars and tiny islands, and watched the preparations for the fording. Numb to all feeling except the bitter anger she nursed toward their tyrannical leader, she gazed with disinterest at the enormous flat plain stretching on both sides of the river, golden now with huge patches of blooming sunflowers. It was timberless, but they'd found that the grass was good for grazing and buffalo chips were plentiful. The water in the Platte, though muddy, was potable, and as they'd followed the river, the travelers had dropped handfuls of cornmeal into pails of it, letting it settle overnight. Yet even by dawn, the water still had an alkali flavor and brimmed with minuscule wildlife.

That morning Private Belknap had stared at a dipperful and snorted in disgust. "Why, it's full of animals!"

Peering into the water in curiosity, Peter had called to her. "Look at this, Theodora! We've grown some little beasties in our buckets overnight."

Theodora had barely glanced at the water. "I'm sure Julius knows what he's doing," she replied without interest. "Besides, Captain Roberts has already given me his official permission to drink it."

The look on Peter's face had told her that the uncalled-for sarcasm surprised and puzzled him, but she hadn't bothered to explain the promise that the captain had so brutally coerced from her. Each evening she'd entered in her diary every un-

141

feeling word Blade had uttered. She'd use that diary someday to show the world what a wretched, uncaring scoundrel the captain really was.

She returned now to her breakfast chores, slipping into the silence that she kept about her like a thick, hand-stitched quilt. It was over a week since Tom had died—days filled with an unrelieved anguish so intense that it blocked out all other sensations. She felt remote, set apart from the world that had always been the source of joy. No longer did she wake up thrilling to the sight of the early dawn breaking over the far-off horizon. Or stop to watch a prairie falcon circling high above her in a wide, graceful arc. Or wonder at the heart-stirring beauty of a black-tailed doe and her fawn as they migrated westward toward the mountains. By her own choice, she spoke only when she had to, preferring to remain alone in her self-made endless night of withdrawal.

It was the first Wednesday of July, and they were preparing to cross the South Platte. The river was only about six hundred yards wide, but it was rapid, high from the spring floods, and known to have a quicksand bottom. After a long consultation with Ezekiel Conyers, Blade carefully chose the point of entry. Sergeant O'Fallon directed two troopers to fashion poles, sharpened at one end and long enough to stand above the surface of the water when driven into the bottom. These were laid out in a pile on the sandy bank.

"Who's going first?" Lieutenant Haintzelman called to Zeke, who stood slightly downriver from him and Theodora.

Conyers slipped his Kentucky rifle into his scabbard and let his mount's reins dangle on the ground. As Zeke walked toward Peter and Theodora, the roan followed him like a trained puppy. "The Cap'n'll go first." His tone was calm and matter-of-fact, as though there were no question about it.

Everyone watched Blade wade barefoot into the muddy current with the bundle of sticks under his arm. He was dressed in leather breeches that had been hacked off at the knees. Using one of the sticks and the soles of his feet, he carefully tried the shifting bottom until he discovered the firmest ground, and then planted the pole. Without wasting a moment, he rapidly but cautiously made his way deeper into the water, choosing the safest ground as he went, then driving the poles into the murky riverbed to mark the track. The water came up to his knees, then his waist.

"Why doesn't he just dive in and swim it, Zeke?" Peter asked. "He's the strongest swimmer I've ever seen. This current isn't half as fast as the Big Blue, and he swam that like it was a flat pond the day he saved Miss Gordon from drowning."

"'Cause a man caught in a current loaded with sand cain't even struggle. That thar movin' sand wave could pull the cap'n under, and he'd be pow'rless to save hisself." Zeke shook his head, and his long gray beard wagged solemnly across his thin chest. "The sand never gives up its dead."

Like a circus audience following the performance of a daredevil tightrope walker, the members of the expedition watched Blade mark the ford. The hush along the shore was so complete that everyone seemed to be holding a collective, baited breath.

All at once the bottom fell away beneath him. Blade sank up to his shoulders in a void of sand and water. Cold fear engulfed Theodora. Despite her smoldering anger, the thought of his death nearly brought her to her knees.

Up and down the bank shouts rang out, and Conyers and Lejeunesse started into the water.

For precious minutes Blade flailed about with his arms. Then he found firm bottom and, without pausing, continued across, planting sticks to mark the route as he proceeded. Theodora released her breath, telling herself that anyone would be frightened at what they'd just witnessed; that the relief she'd felt on the captain's behalf was no more than she'd experience for any member of the expedition.

He reached a sandbar and turned to face them. "It's about medium stage," he called. "We'll ford it here."

When Blade had safely reached the far side, Conyers and two of the French Canadians started across, leading their horses behind them with their boots tied to their saddles.

"Wouldn't it be easier to just ride them over?" Peter questioned Lejeunesse, who had come up to stand beside him and Theodora.

Baptiste's dark eyes twinkled. "*Non*, my friend. The men go across first on foot to pack the sand and make the track more firm and secure. When the horses are led across, they won't be allowed to dally. That's why we watered all the livestock before entering the river, to be sure they don't try to drink, for their hooves will sink quickly into the sand if they stop.''

Peter touched Theodora gently on her arm. "I'll accompany you across, Teddy. I know how frightened you were when we forded the Big Blue. This time I'll stay right beside you.''

Theodora placed her hand over his and squeezed his fingers. "Thank you, Peter. I'd appreciate someone walking across with me.''

Taking care of her had become Peter's unofficial assignment since her brother's death. Earlier that morning, as they'd discussed the fording, Lieutenant Fletcher had offered to be responsible for her safety. Blade had turned on him like an enraged grizzly bear and ordered him to take charge of the pack animals. Nothing seemed to make the captain so angry as the sight of the Southerner in her company.

Fletcher was always a gentleman, demonstrating without words his sympathy and understanding. He'd press her hand and tell her not to talk. Tell her that he, for one, understood her need to be left alone. Unlike that bully of a captain, who never once asked her if she welcomed his persistent attentions.

Theodora had dressed in a pair of Tom's breeches and one of his old flannel shirts, for she'd been instructed by Blade to change out of her skirt. She really wasn't afraid to cross the river. To be swallowed up by the muddy current would be a blessing. She smiled at Peter, trying hard not to show her utter hopelessness. Tom was truly gone. The world would never be the same again.

Before it was time to cross, Blade returned to the near bank. "Lieutenant Haintzelman, you'll lead Athena over with your own horse. Lejeunesse will take care of War Shield for me. Remember, once you start, don't stop for any reason. Don't even slow down. Keep the animals moving as fast as you can and stay as close to the poles as possible.'' He turned to look at her. She had been pointedly ignoring his presence. "You'll go with me, Miss Gordon.'' His voice was aloof, and he seemed to take no notice of the sudden glare she directed at him. "Get your boots off. Your stockings too.''

"Peter has already promised to take me across. Don't waste

your valuable time on me." Theodora wished the scorn in her words could prick his hidebound exterior, but she knew that was impossible. She had repeatedly tried to show the captain that she wanted nothing to do with him, but he continued to pester her with his unwelcome solicitations.

"You heard my orders. Now get your boots off."

Theodora dropped to the sandy bank without another word and reached for the heel of her riding boot.

Crouching before her, Blade brushed her hand aside and took hold of one boot. He held her calf firmly with the other hand and tugged. His breeches were soaking wet, and the water glistened in beads on the thick mat of hair on his chest. His black eyes were piercing in the bright sunlight, and he looked at her with the same immutable determination he'd displayed for the past week, his square, obstinate jaw thrust forward in a gesture of absolute authority.

Dear God, how she hated him! This man who wouldn't leave her alone. Who refused to let her enjoy the comfort of her empty silence. Who kept insisting that she talk, that she work, that she eat, that she sleep, when all she wanted to do was be left by herself.

She tried to jerk her foot out of his hand. "You don't have to do that. I can get my own boots off," she snapped.

Blade ignored her, deftly tugging off first one boot and then the other, and handing them and her stockings to Julius. "Put these in the wagon, Twiggs. They can ride across with you." Then he stood and grasped Theodora's waist in his strong hands. With an easy swing of his arms, he lifted her and set her on her bare feet. "You're going to cross with me, Miss Gordon. Give me your hand."

Reluctantly, she placed her hand in his. "I'm not a child," she complained. "You don't have to treat me like one." With embarrassment, she suddenly realized she was behaving exactly like a three-year-old.

Still, she continued to pull against his grasp until they reached the water. Once in the river, however, Theodora immediately became quiescent. By the time they were waist-deep, the heavy, sand-laden current completely engulfed them. It would have pushed Theodora along in its powerful wake had it not been for Blade. She understood now why she had to wear the old breeches and shirt, for her soaked riding skirt would have weighted her down and slowed her progress dangerously. The shifting, sludgy bottom covered her feet with every step she took, and the suck of the mud on her bare toes each time she pulled them free seemed to be a living thing, trying to entrap her. The thought of being covered with sand and buried alive in the mucky bottom made her heart pound. Her breath came in ragged gasps.

All at once her fears became reality.

The shifting bottom slid out from beneath her, and she slipped under the yellow water. In mindless panic, she clutched Blade's arm, her grip tightening on his strong fingers.

He lifted her up above the water, steadying her while she gasped for air. "Don't be afraid, *vehona*. I've got you." His calm voice was soothing. "We just need to keep moving, that's all."

Terrified, Theodora looked up into his steady gaze and recognized the reassurance there. She nodded mutely. The moment he set her back down on the bottom, she began to walk beside him again, forcing herself to put one foot in front of the other, in spite of the terror of knowing the entire riverbed could move out from under her at any moment.

When they reached the safety of the north side at last, Blade released her hand and nodded to Peter, who was leading the two horses out of the water immediately behind them. "Lieutenant, see to Miss Gordon," he said with impersonal detachment.

Dripping wet, her heart still racing, she watched the captain's broad back as he turned away. She glanced up at Peter, only to catch him shaking his head in commiseration.

After the advance party had safely forded the South Platte, Twiggs drove the light Yankee spring wagon across as quickly as possible, never allowing the mules to stop. The remaining livestock were led across by the troopers, with the loss of only one contrary mule, which stopped from fear, sat down, and refused to budge. The men hollered colorful oaths in three languages at the recalcitrant beast and tugged on it with ropes in an attempt to drag it out, but it became so enmeshed in the miry bottom that the struggle to free it only served to imprison it further, until the only recourse was to shoot it.

At the sound of the rifle blast, Theodora shuddered.

"Come on, Teddy," Peter said to divert her attention. "We'll ride ahead. We should be getting some change of scenery before too long."

She turned a melancholy half-smile on him. How she appreciated his tact and forbearance. Of all the men on the campaign, only the captain pushed her. Annoyed and irritable, she tried to bat him away, as one would a pesky horsefly, but he just kept coming back at her, tenacious and unrelenting. Good Lord, how she despised him!

The travelers left the south fork of the river and struck out over the high prairie for sixteen miles, till they descended the high bluffs that bordered the valley of the North Platte. They windlassed the wagon down the jumble of rocks and entered Ash Hollow, its deep canyon cut by a small, clear spring. The days were long and hot and dry. A constant wind blew across the plains, its velocity never varying. But the face of the land began to change. They approached a stratum of rock, cut and shaped by countless seasons of wind and rain. A series of sharp cones and peaks like chimneys rose in the western horizon. Clouds of dust spiraled upward in the distance, caused by enormous herds of buffalo as they moved toward the river for water. Conyers estimated that there were at least ten thousand of the beasts, extending for miles in all directions and leaving a small open space around the voyagers as they advanced.

One evening, as Theodora sat apart on a box in front of her tent, absently brushing her hair and watching the men gather around the fires for their last cups of coffee, Blade came over to her. He nodded and politely touched his hat brim. "I wondered if I might speak with you a moment, Miss Gordon?"

She glanced up briefly, then resumed her brushing. "My wishes have never stopped you before, Captain."

He ignored her unfriendly remark, crouched beside her, resting on his haunches, and pulled up a long blade of grass. "I'd like to ask a favor of you."

Suspicious, Theodora held her brush in her lap and looked down at him, but his head was bent and the wide brim of his hat blocked his face from her view. He chewed on the grass and waited patiently for her reply. Sensing he would wait indefinitely, she responded at last. "Just what is it you'd like to ask, Captain Roberts? I'm not a mind reader."

He looked up, met her gaze, and grinned engagingly, his even white teeth flashing beneath his dark mustache. His face was deeply bronzed from the days in the sun, and creases framed the corners of his eyes where he'd squinted against its glare. "I was hoping you'd be willing to assist me with the mapmaking. I could use some help in the evenings recording the information we gather during the day. It's more than enough work for two people, as you learned when you helped me and Tom in the past."

She resumed her task with the ivory-handled brush. "I'd rather not. I have enough to keep me busy just gathering my specimens and making my drawings."

Resentment grew inside her at his brassy request for assistance; he was too arrogant to realize how much she disliked him. She'd made a point of writing in her diary beside the fire each night, hoping he'd wonder what vitriolic accusations she penned with such obvious relish. But he'd only regarded her with those mocking black eyes, a faint smile playing about his lips.

"I understand the hardship it would impose, Miss Gordon. It'd mean giving up most of your own work. Naturally, I'd free you from your mess chores." Blade took off his hat and ran his hand through his straight, thick hair. "Another trooper could help Twiggs and Belknap, giving you some extra time. But mostly you'd be working with me."

"Why?" she asked. She stood, the brush clenched in her hand, and he rose with her. "Why should I want to help you, Captain? Now that Tom is gone, the maps are totally your responsibility. Why should I give up my own important work to assist in yours?"

Blade twisted his hat in his strong hands. It was clear how hard it was for him to ask anyone for help. He was a man who'd always handled his own problems. He slowly expelled a breath and met her irate gaze with candor. "For the sake of the expedition, Miss Gordon."

She gave a soft, unladylike snort and turned to go inside her tent. "You can draw the maps, Captain." She looked back over her shoulder at him. "It's what you've been trained to do."

"Yes, Theodora, I could do it without you. But at the expense of valuable time. Time we can't afford to waste at this early stage of our journey. I've seen you work with Tom, and you're a talented artist. You also understand enough of cartography to be able to contribute immeasurably to the success of our mission. I'd appreciate it if you'd set aside your feelings and help me with this work."

"Now how could I possibly do that, Captain? Being a mere female, as you so succinctly pointed out, who's ruled by her emotions?"

Theodora placed her hand on the tent flap, intending to reject his request out of hand. Then suddenly a thought occurred to her. "At the end of this trek, who'd get credit for the maps we've drawn?"

Blade smiled. He took her hand from the canvas and pulled her around to face him. Retaining her stiff fingers in his long ones, he ran his thumb lightly over her knuckles. "If it's your wish, you can share the credit for our work, Miss Gordon."

"How about sharing the credit with Tom?"

At his look of surprise she continued in a rush. "I'm serious, Captain Roberts. Are you willing to have Tom's name on these maps when they're published? Will you agree to share the fame of your accomplishments with my brother?"

"Of course," he acceded immediately. "Every map you draw will be printed with Thomas Gordon's name on it. And my report will include his name as well. Will that satisfy you?"

The thought of fulfilling Tom's dream soared within her. At last, through the grief and despair, a glimmer of hope arose. Her lips trembled as she repeated her dying brother's last words. "That sounds like a deal to me, Roberts."

From that evening on, Theodora joined Blade in his tent after supper to assist in the scientific work of the expedition. While the others sat around campfires, smoking and telling tall tales, the two would enter in their journals the lay of the land and the flora and fauna observed that day. In addition, she helped with the mapmaking, using the astronomical observations that he gave her. They studied the heavens together

through the telescope each night, and Blade astounded her wit
his scientific knowledge.

"How did you learn to calculate our location with suc
accuracy?" she asked him one evening, as she bent over th
map table and drew graph lines with the precision Tom ha
taught her. They were working in Blade's tent, and the canva
sides had been lifted up and tied, making the couple clearl
visible to the rest of the bivouac. She found that it hadn't bee
necessary to insist upon this arrangement for modesty's sake
for throughout the camp it was a common means of allowin
the night breeze to blow through the shelters.

Ruler in hand, Blade stood on the other side of the collapsibl
table. "I studied the advanced methods of Joseph Nichola
Nicollet at West Point. I was also privileged to be tutored b
Torrey and Bailey."

Theodora regarded him in awe, for she immediately rec
ognized the names of the leading botanists of the country. "Yo
studied microscopy with Jacob Bailey?" she questioned wit
admiration. That scientist's amazing studies of algae were rev
olutionizing the frontiers of botany. She lowered her head ove
the map once more. "If only I had been born a man," sh
muttered half to herself. "I'd be allowed to study with suc
great minds."

"There are compensations for being a woman, Miss Gor
don."

"If there are, I haven't found them yet," she responded
noting the amusement in his voice but failing to see the levit
in her statement. She glanced up at him and caught the lopside
grin he struggled to control.

Blade reached inside his pocket for a cheroot, his eyes twin
kling. "That's only because you're so damned young."

"I'm not a child, Captain." Theodora laid down the per
stepped back from the table, and tilted her head to look up a
him. "In point of fact, I'm engaged to be married."

A thunderous scowl marred his brow at the reminder. H
leaned over the maps. His deep voice was a low growl. "Ye
and you don't even know what it's all about yet."

Propping both hands on the table, Theodora bent across he
work, until they were almost nose to nose, and glared back a
him. "I'm a scientist, Captain. I've studied biology. I kno

everything there is to know about . . ." She stood back, non-plussed, while he brazenly waited for her to continue. She averted her eyes and finished lamely. ". . . everything there is to know about."

Blade lit his cheroot with slow deliberation, looking over his hands at her all the while. The suppressed laughter in his voice was a blatant challenge. "Somehow, Miss Gordon, I doubt that. But if you'd like to compare notes on the subject—"

"Let's confine our conversation to the business in front of us, Captain," she snapped, annoyed and shaken by the sensual look on his rugged features. The flicker of his match seemed to leap across the table and ignite a tiny flame within her. Shame for the feelings that spread through her body brought warmth to her cheeks. She picked up her pen and returned to the cartography. She had no intention of allowing him to lead her into personal confidences, especially those involving her own confused emotions.

For Theodora, one of the few reasons for living was now the work that would give her brother credit for his attempt to cross the hated wilderness. The farther they traveled from the site of Tom's grave, the more she grew to despise the endless, unvarying plain with its constant wind and its glaring blue sky. In her depressed and beleaguered state of mind, Blade and the land had become one. For he never seemed to be bothered by the merciless rays nor the mile upon mile of vast, treeless horizon. He was as unchanging as the land. And as unconquerable.

His deep rich voice interrupted her somber reflections. "I think we've done enough for tonight, Miss Gordon. Why don't you turn in, and I'll put the instruments and papers away? You look tired." He didn't finish the unspoken words: *and unhappy.* But she felt his concern as he stacked the maps in a pile and started rolling them into a cylinder.

"As you wish, Captain. I'll see you in the morning." Theodora fought to regain the emotional distance she had kept between them for the past ten days. Setting down her pen, she politely inclined her head. "Good night."

The minute she stepped from the captain's quarters, Lieutenant Fletcher appeared. It was apparent that he'd been waiting

for her. He quickly touched his cap in a salute. "I'll walk y°
to your tent, Miz Gordon." He'd made it a habit to stay close
by each evening until she'd completed her work with Blade,
and then visit with her briefly before retiring.

"How'd it go tonight?" he queried.

Stretching, Theodora sighed. To her surprise he was always
interested in the progress of their work. "Same as last night,
Lieutenant. And the night before. This godforsaken land never
changes, does it? The heat. The dust. The constant wind. Those
never-ending, treeless plains. Sometimes I wonder if we're
even moving, or if we've ended up each day exactly where
we started. Dear Lord, how I hate this country!"

Fletcher took her hand, sympathy on his clear features.
"You've suffered mightily, Miz Gordon. I don't know how
you've managed to keep up your courage, especially in the
face of that man's brutal ways."

Theodora looked back at the captain's tent. The glow of the
lantern inside surrounded the tent in a mystical halo. "He's as
savage as the land, isn't he, Lieutenant? And just as unchange-
able. Sometimes it seems he *is* the land. He never seems to
be bothered by the weather, the long hours in the saddle, the
constant worry about Indians. You were right when you warned
me about him at the very beginning of this trip. I know now
that Tom and I should never have left Massachusetts."

"When we reach South Pass, Miz Gordon, we'll meet with
trappers, many of whom'll be headin' back to St. Louis now
that the beaver is about trapped out. Y' could go on back with
them."

Theodora withdrew her hand and folded her arms across her
chest. She stared beyond the circle of the bivouac's campfires
into the darkness and shook her head slowly. "I don't know.
It'd mean giving up Tom's work."

"What good will that do if you're both dead?" Fletcher
admonished. He placed his hands on her shoulders and turned
her to face him. His pale eyes were intense. "You've a good
life ahead of y'. Don't sacrifice it for some notion of makin'
your brother's death meanin'ful. Save yourself, Miz Gordon.
If you're given a chance to go back home, don't be foolish.
Take it!"

She nodded in resignation. "You're probably right, Lieu-

nant. But that decision can wait until the opportunity presents
self. Right now, I'm going to get some sleep. We've got a
ong way to go before South Pass.''

They had left the green valley below the confluence of the
latte forks. Now the rich buffalo grass was patchy, growing
ostly in low spots or along streams. The soil was sandy and
ry. It hadn't rained in over three weeks, and a constant wind
ad followed them since the day of the burial.

That afternoon, without warning, they were hit by a sand-
torm. The wind came in a sudden downdraft, paralleling the
round and picking up everything in its wake: dust, sand, and
mall pebbles. The company sought shelter in a small ravine.
he troopers pulled their yellow scarves up over their noses
o keep from choking on the dust. The horses and mules were
urriedly picketed, the sound of their neighing and braying
uted by the storm. It was almost impossible to see, for the
and struck their eyes painfully, and the sun was completely
lotted out at two o'clock in the afternoon.

In the confusion Theodora lost sight of Peter. She dis-
ounted, retied her scarf over her nose, and pulled her hat
own tightly, bringing its brim over her eyebrows. She huddled
eside Athena and used the mare as a screen, but was unable
o determine which direction led to safety. In minutes Blade
as at her side. She wondered how he'd found her.

"Give me your reins," he shouted through his scarf as he
ulled them from her gloved hand. "Now get behind me and
ress your face close to my shoulder. I'll lead the way, so you
an close your eyes. Just hold on to my elbow."

Grateful for the protection of his body, which shut out the
tinging sand, she followed him into the shelter of the ravine,
here he eased her under an outcrop of rock. He bent over
er, lifted his arms, and braced them above her head, protecting
er with his body from the storm's onslaught. Behind them,
thena and War Shield gave them the shelter of their own
odies.

"There's nothing to be afraid of, Theodora," he told her.
Iis head was bent above her, and though his lips were near
er ear, his words were muffled by the cloth. "It's just un-

comfortable, that's all. Nothing more than a slight inconven
ience.''

Incredibly, Theodora knew from the sound of his voice tha
under his scarf he was grinning. The elements could do thei
worst to him, and he laughed at them, mocking their power
But the feeling of being isolated in the deep ravine by the sand
laden wind terrified her. She was clammy with fear. She burie
her head in her lap.

The storm died as suddenly as it had appeared, and b
evening the men were able to erect the tents. Everyone wa
layered with dust and sand. Their eyes stood out on thei
blackened faces like egg whites. Julius fed them cold jerky fo
supper, but there was the delicious smell of hot coffee as severa
small fires were lit inside the canvas shelters.

The absence of a trooper named Enoch Pilcher was discov
ered at bedtime.

''Dern it all,'' Zeke exclaimed. ''He probably got turne
around during the storm. No tellin' how fer he's traveled i
the wrong direction.''

Blade smacked his dusty hat on his thigh. ''Let's all ge
some sleep. We'll look for him in the morning.''

They spent the entire next day searching in vain for th
missing dragoon. There was no trail to follow, for the sand
storm had obliterated all trace of him.

The following morning, Blade ordered the men to pack u
and leave.

''You can't do that,'' Theodora said. She stood in front o
him, her arms outstretched as though attempting to block hi
way. Her voice trembled with indignation. ''We can't leav
when a man's out there lost. How could he possibly surviv
by himself?''

Blade looked at the terrified young woman who confronte
him so bravely. She had suffered so much. Most women woul
have given up by now, all hope driven from them by such loss
Yet Theodora was ready to do battle once more. As he gaze
into her emerald eyes, sparkling with unshed tears, he realize
she had more courage than most men. The ferocious spirit o
a mountain cat was centered deep inside that slim frame o
hers.

He strove to make his tone as cold and impersonal as pos

sible. "There's no telling how far he's wandered, Miss Gordon. Without a trail to follow, we could stay here for six months and never find a trace of him." He moved to walk around her.

In desperation she reached out and grabbed his sleeve. "Would you have left Tom and me like this, if you hadn't found our trail?"

"Yes," he lied without compunction. He forced himself to ignore her hand on his arm. "This expedition is going to continue as planned, no matter who gets lost."

"You're inhuman," she whispered, the shock on her face undisguised. She released her hold as though she were touching something evil. "Only a savage would leave someone to the fate that poor man will suffer."

When she tried to bolt, Blade grabbed her elbows before she could run. He held her before him and lifted her to meet his angry gaze. "I may be the savage you think I am, Miss Gordon, but I'm getting as many of my men as possible to California alive. We're not going to waste fruitless days here searching for a man who's probably already dead. Now get on your horse before I have someone put you on it and tie you to your saddle."

Theodora refused even to look at him for the rest of the morning. To ensure his full comprehension of her animosity, she asked Lieutenant Fletcher to ride beside her as they pulled out of camp.

Fletcher, pristine as ever in his blue-and-gold uniform, was happy to escort her. He entertained her with tales of his childhood on a fine plantation near Atlanta. "My daddy owns nearly two thousand acres o' choice river bottom land," he told her in his Georgia drawl. "And nearly three hundred nigras. But I was never meant t' be a farmer. Raisin' cotton's much too tame for me."

Ordinarily, Theodora would have listened politely to his boasting, but that morning she was in no mood to humor anyone. Pulling down the brim of her leather hat to reduce the glare of the sun, she cocked her head at him. "Surely you don't condone the institution of slavery, Lieutenant?"

Fletcher was clearly startled by her question. His tawny mustache seemed to quiver in shock. "Cotton is a way o' life in the South, Miz Gordon. And nigra slaves are a necessary part o' raisin' cotton. I refuse t' believe you're one o' those radical abolitionists, who dress in black and quote platitudes from the Bible. Why, you're much too pretty t' be one o' them. Even your golden hair would be an affront t' those pinch-nosed do-gooders.''

"I'll thank you to keep your opinion of my family to yourself, Lieutenant Fletcher," Theodora warned, recalling with a wave of homesickness the somber dress of her gentle Quaker grandmother. "As far as I can see, it's as barbaric to buy and sell another human being as it is to abandon a man in the wilderness." She flicked her reins and urged Athena forward to join Peter Haintzelman just ahead of them.

At the front of the column, Blade turned just in time to catch the climax of the tiff, and he grinned, delighted to know that the Georgian had just ruined his golden opportunity to further his suit with the fiery Miss Gordon. It was about time someone else felt the sting of her tongue, he thought, chuckling to himself.

Abashed at her abrupt words, Fletcher sat stiffly in the saddle, his pale eyes wide as he watched her go. Then he jerked viciously on his reins, pulling the horse's mouth painfully against the bit, and wheeled around to ride back to his responsibilities at the end of the column.

The next day the weary trekkers camped beside Chimney Rock. The men fired their rifles in celebration of reaching the distinctive landmark.

But the spirit of camaraderie did not affect Theodora, who couldn't stop thinking of the lost trooper, Enoch Pilcher, wandering by himself, perhaps slowly starving to death. He'd been abandoned—left just as she'd been forced to leave Tom. How the others could put the man so casually from their minds remained an unhappy mystery.

"Let's go looking for old bones." Peter Haintzelman called to her. "The captain says this area is known to have the remains of the wooly mammoths that once roamed these plains. O'Fallon wants to look, too. Says he'd like to take one back to his grandson."

Struggling to shake off her melancholy, Theodora agreed. She knew Peter was trying his best to cheer her up. "It's better than sitting here. Let's find Sergeant O'Fallon.''

The trio rode to a nearby rock formation, where they hunted for fossils. The sun beat down, baking the rocks and the searchers alike. Theodora frequently stopped her quest to lift her hand, shade her eyes, and gaze out across the prairie. She prayed for a sign of the lost dragoon. After standing for long moments, desperately scouring the eastern horizon, she turned to find O'Fallon watching her with compassion.

"We'd not be likely to find him, *macushla*," he said at last. "Pilcher probably wandered away in the wrong direction. Out on the open prairie there's little to guide you. Even the Indians seldom strike out alone.''

Theodora's fingers were clenched so tightly together her knuckles were white. "I just can't understand how the captain could give up the hunt so easily. Surely, the man deserved more than one day of searching. How can Roberts be so callous?''

"Callous? Faith, is that what you're thinking?'' O'Fallon took a large handkerchief from his pocket, wiped his face, and motioned with the white cloth to a nearby outcrop of rock. "Let's sit over there in the shade for a moment, darlin' girl. I'm going to tell you something you need to hear.''

Together Peter and Theodora walked over to the ledge and sat down in its scant shade. Beside them O'Fallon leaned his carbine against a large rock and, bracing his dusty boot also upon it, propped one elbow on his knee.

"In the summer of '34, the captain was just a second lieutenant. We were part of a campaign led by General Leavenworth, it being the first mounted military expedition into the Great Plains. We set out in June, in blistering heat, with temperatures of a hundred 'n eight in the shade.''

As he continued his story, Michael O'Fallon's forehead furrowed into a deep scowl, and he gazed off into the distance, as if seeing again that terrible journey. "Wearing their wool shell jackets and leather forage caps, the men were baking in their own sweat, like holiday geese stuffed and popped in your mama's oven. The purpose of the junket was to make a friendly visit to the Comanches and Pawnees.'' Suddenly he drew a long, harsh breath. "Jaysus, everything went wrong from the start.''

Theodora took off her wide-brimmed hat and waved it slowly back and forth in front of her face. She never took her gaze off O'Fallon's haunted blue eyes.

"Go on, Sergeant," Peter encouraged. "I've heard about the tragic campaign, but never from an actual participant."

The burly man shook his head in sorrow. "Heaven forgive him, the general was allowing the men to drink from filthy buffalo wallows, despite Lieutenant Roberts's repeated warnings. The green, stagnant water was never boiled or purified. An epidemic of bilious fever broke out among the men, and half the command became sick with dysentery and typhus. Colonel Henry Dodge continued onward, leading the surviving two hundred dragoons out of the original five hundred, including myself and Roberts and Wesley Fletcher, while Lieutenant Colonel Kearny stayed behind to guard the baggage and the invalids. We went into Comanche country up by the Canadian River and parlayed with the Kiowas and the Pawnees. Now then, the Comanch were another story, for they hated all Americans. But we visited a village and, with Blade's knowledge of Indians, managed to free a captive white boy and a black slave. By the time we made it safely back to Fort Gibson, one third of the dragoons were dead."

"Good Lord!" Peter exclaimed. "And all from drinking contaminated water!"

"That's right, boyo. Blade had tried to warn the men, but they'd ignored him. What did a young officer straight from the Point know about traveling across the plains? they asked. Faith, he was trying to tell them he'd been raised a Cheyenne. But Lieutenant Fletcher, in his jealousy of the half-breed, convinced the men to pay no attention to Blade's warnings."

O'Fallon crushed his forage cap in his large hand. His deep, gravelly voice was filled with misery. "General Leavenworth died on the plains along with the rest. The only one left to lead was Dodge, and him deathly ill, and suffering mightily over the staggering loss of lives. In his delirium he remembered that Roberts had been trying to warn him, but not Fletcher's scoundrelly behavior."

"The bastard!" Peter doubled his fists in anger, then looked guilty as he realized he'd sworn in front of a lady. "Sorry, Teddy," he apologized, and a flush colored his tanned cheeks.

"So that's why Captain Roberts insisted I promise not to drink anything until he'd checked it," Theodora said, half to herself. She rose. "And I thought he was insensitive about Tom's death. And the loss of the trooper."

"Far from it, *mavourneen*. He's bitterly regretting your brother's death, and blaming himself for it, I've no doubt." O'Fallon moved toward the horses. "I know for a fact that the captain vowed he'd never have such terrible losses on any expedition he was in charge of. As for Pilcher, bless us and save us, it was a case of putting the good of the greatest number first. It was a decision he had to make, and the captain faces his responsibilities, that much I'm telling you."

"I always wondered why Blade and Fletcher hated each other." Peter whistled. "No wonder!"

O'Fallon shook his head. "The bad feelings between those two go back farther than that. All the way back to West Point. And neither one has ever said a word about it. I don't think even Zeke knows, and he's known the captain since he was a boy. But they'll settle it between them before this trip is over, I'm thinking."

The three fossil hunters didn't go back to camp empty-handed. They discovered an old, gray bone in the red earth and showed it with excitement to the captain on their return.

Lifting it gently, Blade brushed the soft clay off the fossil with his fingertips, then blew on it to remove the last particles of dust. "Unless I miss my guess, this is the jawbone of a Titanothere." He carefully handed the specimen back to Theodora.

All of the men were enthralled with the bone that might be thousands of years old.

"What kind of an animal was it?" Calvin Belknap asked in awe. "Don't look like any jawbone I ever saw."

Perched on her upturned wooden crate, Theodora held the fossil carefully in her lap while everyone crowded around her, trying to get a peek. "Titanotheres were wooly mammoths that once roamed the plains," she explained.

"Now that's one explanation, Miss Gordon." Blade smiled, his white teeth flashing in humor. He pushed his hat back on his dark head, and the gold hoop in his ear flashed in the sun. "My grandfather, Chief Painted Robe, told me how the Cheyenne found this kind of bone many years ago. My people decided that the huge relics belonged to fierce beasts that came down to earth during a terrible storm, when the lightning and thunder crashed over these bluffs above the Platte. The thunder horse chased the giant beasts from the sky, and they stampeded in terror, plunging to their deaths over the cliffs.''

Theodora smiled at the unique tale. ''That might be as good an explanation as any, Captain Roberts. And it's certainly more colorful than mine.''

Chapter 12

"**Y**'all right, Miz Gordon?" Lieutenant Fletcher asked with concern.

Daydreaming, Theodora barely heard his question. The Southerner had wasted no time in joining her after Peter rode to the head of the column to consult with Roberts. Though she'd not spoken a word to encourage Fletcher, he'd been riding beside her for over an hour.

Inattentive to his solicitude, Theodora gazed at the mountains in the distance and longed for the coolness of their forests. The sun beat down on her with all its July intensity, and the land around them appeared more inhospitable than ever. She longed for a cooling rain, for the shelter of dark clouds. Blinking back the tears that threatened to fall, she squeezed her eyelids closed. She yearned for more than just a change in the weather. She wished desperately that she were back home in the sleepy village of Cambridge, surrounded by her friends and neighbors. How she would love to see the verdant hills of the New England countryside once more.

"Y'all right, Miz Gordon?" Wesley Fletcher questioned for the second time, and the sharp edge to his voice cut through her reverie.

She looked at the handsome officer, then back to the distant vista, and sighed. "I'm fine, Lieutenant. Just hot. And tired." She wondered how he always managed to look so neat—the epitome of the dashing cavalry officer in his blue shell jacket and blue trousers with their yellow stripes. Attired in her cotton blouse and split buckskin skirt, she was moist from perspiration. She'd piled her long hair atop her head and fastened it with combs, hoping her hat would keep it in place. During the morning's ride, damp tendrils had come loose and stuck to her neck.

She glanced at Fletcher once again from under her lashes, not wishing to call his attention to her scrutiny. Since her talk with Sergeant O'Fallon and Peter the previous afternoon, she'd reviewed Fletcher's past conversations with an increased awareness. The soft-spoken Georgian had never given her any cause to doubt his courage or his character. Yet despite his impeccable attire and his courtly solicitude, there was something about him that she didn't quite like or trust.

"Do you think we'll make it safely to our destination?" she asked, trying to prod him into revealing his inner thoughts.

Fletcher's blond head snapped up. He glanced at her speculatively. "No, I don't, Miz Gordon. I think we'll lose a lot more men before the journey's up, and we'll ultimately have t' abandon the idea of goin' all the way t' California."

His pessimism surprised her. "Why do you say that, Lieutenant? Don't you believe it's our country's destiny to spread from one ocean to the other?"

Fletcher untied his scarf and dabbed at the beads of sweat above his golden mustache. "Oh, I do, Miz Gordon. I believe in manifest destiny—that eventually the United States will stretch from shore t' shore. But I think we're doomed t' failure this time. For one thing, I don't believe our illustrious captain intends t' lead us all the way t' the Pacific Ocean. It's my belief that Roberts will do everything in his power t' see that we turn back in failure."

"Why on earth would he do that, Lieutenant?" Theodora found his accusation incredible. "The responsibility of this whole pilgrimage is in his hands. Why would he plan its ruin?"

Fletcher smiled, his pale eyes glinting like silver mirrors in the sun. "Because the success of this expedition would spell the destruction of Blade Roberts's people. Of their whole way of life. Right now, the Plains Indians run free from Canada t' Mexico. Their nomadic ways will inevitably come t' an end if white men invade the prairies."

"Surely not, Lieutenant. Why, there's more land out here than could ever be used. Besides, the white man would only ride across it to reach the Pacific shores. No one but the Indians could actually survive in the middle of this forsaken wilderness."

"Trappers live out here, Miz Gordon. The very trail we're takin' is one the early mountain men followed t' reach the beaver. And they followed the Indian huntin' trails laid down before them. But the changes the French trappers brought with them will be minor compared t' what the influx of large numbers of white folk will bring. And our half-breed captain wouldn't want t' see that, I assure y'."

Fletcher's words made her shift uncomfortably in the saddle. She had no idea *what* went on under the captain's thatch of sloe-black hair or in his half-Indian heart, but she'd witnessed his bravery and leadership firsthand. No coward could have marked the ford at the South Platte, nor would the men have followed a craven across its dangerous quicksand bottom. The mountain men and soldiers alike had accepted Blade's decision to continue without the missing trooper. No one questioned his authority, except herself and Fletcher. And although the golden-haired lieutenant made a grand display of his fine Southern manners and his gentleman's code of honor, it was Blade who'd risked his own life to nurse Tom. During that long, horrible night, Fletcher hadn't come near them. Despite the harsh words of condemnation she'd written daily in her diary, accusing the captain of cruel mistreatment, if her life were threatened at that moment, she wasn't certain to which man she'd turn for help.

With a sigh Theodora decided to steer the conversation into safer waters and asked Fletcher about his early childhood on his family's plantation. It was a topic the lieutenant loved to talk about, and the subject of Blade Roberts was dropped, at least temporarily.

The caravan could easily make twenty-five miles a day now, with only a short rest during the noon hour. They were all becoming hardened veterans of the trail. As they left Chimney Rock behind, the terrain grew rough, and in the light spring wagon Julius Twiggs took a terrible jolting. They reached Scott's Bluff early that afternoon. From a distance, the bluff had looked like a fortress guarding the plains, but when they approached it, they found it was an enormous yellow boulder of marl, covered with dwarf cedar and shrubs. The column of dragoons was forced to climb into the uplands, for the escarpment reached the river, and the ravines around the bluff made the route nearly impassable for the wagon. Two hundred yards below was the water. After days of camping without wood in sight, the weary entourage was fascinated to see small stands of Rocky Mountain juniper.

The orders to make camp had just been given, and the daily unpacking begun, when shouts arose from a cluster of soldiers at the north edge of the campsite.

A trooper placed his hands on either side of his mouth and hollered across the bivouac, "Hey Captain! Found somethin' over here! You'd best take a look."

Theodora was working with Julius at the back of the wagon, setting out the kettles and cooking utensils, when the shout rang out. The soldiers near the picket lines milled toward the stand of cedar and the cluster of men quickly blocked her view. Curious, she started to walk toward the commotion.

"Haintzelman, see to the lady!" Blade shouted as he hurried across the dusty campground. Peter loped over to her from the nearly silent crowd of men.

From its center Private Belknap bolted and ran to the base of a juniper tree on the outskirts of the camp, where he knelt on his knees and vomited. He placed his hands on the ground and retched uncontrollably, his body convulsed with deep shudders.

"Stay here with me, Teddy," Peter insisted. He took hold of her elbow and pulled her in the opposite direction.

"What is it, Peter?" She could sense the nervousness of the men, although they spoke so low she couldn't make out a word they were saying.

"It's the missing trooper. They've found him." Behind his glasses, Peter's blue eyes revealed the horror he was trying so hard to conceal.

"Is he dead?" Theodora asked, but she already knew the answer.

"Yes."

When she tried to pull away from his grasp and go over to the hushed group, the lieutenant shook his head and continued to steer her out of earshot of the soldiers. "It's not a pretty sight, Teddy. He was tortured."

Theodora's heart slammed against her chest at his words. Her hand flew to her throat. The revulsion in Peter's voice told her as clearly as if she'd viewed the corpse that the trooper's death had been unbelievably brutal. Dazed, she turned and stared at Belknap's back, still racked with spasms. "Why? Why would they do that to a defenseless man?"

"They have no compassion for anyone taken prisoner." Peter's brow knitted in dismay. "It's the one thing about the Plains Indians I can't understand, Teddy."

Although Peter steadfastly refused to discuss the death of Private Pilcher with Theodora any further, Lieutenant Fletcher was not so fastidious. That afternoon, he described to her in grisly detail the inhuman suffering that the dragoon had been forced to endure, until finally she had to cover her ears with her hands.

"I'm tellin' y' this for your own sake, Miz Gordon," he assured her, as he took her hands from her head and held them down in front of her. "Y' need t' understand the thinkin' of the Indians. What they're capable of doin' with no more twinge of conscience than if they were helpin' their neighbors at a barn raisin'. The savages will execute a prisoner in a vile, sadistic manner, prolongin' his agony. It's just part of their way of life. The monsters are brought up like that from infancy. Even the women and children participate in the butcherin' of their captives. They actually enjoy it. And they never change—no matter where they go, no matter what else they become."

Unable to listen to more, Theodora broke free. She ran to her tent and sat alone in its dim recesses for the rest of the afternoon, seeing in her mind the bloody, broken corpse of the lost private. Bit by bit, the vision changed, until it was Tom's body, not Pilcher's, that she saw hacked into pieces and scattered across the open prairie. In a split second's revelation she knew why Blade had ordered the troop to ride across her brother's grave. Blade understood their inhuman customs. He knew that Tom's body might be dug up and mutilated. Had that happened? Dear God, how could she endure even suspecting such a thing?

The soldiers wrapped Enoch Pilcher's body in canvas and

buried him in the soft clay. Theodora had not been allowed to see his corpse, nor had she wanted to. The tears that had poured at Tom's burial didn't come. She watched the brief ceremony with dry eyes, numb to all feeling except one. Loathing. Loathing for this savage country and its equally barbarous inhabitants. When she looked at Blade Roberts, she didn't see him in his buckskin shirt and breeches. In her mind she saw him bare-chested, his powerful legs in cut-off pants. Her imagination enhanced the gold earring he wore to an armlet of Indian beads, a headband with its eagle's feather, a necklace of wild animal teeth. Mentally, she dressed him in the clothes of a Plains warrior—the costume he really belonged in—and placed in one hand a dripping scalp; in the other, a razor-sharp hunting knife like the one that was used to torture Private Pilcher.

That evening the men were nervous and excitable. The travelers were only one day away from Fort Laramie, and their hopes of reaching its safety without incident had been dashed. Conyers and Blade concurred that the murder had been committed by Gros Ventre warriors. The sentries were doubled. Around the campfires each man cleaned and checked his weapon.

In the captain's tent Theodora bent over the map table, trying to block out all thought of the afternoon's horror. Her fingers trembled as she worked, despite her brave attempt to control her shattered emotions, and she splotched the parchment in front of her.

"Oh, drat," she muttered. She blotted the ink with a cloth in her shaking hand. "I guess I'm a little nervous tonight," she apologized, as she glanced up at Blade beside her. She squeezed her eyes shut and tried to remember how he'd appeared in his full-dress cavalry uniform back at Fort Leavenworth the night of the farewell ball. Was that really just five weeks ago? she asked herself in disbelief.

When she opened her eyes again, the genuine concern in Blade's gaze disturbed her, making her feel confused and ashamed. His deep voice was filled with kindness. "The Gros Ventres are miles away from here by now, Miss Gordon. The signs indicated only a small hunting party. They won't attack a camp of armed men, fully alert and ready for them.''

"I'm sure you can predict those savages better than most men, Captain Roberts," Theodora blurted out, and they both knew the bitter words she'd left unspoken: *Because you're one of them.*

Bending over her, Blade reached out as though to bridge the widening chasm between them. "Theodora, don't convict me of Pilcher's murder. I'm not—"

She jerked away before his fingers reached her. "Don't touch me," she gasped, her breath coming fast. She stepped back and flung up her hands, as if to ward off a demon. "Please— just don't touch me."

"Then don't look at me with fear in your eyes," he ordered curtly. He straightened his broad shoulders and stared down from his full height. A muscle tightened in his stubborn jaw. He had never appeared so proud and aloof. Anger edged his sharp words. "I'm not a savage, Miss Gordon."

"Oh, no?" she asked. "Aren't you capable of participating in what happened to Private Pilcher? Weren't you raised in such barbarity? Can you deny that you're one of them?" Her fingers trailing along its edge, she moved around the table until it provided a barrier between them.

As he watched her haunted features, Blade stood immobile, unable to deny her hysterical accusations. He was capable of torture and he knew it. "Yes, Theodora. I am Cheyenne. But don't judge a people—a whole way of life—by one incident."

"One incident! My God, when I think of how that poor man must have suffered!" Theodora covered her face with her hands and sank down on a camp chair, her sobs filled with an unbearable grief.

In two strides he was beside her. He reached out, wanting to hold her, to comfort her, yet knowing that his very touch would bring a look of revulsion to her tear-filled eyes. Instead, he pulled a handkerchief from his pocket and pressed it into her moist hand. "Try not to think about it, Miss Gordon. It's over. The pain is over for Pilcher. Let it be over for you, as well. Don't dwell on it. Peter never should have told you so much about it."

Theodora shook her head and wiped her eyes. "It . . . it

wasn't Peter. He refused to say anything. Fletcher told me about it.''

Blade clenched his fists. "God*damn* him. I should have known." He swung around to face the map spread out on the table, carefully hiding the rage he felt toward the infuriating Southerner. With an enormous effort he managed to keep his voice cool and disinterested. "Do you think you can work some more tonight? Or do you want to stop for the evening?''

Theodora blew her nose and squared her shoulders. "No, I won't quit. The task will occupy my mind. If I go back to my tent, I'll have only my thoughts to keep me company. And that's the one thing I fear the most.''

Blade returned to the far side of the table and looked across at the courageous young woman, offering her the security of its width between them. How ironic, he mused with bitterness, that since he was twelve years old, he'd thought all white women were alike, simpering about their salons in tightly laced corsets, feigning fatigue at the slightest exertion in the belief that it made them more alluring. The only exception he'd ever known was his spunky French grandmother. Until he'd met this exasperating New England bluestocking. She was as resilient as she was tenacious, bearing up under the bone-jarring pace of the march, helping to cook for forty men, raising her own tent, collecting her botanical specimens, even working on his maps. She was the only female he'd ever met who dared to challenge his male authority, or share his scientific interests, or match his vibrant love of life with her own totally feminine joy in the world. With one wide-eyed look from those astonishing green eyes she could fire his blood. She was intelligent and compassionate, with an innocent sensuality that brought an ache of desire each time he looked at her.

He wanted her.

And she despised him.

Not for what he'd done, or for what he'd failed to do—but for what he was. The intense dislike for him she'd expressed at the beginning of their journey had now turned to cold, passionless contempt.

He picked up a compass and twirled it on the table top, studiously maintaining his outward calm. "Tom would have been very proud of you, Theodora. Don't underestimate your

wn strength. Or your own importance. Your cartography work
s excellent. These maps will assure the safe movement of
vagons across the prairie. The help you've given me has been
nvaluable.''

Jamming the balled-up handkerchief in the pocket of her
tress, she peered suspiciously up at him. "Do you really want
vagonloads of white people crossing the plains, Captain?"

Blade quirked an eyebrow, trying to fathom her reasoning.
"That's the point of this whole expedition, isn't it?"

"Yes, but is it what *you* want? Wouldn't it be better for the
ndians if the white man never comes?" The doubt in her eyes
varned him that, though she was prepared to hear his denial,
he wasn't about to believe it.

He laid down his pen, reached into his shirt pocket, pulled
ut a cheroot, and lit it. Soon the tent was filled with the
iromatic scent of its smoke, and he inhaled it with appreciation.
"It would've been better for the Indians, Miss Gordon, if the
white man had never arrived on these shores at Plymouth
Rock. But that doesn't change history. White men will cross
he Great American Desert, and nothing on God's green earth
s going to keep that from happening. The best we can hope
or will be a peaceful passage to the West. And the U.S. Army
emains the best hope for that. If I can determine the safest,
astest overland route, I will prevent needless deaths on both
ides.''

Theodora stared up at him from her seat. She leaned forward,
er hands clenching her knees. "Who are you, Captain Blade
Roberts?" she asked in a hoarse whisper. "Are you a Cheyenne
varrior or are you an army engineer? Or are you somehow—
nagically—both?"

Blade grinned as he held the butt of the cigar in his teeth.
"You forget my French antecedents, Miss Gordon. Those
uave, romantic devils who charmed the ladies of New Orleans
ight out of their—"

"I get your point, Captain," Theodora interrupted. Jumping
ip from the chair, she grabbed a ruler and leaned over the map
able. She kept her lids lowered, her gaze locked on the sheets
of paper before her. Never would she let him see the effect
ipon her of the image he'd conveyed. If with mere words he
:ould kindle that yearning need to seek the solace of his arms,

what fire could he light within her with his touch? Pushing aside the memory of his wet, bare skin beneath her cool fingers the day he'd taught her to swim, she took a deep breath. "Now, what was the height you'd determined for the bluff again?"

He followed her lead and turned his attention once more to the parchment in front of him. "Two hundred feet from its base."

They worked together for more than an hour, making remarkable progress. Finally, Blade leaned both elbows on the table and gazed at the top of the head bent over his maps. "I'll walk you to your tent, Miss Gordon, before I check on the pickets. We're all going to need our rest tonight. We'll reach Fort Laramie the day after tomorrow."

In the morning, the voyagers windlassed the wagon down the dangerous slopes to the Platte. Theodora stood on the top of the bluff, watching the men as they strained to ease the Yankee spring wagon over the precipitous ledges. She turned and looked back across the valley they had just crossed. Far to the east, she could see the outline of Chimney Rock, twenty-three miles away. And farther still lay Tom's grave.

"I have to go now, Tom," she told him, straining to see the eastern horizon. "But I'll come back to take you home to Papa. I promise."

Go now, Teddy. Cherish our dream. Do everything we came out here to do. Don't let my death be in vain.

Tears streamed down her cheeks as she heard him speak to her. That was what she'd been waiting for. She had to hear him tell her it was all right to leave.

"I'll continue your work, Tom," she vowed as she lifted her face to the heavens. "The maps will be published with your name on them. The world will know that you gave your life serving your country."

She turned and nearly bumped into Blade's broad chest.

"I thought I heard you talking with someone," he said in a puzzled tone. His glance swept the empty bluff.

Theodora raised her head, unashamed of the tears. "I was saying farewell to Tom."

Startled, Blade searched her grass-green eyes. His heart

soared at the serenity he found in them. "And he said good-bye to you, didn't he?"

When she lowered her head and nodded, he released a long, ragged sigh of relief. He knew at last that he'd won the battle. Theodora had accepted her brother's death. She had chosen life.

Discovering that the North Platte was too deep to ford, the men once again took the axles off the wagon and converted it into a bullboat. They used the nearby cedar to make long-overdue repairs on the wheels, which had frequently been soaked overnight to prevent the dry wood from cracking. The jittery procession followed the river bottom all that day, and the next afternoon it reached the safety of Fort Laramie.

The fortress stood twenty-five feet above the water on the north bank of the Laramie River. Tipis were pitched around its high walls, and as the caravan rode between the lodges, Theodora could hear the strange sounds of an Indian dialect.

In near panic she looked at Blade, who'd accompanied her all that afternoon.

"Indians!" she gasped. Her palms started to sweat in her leather gloves.

"They're Sioux," Blade reassured her as they rode toward the fortress. "Don't worry, Theodora. They're friendly, or they wouldn't be here. But if you're really frightened, you can ride up here in front of me. I don't think War Shield will founder under the extra weight. Stagger a little, maybe, but not collapse completely."

She met his teasing gaze in surprise. A devilish half-grin played on his mobile lips. He'd pestered her to eat three solid meals a day, and she'd already replaced the pounds she'd lost the first week after Tom's death. "I don't think we'd better risk it, Captain Roberts," she told him primly, holding back a smile. "As large as you are, I might just be the straw that would break the stallion's back."

Behind the fort and its surrounding lodges loomed a back-drop of black hills, with the peak of Laramie Mountain standing out clearly against the western horizon. The air was so clear that the fort and its background seemed to take on an other-worldly appearance as they cantered up to it.

"It looks as though it were put here by some magic spell," Theodora told Blade in awe. "It doesn't seem to belong, yet it appears as though it's always been here."

Blade chuckled. "No magic spell put that post there, *vehoka*. Its real name is Fort William for Old Bill Sublette, a trapper who built it with the help of his partner, Robert Campbell. The American Fur Company bought it, hoping to gain control of the Platte route to the mountains. Except for Bent's Fort and Saint Vrain, it's the major force in fur trading today."

As they wended their way through the scattered lodges, Theodora stared in apprehension at the Indians, who stopped and watched them. She cringed each time she heard one speak, fearing that the Sioux would turn on them and hack them to pieces in one swift, overwhelming rush of mayhem.

Recognizing her nervousness, Blade sought to distract her. "I've been meaning to thank you for all the help you've given me with the maps, Miss Gordon. And to tell you how brave you were back there, when we crossed the quicksand at the South Platte fording. It takes real courage to walk into a sand-laden current and to keep moving across a shifting river bottom. You should be proud of yourself."

Theodora blushed at his words, pleased to receive praise from a man who seldom gave it—and never when it was undeserved. "Thank you, Captain," she said. So the hard-headed captain had changed his mind about her at last. This was progress, indeed. She gave him a victorious smile. "Perhaps you're not so certain now that I should never have come on this journey."

He regarded her thoughtfully. "I'll answer that question when we reach California, *vehona*. Until then, I'm afraid my original opinion about a white woman crossing the wilderness still stands." He shifted in his saddle, about to urge War Shield forward, then changed his mind. He glanced at her again, merriment sparkling in his eyes. Pulling his mount even closer to hers, he spoke so low that no one riding behind them could possibly hear. "But I wouldn't have missed that swimming lesson for anything in the world."

Without giving her a chance to reply, he slapped Athena gently on the flank, and they galloped their horses up to the welcoming walls of Fort Laramie.

Riding through the security of the arched main gate, Theodora spotted a scraggly garden of turnips, peas, and onions going to seed. She could have wept with joy at the homey scene. The fort was made of thick cottonwood logs, with blockhouses at two corners. To her relief the walls appeared at least fifteen feet high and were surrounded by a palisade of sharp wooden stakes. On one side of the square she noted storerooms, offices, and living quarters; on the other was the corral.

Three men in the center of the square watched them ride in. Two were dressed in baggy, unpressed business suits. The third, attired in buckskins, came up to Blade as he dismounted and grasped his hand. The wide grin on his handsome face told Theodora that the two men were old friends.

"Welcome to Fort Laramie, Blade. We've been expecting you for several days now. I hope you've brought some mail from New Orleans."

"I've got some letters for you, Lucien," Blade replied. "Your family's well, but misses you. And as you can see, we have a lady traveling with us." Reaching up, he placed his strong hands on Theodora's waist and swung her down from the saddle.

As she sailed through midair, Theodora laid her hands on his shoulders. His muscles tensed and flexed beneath the light touch of her fingers. Against her will, she looked into his eyes for fleeting seconds, forcing herself to ignore the message she read in them. Then her boots touched solid ground and she regained her composure.

"Miss Gordon," Blade said in a polite, unruffled tone that belied the hunger she had seen in his gaze, "may I present the fort's *bourgeois*, Lucien Fontenelle."

Theodora had learned that the mountain men, influenced by the years of French control over the unmapped prairies and plains of North America, called their leader *bourgeois*, or "boosh-way," as Zeke pronounced it.

"Mademoiselle, we are deeply honored," the fort's commander said. "Like the captain here, I have foregone the luxuries of a wealthy life in Louisiana for the adventures of the wilderness. But seeing you reminds me all too well what pleasures I have missed." To her surprise, Fontenelle took her outstretched hand, bent over it, and kissed it. He straightened, flashing a winsome smile. His eyes, like Blade's, were dark. His long brown hair was pulled back and tied with a leather thong. "This has been a summer of surprises," he continued. "Until this month we've never had the pleasure of a white woman's company at the fort. Now, you are the third one to grace our humble lodgings within three weeks."

"Other white women?" Blade questioned his friend in surprise. "Here at Fort Laramie?"

"*Oui*. Two missionaries and their wives, traveling with a party of trappers, stayed with us briefly only two weeks ago. One was a beautiful blonde." Looking over at Theodora, he smiled once again, then placed his thumb and forefinger together, brought them to his lips, and kissed them with a smack. "*Voilà!* Now we entertain another *petite ange*."

"These are my clerks," Fontenelle said. He turned and waved forward the two businessmen, who shook hands with Blade.

The square was filled with black-haired children, who watched Theodora with dark, almond-shaped eyes as they talked excitedly in their Indian language. A few bold ones approached her, followed at a distance by their more timid playmates.

Fontenelle clapped his hands. "Off with you now!" he said in a mixture of Sioux and French. "*Voyoux!* Leave the lady in peace." He turned and shrugged in apology. "Our children are merely curious, that's all, mademoiselle. Most of the sixteen *engages* hired by the American Fur Company to work here are married to Indian women, and the children have almost never seen anyone like you before. But come, let's get out of the sun. Sit here under the shade of the porch while Captain Roberts and I share our news."

The coolness of the porch was a welcome relief. Theodora took off her hat and smoothed back the strands of fallen hair. In clusters the children returned to their play in the busy square, climbing over stacks of buffalo robes, boxes, and cartons. Their happy cries reminded her of the sounds of children playing outside her window in Cambridge. "The youngsters don't bother me at all, Monsieur Fontenelle. It's only natural for them to be curious."

A jovial grin split his face at her open acceptance of the

children's mixed heritage. "Splendid. Then you will join us for a feast this evening, Mademoiselle Gordon?"

Theodora looked at the captain before she replied.

Blade stepped onto the wooden porch, his gaze roving about the noisy fort. "We'll make camp along the river, Lucien. The men have lots to do, including the repair of broken equipment and the washing of clothes. We'll need to stay several days. We'll be happy to accept tonight's invitation."

The afternoon was spent reprovisioning the wagon and packs. The boxes piled high in the square contained blankets, calicoes, guns, powder, lead, glass beads, small mirrors, rings, vermilion for painting, and tobacco. Blade scowled at the many cases of alcohol. He knew the liquor would be diluted with water and sold to the Indians, who'd trade a year's worth of furs for a single keg. He also realized that Fontenelle was forced to barter it in order to compete with the itinerant traders who wandered the plains and sold the drink for a quick profit.

Early that afternoon Blade and Theodora worked on the cartography, wanting to get it done before the merrymaking began. While they concentrated, three Sioux braves stepped uninvited into the tent. The Indians stood silently watching them. The captain glanced up only for a moment, then went back to work. Startled, Theodora straightened. Rigid with terror, she stared at the men. They were attired in breechclouts, their naked chests, arms, and thighs an affront to her New England modesty.

"Wh—... what do they want?" she asked, swallowing the fear that choked in her throat. They met her gaze with implacable calm.

Blade continued his calculations. His deep voice was tinged with amusement. "They're just curious, Miss Gordon, that's all. They don't mean us any harm. Just go on with your work as though they weren't even here."

She found it impossible to ignore them. Her hand shook as she tried to map Blade's information. Peering at them from under her lids, she realized that one of them wore a scalp lock hanging from the handle of his war ax, and she recalled that the lost trooper had been scalped. She clutched the edge of the table and fought the wave of dizziness and nausea that came over her. Beads of perspiration broke out on her forehead and over her upper lip. Her tongue stuck to the top of her dry palate.

"Blade, I . . . I think I'm going to faint."

In one swift movement he dropped his pen and caught her sagging form, cradling her head against his chest. He spoke to the braves in clipped, guttural words. As they left the tent, he lifted her in his arms and carried her to a camp chair. He knelt in front of her and took her hands. "It's okay. They're gone now."

Drawing a deep, shuddering breath, Theodora gazed into his anxious eyes. "I'm . . . I'm s-sorry," she stammered. "I just keep remembering that trooper and what they did to him."

"*They* didn't do anything to him, Miss Gordon," he corrected in a terse voice. "A Gros Ventre hunting party murdered Pilcher. The Sioux happen to be allies of the Cheyenne."

"Good Lord," she cried, "what difference does that make? They're all vicious savages, aren't they?"

His tone revealed a glacial anger. "Yes, I guess in your eyes we are, Miss Gordon." He dropped her hands into her lap, rose with the grace of a mountain cat, and returned to the map table.

As soon as the sun began to set, the squaws set up long trestle tables in the fort's square. Huge racks of buffalo meat were skewered on sharp sticks and placed over open fires. The women, mostly Oglala Sioux, stirred an aromatic broth in enormous kettles into which they dropped fresh vegetables from their gardens. The smell of the stew permeated the air, tantalizing the travelers.

Relieved for once of his cooking duties, Julius Twiggs sat beside Theodora on the wooden porch, enjoying the slight breeze. "Can rest my weary bones at last, Miss Theo," he said as he rocked back and forth in a worn bentwood rocker. "Tomorrow come soon enough."

From her place on an old caned chair Theodora looked at his wrinkled face, its cocoa color heightened by his white grizzled hair. "You've earned a rest, Julius. From now on I'll give you more help with the cooking."

"No, Miss Theo. You work with Captain. Very important."

Theodora flushed at the mention of Blade, remembering his

anger at her comment about the Indians earlier that day. After her condemnation of the Sioux, they'd finished the cartography, but they'd spoken only when necessary. He'd been cold and distant and proud, and Theodora had felt an aching loneliness as she'd worked beside him.

Why should she feel guilty? she asked herself, listening to the creak of Julius's rocking chair. It seemed to measure out the slow, uninspired half-life she'd been living since Tom's death. She'd felt miserable for so long that she didn't know why Blade's aloofness even bothered her.

When she'd called the Indians savages, she'd *meant* to include him. And they both knew it. Suddenly she was overcome with shame. He hadn't been responsible for Tom's death or Pilcher's ghastly murder. She was using him as a scapegoat to relieve her own guilt. It was her own carelessness that had caused her and Tom to get lost on the plains that afternoon two weeks ago. And God knew, she'd give anything to live that day over again. Why then couldn't she offer Blade the same understanding and forgiveness that she knew she must eventually give herself? She had to put the past behind them and give the half-Indian captain a chance to prove himself.

Her solemn reverie was interrupted when Peter joined them. He smiled companionably, for they hadn't had a chance to speak to each other all day. "Well, I guess I'd better take my turn in the river, before we're called to eat," Peter said.

Theodora returned his good-natured smile. "I spent part of the afternoon washing myself and my clothes there. And I can assure you, that water feels wonderful after the dry days on the trail."

Twiggs flashed his gold tooth at them. "Hallelujah, don't this beat all? Bathing, and laundry, and women's cooking. Yes, sir. In the lap of luxury now. Might stay in this chair and never get up. No how. Just stay here and rock for the rest of my life."

"That does sound mighty good," Peter agreed as he turned to go. "But I, for one, am looking forward to a meal."

Supper that night was good enough to tempt a saint during Lent. Everyone ate until they were too full to move. Then one of the fort's *engages* appeared with a fiddle tucked under his chin. As he filled the night air with its sweet, melodious sound,

a corporal pulled out his harmonica and joined the serenade
Spontaneously, the French Canadians began to clap, and the
left their places at the tables and formed a double line. On
after another the soldiers joined them, egging each other on a
first one man and then another broke into an impromptu dance
skipping down the column and showing off his skill with
wide now-top-that grin.

As the players struck up "Jimmie Crack Corn," Peter came
up to Theodora and bowed formally. His blue eyes twinkle
behind his spectacles. "I'd be honored if you'd dance with
me, Miss Gordon."

"Oh, Peter, I'd love to," Theodora exclaimed. "But I don'
know how."

"That's no problem. Come on. I'll show you."

Leading her between the two rows of men, Peter swun
Theodora on his arm. It was amazingly simple. All she had t
do was skip down to the center, let Peter swing her around
and then sashay back to the end of the line. After Peter, Lieu
tenant Fletcher asked for a turn.

Theodora danced with everyone, including Zeke, kickin
her heels and laughing out loud for the first time since Tom'
death. Fontenelle had generously provided several bottles c
wine and a keg of brandy, and she felt giddy and excited fron
the alcohol's effect.

The men never let her stop, each one claiming a turn, unt
she was completely exhausted.

"Wait! Wait!" she cried at last, fanning herself with he
hand. As she gasped for air, she plopped down in the rocke
on Fontenelle's porch. She put up one palm in a plea for mercy
"No more!"

Although he was the only man who hadn't asked her for
dance, Blade was immediately at her side. At a quiet shake c
his head, the men acceded, boisterously finishing the reel them
selves, until everyone agreed that it was time to stop and catc
their breath. When the music died, Blade bent over and spok
in her ear. The fresh scent of his skin and hair mingled wit
the spicy aroma of the cheroots in his shirt pocket. His dee
voice sent waves of longing through her. "I'll escort you bac
to your tent, Miss Gordon. I believe the party's over."

Realizing it was, indeed, time to go, Theodora smothere

a sigh. She forced her tone to be light. "We'll regret our carefree ways tomorrow, Captain, but I can't remember when I've had so much fun."

"If the men don't get to bed soon, they'll sleep right through the morning. And until you say good-night, not one of them is going to turn in." Blade reached behind her and dropped her shawl across her shoulders, his strong fingers lingering in a gentle caress.

Theodora flushed at the sensuous quality in his voice. She stood and took the ends of the woolen shawl in her fingers. By now the effect of the wine was slight, for she'd nearly danced its euphoria away. Only a soft, warm glow remained. "Good night, gentlemen," she called, curtsying to the men who stood around the tables talking. "I'll see you in the morning."

At her words Lieutenant Fletcher hurried toward her. He stopped abruptly when he saw Blade. The two officers stared at each other in a silent confrontation, and the space between them crackled with animosity. Then Fletcher bowed to Theodora and backed away.

Blade placed her hand on his arm, nodded to the watching crowd, and led her through the square and out the fort's gate.

For the first time that night Theodora noticed the summer moon. It was full and ripe, like a huge peach suspended high in the sky. She gazed up at it and hummed one of the tunes they'd played, swaying slightly to the melody as she walked beside him.

"I take it you enjoyed the dancing," Blade said, his voice so soft she could barely hear the words.

"Very much. And to think I'd never danced the Virginia Reel in my entire life until I came to Fort Laramie. Imagine such a grand debut right here in the middle of nowhere."

"We're not exactly, 'nowhere,' Miss Gordon. My tribe camped many times in this area when I was a boy." In the moonlight she could see the smile that hovered at the corners of his mouth. "This spot is a major crossroads," he continued. "The Northern Cheyenne took the north-south trail countless times in the past and still do. The east-to-west route was an old buffalo trail that the Indians took on their hunts. The beaver trappers followed it into the mountains."

"I'm sorry," Theodora said, thankful that he hadn't taken offense at her remark. "I forget sometimes that all of this is quite familiar to you."

They walked past the cluster of Sioux tipis toward the row of military tents by the river. Silvery light bathed the landscape, making the dark silhouettes of the tents stand out against the pale water.

Partly to cover her embarrassment and, in part, to make up for her narrow-minded remarks of the afternoon, Theodora peered up at the tall man beside her. "What was it like? Being brought up . . . as an Indian?"

He swung her around to face him. The moon lit his strong features, accentuating the high cheekbones and straight nose. "I wasn't raised *as* an Indian, Miss Gordon. *Nazestae*: I am Cheyenne. At least half of me is. And I'm damn proud of that half. My Cheyenne family gave me a childhood filled with love and acceptance. They expected me to behave with courage and honor." Hearing the others draw nearer, he took her elbow once again and led the way down the dirt path. "There were times, growing up, when I was the butt of pranks by the other Indian boys because of my French heritage, but my Indian family taught me to be proud of who I was. What I learned at my grandfather's side about the meaning of being a Cheyenne stood me in good stead when I was in New Orleans, and once again the target of ignorance and prejudice."

Theodora winced at his words, for she knew that she was as guilty of bigotry as the others in his past. She hoped he'd accept her next words as a peace offering. "That must have been very difficult, Captain. Trying to adapt to such a totally different culture."

Responding to the compassion in her voice, he slid his fingers down her arm and caressed the palm of her hand with feather-like strokes. His light touch sent waves of pleasure through her. She laced her fingers in his, afraid to say anything lest her voice tremble and betray the devastating effect he had on her. Since she'd met him, she was both frightened and attracted at the same time, and this confusion had only deepened during the weeks on the trail.

As they reached her tent, Theodora peered up at him, surprised to find delight at her response gleaming in his eyes.

He took both her hands and lightly rubbed his thumbs across her knuckles. His dark brows drew together in thought. "Life's never easy. But a man doesn't back down from a difficult situation. No one ever solved anything by running away."

Together, they turned and looked back at the fort. Like a medieval castle with its peasant huts huddled around it, it stood high above the water's edge.

"It's really beautiful tonight, isn't it?" she whispered. "It looks so strangely peaceful."

Slowly, he pulled her to him. His voice was velvety soft as he bent over her, and she felt his cool breath fan her lowered lashes. "Don't worry about the nearness of the Sioux, little bluestocking. They're friendly. Just very curious."

"So I learned this afternoon when they came into your tent. Are the Sioux and the Cheyenne tribes similar?" For no reason she trembled as she watched the mobile line of his upper lip under the thick mustache, and she tried to keep her mind on their conversation.

His even teeth flashed in a smile, and she detected a hint of amusement in his deep voice at her sudden interest in Indian customs. "There are many similarities, *vehoka*. But each tribe tends to pay more attention to the differences. Little things are very important to the Indian. Take, for example, just moving about inside the lodge. No one with any manners would ever walk between the fire and another person. It's not polite." The creases around his dark eyes deepened as he chuckled softly. "Even a child knows that a civilized person always walks behind his host. There are countless rules of daily life that a white man has no knowledge of. That's why the Indian has always complained of the white man's bad manners. The ignorant *veho* just doesn't know how to go on."

"Sounds very complicated," Theodora replied as she searched frantically for something more to say. She dragged her gaze from his mouth to discover he was watching her with a quizzical look, no doubt wondering at her total change in mood from earlier in the day.

"It is," he answered with a wry grin. "Every bit as complex as learning to take tea and biscuits with my grandmother in her fancy Louisiana drawing room."

Shocked, Theodora tried to picture him as a twelve-year-

old, with two long black braids and a hoop in one ear, dressed
up like a little Southern gentleman and sitting down to afternoon
tea with his starched and proper grandmother. She burst out
laughing.

Seeing her upturned face brimming with merriment, Blade
felt the need for her flame up inside him. Her musical laugh
triggered a hunger he'd held tightly under control since the
morning he'd found her sleeping beneath her petticoat tent.
The day before her brother had died of cholera. He'd been
afraid since then that he'd never again see her as she was now,
her eyes filled with laughter. God, how he wanted her. Perhaps
if Tom hadn't died . . . if Pilcher hadn't been so savagely mur
dered . . .

He ignored the sounds of the camp around them. Sliding his
hands over her shoulders, he gently rubbed her collarbone.
"I'll go inside and light your lamp," he said, his voice husky.

Frightened by the magnetism that pulled her to him, Theo
dora slipped away from his touch. Her voice sounded high-
pitched and slightly frantic to her own ears. "Oh, you don't
have to. I can find the lantern in the dark. I know right where
I left it."

He didn't answer. Instead, he lifted the tent flap and went
inside. "Where is it?" he called.

"Right beside the center tripod." She stood to one side of
the opening and held back the canvas, allowing the moonlight
to illuminate the shelter.

Blade knelt in the middle of the tent and groped in the
darkness. Then he struck the match with a snap, and the soft
glow of the lantern filled the interior, throwing long shadows
across the canvas walls.

In the doorway, Theodora froze.

The sharp intake of her breath brought Blade to his feet. He
saw it instantly.

There on her bedroll coiled a huge rattlesnake. Its beady,
malevolent eyes glinted in the moving light. Its jaws were
opened wide, revealing twin sabers of death.

Chapter 13

The sound of the snake's rattle filled the tent. With one swift, fluid movement, Blade pulled his knife from its sheath and hurled it. The serpent lunged the instant the knife left his hand and met the cold steel in midair, openmouthed like a lover. The force of the razor-sharp blade split its jaws apart. The forward momentum of the knife carried it, with its gruesome cargo, across the shelter, and the blade struck the taut canvas side, impaling the prairie rattler. The long slithery body writhed and twitched convulsively, its death throes the syncopated rattle of a baby's toy.

Theodora stared transfixed as the rattler's agony gradually ceased and the tent became still. She turned to Blade and tried desperately to breathe, but it was as though someone had knocked the wind out of her. Her vision blurred and a gray fog enveloped her.

"Blade," she whispered. Her voice sounded faint and far-away. She stretched out her hand, trying to reach him where he stood halfway across the tent. Valiantly, she fought the darkness that closed in on her, then took one tottering step and pitched forward.

Blade caught her before she reached the ground. He pulled her to her feet and cradled her head against his solid chest. The feel of his strong arms around her brought a stab of poignant longing to Theodora. A yearning for the safety of her home and family nearly doubled her over with its intensity, and had she not been held upright, she would have crumpled in a heap. Deep sobs wracked her.

"Oh, Blade." She wept against his soft buckskin shirt. "I o-only I could go home. If only I h-had never c-come to this horrible place."

"Hush," he whispered. He kissed the top of her hair and buried his face in her curls. "Shhh, *zehemehotaz*. It's all right." He swayed back and forth, comforting her.

"You were r-right. I . . . I n-never should h-have come. I should h-have listened to you. But I was too stubborn. I don't b-belong out here." Theodora pulled her head back and wiped her cheeks with her palms. She looked up at him and her voice cracked as she spoke. "If I had listened to you back at Fort Leavenworth, Tom would be alive today." Her lips trembled uncontrollably, and she covered them with her fingers. She bent her head, resting it against Blade's chest. "Dear God, why couldn't it have been me instead of Tom?"

"Don't, Theodora. Don't do this to yourself." Blade's arms tightened around her. His voice was hoarse with an inner anguish. "No one's to blame, least of all you. You had no way of knowing the risks involved. I'm the one responsible for this expedition and for every member in it. Don't ever blame yourself for your brother's death."

She lifted her gaze and recognized in his eyes genuine concern for her. Had it always been there? she wondered. Was his intention from the very beginning to protect her from harm? This fierce soldier who'd stormed and railed at her after Tom's death—what would it be like to be cherished by this strong, dominant male? Instinctively, she knew that once he gave his love, it would be a commitment he'd never break. He was the kind of man who valued his word above his life. A man of tremendous pride. Not one to be flirted with or teased, the way the young ladies back home enjoyed leading on their beaux in order to satisfy their own shallow pride with a proposal they had no intention of accepting. One move on Theodora's part, one tiny hint of willingness, and Blade would possess her. Completely. Somehow, she sensed it, even though—despite her avowal to the contrary—she knew only the most basic physical facts about the mating of human beings. With him, it would be total and consuming, without the restraints dictated by the white man's upright and rigid social mores. She knew she must pull away from him now before it was too late.

She tried to step back. "I'm all right, Captain. I can stand my own now." Her gasps for air were short and rapid, matching his own labored breathing.

But Blade didn't release her. He pulled her nearer. His mouth was warm and gentle as it brushed her lips, then moved across her wet cheeks and eyelids. "Theodora," he whispered into her ear, his voice thick with desire, "don't push me away. Let me stay with you. Let me comfort you."

Her heart thundered beneath her ribs. She knew what he wanted. She wanted it herself. As of their own volition her arms moved around his neck and she raised her lips to his. It was wrong, but she needed him. His strength enveloped her, promising her a haven of warmth and security from the frightening world that threatened to engulf her.

"Blade, I—"

"Shhh, don't talk," he commanded. His finely molded lips came down to meet hers.

Through the stillness that surrounded them, Wesley Fletcher's Georgia accent sliced with biting clarity. "Is everythin' all right, Miz Gordon?"

The embracing couple stopped, their mouths frozen a fraction of an inch apart. They turned their heads in one simultaneous motion. Fletcher stood in the open entrance, illuminated by the yellow glow of the lantern light.

In her shock Theodora would have leaped back from Blade, but he held her tightly to his chest.

"What the hell are you doing here, Fletcher?" The captain's deep baritone was an ominous growl.

Fletcher looked from one to the other, a tawny eyebrow lifted in judgment. "I was merely checkin' t' see if there was anythin' the *lady* needed." Then his gaze took in the snake pinned to the sagging wall of the tent. "Good God!" He walked over to the reptile and whistled in amazement. "It must be six feet long!"

Blade at last allowed Theodora to move away from him. "We haven't had a chance to measure it yet, Lieutenant." His clipped words conveyed an unspoken warning. Going over, he pushed Fletcher aside, lifted the snake with one hand, and withdrew his knife. The muffled shake of the rattles was like the sound of drums in a funeral dirge.

The captain carried the snake to the opened tent flap an
hurled it across the grass. "Lieutenant Haintzelman!" F
shouted. "On the double!" He turned back to Fletcher. "Now
if you'll excuse us, Lieutenant, I'm sure you have pressin
duties to attend to while I escort Miss Gordon back to the safet
of the fort for the night."

The next morning Zeke charged into Blade's tent. Outraged
he waved a burlap bag he held clutched in one hand.

"Lookee hyar, Blade," he said in disgust, and threw th
sack on the dusty floor. "I found this down by the river, shove
under some rocks. Only the lily-livered varmint who done
didn't quite git it covered up. Must've been in a pow'rful hurr
to have left it only partly hidden."

Blade reached down and grabbed the bag, his curiosity high
for Zeke seldom raised his voice. He opened one end, whic
had been tied together with a leather thong woven through slit
in the burlap, and immediately understood Zeke's outrage. Th
sack had been used to transport a very large snake. Part of it
rattles had broken off and remained caught in the folds of th
coarse material.

A fire raged through Blade. "The son of a bitch," he snarle
savagely. "When I catch that bastard, he's going to beg m
to kill him." He wadded the sack in his fist and shook it a
Zeke. "Was there any sign of who left this?"

"Yep, and this time the polecat warn't so smart." The eagl
feather in Zeke's hat bobbed as he shook his head. "Thar wa
a heel mark in the dirt. It were a soldier's boot that made it."

Blade tossed the bag on his bedroll and headed for the tent'
entrance. "Let's go take a look," he said, his rage threatening
to demolish his usual composure.

Zeke grabbed his sleeve. "Whoa now, Blade. 'Tain't no
use in announcin' this to the whole world. Whoever done it is
sartain to be watchin' us. Let's jest mosey down to the riverbank, nice and easy. No sense in givin' the ornery rat a
chance to skeedaddle."

But their caution was in vain. Whoever had left the sack
had tried to retrieve it and, finding it gone, had removed all
trace of boot marks around the rock. This time they found the
soft imprint of a moccasin instead. Blade and Conyers carefully

questioned each mountain man and dragoon, but no one recalled seeing anyone near that part of the riverbank.

The long, upward incline of the high plains became apparent
beginning the seventh week of the journey. The sojourners,
refreshed from their two-day stay at the fort, traveled northwest
along the divide between the Laramie and North Platte rivers.
Groves of cottonwood dotted the open prairie, and pine trees
grew on the higher slopes of the streams that fed into the Platte.

The news of Miss Gordon's near brush with death had swept
the camp the night it occurred, and Lucien Fontenelle had
insisted that she sleep in a room in the fortress. Shaken, Theodora had gratefully accepted his hospitality.

She remembered with nostalgia the small cell in Fort Laramie's northeast bastion, with its heavy wooden door and its
tiny bed, no more than a crude platform nailed to the wall.
Through a window slit she'd seen the light cannon that stood
guard beyond it, and for the first time since leaving Fort Leavenworth, she'd felt truly safe.

"Why not wait here at Laramie, Miz Gordon?" Lieutenant
Fletcher had asked the next morning. "Y' can go on back t'
Leavenworth with the supply wagons that'll be comin' from
Green River after the rendezvous. Y' wouldn't have t' stay
more'n a few weeks at most, and then you'd be headin' for
home. Fontenelle would be delighted t' take care of y' till the
fur traders come through."

The regard on Fletcher's attractive features touched her. It
was clear he had only her best interest at heart, for he'd made
no secret of his enjoyment of her company. She touched his
blue sleeve in an effort to convey her gratitude. "As much as
I'd like to remain in this friendly haven, Lieutenant," she told
him with regret, "I have to continue the journey west. Staying
at the fort will never get Tom's name on the maps and journals
that will be published once we return to the East."

"I think you're makin' a grave mistake, Miz Gordon. After
all that's happened, I'd feel much better knowin' y' were safely
on the way back t' your father." Fletcher lifted her fingers
from his arm and squeezed them gently. "Think how he'd feel
if he lost not only Tom, but you as well. I doubt any parent
could survive such a double tragedy. Let Roberts worry about

the topographical work. That's not your responsibility.''

Theodora was troubled by the thought of causing her father more grief, but in the end she knew she had to fulfill the obligation she'd taken upon herself, regardless of the pain involved. And though he'd been clearly disappointed in her decision, Fletcher had accepted it with his unfailing courtesy. Never once had he mentioned the compromising position he'd found her in the night of the rattler's attack—no doubt believing that she'd fallen into Blade's arms in sheer terror. She was thankful for the lieutenant's tactfulness and reassured herself that he was at least partly correct. It'd been fear that had propelled her into the captain's arms. But an entirely different emotion, one she refused to examine too closely, had kept her there.

Baptiste Lejeunesse rode beside her now. The burly French Canadian had been her shadow for the last five days. Directly behind her was Lieutenant Haintzelman; up ahead, she could see Fletcher in his impeccable uniform. Captain Roberts rode in his usual place at the head of the column, ramrod straight in his fringed buckskins and dusty cavalry boots.

Yes, she admitted to herself, Fletcher's assumption had been correct: she'd fallen into Blade's arms in fright. But both she and the handsome captain knew that was only the beginning of what had happened between them. Blade had never mentioned her willingness to surrender to him that night. Since the incident, he'd been as discreet as the gentleman he was supposed to be. Perhaps he'd belatedly remembered his promise to Colonel Kearny to protect her virtue. Or perhaps he regretted his attempt to seduce her once he realized what an easy conquest she'd be.

Theodora clenched her teeth. Shame on you, an engaged woman, for kissing another man, she scolded herself. For *wanting* another man.

She bit her bottom lip as the image of Martin Van Vliet rose before her. She hadn't thought of her fiancé since before Tom's death. When she'd accepted Martin's proposal, she'd been certain that she loved him, that he would be the perfect helpmate and companion. But she had never felt with Martin the deep, all-encompassing need that Blade aroused within her.

She was aware of his every movement, even though she

forced herself to keep her gaze averted. She was afraid he would read in her eyes her deep longing, the driving need to beg him to take her into his arms once again and finish what had been left so frustratingly incomplete that night at Fort Laramie.

They rode in a fine, misty rain that had plagued them since leaving the fort. The mornings had been unseasonably cool and foggy for July. Conyers had assured them that this weather wouldn't last, for the trail would soon lead them into a rocky desert. In the distance an approaching dark spot from the north signaled the arrival of buffalo at the river.

When the travelers encamped that afternoon, they were soon surrounded by an immense herd. Since the bivouac was downwind, the animals left only the immediate land around the campsite empty in their push to reach the water. Some of the shaggy beasts stood in the sluggish current up to their knees. Others slowly moved across to the southern bank. Theodora decided to get a closer look at the *Bison bison*, for Conyers had informed her that it would probably be the last great herd they'd encounter.

"I'm going to do some sketching," she told Peter, who was about to carry her packs into her tent. "I'll be on that rise over there."

Haintzelman peered through his spectacles in the direction of her pointing finger. A raised hillock not far from the campground provided an excellent view of the bison. "Okay. Just be careful, Teddy. The captain doesn't want you out of eyesight."

"*Oui*, Mademoiselle Gordon," Baptiste agreed. He'd been checking the anchor pins of her tent and looked up when she spoke. "I'll go along with you. I would like to see you put those great hairy beasts down on paper."

Gathering her sketch pad and pencils, Theodora smiled a welcome to Lejeunesse. She knew the captain had ordered the voyageur to keep a close watch on her, and she appreciated the good-hearted way he'd given up his position in the advance party and taken on the responsibility for her welfare. Immediately after the horrible fright she'd been given by the rattlesnake, she'd needed to know someone was within call. "Come on," she invited him. "I'd enjoy the company."

Side by side, they trudged up a grassy rise that separated the camp from the grazing buffalo and sat down on the hillside.

Lejeunesse sprawled on his back in the thick prairie clover with a relaxed grunt and pillowed his head on his cupped hands. He placed one heel on a bent knee. With a bright purple flower tucked behind his ear, he grinned in satisfaction at Theodora. "*Ah, mon Dieu, ma fille*. We have to work so very hard, *n'est-ce pas?*"

She shook her head in mock reproach at his loafing and inhaled the sweet perfume of the *Petalostemum purpureum*. "You really don't have to follow me everywhere I go, Baptiste. I'm no longer frightened of everything that moves in the grass."

"The *bourgeois* says to watch you, chérie. Who am I to dispute such a wise *capitaine?*"

Theodora laughed at his teasing and looked around for the right scene to sketch.

To the north of them the bison milled quietly, some lying down chewing their cud, some grazing on the open plain. The calves, in the center of the herd, were a light sandy color, the yearlings darker. Spike bulls, the four-year-olds whose horns had smooth, clean points, wandered in and out of the clumps of cows. Many approached near nudity, for their thick wooly hair had been shedding in the heat of mid-summer. The shaggy, uneven patches of hair, ranging from blond to dark brown to black, made the bulls look even more ferocious. Conyers had told her that a ten-year-old bull could weigh just short of a ton and stand six feet high at the shoulder. From muzzle to rump he would be ten feet long. The sheer bulk of the huge animal was awe-inspiring.

At the edge of the herd a large bull and a small calf were nibbling the grass side by side, and Theodora eased slowly closer, moving bit by bit, until she reached a large boulder. Then she perched on it and started to draw.

The morning's drizzle had cleared while they were setting up camp in the late afternoon, and now white, puffy clouds scuttered across the deep blue sky. The pastoral setting, with its rolling green plain stretched out beneath her, dotted by the dark brown and black of the placid buffalo, was idyllic for sketching, and Theodora worked on her renderings of the peaceful scene in deep concentration. For the first time in many, many days she felt a small measure of contentment.

"Where's Miss Gordon?" Blade demanded of his aide-de-camp, who was vigorously currying his horse.

Peter looked over the mare's back. He grinned and jerked his head, apparently amused at the worry his commanding officer's voice betrayed. "Right over there with Lejeunesse, Captain. She's drawing the buffalo. Though why anyone would want a picture of those ugly beasts is beyond me."

Blade looked where Haintzelman indicated and spotted the sparkle of her golden hair in the sunshine. Not far from her lounged Lejeunesse. Standing beside War Shield, Blade absently slid his reins through his hands as he took in the scene of the lovely woman bent over her sketch pad in total absorption. A scowl creasing his forehead, he pulled on the lines and, leading his stallion behind him, headed for the rise.

The uneasiness that had plagued Blade since Fort Laramie remained with him as he walked toward Theodora. He'd issued orders that she was never to be out of Baptiste Lejeunesse's sight, even though it had meant removing the French Canadian from the advance hunting party, and thereby announcing to the would-be killer that someone—possibly a soldier—was under suspicion. Not even Lejeunesse knew why he'd been instructed to watch over her, but he'd accepted his new responsibility with bawdy enthusiasm. He'd even slept outside her room at the fort, his enormous bulk sprawled on the splintery wooden floor like some great hibernating bear.

Approaching the rise, Blade could see him close by Theodora now, his long curly black beard spread across his chest, his white teeth gleaming in a self-satisfied grin that was visible even from this distance.

Suddenly there was a sharp crack. From the corner of his eye Blade saw a gray blanket flap on the far side of the herd.

As the sound shattered the still afternoon, the buffalo rose in one giant wave. A calf bawled in fright. A huge bull pawed the ground and snorted.

Blade leaped on War Shield as Lejeunesse rose to his feet, his long rifle in his hand.

In a mindless mass, the buffalo milled outward in a large,

spiraling circle. Then one old bull pulled in front and headed directly toward the couple on the hill. Behind him, at a dead run, followed the herd.

In her concentration Theodora barely heard the noise that disturbed the buffalo, but in an instant Lejeunesse was running to her.

"Mademoiselle," he called. "Come quickly with me." He grabbed her arm and pulled her beside him. They flew across the grass, heading for camp. But they were no match for the bellowing, frightened herd. "Wait here," he shouted as he pulled her to an abrupt halt. "I'm going to try to turn them."

Theodora stood frozen in terror as Baptiste raced back toward the approaching buffalo. Then he knelt on one knee and fired at the lead bull. It staggered, righted itself, and continued to come straight at him. Baptiste was reloading when the herd overtook him. Theodora strained to keep his dark head in view, but the blur of horns quickly blocked out all sight of him as the hurtling mass of buffalo crushed him beneath its hooves.

The sound of approaching death was the roar of bedlam. The buffalo were so close she could hear over the thundering hooves the hollow clatter of their horns as they bumped against each other in their crazed flight.

There was no chance to outrun them. She didn't even try. Death wouldn't be easy, but it would be quick.

Then some instinct made her turn, look over her shoulder, and understand Blade's unspoken command. In an instant she readied herself. As he rode by, she grabbed his outstretched hand, put her foot on his boot, and using the power of his arm, vaulted up behind him. Suddenly, the buffalo were all around them, carrying War Shield forward by the sheer force of their momentum. Theodora clung to Blade's waist and locked her hands in his belt, her face pressed against his back. Clods of dirt sprayed around them. Mile after mile they rode at terrifying speed in the vanguard of the closely packed animals. The great stallion strained ahead as he strove to outrun them, his eyes wide and bulging from the exertion, his coat lathered and slippery. He stumbled once but caught his balance.

Theodora closed her eyes. The thought of being trampled under those deadly hooves made her clutch Blade so tightly she could feel his ribs beneath her forearms. Her heart pounded in rhythm with the galloping horse.

The ride was endless. Over hillocks, through gullies, down steep ravines, into wooded coulees—as by instinct the buffalo made for terrain too rough for a horse to cross. Theodora knew she would never forget the ghastly sound of their clattering horns.

If she survived.

She realized that War Shield was coming to the end of his endurance. He was snorting for breath and bathed in foam. The mighty horse raced with all his heart, but even he could not possibly match the stamina of the buffalo.

Then, as suddenly as the stampede began, it slowed. Clusters of buffalo began to spread apart and a clearing around the great stallion opened up. Using this small space to his advantage, Blade wheeled his tired mount down an empty gully. As the horse came to a halt, Blade threw his leg over War Shield's neck and slid to the ground. Reaching up, he lifted Theodora from the horse's back.

"Thank God—" she began, only to feel his hand clamped firmly over her lips.

Without a sound he pushed her flat on her back in the grass and followed her down. He yanked on War Shield's reins as they fell. The stalwart horse folded his legs and rolled to his side next to them. His deep chest heaved with exhaustion.

Blade lay across Theodora and shielded her with his body. Trapped by his bulk, her hands pinned between their chests, she twisted and turned in an effort to free her mouth.

"Be quiet," he warned softly in her ear. "Don't make a sound."

Chapter 14

Confused and frustrated, Theodora lay on her back and looked up at Blade, but he wasn't paying any attention to her. He was listening to something on the plain above them. Over the noise of the buffalo came a blood-chilling cry. A second howl pierced the din, and she understood at last what was happening.

At the ghastly sound of the hunting cries, she grew as still as a trapped jackrabbit beneath Blade's muscular body. He seemed to sense her sudden acquiescence and withdrew his hand from her lips without even glancing down at her. When he braced himself on his elbows and moved aside a fraction, the pressure on her ribs eased. She pulled her hands out from under his hard chest, rested them on his shoulders, sucked in air, and prayed she wouldn't start to choke on the dust.

"Gros Ventres."

The whispered words filled her with terror. Frantic, she stared up at him. Images of the trooper's mutilated body as Fletcher had described it sprang to mind; she gagged in panic and clutched at the long fringes on Blade's shirt. His gaze flew to hers. His calm eyes conveyed a silent message of reassurance. He took her hand and lifted it to his lips, then without a word released it and pulled away to load the rifle he'd jerked from its scabbard. They lay on the ravine's incline side by side, her buckskin skirt caught under his hips, and listened to the herd gallop around them. At last it was quiet.

Blade eased his head above the embankment, then slid back down.

"Are they gone?" she asked in a broken whisper.

"For now. But they'll be back to butcher their kill." He stood and War Shield rose with him. Reaching down, he pulled her to her feet. He ran his hands over her quickly, checking for injuries. "Can you keep going?" he asked. "We can't stay here."

She nodded. "Yes, I feel fine."

"Then let's get the hell out of here."

Trailed by his gray stallion, Blade crouched down and led Theodora by the hand. They cautiously worked their way along the ravine in the opposite direction of the scattered buffalo carcasses. The light was fading as they crept from the ditch. He lifted her up on War Shield and then mounted behind her. "We'll ride for a while," he told her, as he encircled her with his arms. "But slowly and quietly."

They rode the big horse at a walk until it was almost dark, the only sound the clip-clop of its hooves on the hard-packed ground. In terror, Theodora strained to hear any noise that would indicate they were being followed.

Then from behind them in the distance the wail of a solitary war whoop pierced the twilight's calm.

She stiffened and clutched Blade's wrist. "What's that?" she cried.

He answered softly, his head so close that the hoop in his ear touched her cheek. The nonchalance in his calm voice slowed the panic building in her chest. "They've found our sign. But they won't be able to follow it till daylight."

Blade rode into a wooded coulee with a tiny stream running its length. Bright yellow goldenrod spread along both banks, still visible though masses of nimbus clouds overhead promised a moonless night.

"We can rest here. I want to take a look at your legs before the light's completely gone."

Their entry into the haven of cottonwoods disturbed a flock of grouse, who'd come for their evening drink. The agitated birds fluttered at their approach, reluctant to leave the water.

Blade dismounted and reached up for her. His hands spanned her waist as he lifted her down and set her on her feet. Before she could say a word, he raised one side of her leather skirt with both hands, and at her sudden shocked intake of breath, his determined gaze locked with hers for a fleeting second before moving with deliberation down the pantaloon on her thigh to her calf encased in her riding boot.

"You can't—" Theodora stopped short as she looked down at herself in bewilderment. A neat slice had been cut through her right boot at mid-calf by a buffalo horn. She hadn't even felt it happen. At Blade's direction she sat down on a large, flat rock.

He squatted on his haunches in front of her. Worry etched a deep crease between his dark eyebrows, and his firm mouth was taut with apprehension. He eased the boot off with cautious fingers and rolled down the gray woolen sock.

"Doesn't look too bad," he said with open relief after he'd examined the wound. "Just a graze. The leather of your boot plus the thickness of your sock saved you from a deeper cut. Now let me see your other leg."

Astonished, Theodora looked at her left boot. It was criss-crossed with similar cuts. Miraculously, when Blade removed it and stripped away her sock, they found she had only three superficial lacerations.

He grinned up at her, his eyes alight with teasing admiration. "Your boots are a loss, but it's a small price to pay to protect those gorgeous legs. I'd gladly meet the cost of another pair for a second peek."

In spite of herself, Theodora smiled at his rakish attempt to comfort her. "I didn't feel a thing when it happened," she replied, suddenly aware of his callused fingers on her skin. Her bare leg rested in his cupped palm, and she removed it in an effort to restore order to her suddenly confused thoughts. "All I could think about was hanging on for dear life," she added in a blatant attempt to redirect the conversation.

Blade placed his hands on his knees, a provocative smile on his deeply tanned face. "Well, you did *that* like a trooper." He stood, eased down beside her on the boulder, and ran his fingers lightly across his outer right thigh. Blood soaked his buckskin trousers. He lifted the soft leather away from the wound with the point of his knife in an attempt to survey the extent of the injury. The cut was above his riding boot and much deeper than Theodora's.

"You're badly hurt," she exclaimed. She jumped up and tried to examine his leg.

He brushed her hand aside. "It's nothing. Just a small gash. We're both lucky to come out of that stampede without being sliced to ribbons. I have a flask of whiskey in my saddlebag. I'll get it and pour a little on these cuts."

As he started to rise, Theodora tried to push him back down with both hands on his broad shoulders. He quirked an eyebrow, shrugged, and remained seated.

"You stay there. I'll get it," she told him. She padded across the grass on bare feet and removed the flask from his bag. She returned and knelt beside him. The slash on his thigh was deep and jagged, and she cringed at the thought of the alcohol burning into the open flesh. Her words were softened with commiseration for the added pain she was about to inflict. "I'll pour it directly over the wound if you think you can hold still."

His voice was tinged with amusement. "I wouldn't dream of moving a muscle with such a beautiful nursemaid beside me."

She stared with surprise into jet eyes sparkling with laughter. How could he flirt at a time like this? They had just narrowly escaped death, and he was as cocky as a cavalry officer dallying with a Southern belle.

Deftly, Blade cut away the buckskin pant leg below the wound. Then he pulled a cheroot from his shirt and lit it. He exhaled the smoke with a long sigh of appreciation, and the spicy aroma swirled about her head. "I'm ready," he quipped with insouciance. "Do your darndest."

True to his word, Blade didn't move while she poured the alcohol over the deep cut. He seemed oblivious to the pain, for he watched her face rather than her trembling hands as she ministered to his wound. She kept her eyes lowered and hoped he wasn't recalling, as she was, the time he'd found her lost on the prairie.

For days after Tom's death, she'd forgotten completely that the audacious captain had unbuttoned her dress and caressed her in such an intimate way. It was as though the memory of that terrible day had been blocked out in self-preservation, for it had been that same day that Tom had fallen deathly ill. But with Blade's close proximity and the marvelous scent of his

tobacco smoke to taunt her, the events of her rescue and sub-
sequent apology were now as clearly in her mind as if it had
been only yesterday. A blush warmed her cheeks. Rising, she
stood back and surveyed his sinewy thigh. "Should we tie a
tourniquet on your leg?" she questioned, and forced herself
to meet his probing gaze.

"No, the bleeding's stopped."

"At least let me put a bandage on it."

In the stampede one sleeve of her cotton blouse had torn
away at the seam. It drooped over her bare shoulder, hanging
by a few threads. She ripped it loose and slid it down over her
wrist. After tearing it into strips, she wound the cotton material
around his injured thigh and tied it securely.

Blade jabbed the cigar into his mouth, stood, and took the
bottle from her tight grasp. "Let's get your cuts taken care of
and get out of here." But while he was dabbing the whiskey
on Theodora's calves, another war howl pierced the stillness.

"Get down," Blade ordered. Without ceremony, he shoved
her onto her stomach under him. He grabbed the rifle propped
on the rock at his side. The barrel touched her cheek and she
tried to jerk her head away from the hard, cold metal.

He paid no attention to her, concentrating instead on the
sounds around them. "Dammit," he said in a low voice. "I
didn't think they'd track us so far before dark. We're going
to have to sit this one out real quiet. With the cloud cover they
shouldn't find us tonight, at any rate."

The hours stretched on in silence. The fugitives spoke in
whispers and only when necessary. They drank quietly from
the stream, flattening themselves along its shallow bank like
forest animals. Blade eased off War Shield's saddle and blanket
and made a bed for Theodora. He helped her pull her socks
and ruined boots back on. Instead of replacing his own slashed
boots, he stowed them with his gear and drew on a pair of
moccasins. Then he cut off his other pant leg to match the
first.

They couldn't chance a fire, but chewed on jerky from his
saddlebag. The night was cool for July, and when a misty rain
fell, Blade took his long cape and pulled it over their shoulders.
They sat on his bedroll, huddled together for warmth.

Wisps of fog drifted around them, thicker and thicker, until it seemed they were the only ones alive on the earth, so isolated were they in the silence. At last in the early morning hours, Theodora fell asleep, her head resting on his good leg.

She awoke to the soft call of her name. At the recollection of where she was, she jerked upright. Blade had slipped her head onto his bedroll and covered her with his cape. He stood beside War Shield now, fastening the saddle girth. It was sunrise, but though daylight had come, they were still surrounded by unpenetrable fog.

"Did you sleep?" she asked him softly, abashed at the possibility that they might have been lying side by side like husband and wife.

He glanced at her. "No, I thought one of us had better stay awake in case we had company." Though his words were unemotional, he seemed to read her thoughts, and his eyes twinkled.

Through the mist came the monotonous, plaintive call of a bird. Theodora cocked her head and placed a finger to her lips. "Listen," she whispered. "A *Fringilla querula*."

Blade met her delighted look with a scowl. "Sounds like it, doesn't it?"

His tone was so noncommittal she wondered at his inability to identify such a distinctive wail as the mourning sparrow's. A second one answered its call, and Blade stared in its direction, as if trying to pierce the white shroud that enveloped them.

He came to stand beside her, then bent and spoke softly in her ear. "Theodora, I'm going to reconnoiter our position. While I'm gone I want you to remain absolutely still and silent. Do you understand? No matter what happens, no matter what you hear, don't move and don't make a sound."

"No sir!" she hissed. "You can't leave me here alone!" She grabbed his arm with panic-stricken tenacity. "I'm coming with you."

Blade pried her hands off and held her in front of him. "You'll stay here and you'll follow orders," he responded tersely. "If we're surrounded, as I think we are, your ability to keep quiet may save our lives."

Recognizing the absolute finality in his voice, Theodora nodded. Her heart dropped to the pit of her stomach, but a cold, detached calm enveloped her. The first thing she'd learned about the captain was that he expected his orders to be obeyed without question. The second was that his orders were usually right.

He tied War Shield to a nearby bush, rechecked his loaded carbine, and disappeared into the fog.

For long moments after he'd left, she stood by the stream, alone and paralyzed with fear. With Blade gone, she felt abandoned. Belatedly, she realized he hadn't even left her his knife. The mournful wails of the sparrows continued, interspersed with the melodic notes of bobolinks and the caws of ravens. The birds seemed to be talking to one another, coming ever closer; just as suddenly, they began moving away.

She stared into the mist, unable to see anything. Then out of the fog stepped an Indian warrior. For a brief second their gazes met. The cold-blooded ferocity in the savage's eyes pinned her to the spot. She started to scream, but remembered Blade's orders. Clasping her hand to her throat, she sank to the grassy bank on buckling knees.

The Gros Ventre was naked except for breechclout and moccasins. He held a tomahawk in one hand and a war shield in the other. With the cunning of a wild predator, he crouched and searched the mist for her protector. When he realized she was alone, he smiled and looked from her to the great stallion tied nearby, as though unable to judge which was the finer prize. At the sight of the intruder, War Shield snorted and danced about; he jerked his head up and down against the tether and whinnied a warning.

Just take the horse and go, Theodora begged in silence.

The brave stepped toward her. She could see his decorated shield of buffalo hide clearly. Its upper part was blackened to represent a storm cloud pierced by lightning; the lower half carried the head and claws of a mythical bird. Summoning all her courage, she raised her face to meet his eyes. His look of ecstatic triumph kindled a rage inside her, and with it, resolution. She wasn't going to meet death on her knees. She pushed herself up with her hands and raced for War Shield.

The Gros Ventre reached her as she touched the stallion's bridle and yanked her back by the hair. His buffalo shield fell discarded at their feet. He held her imprisoned in front of him with one hand encasing her skull in a viselike grip. The feathered tomahawk in his other fist danced about, only inches from her face, then joined the shield on the ground.

No matter what he did, she wouldn't cry out, she promised herself. If there were more Indians around, she wouldn't give Blade away to them.

The brave's waist-length hair was as dark and sleek as the otter fur that bound his side braids. Black paint was smeared on his face and chest. Incredibly, he grinned at her. He loosened his tight hold on her head and wound a lock of her hair around his hand, staring at it in curiosity. With a grunt of victory, he reached down to grab her thigh. At the feel of his questing hand beneath her skirt, Theodora shoved and twisted in a futile attempt to break free. Her breath came in short gasps, but she didn't scream. With a flip of his hand, the Gros Ventre sent her sprawling backward across the grass and followed her down. He pinned her to the ground with one hand entwined in her long hair and thrust a knee between her thighs. Using a knife now held in his free hand, he split the side of her riding skirt.

Don't make a sound! Don't make a sound! Theodora chanted to herself over and over. The only noise in the mist-shrouded clearing was the ripping of the buckskin and her rasping struggle for breath. She fought back with all her strength, pushing and clawing at his chest and arms. The painful hold on her hair and the weight of his hips on hers held her fast. As panic overcame her, she knew she was going to scream despite all her brave intentions. When the savage tore open the leg of her pantaloon with his knife, she opened her mouth to cry for help.

There was a short, strangled grunt. The Indian was lifted off her before the scream left her throat. Without a sound his knife was pried from his fingers and hurled across the clearing. In frenzy, he tore with both hands at the muscular arm pressed against his windpipe, which relentlessly squeezed the life's breath from him. He kicked his feet in an attempt to trip his captor, but was blocked with ease as his attacker pivoted with him. The brave's face turned purple and hideous in his death struggle. His eyes bulged in incredulous denial, and a gurgle bubbled up from his crushed throat. His body writhed and twisted, then dangled inert from that powerful stranglehold, the toes of his moccasins barely scraping the ground.

Blade tossed the body aside. Lifting Theodora, he held her with outstretched arms. In her shock she tried to pull her severed skirt together over the exposed flesh of her leg. Her blouse had lost its buttons and gaped open to reveal her lacy camisole.

"Did he hurt you?" His voice was filled with an awful dread. With lightning speed, he looked her over, checking her torso, arms, and legs before enfolding her in his strong embrace.

She wrapped her arms around his neck and clung to him. "No . . . n-no . . ." she stammered, the words catching in her throat. "He . . . he . . ."

"Theodora, did he hurt you?" He pulled her hands down and held her in front of him. His eyes searched hers, the tender concern in his gaze undeniable.

She shook her head as two tears slid down her cheeks. She stared at him in bewilderment. One moment he was an inhuman engine of death, capable of killing a man with his bare hands without hesitation. The next, he was as compassionate and gentle as her own father. She pushed aside this irreconcilable paradox. Because of him, she was still alive.

Once convinced she was unharmed, he picked up his carbine from the ground, put his arm around her waist, and turned toward his stallion. "We're leaving now."

Leading her to War Shield, he tossed her up and mounted behind her. He wheeled the stallion past the grotesquely sprawled corpse and headed out of the coulee.

They raced for miles across the plains, away from the rising sun as it gradually burned through the dense fog. Finally, Blade pulled his horse to a halt and dismounted. He lifted her down. "We'll walk for a while and give War Shield a rest."

"Will they follow us?" Theodora asked, astonished at the pace he'd set. She looked back over her shoulder, half expecting to see a war party hurtling out of the waning mist.

"No. I led them the other way. Those weren't birdcalls you heard back there. The Gros Ventres never expected a Longknife to know their tricks and turn the tables on them, so they were easily fooled." Blade's words were clipped and harsh as he continued. "All except that clever buck who found you. But he paid dearly for his cunning. He'll never walk his ancestors' hunting grounds."

She glanced up at Blade. He'd lost his hat, and his black hair, which had grown well past his collar, was as thick and straight as the dead Indian's. It reminded her that he and the Gros Ventre had forefathers who were much the same. "You mean in the Indian's afterlife?" she questioned in confusion. "Why not?"

His answer came in a low, terrible voice. "Because I strangled him. That's the one thing a warrior fears most, for his spirit is unable to leave his body at the moment of death. It remains forever trapped inside his corpse, never to find the promised hunting grounds."

"You don't really believe that, Blade?" She skipped along beside him in an attempt to keep up with his long strides.

"That buck believed it, and it was the last thought he had before he died."

Theodora was silent for a moment while she pondered the meaning of his words. "If he hadn't attacked me," she asked hesitantly, "would you have choked him to death?"

"No. I'd probably have slit his throat." Blade shrugged. "For a warrior it's an honorable way to die." He stopped and looked down at her; she could read the unspoken words in his eyes. *Any man who harms you will suffer the worst possible death I can give him.*

They walked side by side in silence until Theodora looked up at him. "It would have been a lot safer just to shoot him."

Blade scowled and looked across the open country. "When you're caught by yourself on the plains, you always save your last shot."

The sun's glare soon replaced the cool fog, and the temperature rose steadily until Theodora was certain it was well over a hundred. She'd tied the ends of her torn blouse together in an effort to keep herself covered and protect the fair skin on her neck and chest from sunburn. There was nothing she could do for her bare arms, for her other sleeve had been torn off as well. Her skirt hung in tatters. Her wide-brimmed hat had been lost in the first mad rush of the buffalo, and the afternoon heat plastered her hair to her head. Despite her efforts, she knew she'd be blistered and burned the next day.

Although he was without a compass, Blade seemed to have no difficulty determining their direction. With the sun as his guide, he rode without pausing across the dry land of cactus, greasewood, and sagebrush, and Theodora gradually realized that he was heading west.

"Shouldn't we turn north soon?" she questioned at last from her place in front of him on War Shield. She believed the stampede had driven them southward, and the members of the expedition had to be miles due north.

Blade looked down at her cradled in his arms. His sensual mouth twitched with amusement that she would question his ability to travel on the unmarked plains.

"With that herd of buffalo as large as it was, there'll be more Gros Ventres to the north of us. If we went that way we'd run right into them. Anyway, Conyers will be leading the men westward as quickly as possible."

At the thought of the others leaving them behind, she sat up straight. "Won't they wait for us?" she cried, unable to keep the fear from her voice. "Peter told me never to move if I became lost. To wait until a search party found me. If we keep going like this, they'll never find us."

Blade chuckled and bent closer. She felt the tickle of his mustache on her ear as he spoke. "That's good advice if you're lost, Theodora. But I know exactly where we are. And Zeke knows I can easily find my way back."

Certain that a search party would be looking for them, she clutched his sleeve. "They can't be sure you're alive, Blade. For all they know, I could be out here by myself, just wandering around."

The amused look on his face disappeared. He hesitated, then spoke slowly, as though choosing each word. "They won't think that, Theodora. Zeke will know that if I'm not alive, neither are you."

"How can you be so certain?"

"I just am." His abrupt tone invited no further questions.

The silent duo entered the barren country Conyers had predicted two days before. They rode through a wind-burned, sun-scorched land of ash-colored soil and stratified rocks. To the south lay the Medicine Bow Range. Across the sandy ground clumps of tough, wiry sagebrush grew everywhere, making the air smell like a mixture of camphor and turpentine.

By late afternoon Blade had found an isolated grove of

willows and cottonwoods beside a creek. The melted snow was icy cold. Clumps of bunch grass, though sparse, provided forage for War Shield.

A small flock of wild turkeys ran away as they drew near, and the explosion of Blade's carbine sent them into a panic, some trying to alight in the branches of the nearest trees, others attempting to hide in the breaks. That afternoon Blade roasted a plump hen over a fire. Nothing had ever tasted so good to Theodora, despite its flavor of sage.

They said little while they prepared camp. After supper Theodora sat watching the fire, and Blade walked the camp's perimeter. With a feeling of bafflement she recalled his sudden change of mood that afternoon, when he'd curtly cut off her questions. How would the men know she wasn't out here alive and alone? Without the captain, everyone knew she'd be totally helpless, at the mercy of any hostiles that might find her.

In a sudden flash of insight she realized with brutal clarity what Blade had refused to put into words. He would kill her before he allowed her to be left alive and alone without him. And Zeke knew it. Blade hadn't shot the Gros Ventre because in hand-to-hand combat, with no time to reload, he'd saved his last shot for her.

When he returned to the fire, she met his gaze with dread at the unspeakable bond between them. In the next few days he would be her savior or her executioner. Her very existence was tied to his in a way that couldn't be broken. She'd never felt so helpless. It was as though she were no longer a person in her own right, but an unwanted appendage to another human being. No wonder he'd fought so hard to keep her from coming on this journey! She'd been a yoke across his shoulders from the beginning. Had the congressmen back east realized what a liability she'd be? Had they even cared? Or had the possibility of a white woman crossing the country meant more to them than her safety? No one had mentioned the danger to either her or Tom. They were told they'd be escorted by a half-troop of the finest U.S. dragoons. Her scholarly father had been convinced they would be well taken care of, or he'd never have allowed them to go.

Humiliation burned on Theodora's cheeks, and she turned away from the tall man beside the fire.

Blade watched her withdraw into herself and understood her torment. He'd hoped she wouldn't realize their predicament—at least not until they were safely back with the others. He had every intention of rejoining the expedition. But if worse came to worst, and they were overrun, he knew he wouldn't hesitate to kill her before he allowed the Gros Ventres to take her alive.

Chapter 15

With his dark blue cape for a blanket, Theodora lay on the ground beside Captain Blade Roberts and stared up at the stars. Unlike the previous evening, no clouds obscured the sky, nor did rain force them to huddle together for protection. Yet since nightfall she'd remained close enough to reach out and touch him. She knew he was awake now, though he'd been silent since she'd edged closer to him in the dark.

"How's the sunburn?" His tone was as tender as a lover's touch.

"A little uncomfortable. Enough to make it hard to fall asleep."

He chuckled sympathetically. "Sorry there's nothing in my saddlebag for it. That's one problem I've never had to worry about. But you wouldn't have gotten so badly burned if I hadn't used your sleeves for bandages."

"Nonsense." She turned her head, pillowed on his blanket, to look at him. "It was my idea. Besides, your wound is a lot more serious."

Theodora didn't regret the loss of her sleeves. After eating the turkey he'd roasted for them late that afternoon, she'd insisted on checking his wound.

Then she'd turned to her own needs. She felt grimy from the long day under the hot sun. She wanted desperately to go farther downstream to wash, but that privacy was denied her. He vehemently insisted that she stay within eyesight.

"If you want to bathe, I'll turn my head," he'd said with matter-of-fact aplomb, not looking up from the inspection and cleaning of his carbine. "But if I hear anything strange at all, don't count on keeping your modesty. Our first priority is staying alive."

In the end she'd compromised and removed her tattered blouse and ripped skirt. Dressed in camisole and torn pantaloons, she sat on a boulder and splashed cold water on her burned arms, neck, and face. She indulged in the luxury of washing her hair with a bar of soap he'd provided from his saddlebag. She scented the rinse water with wildflowers she'd found on the bank and poured it over herself, delighting in the icy tingle.

Refreshed, she waded out of the stream, but before she could replace her blouse, Blade walked over.

"I want to take a look at that sunburn," he said. He touched her lightly here and there on her neck and shoulders and arms to determine just how badly she was burned. She felt stripped and vulnerable in front of him, until his nonchalant manner gradually allayed her fears. Satisfied, he ran his forefinger lightly down the bridge of her sore nose. "I've never seen such a red little bluenose," he teased. "You sure you're not really part Indian?"

She lifted her eyebrows in mock disdain. "Do I act like one?"

"Sometimes." His ebony eyes sparkled with amusement. "When you lose that fiery temper of yours, I'd swear you were part Comanche."

"Not Cheyenne?"

"My people are much too civilized to threaten to cut off someone's—"

"Do you have a comb, Captain?" she interrupted, and he produced one with a mocking grin. But he'd kept to safer topics after that, and his easy manner had helped her relax and accept their unorthodox situation.

Now as she lay on the bedroll he'd given up for her, she knew she should keep her distance from him, but the close call with the buffalo, Baptiste's death, and the attack by the Gros Ventre, followed by the awful realization that Blade literally held her life in his hands, had left her nervous and fearful. Though the night sounds didn't seem to bother him at all, each tiny noise brought her upright. She was afraid he might fall sleep and miss something, or someone, creeping up on them. His leg bothered him, she knew, for he'd favored it ever so lightly when he'd crouched beside the fire to cook the wild turkey. She also knew he hadn't slept in over twenty-four hours. Still, she couldn't let him go to sleep. Not yet.

"Will you use the constellations to plot our trail tomorrow?" she asked, and ignored her guilty conscience at purposely keeping him awake.

"Mmmm." He sounded relaxed and comfortable.

"Have you found the North Star?"

"Yes, Theodora." His deep baritone was warm with suppressed laughter. "It's right up there, see it?"

"Where?"

"There." He scooted next to her and pointed heavenward so she could sight up his arm. Then he laid back down beside her, their heads almost touching. He pointed again. "And over here's Pegasus."

"Yes, I see him flying through the night," she whispered with delight. "How incredibly beautiful it is. The air's so clear out here, you want to reach up and try to pluck a star right out of the sky."

"They do look close, don't they? Have you found Ursa Major?"

"No, where?"

"Look. Almost directly across." He slid his arm beneath her, careful not to scratch her sunburned neck, and cushioned her head on his shoulder; with the other hand he pointed out the three stars on the Big Bear's tail.

"Yes, I see it." Content and secure, she nestled against him.

He bent his head to look down at her, and she felt his breath on her cheek as he spoke with a note of admiration. "You're so fascinated by the world around you, Theodora. Were you always interested in the natural sciences?"

"Always," she answered. "That's what happens when you belong to a family of botanists. Papa would carry me around in his arms just like any parent, but instead of saying, 'Oh, look at the pretty flower!' he'd say, 'Look, dearest, at the fine *Paeonia officinalis*.' I grew up labeling plants and trees the way other children learn nursery rhymes."

Blade chuckled deep in his chest, and Theodora felt the vibration against her arm and back. It sent a shivery feeling through her, as though she'd eaten something cold and delicious.

"The other children must have thought that strange."

"Oh, *strange* isn't the word," she conceded. "Tom and I were considered downright bizarre. He was always frail and sickly. I was healthy, but skinny as a rail and with my nose always buried in a book. What a pair we must have been!"

"Were you lonely?"

"Never. Our house was always filled with visiting faculty members. And though the children our age had little in common with us, our adult guests were enchanted by what they labeled our 'precociousness.' My father entertained some of Harvard's greatest scholars in our front parlor, and as long as we were as quiet as church mice, Tom and I were allowed to stay and listen."

Wanting to keep her talking, Blade lay as still as a mouse himself. The feel of her soft body against his, the gentle rise and fall of her breasts as she breathed, made him as randy as a buck at mating time. This was not the moment to make a sudden move and scare her off. "What about your mother's family? Were they also so erudite?"

Under his cape Theodora giggled and folded her arms across her waist. "My, my. I'm not the only one who can use two dollar words." She snuggled closer to him, relaxed and comfortable. "No, but my Aunt Prudence came over frequently to see that we received proper guidance in the study of biblical and ecclesiastical subjects, as well as the academics. She was a terror, but I liked her."

"Why?"

"Well, for one thing, we had our blond hair in common. But because she was a minister in the Society of Friends, she always kept hers decently covered and out of sight. I'm sure she felt God had specifically punished her by giving such coloring to a woman who believed it was virtuous to wear only drab grays and browns. She'd look at me, cluck her tongue and say, 'I don't know what I'm going to do with thee, girl. With thy golden curls and green eyes, thee's an affront to the elders when they see thee on the street. Cover thy hair and eep thy eyes down. And try not to look so—so vivid!' "

"And you didn't agree with her?"

"Oh, no!" She laughed out loud at the memory. "Nor did ny Episcopalian father. He always wanted me to wear my hair lown whenever she came. 'If the Almighty hadn't wanted nankind to be so many different colors,' he'd say, 'He vouldn't have created us that way.' " She tilted her head up o look at him. Their lips were inches apart. Her eyes were sparkling. "Don't you agree? Look at the flowers! Wouldn't t be awful if they were all one color?"

"Terrible," he replied. "What would life be like without your gorgeous blond hair?" He kissed her forehead at the hairline. "Or your marvelous green eyes?"

Slowly, Theodora closed them, as if in expectation. With a feather-soft touch, he kissed each lid.

He drew back slightly and looked at her. She raised the lush fans of her lashes and watched him with intensity, as though holding her breath in curious anticipation. With the tip of a finger, he followed the graceful curve of her cheekbone to her sensitive lips, tracing a path as light as a whisper across her sunburned skin. "I don't want to hurt you," he murmured.

"You're not." She closed her eyes for his kiss.

Blade looked at her as she lay waiting for him with such trust. He didn't want mere gratitude for saving her life. And he was determined not to take advantage of the situation. He shouldn't kiss her now, when she was totally dependent on him. He wouldn't.

How could he help himself?

With infinite gentleness, he pressed his lips against hers in a brief kiss that demanded nothing in return. Then kissed her again and yet again as a bee returns to the blossom, drawing in the sweet nectar, each kiss longer and deeper and more demanding. He savored the satin-soft feel of her lips, the scent of wildflowers in her hair, the exquisite pressure of her breasts against him. He followed the finely molded line of her lips with his tongue until they parted hesitantly. When he thrust his tongue into her mouth, the warm softness of her brought an ache so deep inside that he groaned.

He pushed his cape aside, as he pushed the last warnings of his conscience to the back of his mind, and slid his hand from

her waist up her ribs. She was as slim and supple as a willow
shoot. Her fingers were buried in his hair, and she fondled him
with such light strokes he could feel the muscles of his shoulders flex and ripple in yearning anticipation of her touch.

Her torn, buttonless blouse was no hindrance for his searching fingers. He pushed aside the ends to cup the globe of one
rounded breast. Beneath her camisole, it grew firm and full at
his caress. He moved his lips to her jaw, raining light kisses
across her cheek and down her neck, to flick his tongue in the
hollow at the base of her throat.

"Blade," she gasped, and he thrilled at the husky, breathless
sound of his name on her lips. He returned to devour her mouth,
kissing her passionately, demandingly, his hand beneath her
shoulders moving down her back to bring her hips closer to
his aching need. She responded with a light touch of her tongue
on his lips, and he drew it inside to greet it with his own.

He pushed the lacy camisole down and found the fine batiste
of her chemise, the last sheer barrier between his work-
roughened fingers and the silken smoothness of her breast.
Beneath his thumb its crest became hard and firm. He lowered
his head and suckled her through the thin chemise, laving her
till the damp material clung to her rosy peak. He heard her
soft cry of surprised pleasure and moved to explore her other
breast, her nipple a taut, sweet bud against his tongue.

She arched against him, a sigh of unfulfilled need torn from
her throat, and he slid his hand down her hip, her soft leather
skirt bunching as he pushed it aside. "*Nameo, nihoatovaz*,"
he whispered, telling her of his hunger for her.

Theodora felt him touch the waistband of her pantaloons
and hurtled through the dizzying, all-consuming plane of sensual delight to earth and reality. Blade was murmuring to her
in Cheyenne. The strange sounds pierced the passion-induced
mists of her befuddled mind. Although the words were unfamiliar, she sensed his meaning. *What was she doing?* she asked
herself in horror. He was half savage!

The warnings of Wesley Fletcher echoed in her frightened
mind: *The monsters are brought up that way from infancy.
And they never change.* As Blade's hand moved down her
thigh, she clamped her legs together and shoved against his
chest with all her might.

"Blade, no!" she cried, her voice high-pitched and terrified. "Stop it! Stop it!" She pounded against him with her fists, not noticing in her frenzy that he'd ceased the minute she'd spoken.

"Theodora, I've stopped," he said, his words low and calm. He released her and drew back, a scowl on his rugged features. "Why the sudden terror? I wasn't going to force you. I'm not savage."

At his words she jerked her head as though he'd struck her across the face. In spite of herself she knew her thoughts were transparent in her eyes. She bit her lip and lowered her lids. Ashamed of what she'd thought, she looked away.

But he knew.

"I'm sorry," she said lamely. "I . . . I was frightened."

"Of the brutal Indian," he completed for her, his sarcasm as sharp-edged as his bowie knife.

Still she kept her face averted. "No, no. You've been nothing but kind."

"Maybe that's the problem." Grabbing her wrist, he stood and pulled her up beside him. His jet-black eyes blazed with anger. "Maybe I should show you how rough a savage can really be. Then you'll have someone to compare your genteel, blue-blooded fiancé with. If you're going to be frightened, I'll give you something to be frightened of."

Theodora jerked on her arm, trying to break free of his hold. She glared at him with tears of rage and fear. "Go ahead," she cried. "Act like the monster Fletcher always told me you were."

His jaw tightened and a muscle in his cheek twitched. In the moonlight, the rugged planes of his face were set in stone. Without a word, he released her hand. Theodora took a quick step back. She'd never seen anyone so boiling, God-awful mad. If he'd pulled his knife or picked up his rifle, she'd have swooned to the ground in a dead faint, certain he was going to murder her.

Instead, he turned his back on her and walked toward the stream.

She tried to call him back, to apologize for her heedlessness, but she choked on the words.

He didn't even look over his shoulder. His voice was terse.

"Go to sleep, Theodora. We've got a long ride ahead of u
tomorrow."

The next morning they were up before sunrise. At Blade'
curt instructions, Theodora fastened her hair in two long braids
She was clean from splashing in the icy brook the afternoo
before, but her clothes were in tatters. She wrinkled her nos
in distaste at her wardrobe, and then touched that tender ap
pendage with a hesitant finger.

"Ouch," she muttered to herself. She lightly probed he
sunburned arms with a fingertip.

"Come here, Theodora." Blade was standing ankle-deep i
the cold stream. He'd shaved off his mustache. Water drippe
from his black hair and glistened on the muscles of his arm
and chest. His hacked-off breeches were damp against his we
legs, and she suspected he'd gone swimming stark naked whil
she was still sleeping. She envied him his ability to bath
completely when she had to settle for a sponge bath. Mor
than that, she resented his hostile silence during their breakfas
of cold turkey and water.

"What do you want?" she snapped in irritation.

"Theodora, come over here," he repeated in the low voic
of authority.

She read the determination in his eyes. With a show o
bravado she sauntered over to the creek's edge. She hadn'
pulled on her boots yet, for they were in worse shape than he
clothing and kept falling off when she walked. She stood i
stocking feet and hesitated.

"What is it?" she questioned suspiciously.

He stood with his strong hands planted firmly on his lea
hips. "Take off your stockings and get in this water."

Certain he'd lost his mind, she shook her head. "I'll do n
such thing!"

With lightning speed he reached out and pulled her, ankle
deep, into the stream. She gasped as her woolen socks soake
up the snow melt. He bent down, scooped up a handful o
mud, and dropped it on top of her head.

"What are you doing?" she screamed as she thrashed about

He held her effortlessly by one arm. Without a word h
continued his work, dropping mud by the handfuls on her hai

d bare arms. Then he took his muddy fingers and spread the
uck across her face until her cheeks, forehead, chin, and nose
ere covered with it.

"You're crazy!" She squealed as each cold, gooey blob fell
n her. "I just washed my hair yesterday!" With a doubled-
p fist, she took a wild swing with her free arm, hoping to
nock the smug grin off his face, but he held her at arm's
ngth. "Stop it!" she screamed.

Finished, he set her free.

Her arms flew in frenzied circles as she tried to hit him. He
huckled maddeningly and dodged her blows with ease. Seeing
e fruitlessness of her attempt, she changed tactics and reached
own for a handful of mud. She flung it at point-blank range.
struck his broad chest with a thunk.

She'd caught him by surprise. His black eyebrows rose as
e regarded her in astonishment. Then he tossed his head and
rinned in sudden admiration. She followed up with a second
andful, but he jumped aside and whooped in mirth when a
aird only grazed his bicep. "You rat!" she hollered. "You
w-down skunk! How dare you do this to me!" She stooped
o gather more ammunition.

He gave a shout of laughter and grabbed both her arms,
winging her around and holding her against his muddy chest.

"Theodora, calm down," he said, still laughing. "I'm
rying to keep your sunburn from getting any worse."

"What about my hair? Do you think it's going to blister
oo?" she cried in rage as she struggled against him.

"That bright mop of yours would be visible for miles. If
omeone sees us from a distance, I want him to think we're
oth Indians." When she ceased her struggles, he released her
nd she turned to face him.

What he said made sense. Partially mollified, she folded her
rms across her chest and glared at him. She was covered with
mud. It dripped down her braids and slid across her back. She
ould feel it on her upper lip when she spoke. "Well, why
lidn't you just say so in the first place?"

"I wasn't sure you'd go along with the idea. I was afraid
you'd think I was just trying to get even for last night." His
esponse was a calm, measured appeal for peace between them,
out his lips twitched suspiciously.

She frowned and watched the mire on his chest slowly sli across his flat belly to the edge of his trousers. She sniffed indignation. "Well, if I'd scored my last volley, I *might* co sider us even."

Blade flung his arms wide. "Here. Take your best shot. I just stand here and you can have at me." His carefree g was dazzling.

She fought a reluctant smile. She'd never felt more ridic lous. She looked down at the muddy bank, then raised her l to catch the look of anticipation in his raven eyes.

"That's letting you off too easy," she said with a rue laugh. "I'll wait and let you have it someday when you're n expecting it."

Though his eyes still sparkled with mirth, his expressi grew solemn. "And I'm sure some day you'll do just tha Miss Gordon."

Chapter 16

They were traveling in the Black Hills of Laramie, a grueling range of high, stony mountains named for the distant effect of their cover of dark red cedars and pines. Theodora spotted the phoebe and the sharptailed grouse. Blade pointed out the mountain bluebird, written of by Thomas Say in his journals, and she realized with renewed surprise how many interests she and the rugged captain had in common.

Blade was an excellent tracker. Early that morning they came upon a trail of horses, and Theodora, behind Blade on War Shield, urged him to stop and take cover. "If it's the hunting party," she said in his ear, certain they were about to be attacked from all sides, "they could spring upon us without warning."

"It's not the Gros Ventres," he told her. "It's only a small herd of wild mustangs."

"How can you be so sure?"

"Look at their sign." He pointed to a single area of dung. "A wild herd always stops to relieve themselves in one spot. If it was a party of Indians, their horses would be kept in motion, and their droppings would be scattered along the trail. Also watch how the trail passes under the limbs of the trees, too low for a man on horseback."

They climbed ever higher on a plateau of grama grass mixed with mountain sage. But the terrain of gullies, knife-edges, sage, greasewood, and alkali, increasingly steep, was relieved by small, sweet creeks flowing among tall cottonwoods—if only one knew how to find them.

And Blade had the knack of doing just that.

"You know this land so well," Theodora stated in wonder. "How can you possibly know there is water from so far away?"

He smiled at her amazement. "There are many indications of water, Theodora, if you know what to look for. Deep green cottonwood or willow trees growing in depressions, water rushes, tall green grass. There's the fresh tracks of animals all heading for the same location, or the flight of birds and waterfowl moving toward the same point."

They halted for a midday rest; she was already weary from the pace he'd set. A brook ran through the shaded bower, festooned with vines and filled with the sweet melody of bird song.

He lifted her down and began to unsaddle War Shield. "Besides," he added, "I've been in this area many times."

"Is it your people's land?"

"Not here. For hundreds of years no tribe has ever claimed or dominated it. It's a crossroads, a no-man's-land. Vast herds of buffalo bring many tribes to hunt. Snakes and Bannocks from the west, Utes from the southwest, Arapaho, Crows, Pawnees. Sometimes the Blackfoot and Gros Ventres," he added with a grim smile. "Now the Sioux. And of course, my people. All the tribes raid one another indiscriminately, then arrange temporary prairie truces so they can trade—frequently the goods they've just stolen."

Theodora looked around her. It was a good year for traveling west. The snowpack in the high mountains was greater than usual, and the rivers were running high; the little stream in their glade was no exception, and Blade caught several catfish with a hook and string he unearthed from his saddlebag. He set the fish to bake on the coals of a small fire. They had few bones and would make a delicate and delicious meal.

He allowed her to wash her hands before eating, but when she looked longingly at the crystal water bubbling over the smooth stones and then down at her mud-covered arms, he shook his head. "Don't even think it," he warned her.

Humiliated, she avoided his eyes and wondered just how ridiculous she must look. It hadn't been as bad riding behind him, which she'd insisted on doing that morning. Now, sitting across from him in the peaceful glade, she felt like a human mud pie. Covered in dried mud, her blouse gaping open over a smudged, tattered camisole, her skirt ripped almost to her waist and revealing a dirt-spattered and torn pantaloon leg, she delicately held the baked fish wrapped in a leaf and tried to ignore the uncomfortable scent and feel of herself. How he could keep from sniggering was beyond her. From his polite manner he might have been enjoying *dejeuner* with a sophisticated New York socialite. His sense of empathy and fair play helped her retain the few shreds of dignity left to her.

When they were ready to leave, Blade mounted and reached down to help her up. They were close enough for him to inhale the aroma of her unique disguise.

"Phew," he said in a stage whisper. He shook his head and wrinkled his nose.

Mortified, she looked into his eyes and saw the teasing glow alight in their sooty depths. She laughed out loud in spite of herself. "You've no one to blame but yourself," she told him as she wrapped her dirt-caked arms around his waist with vengeful satisfaction. She purposefully rubbed her grimy cheek against his back. "Since it's your idea, it's only fair that you should share some of the glory."

"Valor of this kind should get me another promotion," he declared as he pressed his heels to the stallion's flanks, and they took off at a quick trot. "Not to mention a presidential commendation."

Only a few hours later Theodora saw the outline of a rider on the ridge above them. "Blade," she said in a hushed voice over his broad shoulder, "look over there to our left."

"I see him. He's been following us for more than an hour." His words were quiet and unconcerned.

"Is he Indian or white?" she questioned.

"He's one of my people."

She pressed her forehead against his spine. "Thank God!" Then a thought occurred to her. "Do you know him?"

"I'm not sure. In the glare of the sun I can't make out his features. He's not certain about me either. He knows I'm Indian, but he probably can't figure out what the heck I'm doing out here without any identifying feathers or paint—with a woman—and riding a white man's horse to boot. He'll be moving up for a closer look. When he does, I want you to keep your eyes down and say nothing.''

The brave followed a ridge that ran at an angle to their path. As he came nearer, Blade halted and shouted something to him in Cheyenne. At his words the warrior galloped toward them at a dead run.

Theodora hid her face behind Blade's broad back, thankful his shoulders were so wide. Terrified, she waited for a hail of arrows to rain down upon them. She heard the brave pull his horse to a stop directly in front of them, and the two men spoke in quick, clipped phrases. Desperate to know if they'd encountered an enemy, she cautiously peeked over Blade's shoulder. The expression on the newcomer's face gave her the answer. He was a friend. He spoke to Blade earnestly and with animation, as though trying to catch up on many years of separation, and Blade was talking just as fast, the excitement in his voice unmistakable. Then the brave noticed her. For an instant, she could have sworn an expression of shock crossed the warrior's face. But the next moment he looked back at Blade, his expression inscrutable.

"Theodora, this is Black Wolf," Blade said. "He's a Fox Soldier. We were boys in the same village together. My tribe is camped a few miles ahead in a small valley, just as I hoped. He'll escort us there.''

Nervously, she smiled at the warrior in an attempt to convey her friendliness. She prayed he wouldn't suspect her fear of him, but he'd already turned his horse and was riding before them across the high plateau.

Black Wolf led them into a valley with tipis scattered across its base. As they drew within sight, several young men mounted their painted horses and raced out to meet them, calling to them as they came. The escorts rode beside the new arrivals, talking excitedly.

The Cheyenne camp was pitched in a broad river bottom protected by stands of trees. The lodges stood in a great circle, its diameter more than a half mile across. Columns of smoke rose from cooking fires in the still afternoon. As they approached, Theodora could see groups of men sitting about in the shade of the lodges, whose skins had been raised to allow the warm breeze to blow through them. Some men smoked and talked; others worked at different tasks with bows, arrows, pipes, or whetstones. A few boys sat nearby, as though eagerly listening to their elders. About the camp groups of small children played, while their mothers worked over hides staked across the grass.

One of the young bucks riding beside the visitors gave a whoop and raced ahead, calling to those in the camp, no doubt telling about their arrival. From the tipis older women came out to see who the visitors were, pointing and chattering with excitement.

The newcomers rode directly into the village. Blade pulled to a halt before a large tipi, painted yellow and decorated with blue stars on each side and a large green crescent moon over the door.

In the shade of the lodge sat two men, one with a pipestem he was fashioning in his wrinkled, leathered hands. Laying the stem of hard red stone carefully aside, he rose with astonishing grace for his age. He spoke directly to Blade, and Theodora marveled at the depth of welcome in his voice.

Blade dismounted and clasped the elderly man's forearm. They talked softly, urgently. The old warrior shook his head, as if in disbelief, then turned to the middle-aged man who'd been sitting beside him. The oldest man spoke with such pride that Theodora could easily understand the meaning the strange words conveyed. He was Blade's grandfather. Tears sprang to her eyes at the poignant reunion, for that the two men loved each other was without question. A woman emerged from the lodge; she gasped at the sight of Blade and ran to him. They clasped each other's arms in joy, each talking excitedly. She was tall and slim, slightly younger than Blade, with enormous brown eyes that sparkled with happiness. Her lustrous black hair was parted in the center and fell in two thick braids down her back. Turning, she looked up at Theodora. She spoke to Blade with a graceful gesture, as if to say, "Who is this guest you've brought to us?"

A smile playing across his mobile lips, Blade answered the woman, and Theodora wondered what he'd said about her. Then he walked over to War Shield and lifted her down. "This is my grandfather, Chief Painted Robe," he said as he led her before the eldest man. He motioned toward the other warrior.

"And this is Broken Jaw, my uncle. He is a war chief of the Bull Soldiers." He took the lovely Indian woman by the hand and pulled her forward. "And this is my cousin, Snow Owl."

Theodora looked at the waiting group and straightened her spine. All around them, men, women, and children gathered, silent except for the whisperings of children. "How do you do," she said formally, and smiled at them.

No one said a word. They stared at her in shocked amazement. If she'd been a Hottentot from deepest Africa, they couldn't have looked more astounded. Theodora wondered if she should offer her hand in an effort to breach the chasm between them. She started to lift it, looked at their appalled faces, and stopped. Was it her imagination, or had they collectively taken a slight step backward? Acutely self-conscious, she dropped her hand to her side. She glanced up at Blade, who looked as though he could barely keep from bursting into howls of laughter.

"You'll have to forgive my family, Theodora," he said, scarcely able to contain himself. "They've never seen a white woman before."

As she looked from one pair of dumbfounded eyes to another, she realized the cause of their astonishment. In her nervousness she'd forgotten her own appearance. She was covered with filth. Her hair was encrusted with mud. Her face was smeared with it, as well as her arms and neck. Her dirty, ragged clothes hung about her mud-spattered person in disarray. No doubt the only thing "white" about her was the teeth she'd flashed in a too-wide, overfriendly smile, and the whites that encircled her green eyes. She swallowed her humiliation. "And they haven't seen one now," she gritted at him through clenched teeth.

Bravely, Snow Owl stepped closer. Her huge brown eyes were filled with compassion for this pathetic apparition that might have climbed up from the bowels of the earth to stand in their midst.

She wore a dress of soft antelope skin decorated with elk tusks. The long fringes at the hem of her skirt, which came to mid-calf, almost reached her beaded moccasins and, when she moved, revealed leggings that were pulled over the moccasins and tied below the knees. The sleeves were a cape that hung down to her elbows, ornamented with colorfully dyed porcupine quills.

"*Bonjour*, Mademoiselle Gordon," she said in halting but correct French. "We are most happy to meet my cousin's friend." Though Snow Owl spoke with an accent, Theodora understood every word.

"She speaks French!" she exclaimed to Blade. She turned again to the woman. "*Vous parles français!*" she said.

Blade and Snow Owl laughed. "Theodora, may I reintroduce Madame Pierre du Lac. Her husband is a French trapper. My cousin is visiting her family for the summer but will join her spouse at the rendezvous in a few days."

Then Painted Robe spoke, and Theodora turned to look up at him. He was as tall as his grandson, deep-chested, a powerful man despite his age, which she guessed to be in the early seventies. His long gray hair fell past his shoulders, the side braids decorated with otter skin. His scalp lock was braided and adorned with a cluster of eagle feathers, although he didn't wear the long war bonnet she'd seen on a Sioux chief at Laramie.

"My grandfather welcomes you to our village," Snow Owl translated for her. "Because you come as a friend of Blade Stalker, you will be one of our family. My lodge will be your home."

"Tell Chief Painted Robe that I am honored to be a member of Captain Roberts's . . . er, Blade Stalker's family."

Looking at the chief, she could see the dignity and generosity with which he'd spoken. In spite of her fantastic appearance, he'd offered her his home with more grace than most so-called civilized gentlemen could have mustered under such outrageous circumstances. She understood now why Blade always spoke of his grandfather with such respect and admiration.

Painted Robe motioned for Blade and Theodora to enter the lodge, then went before them. Stooping, Blade stepped inside.

"I'll never forgive you for this," she hissed over his shoulder as she followed him.

"I'd planned on letting you bathe in the river before entering the village," he apologized in a soft tone. "But with Black Wolf following us for the last hour, I decided it wasn't the right time to stop."

Unwilling to relinquish her anger while she remained in such a dreadful state, she snapped at him, ''Where should I sit?''

''Over there.'' He sat down next to his grandfather, and she obeyed with reluctance, sitting across the fire from them.

''I want to wash up immediately,'' she demanded in a low voice.

''Be quiet,'' he murmured. ''First the formalities. And don't move. Everyone's already convinced you're half savage. An outburst of bad manners from you and they'll never get over their initial prejudice.''

With surprise Theodora realized she was the only woman present, for Snow Owl had remained outside with the others. Beside Blade sat his uncle, Broken Jaw, who studiously avoided looking at her, as though he was uncomfortable being in the same tipi with such a strange creature.

With obvious ritual the men shared a pipe. Painted Robe spoke for a long time, then Broken Jaw, and finally Blade. During the long wait Theodora began to shift uncomfortably. The mud on her skin itched, and she tried to scratch surreptitiously. No one in the lodge paid her the least bit of attention. At last, Blade rose and motioned for her to follow him outside.

As they returned to the bright sun, Blade called to Snow Owl, who was working nearby, pounding dried roots with a maul. She approached with a smile.

He spoke in French for Theodora's benefit. ''Our guest would like to bathe before eating.'' Then he continued speaking to his cousin in Cheyenne.

Snow Owl reached out and took Theodora's hand. ''Come with me. Many of the women will be going down to the river to swim. I will get a few things from my lodge, and we will go together.''

Torn between the raging desire to bathe and the fear of leaving Blade, Theodora looked up at him.

''It's perfectly safe,'' he reassured her. ''Only the women and girls will be there. No Cheyenne male would be so foolish as to go near their bathing spot. It's forbidden by our customs.''

Relieved, she turned to Snow Owl with a smile. ''There's nothing I'd like better.''

The water was cool and invigorating in the afternoon heat. Theodora dove again and again into its clear depths, relishing

e feel of it against her sunburned skin. All around her, young
dian women and girls swam like bronzed mermaids, splash-
g and calling to one another. Then they dressed and climbed
the nearby rocks to sit and comb their long straight hair,
hich cascaded to their hips like glossy, sable veils.

Emerging from the river in dripping chemise and pantaloons,
eodora looked with disgust at her pile of damp, torn clothing.
ough she had attempted to wash the blouse and skirt, they
ere in such bad condition she hated the thought of putting
em back on.

"Here, Little Blue Nose," Snow Owl called to her in
ench. "I have brought you a clean dress and moccasins,
nce your own clothes were ruined by the Gros Ventre cow-
d."

Theodora accepted the clothes with a grateful smile. "Oh,
now Owl, how good of you to lend me your own things."
'ith delight she stroked the tunic of antelope skin. Snow Owl
:ld up a blanket to provide privacy, and Theodora stripped
f her bedraggled undergarments. Quickly she slipped on the
ess. She sat down on the grassy bank and pulled on the
occasins, amazed at how soft and comfortable they felt.

"This is also for you, Little Blue Nose."

Theodora took the hairbrush Blade's cousin held out. It was
ade from the tail of a porcupine. The skin was stretched taut
ver a stick and the quills trimmed off evenly.

"How ingenious," Theodora said. She glanced up at Snow
wl as she brushed her wet hair. "Who did you call 'Little
lue Nose'?" she questioned.

"You," Snow Owl answered with a smile. "It's the name
y cousin called you. He said in your language it means a
ise woman of great medicine. He told us that you are different
om most white men and women. That like our people, you
now and respect our little animal brothers and sisters, as well
s the plants and the trees."

Theodora flushed with pleasure at the praise, though the
ompliment in being labeled a bluenose was somewhat du-
ious.

As she continued to brush her hair, several women moved
earer. They were drawn, she suspected, by the unprecedented

sight of her blond locks. When she smiled a welcome at ther
they sat down beside her on the grassy bank.

"This is Deer Walking Fast," Snow Owl said, touching
woman lightly on the shoulder. "She is the wife of Blac
Stalker's cousin, Bald Face Buffalo."

Theodora's smile was immediately returned by a tall, angul
woman in her early thirties. The Cheyenne woman spok
quickly to Snow Owl, who translated for her.

"Deer Walking Fast wants to know if you color your ha
like we dye the porcupine quills. She knows you are a medicir
woman and hopes you will show her which plant changes yo
hair to the yellow of the flower that follows the sun with h
face. She is a talented quiller and could use such a dye."

Theodora laughed. "My hair's not dyed. I was born wit
this color."

When Snow Owl translated this unbelievable news, th
women cried out in dismay and sympathy. They clucked the
tongues with compassion. Theodora sensed what they wer
murmuring to one another. Clearly the birth of such a strang
baby must have caused tremendous heartache to the parents

"I had a brother with yellow hair, too," Theodora offerec
hoping to allay their consternation.

After this tragic announcement had been explained, anothe
woman, with a face as round as a full moon, spoke solemnl
and Snow Owl translated her words to Theodora. "Two Moor
Rising says your parents must have been very brave people t
face such a tragedy twice."

Theodora was momentarily speechless. "Tell Two Moon
Rising that her concern for my parents is deeply appreciated,"
she said at last, "and I will convey her thoughts to my fathe
when next I see him." She ruthlessly quelled the laughte
bubbling inside her at the idea of what her learned father woul
say when she told him about this fantastic conversation.

"Two Moons Rising is the wife of Blade Stalker's cousin
Weasel Tail. She has a new baby boy only four weeks old."
Snow Owl pointed to a board of hardwood, lined with sof
buffalo hair, propped against a boulder nearby. "She is ver
proud that her first child is such a fine son. He will be brav
and strong like his father and count many coups."

Theodora noticed for the first time that a baby was strappe

the unyielding board by leather bands, which bound his legs
traight. He was sucking his finger and staring at her with
urious black eyes.

"He is a beautiful child," Theodora said.

As quickly as this praise was made clear, Two Moons Rising
rought the baby over and placed him, board and all, in Theo-
ora's lap, beaming with pride. The baby gurgled and cooed
s Theodora touched his tiny fingers. "What's his name?" she
sked.

"We call him Potbelly," Snow Owl replied. "Later, his
arents will decide upon a better name for him."

The women nodded and laughed, clearly delighted at Theo-
ora's appreciation of the tribe's new baby boy.

Deer Walking Fast, who had quietly left the group, returned
arrying a round clay bowl. Graciously, she knelt beside Theo-
ora and offered it to her.

Theodora took the pot from her hands and looked at its
contents. Dirt from the riverbank had been gathered and mixed
with water to form a smooth mud. Perplexed, Theodora looked
up to find all the women smiling at her in expectation. "What
is this for?" she asked Snow Owl, holding the bowl out at
arm's length.

The lovely woman pushed it closer to her in a gesture of
open generosity. "It is for you, Little Blue Nose. Since it is
your custom to spread mud on your body like we decorate our
own with paint, Deer Walking Fast has mixed it especially for
you."

Theodora gazed at the waiting, eager faces. Slowly, from
deep inside her, laughter rose. She hugged the clay pot to her
as she tilted her head back and howled with glee. "Oh, Snow
Owl," she gasped between giggles, "I didn't put that awful
stuff on myself. Blade . . . Blade Stalker . . . smeared it on me
to make me look like an Indian woman. He didn't want anyone
to see my yellow hair from a distance, so he covered it with
mud."

When Snow Owl told the others what Theodora had said,
they joined in the merriment. The thought that Little Blue Nose,
covered with grime, was supposed to look like one of them
sent the women into convulsions of laughter.

"Blade Stalker has been away from our people too long,"

Snow Owl explained through her giggles, though it was ob
vious she didn't for one minute believe such a fantastic ex
planation. It was clear they all thought Blade Stalker had playe
some clever prank on her, and they thoroughly enjoyed th
trick.

I'll get even with Blade Stalker for this, Theodora told her
self, even as she wiped the tears of laughter from her eyes
Somehow, someday, I'm going to turn the tables on him.

Chapter 17

The women returned to camp, talking and laughing among themselves, while Snow Owl busily translated for Theodora's benefit. Young children saw their mothers approach and raced toward them, shouting with excitement.

"Come," Snow Owl called to Theodora. "The men are playing *ohoknit*." She ran with her guest toward an open space at the side of the camp.

Two groups of young men armed with curved sticks were racing after a flattened ball about four inches in diameter.

"What are they doing?" Theodora asked.

"They are playing a game called Knocking the Ball," Snow Owl explained. "They must drive the ball between the two embankments at their opponents' end of the field. If the ball passes outside of either mound, it counts as nothing. Black Wolf has just scored."

Theodora watched with curiosity. The level space of ground was about a quarter mile long, with two hummocks of dirt heaped up at each end to form a goal. Most of the players stood at either end of the field, but she noticed Blade and Black Wolf, on opposite teams, waiting at the sides.

"What will they do now?" Theodora questioned.

"Weasel Tail and Bald Face Buffalo will each try to strike the ball with his stick and knock it to the fastest runner on his side. Watch."

At a signal from one of the braves, the two leaders in the center struck the ball. With a resounding crack, Weasel Tail hit the ball and sent it crashing to Blade. Another brave tried to intercept it and smashed headlong into him. Blade Stalker kept his balance and shook off the charge like a maddened young bull. With fluid, graceful movements, he dodged another man, caught the ball on the curve of his stick, and raced toward his goal, while the other team chased after him pell-mell.

Spectators on the sidelines roared their approval. Once out in the open, no one could catch Blade Stalker. He outran them all, including Black Wolf, who turned and scowled at the cheering crowd. The Fox Soldier glared at Theodora as she called encouragement to Blade, then turned and said something to another man. The second brave looked at her and shrugged as if to say "She is none of our affair."

"Black Wolf does not like to lose," Snow Owl remarked, for she too had noticed the look of contempt he'd aimed at Theodora. Then she spoke in Cheyenne to a woman nearby, whose soft reply conveyed embarrassment.

"Whirlwind Woman is Black Wolf's wife," Snow Owl told Theodora. "But she is not happy. He does not treat her well."

The young woman was at most only seventeen. Theodora couldn't imagine the sweet-faced girl living with the angry man who was possibly fifteen years her senior.

"She doesn't care for him?" Theodora asked cautiously, not wanting to give offense by prying.

"Whirlwind Woman loved another young man. But her family gave her to Black Wolf when he saved her brother's life in battle. She is a dutiful daughter, so she shares her lodge with Black Wolf. But her heart is not there, and he knows this."

A roar from the crowd brought Theodora's attention once again to the field. The men were dressed in breechclouts and moccasins, and their bodies glistened with sweat. Blade Stalker was easy to follow. His shock of ebony hair, though well down the nape of his neck, was much shorter than the hair of the other men, whose long braids came to the middle of their backs. And only he had the mat of black hair on his chest.

At the crack of the sticks, Blade Stalker once again took possession of the ball. He was hurtling down the open space when Black Wolf stuck out his stick and tripped him. The groan of disapproval from the spectators told Theodora that this tactic, though not forbidden by the rules, was considered less than skillful. Blade Stalker crashed to the ground, rolled, and came up again with the grace of a mountain cat. He charged after Black Wolf, closing the distance with ground-devouring strides. With a clever feint, Blade Stalker snatched the ball on the end of his stick and bounded for the far goal. After him raced the entire opposing team. The crowd's cheers rose to a crescendo.

"Run, Blade, run!" Theodora screamed with excitement.

On his heels came Black Wolf. He smashed viciously at the ball with his curved stick. But little by little Blade Stalker pulled ahead and raced in solitary victory to the far goal, where he drove the ball solidly and accurately between the two mounds.

"Hooray!" Theodora cheered as the crowd shouted its approval.

When the game broke up, Blade came over to her with a grin of triumph.

"You were wonderful." Her voice was filled with appreciation of his victory, his prowess. Her green eyes shone.

"Thank you," he replied, noting her costume with pleasure. He feasted his eyes upon her. "And you look beautiful."

She'd brushed her tresses till they shone. Her hair fell in loose waves down her back to her waist, where they ended in a riot of curls. Someone had helped her fasten two side braids with white rabbit fur, and the softness of that fur vied with the creamy smoothness of her cheeks. Without her restrictive undergarments, the dress she wore clung to the firm, rounded curves of her breasts and hips. The memory of his hands exploring those soft curves brought a surge of lust. He basked in the admiration glowing in her marvelous eyes, wanting to draw her near and hold her slim frame next to his hungry body. He wanted to hear his praises sung from her honey-sweet lips as he covered them with kisses. He yearned to hear her tell him that he was not a savage, that she was not afraid of him, that she desired him as much as he did her.

As though reading his thoughts, she spoke in a husky voice. "You look pretty spectacular yourself."

Without the thick mustache, his firm lips seemed molded for sensuality. She'd never been so aware of his commanding physical presence. His broad shoulders and upper arms were striated with muscles, the pectorals firm and hard. She tried vainly to keep her gaze from drifting down his flat stomach and lean hips to his bare, sinewy thighs and calves. He was magnificent, proportioned like a Roman gladiator: bronzed, rock hard, and all male.

"Theodora." His voice sent waves of longing through her. He took her hands, and she marveled at how small and pale they looked in his strong ones. She remembered the feel of his callused fingers as they'd stroked her bare skin. Her heart started an erratic thumping against her ribs. With reluctance she dragged her gaze to meet his, knowing he would read the desire in her traitorous eyes.

"Come here," he said. His midnight gaze was hypnotic.

She moved closer, drawn by a force too powerful to withstand, until her breasts nearly touched his bare chest. What hold did he have over her, she wondered, that he could pull her to him merely by the strength of his will? She was tired of fighting him. Just when she thought she'd exorcised him from her mind and heart, he battered down her wall of resistance once again and scattered her doubts and her Yankee horse sense like so many corpses littering a deserted battlefield.

"We can't . . ." she began, then stopped at the mocking challenge in his eyes. "I can't . . ." she amended, as she tried to withdraw her hands from his clasp. She was interrupted by the sound of a sharp slap and a muffled cry of pain. They both turned to see Black Wolf pull his wife back into their lodge by her long, satiny hair.

"He's beating her!" Theodora exclaimed. "He's taking his failure to best you out on his young wife."

"Which proves that, despite his many coups, he's a coward at heart," Blade answered with a scowl.

"Aren't you going to do something?" she demanded.

"A Cheyenne husband has the right to chastise his wife, Theodora."

"Chastise! How can you defend such a primitive custom?"

"A custom even the white man indulges in," he answered with irritation, obviously stung by her derision and uncomfortable at the accuracy of her barb. "I've seen the same behavior before—from Boston to New Orleans. It's not pleasant, but it's a fact of life."

Theodora recognized the common sense of what he said. She also realized that there was little either of them could do to change the behavior of others. She couldn't even talk to Whirlwind Woman unless Snow Owl translated for her. She acceded to his logic, but the spell between them was broken.

All around them the village was alive with activity. Children went from lodge to lodge carrying messages of invitation for the feasts that were to take place that evening. Over the cook fires women prepared the meal. In the nearby hills great clouds of dust arose as horses were driven into the camp under the watchful eyes of the young boys who had been guarding them. Some were tied in front of the tipis, to be close by in case of sudden need. Others were set loose to graze in the meadow.

All of Blade's family were invited to the feast in Snow Owl's lodge. Snow Owl, with the help of Deer Walking Fast and Two Moons Rising, prepared a stew of buffalo meat, squash, beans, and a sprinkling of wild onions in a buffalo paunch. The bag was suspended from sticks set in the ground over the open fire. Then red-hot stones were placed inside the tight vessel until the stew boiled. Snow Owl also added a handful of small roots about the size of large peas to the simmering meat. She told a questioning Theodora the root was called *aistomimissis*, which translated to mean "small and tasteless." However, Snow Owl assured her it was a favorite food of her people. When she saw Theodora's interest in the unfamiliar plant, she gave her a few to save.

Other cooking pots were made of fired clay, as were some of the small, flat dishes used for eating. Fresh plums, elkberries, and bullberries were placed in bowls carved of horn. Thin, rectangular cakes made with red and black currants were taken from small rawhide sacks and placed on a carved wooden platter.

At the appearance of a lovely young girl, Snow Owl stopped her work and turned to Theodora.

"This is Gray Fawn," she told her. "She is the wife of Bald Face Buffalo."

Confused, Theodora looked back at the tall, angular woman who stood at the cooking pot beside Snow Owl, and then at the newcomer. Gray Fawn couldn't have been eighteen, and she appeared to be about seven months pregnant.

"I thought you said Deer Walking Fast was married to Bald Face Buffalo," Theodora said in confusion.

"She is," Snow Owl explained as she stirred the stew with a horn ladle. "Gray Fawn is his second wife. She is also the younger sister of Deer Walking Fast."

"She doesn't mind?"

Snow Owl's brow puckered. "Which one would mind?"

"Well, either one of them!" Theodora exclaimed in disbelief.

Behind her Blade chuckled. She glanced at him seated cross-legged on a buffalo robe. Now *that's* not a white man's custom, her expression told him, though a smile hovered on her lips.

"Oh, no," Snow Owl replied. "Deer Walking Fast is pleased to have the help her sister can give her with the work, and Gray Fawn is happy to have the guidance and comfort of her older sister while she is carrying the baby. Later, Deer Walking Fast will ease the load when her sister has a new child to care for."

"No doubt Bald Face Buffalo is pleased with *both* of them," Theodora said wryly.

"Yes, of course," Snow Owl answered, happy that at last the ignorant newcomer understood the mutual benefits of the arrangement.

With a muffled snort Blade stood and left the tent, his shoulders shaking with laugher. But he was back shortly with a small boy perched on his back. "Theodora," he said, "this is Tall Boy, Snow Owl's son. His other name is Phillipe du Lac. He's been playing with his friends all day, so you haven't had a chance to meet him."

Riding piggyback, a young boy of about five, who might have been Blade's own son, peeked over his shoulder. With his mixed heritage, he could easily have belonged to a French family.

"*Allo!*" Theodora said to the child in the hopes he might understand. Like his older cousin, he had raven-black eyes and hair, and his cheekbones, though high, were not as wide and prominent as those of the other members of the tribe. In New Orleans, dressed in the costume of a wealthy gentleman's son, he would have passed almost without notice, except for the

inborn pride and natural arrogance that all Cheyenne males
seemed to have from infancy.

"*Bonjour*," he promptly answered, then began chattering
excitedly to Blade Stalker in Cheyenne. Clearly, a woman—
no matter where she was from or what color her hair—was
not nearly as interesting to him as this new cousin who had
played *ohoknit* with such skill and cunning.

It was time to eat and Theodora found she had much to learn.
When she sat down between Blade and his cousin, Bald Face
Buffalo, everyone stopped what they were doing and stared at
her in astonishment.

"What did I do wrong?" she murmured to Blade under her
breath as she looked straight ahead.

His voice was filled with suppressed laughter. "You're sitting on the men's side of the lodge. The other side is reserved
for the ladies."

One look verified his statement.

Without another word Theodora moved across to sit with
the women. She heard a collective sigh spread through the tipi
as she sat down. Blushing with mortification, she bent her head
over her food. What did they think she was going to do, for
heaven's sake? Attack one of the braves?

She heard Blade speaking and deduced that he was explaining to his family that she'd acted from ignorance and not from
wanton boldness. In the hope of smoothing over her gauche
behavior, she looked up and smiled widely at the men one at
a time. Painted Robe's impassive face gave no hint of his inner
thoughts. Broken Jaw, Blade's uncle, nearly flinched as her
eyes met his. She was certain the middle-aged man was more
outraged at her attempted apology than at the initial discretion.
His eldest son, Bald Face Buffalo, ignored her completely.
But when she met Weasel Tail's gaze, the younger son returned
her smile, his dark eyes lighting with a glow that bothered her
more than Broken Jaw's obvious censure.

"Eat your meal, Theodora," Blade ordered curtly, his
expression no longer so amused.

Outraged at his tone of voice, she glared at him. "That was
my intention from the beginning."

She didn't say another word, but let the family talk drift
over her while she enjoyed the peaceful scene. She looked

about the tipi, feeling strangely content and at ease, despite the armaments that hung by the doorway—hunting knives, tomahawks, bows, and quivers filled with arrows. It was impossible to forget that theirs was a warrior culture.

The meal was delicious. After it was over Theodora stayed with the women and helped Snow Owl and Deer Walking Fast clean up and put things away. Two Moons Rising nursed the infant, still strapped to its board, but when Potbelly began to cry despite her attempts to hush him, she took the baby outside the lodge, far enough away that he couldn't be heard.

"Why did she do that?" Theodora asked Snow Owl.

"The first lesson a child must learn is self-control. He must be quiet in the presence of his elders."

Gray Fawn sat on a buffalo robe, weaving a tiny basket from spike rushes. Snow Owl explained that it would be attached to the head of the baby-board to provide shade from the sun for the new infant. Next to her, Deer Walking Fast was quilling a shirt. The men sat by the fire and talked, while Tall Boy leaned against Blade's shoulder and listened to every word they said. From the corner of her eye Theodora watched the child put his chubby arm around Blade's neck and whisper animatedly into his ear. Blade seemed to enjoy the youngster's attention. She'd never seen the stern captain so relaxed and happy. She waited to hear Snow Owl correct her son's behavior, but the lovely woman only glanced over at him every once in a while and smiled. Had it been a white family, the five-year-old would have been sternly lectured for bothering a grown-up.

Suddenly everyone in the lodge, including Tall Boy, grew very still.

"What's happening?" Theodora whispered to Snow Owl.

"Ah, my grandfather is going to tell a story now," she replied. "I will translate what he says."

Theodora listened as Snow Owl quietly retold Chief Painted Robe's story in her ear. It was a wonderful tale of chipmunks who talked and acted like humans. Its moral encouraged children to show the traits of independence, perseverance, and valor. As the story was told Theodora watched Tall Boy. He listened enraptured, never taking his eyes off his great-grandfather, nor speaking a single word. How much better a way to guide a child, she thought, than to try to beat the lesson into him with a stick. She looked at Blade and their eyes met. This was how he'd acquired his traits of manliness and courage. Like the hero in the story, he was energetic and brave, impatient of control or restraint, and, no doubt, fierce and cruel when need be. The influence of his grandfather had been pervasive. In some ways Wesley Fletcher had been right: *They never change, no matter where they go*. Theodora realized that for Blade his family would be the most important thing in his life—not career, or power, or wealth. He would treasure his wife and children. And woe be to the person who tried to harm them. His intent gaze seemed to say: Now you begin to know me, *vehoka*, little white woman.

When the story was over, the guests departed. The families said their good-byes, and Theodora stood with Blade outside the tipi's opening and watched them return to their homes. Throughout the village people moved to their own lodges after the feasts with relatives and friends, talking and laughing as they went. Far off, a plaintive, haunting melody could be heard as it floated across the nearby meadow. The evening grew gradually quieter. A horse neighed, a dog barked, a woman laughed, and then all was still and peaceful.

"It's lovely," Theodora said in a whisper. "I actually thought I heard someone playing a flute in the clearing by the river."

Blade slipped his arm around her shoulders. "What you heard was a young man playing for the girl he loves. He probably had the flute made by someone with special powers. If the *tapen* works, it will charm the maiden and she will love him too."

"And what did the young girl do when she heard him this evening?"

"She came to the door of her mother's lodge and listened. When he saw her standing there, he knew that his love was returned. Tomorrow he'll wait for her in front of her family's tipi."

"And?"

"And they'll talk. Just like young people do all over the world. But he may have to stand in line, for sometimes there are as many as four or five suitors waiting to court a pretty girl.'' He looked down at her, half smiling. ''Sound familiar?''

''Not to me. Martin was the only beau I ever had.''

He bent closer to her, his low voice as sweet as brown-sugar candy. ''That's because you hadn't met me yet.''

Theodora chose to ignore his comment. ''What happens when the lady makes up her mind?''

''Once the brave is sure of her affection, he sends someone to ask for her in marriage. He'll send a gift of horses with the messenger, who'll leave them tied in front of her mother's lodge. If the father refuses the young man's suit, the horses are returned within twenty-four hours.''

''Oh, poor girl.''

Blade slid his hand from her shoulder and stroked the base of her neck with his long fingers. ''Usually the parents accept the man their daughter has chosen. If they don't, it's because they feel he can't take care of her. If she's willing to wait, he'll have a chance to prove himself in future hunting and raiding parties.''

Through the open doorway Theodora could hear the others preparing their beds. A thought that had nagged her all evening intruded again on her serenity. ''Where will I sleep?''

''We'll sleep here in my cousin's lodge.''

The memory of the previous night brought their gazes together.

''Captain Roberts,'' she began formally, determined to ignore the blush she knew stained her cheeks, ''I'm sorry for the terrible name I called you. I'd give anything to take back what was said—and done. It was my fault as much as yours. I'm just thankful we didn't . . .'' She couldn't finish. The words stuck in her throat, and she swallowed painfully.

His fingers slipped into her hair at the nape of her neck. ''I have to disagree with you there, little bluenose. I can't take back anything I said or did. And I'm not grateful we didn't—''

''You told them my name was Little Blue Nose, didn't you?'' she interrupted. She shook her head in reproach. ''How could you do that?''

Ever so gently he moved his hand up the back of her neck and let the strands of her hair slide between his fingers. ''My people always give a person a name that means something. As far as I'm concerned, you are a little bluestocking, for you've studied the natural sciences. To my people that knowledge means strong medicine.''

''What's wrong with just plain Theodora?''

''Now what does that mean?'' he said. He seemed to be goading her.

Self-conscious, she peeked up at him beneath her lowered lids. ''In Greek, it means 'God's gift.' ''

The corners of his mouth twitched. ''Exactly. Somehow I thought you'd prefer the others to call you Little Blue Nose. On second thought, *Meatozhessomaheo* fits you even better.''

She flushed at the possessiveness in his deep male voice. ''And where does the name Blade Stalker come from?''

''Ask Snow Owl. If I told you, you'd think I was boasting.''

''I know you left the tribe when you were only twelve. You certainly couldn't have earned such a ferocious title at that age.''

''It does sound farfetched, doesn't it?'' he agreed. With his hand entwined in her curls, he pulled her steadily toward him. He kissed her lightly, gently on the mouth. ''We'd better go in now,'' he murmured against her lips, ''or I'll never get any sleep.''

They entered the lodge to find that Painted Robe had already retired. His place was at the back of the tipi, directly across from the doorway. Four feet or so from his bed on the earthen bench that encircled the lodge was Snow Owl's mattress. And close by hers lay Tall Boy, who was already sound asleep. Between the mattresses were tripods made of slender painted poles that supported the backrests for each bed. The vacant spaces created by the tripods were used as small cupboards to store various household items. On the opposite wall, two beds were placed close together, each with its own back and footrest. From each of the tripods that supported the rests, a buffalo robe was hung on a beaded leather loop. The robe dropped down to cover the backrest and bed, creating a soft hammock to lean against. Both mattresses were covered with several thick fur robes.

It looked as sinfully inviting as a pillow-strewn harem.

Blade spoke quickly in Cheyenne to Snow Owl. She looked

in open surprise at Theodora. It was obvious she'd taken for granted that the two would sleep next to each other.

Theodora's cheeks burned. Why shouldn't Snow Owl believe that about her? She was traveling unchaperoned around the countryside with a man who was neither her father nor brother. When Blade's cousin started to move one of the beds, Theodora hurried to help her. The mattress was made of willow rods strung on lines of sinew, which gave it flexibility. Together they folded it up like a bedroll, then unrolled it on Snow Owl's side of the lodge. Over this wooden frame they spread a mat woven of tule stems, and topped it with two buffalo robes. Theodora plopped down on the bed and promptly removed her moccasins. She smoothed her hand across a soft pillow made of deerskin and stuffed with animal hair. One side was embroidered with beautiful porcupine quillwork, and she realized from the scent that the leaves and stems of a mint plant, mixed with the needles of sweet pine, had been placed inside. Such luxury seemed wicked and filled with sensual connotations.

She felt Blade watching her and looked across the tipi at him. He was sprawled on his bed, his long legs stretched in front of him, his shoulders propped against the fur-covered backrest. The back of his head rested in his cupped hands. He'd slipped off his deerskin shirt and moccasins. The sight of his bare feet and legs seemed even more intimate than seeing the dark hair on his chest and underarms.

"Thank you," she mouthed silently.

"You're welcome," he returned just as quietly. His lopsided grin was back. But the slight shake of his head revealed that he already regretted his gentlemanly behavior.

Early the next morning, Theodora helped Snow Owl fetch water from a nearby stream. Carrying the water paunches with the other women, she saw the men and boys emerge from the lodges and head toward the river. Blade walked with Painted Robe and Broken Jaw. Tall Boy tagged behind them.

"They are going to swim," Snow Owl told her. "They do it every morning, even in winter, for good health. It will make them strong and well and wash away all sickness. We will bathe this afternoon, while the men are away hunting."

As they returned with the fresh water, the camp was coming

to life. Women prepared the meal. Young boys rode out into the hills, taking the horses that had been tethered near the lodges for safekeeping. These would be turned loose to graze. When the men returned from the river, they grabbed some food and prepared to leave on the day's hunt.

After the dishes were cleaned and stored, Snow Owl invited Theodora to come with the women on a cherry-picking foray. Theodora thought Blade planned to leave that day, but the idea of spending time relaxing sounded very appealing. Besides, she also knew how much the captain enjoyed being with his family.

She found Blade in the meadow by the river, working with a spotted pony. He ran his hands over the filly as he talked to her, then led her about with a rope halter.

"She's a pretty little thing," Theodora called as she approached. "What's her name?"

"Whatever you want to call her," Blade replied. He held the halter tight and patted the pony's velvet nose. "She's yours."

"Mine?" Theodora's voice squeaked in surprise and delight.

"A gift from my grandfather. He saw us both ride in on War Shield. Being a chief, he couldn't allow us to leave without a mount for you. He has many horses. He let me pick one out for you. I'll work with her this morning while you pick cherries. By tomorrow she'll be gentle enough to ride."

She laughed at his perspicacity. "I was just coming here to ask if we could stay another day." She looked around her at the open vista. Since leaving Fort Leavenworth, she'd learned to ride with skill and endurance. The freedom to gallop across the open prairie, as unrestricted as a wild animal, had become a part of her life. She'd learned to shoot a carbine, cook over an open fire, pitch a tent. The thought of returning to the rules and regulations of New England society seemed as uncomfortable and confining as outgrown shoes.

"Do you think I'll ever be the same again?" she asked him.

He turned to look at her with a questioning gaze. When he realized her meaning, he shook his head. "No."

"Will you teach me to shoot with a bow and arrow?"

"Yes. This afternoon, when you come back." He relaxed his tight hold on the halter and took a step toward Theodora, his eyes betraying his intent. But the filly resented the sudden lack of attention. She snorted and reared up. He pulled the pony down, coaxing her with soft Cheyenne words. She whickered again in reproach, then quieted, shaking her mane.

"What did you say to her?" Theodora demanded. "She certainly obeyed you promptly enough."

His eyes twinkled. "I told her she'd better mind me or I'd trade her for a stud. I can only gentle one hardheaded female at a time."

At his words Theodora turned on her heel and raced back across the meadow. "I'll name her Spitfire," she called over her shoulder, trying hard to keep the gaiety from her voice.

His sudden shout of laughter rang out in the cool morning air.

Chapter 18

⟡⟡⟡

The idea of an outing with feminine companionship, after so many days of only male company on the trail, was too good for Theodora to resist.

With them came Two Moons Rising, who carried her son on her back, still strapped to his board. Behind them was Deer Walking Fast, two large baskets held in her thin arms. Her sister walked beside her, moving slowly but not as awkwardly as Theodora would have expected, considering her advanced pregnancy.

"Does Deer Walking Fast have any children?" she whispered to Snow Owl.

"An older boy who helps herd the horses. Spotted Coyote did not come to the feast since he was guarding them during the night. Deer Walking Fast lost an infant girl this past winter. It is very hard when the babies are born during the cold time. Many are too weak and cannot survive the bitter wind and snow that blows across our land. She and Bald Face Buffalo will wait a year before she has another child. Our people know that it is not good for a woman to have children too close together."

"Your people are very wise," Theodora answered. And the men are very caring, she added silently. She thought of the women she'd seen back home, worn out with childbearing, one pregnancy coming right after another.

Snow Owl looked around at the nearby riverbank and the thick bushes and small trees laden with fruit. Her large brown eyes glowed with happiness. "*Meanesehe*, the season when

the cherries are ripe, is a good time, for we enjoy our Brother
Sun's warm light. It brings us food and game, and we can eat
our fill. We will prepare some of the fruit we gather to save
for the wintertime. But some we will eat now, too.''

The group of women grew larger as others, young and old,
joined them. Most carried baskets. Some had brought intricately decorated parfleches. The chokecherries grew right
alongside the river, and several of the younger girls took off
their moccasins and waded to the other side of the trees to strip
off the delicious fruit.

Theodora worked alongside Two Moons Rising. The plump
young mother had hung her baby in his board on a nearby low-
hanging branch. Every once in a while she'd turn and coo to
him as she picked the red cherries. Laughter and noisy chatter
began to fill the air, reminding Theodora of the time she'd
picked strawberries with Nell Henderson and the dragoons back
at Fort Leavenworth.

They'd barely begun to work when the chatter of the women
was pierced by a shriek of terror. Other screams followed,
and the girls who'd been wading in the river splashed to the
bank, calling out in fright as they came. "*Voxpazena-nako!
Voxpazena-nako!*''

Unable to understand them, Theodora turned to find Blade's
cousin. Snow Owl had moved farther upstream with Deer
Walking Fast. She cupped her hands to shout. "Run, Little
Blue Nose. It is a bear!''

A loud crash reverberated as a tremendous grizzly smashed
through the bushes. The women screeched and raced into the
meadow. The last one to understand what was happening,
Theodora found herself alone on the bank. The bear stood up
on its haunches and roared, enraged that its cherry picking had
been disturbed, perhaps even believing it had been cornered
by the girls, who had so innocently approached from the rear.
The bear looked ten feet tall. It was buff-colored from the
summer sun, and its massive paws flailed the air, the long,
curved claws slicing like daggers.

As Theodora turned to follow the others, she heard the wail
of a baby. It was Potbelly. In her rush to escape Two Moons
Rising had forgotten her infant son.

The bear heard the infant's cry at the same moment. It

pivoted. Its nostrils twitched; its small eyes searched for the source of the noise. Without pausing to think, Theodora raced toward the board that spun lightly in the morning breeze. She snatched it off the branch and held it protectively to herself. As she whirled about to escape, she looked straight up into the face of the roaring grizzly. Its mouth was open, showing long yellowed fangs. Saliva dripped from its pink gums and jowls.

"Run, Theodora!" Blade shouted. Suddenly he was almost beside her, his rifle in one hand. With the other he swept up a basket of cherries and hurled it at the beast, hitting it squarely on its snout. The fruit rained over the four of them like scarlet hail. With a roar of outrage, the bear turned from Theodora and grabbed Blade, snatching him up like a child in a bone-crunching hug.

"Blade!" Theodora screamed. She stood frozen in panic as she clutched the baby and his board to her chest.

The roaring of the grizzly bear shook the ground. Theodora knew there was no hope for Blade. Then the blast of the carbine echoed in the brute's mouth. Blood and bone and brains spewed from the back of the animal's head. Blade had jammed the rifle muzzle between the bear's jaws and discharged it against its soft palate. The huge grizzly dropped him and lurched backward toward the water. In less than three steps it crashed to the muddy bank.

"Blade!" Theodora cried in horror. She raced to where he lay facedown in the short grass. After placing the baby-board on the bank, she gently turned him over. He was unconscious. His bare chest and right shoulder were gashed in ribbonlike slices. Blood poured down his side and puddled on the green grass. "Oh, my God, no!" she wailed. She lifted his head and placed it tenderly on her lap. "Don't die, Blade!" she sobbed, tears streaming down her face. "Don't you die, too!"

The first to return was Snow Owl and Two Moons Rising. Snow Owl knelt on the grass and placed her ear on Blade Stalker's chest, listening for a heartbeat. Cautiously, Potbelly's mother picked up her infant. As she held the baby in his board, she stood and stared down at the fallen man.

"He is alive," Snow Owl said. She called to the other women, who were cautiously returning. With them came the older men who had not ridden out to hunt that morning.

In their midst, Painted Robe hurried across the meadow. He knelt beside Blade Stalker as he listened to the excited talk of the women. Then he lifted his grandson in his arms and carried him back to the village. Sobbing, Theodora followed beside him with Snow Owl's arm around her.

Chief Painted Robe laid Blade Stalker on his own bed. The wounded man was now conscious, and they spoke quietly.

"My cousin has asked our grandfather to let you care for him. He says you have strong medicine," Snow Owl translated.

Tears coursing down her cheeks, Theodora knelt beside the mattress. "I'll need your help," she replied.

"My grandfather says you have a brave heart. We will do whatever you wish for *nis' is*, my cousin."

Blade was watching Theodora silently. Only his stillness betrayed the horrible pain he suffered.

In anguish Theodora realized she had nothing but soap and water with which to cleanse the four bloody slashes that ran across his chest and shoulder. She had used up all the alcohol in his saddlebag in tending the cut on his leg.

"First, I want fresh water from the river to clean out the cuts. Then I'll need something to sew them with. Also, we must see if there are any broken ribs."

Snow Owl worked with her. Kneeling on each side of him, they cautiously felt his rib cage. "*Maheo* has protected you," Snow Owl told her cousin. "There are no broken bones. Only a man as strong as Blade Stalker could withstand the fierce hug of the *voxpazena-nako* and not be crushed." She sat back on her calves and looked at Theodora. "I will help you sew up the cuts, Little Blue Nose. I have done this before for my husband."

Together they cleansed the wounds, careful to remove all bits of fur and dirt embedded in them. Then, using a bone needle and fine sinew, Snow Owl stitched together the torn flesh that Theodora held in place. Even during the sewing, Blade didn't make a sound.

"The end result isn't going to be pretty," Theodora warned him as she wrapped a soft deerskin tightly around his chest, under his arm, and across his shoulder.

His voice was weak, but he flashed his lopsided grin. "I never spent a lot of time worrying about my good looks."

"How any man can wrestle a grizzly and then joke about it is beyond me," she scolded him. "Now be quiet and lie absolutely still. I'm going to bind your whole chest very tightly. Even though we didn't find any ribs broken, you may have a cracked one that we can't feel. After that, I don't want you to move. I'm the *bourgeois* now, and I'm giving the orders."

"I've no intention of going anywhere at the moment, princess," he conceded. "As long as you promise to stay right beside me. I don't want you wandering off and getting into any more trouble."

"I promise. Now try to rest."

He closed his eyes for a moment, then opened them. "My grandfather was right. That was a very brave thing you did, *vehoka*."

She placed two fingers against his lips. "Hush. You can tell me how wonderful I am tomorrow."

With the ghost of a smile, he closed his eyes.

By evening Theodora was afraid that for Blade Stalker there would be no tomorrow. An infection had set in, bringing with it a raging fever. She bathed him in cool water, but his skin remained hot to the touch. The wounds were inflamed, and streaks of red spread across his belly and down his arm.

All night long she and Snow Owl took turns sponging him. They lifted his head and tried to get him to swallow the clear, cool water. He was delirious, unable to understand their commands. Most of what he said was in Cheyenne, but Theodora recognized a few words. Throughout his ramblings, he called her name over and over. Theodora and Little Blue Nose and *vehona*—princess.

"Shh, I'm here, Blade. I'm right beside you," she told him in an effort to calm his wild thrashing. But to no avail. The only name he responded to in his delirium was *Zehetoxem-honeheo*—Blade Stalker. When she repeated the phrases Snow Owl taught her in Cheyenne to quiet him, he would lie still for a while, only his hands fidgeting restlessly.

People came to the tipi to ask about his recovery during the evening. They praised the yellow-haired woman who'd risked

her life to save Weasel Tail's only son. But Theodora was onl
vaguely aware of the visitors, though she realized that Chie
Painted Robe stayed awake all night with her and Snow Ow
watching his grandson.

By morning there was still no change.

"We've got to reduce the fever," she told Snow Owl a
she felt Blade's brow. "Bathing him in cool water is no
enough. We need something to bring it down quickly and kee
it down."

Snow Owl's brown eyes were shadowed with concern
"There is an old medicine woman in our village. She know
the plants that help the sick."

Theodora grasped her hand. "Take me to her. She may hav
some herbs that will work."

As they stepped from the lodge, Weasel Tail and Two Moon
Rising met them. The young mother was holding Potbelly
now released from the infant board. A smile creased her roun
face and lit her dark eyes.

The couple questioned Snow Owl about Blade Stalker'
wounds. Hearing her answer, they shook their heads solemnly
The two women turned to resume their errand, but Weasel Tai
intercepted Theodora. He smiled broadly and spoke directly t
her; she realized he was thanking her for the life of his son.

"You're welcome, Weasel Tail," she said, and returned hi
grin. Even though he couldn't comprehend her words, sh
knew he would understand her open smile of friendship.

Abruptly, Weasel Tail thrust a ring toward her, gesturing
that she take it. Two Moons Rising spoke as well and nodde
her agreement.

Touched by their gratitude, Theodora lifted the ring from
his open palm. It was made of horn, intricately carved wit
geometric designs. "Thank you," she said, and smiled at him
again. She slipped it on her finger. "I'll treasure this re-
membrance."

Snow Owl, who had moved ahead and hadn't seen the gift
called to her. "Come, Little Blue Nose. We need to catch
Picking Bones Woman before she leaves this morning to collec
her plants."

They hurried to the far end of the village where a small
lodge stood slightly apart from the rest. As they entered, Theo-

dora saw a wizened old woman sitting cross-legged on a robe
beside a small fire. A network of wrinkles covered her face;
her long, stringy hair was white and coarse. At her invitation
they joined her on the bearskin rug. All around the tipi were
stacks of baskets filled with leaves and clay bowls of ointments
and salves.

Snow Owl spoke rapidly to the old woman. Nodding, the
toothless ancient turned to Theodora. When she replied, her
reedy voice cracked and broke.

"Picking Bones Woman no longer tends the wounds of
warriors. For many years now, it has been forbidden by Short
Eared Rabbit, the medicine man."

"Ask her why healing has been forbidden to her."

"She says Short Eared Rabbit is jealous of her powerful
medicine. As a young woman she cured many brave warriors
who had been injured in battle. But now she is old and those
whom she saved have gone to their place in the sky to hunt.
No longer is she respected as she once was, even though she
still has her bundle of medicines, the secrets of which she has
shared with no one."

Theodora looked into the black eyes, still sparkling with
intelligence. "Does she know the plants that will bring down
a fever?"

At this question Picking Bones Woman gave a wide, toothless grin and cackled mirthlessly.

"Of course," Snow Owl answered for her.

Breathless, Theodora jumped up in her excitement. "Will
she show me where these herbs grow, so I can make medicine
of my own?"

The crone rose beside her. She came only to Theodora's
shoulder for she was so crippled by age she was unable to
stand upright.

Snow Owl rose too. "She says the medicine man will not
be happy. But she is too old to worry about what Short Eared
Rabbit likes. She will show you."

With baskets under their arms the three women left camp.
Snow Owl and Theodora followed the old woman into a woods
where tall fir trees provided shade from the morning sun.

"*Meemiatun*," Picking Bones said, pointing to a diseased
yellow twig growing on a tree.

Theodora's heart lifted as she recognized the tree. "*M* *lampsorella elatina*. Sweet pine."

Snow Owl translated the old woman's words. "This w purify and make stronger the medicine we use."

Picking Bones Woman moved quickly, despite her crouche gait. She led them to a patch of coarse weeds and pulled son up by their roots. "*Maheskoe*," she proclaimed proudly, ar waved them in the air.

Theodora took the plants of the buckwheat family and place them in her basket. "*Rumex crispus*," she said with a smile "Red medicine."

"This is bloodroot. We will make a poultice from these an place it on Blade Stalker's wounds," Snow Owl told her.

Off Picking Bones Woman went, peering about the shade glade, poking under rocks and into clumps of weeds and flow ers. In triumph she yanked a plant from the ground. She grinne and cackled in joy. "*Towaniyuhkts!*"

"Yes." Theodora nodded in agreement. "*Psoralea argo phylla* is related to a species that we know has important me dicinal properties. How will we use it?"

"This is called 'to-make-cold medicine,'" Snow Owl ex plained. "We will use the leaves and stems in a tea to reduc my cousin's fever. We will also grind it to a powder, mix i with grease, and rub it on his body. This is especially good for curing a high fever."

Elated, Theodora added the plant to her store. "Picking Bones Woman is a genius!"

When Snow Owl translated Theodora's praise, the ole woman laughed out loud. She laughed so hard she fell dow with a plop and rocked back and forth, howling with glee.

"What's so funny?" Theodora questioned.

Snow Owl smiled, her eyes dancing with mischief. "I told her we will call her Old Blue Nose from now on, for she has studied the trees and plants just like you. Both of you have strong medicine."

The thought that she and the old crone would share the name Blade had bestowed on her tickled Theodora as much as it did Picking Bones Woman. Despite the overriding need to hurry back to Blade, she laughed as well. She offered her hand to the ancient crone. "Come on, Old Blue Nose. Let's get these medicines prepared."

When they reached Snow Owl's lodge, they found it filled with smoke and fumes. Through the haze Theodora saw a man whose entire body was painted in black and yellow bent over an unconscious Blade. The stranger turned and held his hands over the smoke of the fire, which had pine needles sprinkled on the live coals. He raised his hands toward the roof of the tipi, rubbed them on the ground, then pressed his palms over Blade's unbandaged wounds. Walking around the lodge, he shook a gourd rattle filled with little stones and sang a long, monotonous, high-pitched incantation.

"What's happening?" Theodora cried out in alarm. She rushed to Blade's bed and knelt beside him. Placing a hand on his forehead, she felt his burning skin.

"It is Short Eared Rabbit," Snow Owl explained. "He is trying to release the evil spirits from my cousin's body."

At her words the medicine man threw sweet pine and juniper needles on the fire, causing more smoke to rise in the tipi. He took some dried flowers from a little bundle hanging around his neck and chewed them. Then he spat on his hands and rubbed them over his arms and legs and torso. He laid one hand on Blade's wounds, all the while shaking the rattle over him.

Theodora turned to Snow Owl in near panic. "But it's much too warm in here! Blade Stalker is already burning up with fever! Why did Short Eared Rabbit build the fire even higher?"

"He is trying to purify the lodge."

"Tell him to leave. The tipi is purified by now. I and Picking Bones Woman will attend to Blade Stalker."

When Snow Owl translated this, the medicine man became irate. He spoke to Painted Robe in loud, angry words. He pointed to the old woman in derision. But the chief shook his head and folded his arms. At his calm words, the medicine man threw down his rattle in apparent disgust and, with a bitter retort aimed at Theodora, left the tipi.

Snow Owl knelt beside her cousin. She spoke to Theodora. "My grandfather told Short Eared Rabbit that Blade Stalker believed in your medicine. We are to do exactly what you wish us to do."

* * *

With Snow Owl's and Picking Bones Woman's help Theo
dora worked at a maddened pace. They crushed the leaves and
stems of the plants they'd found, then made a strong tea and
with a small spoon carved from bone, coaxed it down the
unconscious man's lips, drop by drop. After that they mixed
a poultice of the dried, pulverized bloodroot and spread it
carefully over the four mended gashes. Last they rubbed the
ground leaves mixed with grease all over his body. The smell
of the thick mixture was rancid and foul, and Theodora was
thankful for the fragrance of the sweet pine needles Short Eared
Rabbit had placed in the fire earlier.

The feel of Blade's hot skin frightened her. Though Tony
had nearly died of lung congestion as a child, his frequent
illnesses had never included such a raging fever.

During the afternoon Painted Robe left his lodge. He went
to pray to the Great Wise One Above, Snow Owl told her.
Outside the tipi the shaman continued to shake his rattle and
sing. He moved all around the lodge, his voice droning the
prayer songs he was convinced would help Blade Stalker. What
harm could it do? Theodora asked herself.

Deer Walking Fast came, bringing a thin broth in a tall clay
pot. Blade's cousin, Bald Face Buffalo, and his uncle, Broken
Jaw, also came. Gray Fawn avoided the lodge, for fear the
evil spirits in Blade Stalker's body might harm her unborn
child, as did Two Moons Rising, who didn't want to bring
little Potbelly into the tipi either. But Weasel Tail came,
wrapped in a gleaming white doeskin robe entirely without
ornamentation. He grinned at Theodora as though they shared
some marvelous secret. She smiled back, grateful for his kindness and sympathy. As all of them waited quietly, a hoarse
whisper called out in Cheyenne.

It was Blade. He was conscious, though weak. Theodora
bent over him. His eyes were open and alert. His brow was
cool to the touch.

At his words everyone started to smile and nod. They turned
and looked at Theodora, grinning as though she'd played some
clever trick on them all.

Tears sprang to her eyes. "What did he say?" she asked in
relief.

Snow Owl placed a hand on Theodora's arm. Amusement her lovely features. "*Nis'is* said that he hopes you are tisfied, now that you have repaid him for his trick of spread- g the stinking mud all over you."

Theodora turned in a fitful sleep and bumped her arm against e man beside her. She'd slid her mattress next to his so that e would be close if he needed her. She was awake instantly, arful that she might have banged against his inflamed wound. lade lay still, his breathing steady and even, but his lips were y and cracked. She looked around for a water skin.

The last faint rays of sunlight filtered through the open door- ay of the lodge, and Theodora saw Snow Owl dozing on her attress. Until late that afternoon neither of them had really ept in over twenty-four hours, and it was no wonder they'd oth fallen sound asleep. They were alone in the tipi now.

She found the water paunch tied to a lodge pole. Tipping it o, she discovered it was nearly empty.

There was just enough light to make her way to the river. ' she waited for Snow Owl to wake up, it'd be too dark for ther of them to see.

The minute she left the tipi, she was grabbed from behind y strong arms and covered from head to toe with a white oeskin blanket. The robe was wound around her so tightly at Theodora couldn't move. Her attempted cry for help was nly a muffled sound against the doeskin. Whoever held her, ung her like a fallen deer over his shoulder and raced in lence across the village.

Chapter 19

Suddenly her captor slowed, stumbled, and stopped. Through the blanket Theodora could hear the sound of a branch being whacked against his back again and again. His muted grunts gave testimony to the rage of his own attacker and to his reluctance to drop his prize and defend himself.

"Niveevhaneseve!" she heard Snow Owl cry furiously as he continued to beat the man across the shoulders. Without a word he spun Theodora out of his blanket and onto the ground. He fled into the dusk, but not before Theodora had recognized him. Weasel Tail!

"How could he do this to me?" she demanded in indignation. She sat up and brushed the weeds and dirt from her arms. "Just this morning he thanked me for saving his son's life. He even gave me a ring to show his gratitude. And now he tries to abduct me!"

Snow Owl knelt beside Theodora. "You took his ring?" Her voice was filled with condemnation. She lifted Theodora's hand and slid the circlet of bone off her finger. Holding it in her open palm, she stared at Theodora. "Weasel Tail did not give this to you in gratitude. This is a courtship ring. Once you took it, you accepted his declaration of love. When he came this afternoon dressed in his white blanket, we all assumed he was going to the lodge of another family to ask for their daughter's hand. No one realized you had accepted his token."

Theodora looked in astonishment at Snow Owl. "What shall I do?"

"I will return Weasel Tail's ring to him. I will explain that you did not understand our customs. Both he and Two Moon Rising will be very hurt, for she was there when you accepted her husband's offer. Because she came with him, she was declaring that she, too, wanted you for Weasel Tail's second wife. She has no sister and she would have accepted you into their lodge as her own." Snow Owl stood and offered her hand.

Theodora rose on shaky legs. "Let's not tell Blade Stalker about this."

Snow Owl slowly smiled, her brown eyes warm with sympathy. "This is not something that can be kept a secret, Little Blue Nose. Your acceptance and rejection of Blade Stalker's cousin all on the same day will be known throughout the camp by tomorrow. Such scandalous behavior will not go unnoticed. Whatever you do, don't accept any more courtship gifts."

"I won't take anything from anyone from now on," Theodora declared.

When they returned to the lodge, both Blade Stalker and his grandfather were sound asleep. Motioning for silence, Snow Owl pulled Theodora to the side of the tipi. "You must wear the *nihpihist* from now on, Little Blue Nose," she said softly. "This will protect you, even if you are stolen by Weasel Tail or any other man. Put it on."

"What is it?" Theodora asked in confusion as she took the thin rope.

"It is the protective string that all our women wear."

"What does it protect you from?"

Shaking her head at the white woman's naïveté, Snow Owl lifted the fringe of her own dress. Theodora could see a string wound around her leg just above her knee. "From being attacked by a man, Little Blue Nose. If you wear the rope, no brave will force himself on you. It will protect your chastity."

"This little string?" Theodora whispered in wonder. "If I have this on, I'll be safe from every man in the village?"

"Of course. No brave would dare to force himself on a woman who is wearing the *nihpihist*. If he did such a dreadful thing, her male relatives would kill him and there would be no tabu against it." Snow Owl lifted a blanket of deerskin from her bed and placed it across Theodora's shoulders, so that if a sleeper stirred, she would be hidden from their sight. "Lift your dress," she told her, "and let me show you how to put it on."

Obediently, Theodora raised the hem of her skirt. She flushed, for like the Cheyenne women, she now wore no undergarments. Snow Owl seemed to understand her embarrassment. With quick precision, she wound the small rope around Theodora's waist, knotted it in front, and passed the long ends down and backward between her legs. Then she took one end and wound it around a thigh almost to the knee, where she tied the rope to itself. She wound the other end around the other thigh, then smoothed down Theodora's dress. "Now we will not have to worry about you when you leave the tipi."

"I need fear no brave, then?" Theodora was incredulous.

"No male in our tribe would violate the protective rope. But my husband has told me that this is not so for the white people. He has warned me never to allow a *veho* to get near me if I am alone. How a white man can be so dishonorable, I cannot imagine. But I believe my husband."

"Believe him," Theodora told her in an adamant whisper.

"It must be a frightening world for you, Little Blue Nose, to go among your own people without protection. To know that some man might force himself on you."

"I never thought it could be any other way, Snow Owl. I guess your people are just more civilized than we are when it comes to that."

Snow Owl nodded and smiled solemnly. "My people are very wise. Now let's go together and get the water for Blade Stalker."

As soon as Blade tried to move, he realized that he must have cracked at least one rib. The slightest motion brought a jolt of excruciating pain. He ignored it, for no warrior paid the least attention to suffering. Personal sacrifice would gain the favor of the *maiyun*, who controlled the affairs of men.

He'd awakened at dawn to find Theodora sound asleep beside him. She'd squeezed her mattress up against his, and he could hear the soft sound of her breathing. Clutched in her hands was the water paunch, and he remembered, as in a dream, that she'd held it to his parched lips and urged him to drink from it several times during the night. He tried to take it from her hands, only to discover that he was too weak to sit up. With a sigh of frustration he slipped back into the arms of the great healer, *naozistoz*.

When he woke again, the angle of the sun's rays told him it was mid-morning. The lodge was empty. He knew that by now many of the men had left for the day's hunt. Outside he could hear the chatter of women. Over their soprano voices came the excited cries of the children at play. Gradually, he realized that what had wakened him was not these common morning noises but the neighing and stamping of many ponies tethered in front of the tipi. He tried to get up, but fell back on his bed. With painful effort he scooted into a sitting position and propped his shoulders against the soft backrest.

"Oh, you're awake!" Theodora entered the tipi and walked over to him. With a smile she knelt, lifted the water skin, and offered him a drink.

"I can hold it myself, *vehoka*," he said gruffly. His weakness made him cross and irritable, but he wasn't about to admit it, even to himself.

She relinquished the waterskin with caution. "Very well." She watched him drink with wide, solemn eyes, as though afraid he wouldn't be able to manage.

"What's all the commotion?"

"I'm not sure," she answered with a frown. "Snow Owl hasn't had time to translate for me yet, but it looks as though one of the young men has brought a gift of ponies to your grandfather."

"What?" Blade Stalker started to get up, but she pushed him back against the buffalo robes.

Her smooth brow furrowed as she took the water paunch. "You're staying right where you are, Blade Roberts. I didn't fuss over you for two days just to have you tear out Snow Owl's fine stitching."

"What's the brave's name?" he growled between clenched teeth.

"Which brave?"

"The one who brought the horses."

"How would I know?" Her look of indignation was sincere. He relaxed against the furs. "How many?"

"How many what?"

This time he couldn't keep the exasperation from his voice. "How many ponies did the man bring?"

She gazed at him in wonder, as though certain he'd lost his senses. "I didn't count them. What difference does it make?"

"Merely curious. Indulge me." His jaw tensed as he spoke.

"I don't know." She shrugged. "Maybe twenty or so."

He whistled in sarcastic admiration. "Twenty. Quite an honor."

"I think you're still delirious." She pursed her lips in mock reproach.

At that moment Painted Robe entered the lodge. He came and sat down beside his grandson. "Strangling Horse has offered twenty-three horses for Little Blue Nose," he said gravely. "He lost his young wife last summer when she bore his daughter. The child lives with her mother's family, but Strangling Horse would like a new wife to help him care for her. Because of Little Blue Nose's bravery and her great medicine, the family is willing to allow the child to live with them if they are married."

"No, *namsem*, we cannot give Little Blue Nose to Strangling Horse against her will. It would not make a happy family for the little girl."

Painted Robe lifted his gray brows in consideration. "Strangling Horse says that Little Blue Nose wants to marry him."

"He lies!" Blade Stalker sat up, ignoring the piercing pain in his chest.

"What's going on?" Theodora demanded. She put her hand on his arm as though to hold him still. "Is something wrong?"

"Did you tell Strangling Horse that you were willing to marry him?" He realized, even as he asked the question, how crazy the idea was, but he still couldn't keep the anger from his voice.

She stared at him in shock. "Don't be ridiculous! I've never even spoken to him! How could I unless Snow Owl translated for me?"

Relieved, Blade Stalker leaned his head against the fur-covered backrest. He turned to his grandfather. "Tell Strangling Horse that she is honored by his offer, but she cannot accept it. Despite her feelings, she must return to her own people. She has much work to do for them.''

The rugged features of the gray-haired man revealed nothing. ''He will be very disappointed, *nixa*.''

Blade Stalker smiled wryly. ''And so will you be, *namsem*, when you return the twenty-three horses.''

Painted Robe nodded and rose to send a message to Strangling Horse, who waited in his own lodge. ''You rest, *nixa*. I will send our refusal.''

The grizzly bear was butchered and shared by the whole tribe. Its hide was staked out in the grassy meadow beside Snow Owl's lodge to be tanned. Nothing was discarded. Thick steaks were roasted over the fires; the grease was melted down and poured into bags made of buffalo hide. It would keep sweet for months, to be eaten in chunks or used for seasoning and making pemmican. It was also used as a foundation cream to mix with paint. Theodora learned that it was not the best cook who was most sought after by the young Cheyenne brave but the woman who could paint her husband's body in the most brilliant, intricate designs.

The claws were strung on a necklace and presented to Blade Stalker in honor of his great heroism. For the people of the village the killing of a grizzly was a feat of wonder, as its hide was too tough and thick for their arrows to penetrate. Little Blue Nose was given a bracelet made of the teeth. Her bravery in saving Weasel Tail's infant son was greatly honored. Nothing impressed the Cheyenne people more than a show of personal bravery. She was offered many presents, but kept her promise to Snow Owl and accepted nothing. With a wide smile to convey her appreciation, she politely refused each and every gift. Even this act increased the respect in which Blade Stalker's tribe held her, for such generosity and nobleness of heart was compared to that of a chief's. The coming and going of visitors to Snow Owl's lodge was incessant. They spoke in hushed tones so as not to disturb Blade Stalker's rest.

Blade had been left weak from the infection. For two days Theodora fed him a tea made from the tops and stems of the chickadee plant to ease the pain and help him sleep. She tended his wounds, changing the bandages and reapplying the poultice. She checked to be sure the deerskin wrapped around his chest was tight and smooth over his ribs. After she was certain the fever would not return, she washed off the foul-smelling salve.

To touch him was an agony and a delight. The feel of his powerful arms and thighs brought back every intimate moment between them, from the first lustful kiss in the stable at Fort Leavenworth to the magical night under the stars when they'd lain in each other's arms. She watched over him as he slept and marveled at the strong, well-defined features of his face. Was she falling in love with his physical beauty? she wondered. Or was this merely the lust she'd been warned about in her aunt's biblical readings? Everything about him aroused her, made her more aware of her own body, her own feelings. But nothing was as devastating as when he opened his eyes and gazed at her, quietly allowing her to nurse him. The look of naked hunger in his face made her weak.

The second afternoon, as she sponged his face, he kissed her fingers and slid his tongue across the palm of her hand and down her wrist. The blatant sensuality of the touch held the power of a lightning bolt. She snatched her hand away, the sudden intake of her breath a hiss in the quiet tipi. "That's not right," she scolded in a whisper, anxious that his grandfather, who sat just outside the lodge, might come in and see them.

"It's the best I can do at the moment," he apologized, his voice a hoarse croak. "But I'll do better once I get my strength back. Then I'll taste a whole lot more of you."

She knew she should make some crushing remark, but she could think of nothing except the way his lips and tongue and teeth had felt on her breasts. She tried to speak, but all that came out was a low whimper of desire, coupled with her ragged breathing. She tried to rise, but his hand shot out to her waist and held her beside him. She started to struggle, then gave up. "You'll hurt yourself," she warned.

"Then stay here."

"Why?" She was insane to ask, but the words were out before she could recall them.

"I want you to kiss me." His midnight eyes blazed with

undeniable desire, and he leaned forward ever so slightly.
"Kiss me, little bluenose."

She placed her lips lightly on his in a gentle, healing buss.
When she tried to withdraw, he cradled the back of her head
in one strong hand and held her mouth against his own.

"Not like that," he coaxed in a voice raw with burgeoning
passion. "Kiss me the way you know I want to be kissed."

Cupping his face in her hands, she pressed her mouth to his.
She moved her tongue against his lips, and they opened immediately for her. He was ready, waiting to caress her as she
entered. Slowly, she explored his warm mouth, learning each
crevice and fold, while his own firm tongue stroked and encouraged her. Without words, he told her of his aching need.

A low moan of desire rose in her throat, and she slid her
mouth to his cheek. She breathed heavily against its dark stubble, her nose touching the gold hoop in his ear. "Your grandfather could come in at any moment," she warned.

He laughed softly and cradled her head against his neck.
"We wouldn't shock *namsem*. My people don't turn lovemaking into something shameful or evil. We see our little
animal brothers and sisters do it and know it's a natural part
of life. But our kissing would surprise him, for adult Indians
don't kiss each other."

Theodora moved back to look into his eyes, uncertain if he
was teasing her. Tentatively, she touched his upper lip with
her fingertip, running it lightly across the whiskers. "What do
they do?" she asked shyly.

"I'll show you," he promised. He brought her lips down
to his open mouth. His tongue darted inside hers and retreated,
only to return once again. Rhythmically, he thrust in and out
in a manner so suggestive, so erotic, she had no doubt what
he planned to demonstrate. "I'll show you," he repeated
against her lips in a voice hoarse with emotion, "but not until
I'm certain we won't be interrupted."

He must have heard Snow Owl come in, for he released
Theodora and turned to his cousin, who stood inside the lodge.
She watched them with a knowing smile, the teasing light in
her eyes warm with affection.

"I will tell Beaver Claw to take back his forty horses," she
said to them both in French. "But he will be very disappointed.

He is convinced that Little Blue Nose will accept his proposal.''

"What?'' Blade Stalker thundered. "Not a second marriage offer!''

Theodora flushed and stood up. She smoothed her dress self-consciously. "Well, you're not exactly correct about the number.''

Snow Owl laughed. "Not two offers, *nis' is*. Including Weasel Tail's attempt, this is the fourth one. Yesterday, Counts Many Coups tied thirty-two horses in front of our lodge. And he was as certain of his acceptance as the others.''

Painted Robe entered the tipi and looked at his grandson. Blade Stalker could tell that he was upset, though his expression remained stoical. "What is it, *namsem*?'' Blade asked. He had a good idea what had been happening while he was unconscious and braced himself for the worst.

Painted Robe sat down at his place opposite the open doorway. "Little Blue Nose is a brave young woman,'' he said at last. He folded his arms across his broad chest and the fringes on his deerskin shirt swayed. "She is wise in the ways of plants and healing.'' He shook his gray head slightly, as though in disbelief. "But she does not have the virtue of our maidens.''

Blade Stalker sat up straighter against his backrest. "Who says this lie about her?'' he demanded in outrage.

"Many of the braves in the village believe that she cares for them. She does not shyly lower her eyes the way our women do. She meets each warrior's gaze with boldness and smiles openly at them. Each man with whom she has exchanged looks is certain that it is he who has won her heart. Now the young men argue and fight among themselves over which one of them she favors. The girls are upset as well, for many had already told her friends that one or another of the braves was her own choice.''

Furious, Blade Stalker turned to Theodora. "Is that true?'' he snarled.

"Is what true? Blade, you're speaking to each other in Cheyenne. What's happened?''

"What's happened is,'' he snarled in fury, "you've flirted with every brave in the village.''

"I have not!'' she shot back.

"Oh yes, you have! You've looked right into their eyes and

smiled. Young women are supposed to be shy. They're expected to look down in modesty when a man gazes at them. Not exchange long, meaningful looks. Don't you have any more sense than to lead on every male you meet?''

"I didn't lead anybody on," she said, her voice trembling. Teardrops sparkled on her thick lashes. "I was just trying to be friendly.''

He spoke through gritted teeth, his jealousy cloaked as sarcasm. "Yes, so *friendly* that half the men in the village think you want to marry them.''

Unable to understand their words in English, Snow Owl and Painted Robe waited in polite silence. But the unshed tears that glistened in Little Blue Nose's eyes told them she hadn't meant to be so shamefully bold.

"She does not understand our ways, *nis'is*," Snow Owl said tolerantly. "I do not think she meant to be so forward with the men.''

"What should I do now?" Theodora cried.

Blade Stalker sat up painfully and then eased to a standing position. He tried to keep calm, but the thought that most of the young bucks in the tribe were lusting after her nubile body filled him with jealous rage. "You don't do anything except stay in this tipi, do you understand me?" he roared. "You don't go anywhere unless I, Snow Owl, or my grandfather go with you. And if any man between eight and eighty comes near you, you stare at the ground. And you don't smile! Is all of that perfectly clear?''

She glared back at him. "Perfectly.''

By the next morning Theodora was tired of feeling cross and irritable. She discovered that Blade had left the lodge before she'd even awakened. So at Snow Owl's invitation she agreed to help pick blackberries in the nearby woods. As they crossed the open field, she saw him astride War Shield. But it was Blade Stalker, not Roberts. His body was painted, as was the stallion's. Clean-shaven, he wore only a breechclout and moccasins. Around his neck hung the trophy of grizzly claws and a small leather medicine bundle. A war shield rested on one arm, a lance on the other. He rode bareback, without saddle or rifle. He'd even removed the bandages from his chest and shoulder.

"Where's he going?" she asked Snow Owl, who shook her head and didn't answer. Theodora raced through the tall grass after him. "Blade, where are you going?" she shouted.

Reluctantly, he slowed at her call and turned with obvious impatience.

When she came up to him, she thought she'd made a mistake. He was a ferocious stranger. A black streak was painted down his whole body. Two white lines slashed each cheek. He'd even painted over the wounds made by the grizzly.

"Are you crazy?" she cried. "You can't ride a horse yet. Your ribs aren't healed. And where are the bandages? You almost died of that infection. What do you think you're doing?"

"I'm going hunting. I'll be back by tomorrow at the latest." He looked down at her hand on his leg, a smile hovering on his mouth.

"You're not leaving here without me," she told him. She placed her hands on her hips and scolded like a fishwife. "What if you don't come back?"

"I'll be back. And you'll be safe. My family will take care of you while I'm gone." He wheeled War Shield about and started to ride away.

Her heart pounded in panic. She couldn't believe he was actually deserting her. She raced after him. "Blade, come back here!"

But he ignored her cries and urged the stallion into a gallop.

Theodora reached down, picked up a buffalo chip, and hurled it at him. It whizzed past his head. "Come back here, you bastard!" she screamed.

Without slowing his horse, Blade Stalker turned and looked back. Could he have heard correctly? he wondered. She stood stock still, her hands covering her mouth. Obviously appalled, she stared at him, her eyes round and wide in horror at her own profanity.

He leaned forward and urged on War Shield. A slow grin spread across his face. What a woman!

Chapter 20

When Theodora woke up the next morning, Blade was sound asleep beside her on his fur-covered mattress. Attired in only a breechclout, he lay without moving, his body still painted, the string of bear claws around his neck. She rose on an elbow and watched the steady rise and fall of his chest. How had he managed to come in during the night and slip into bed without disturbing her? she wondered in irritation. She'd lain awake for hours worrying about him, certain that he'd reinjured his ribs or torn out the stitches in his chest and shoulder. Terrified that she'd never see him again, she'd prayed until she fell at last into an exhausted sleep. Tossing and turning, she'd dreamed that she was in the middle of a buffalo stampede once again, the sounds of the hooves echoing through the night.

The day before hadn't been any better. When she'd asked Snow Owl where he'd gone, she'd replied serenely, "Hunting."

Painted Robe had seemed as unconcerned as Blade's lovely cousin. Neither was upset that he'd ridden off in his weakened condition, still suffering from his wounds.

Theodora looked around the lodge. Everyone else was sound asleep. Tall Boy lay beside his mother, his arms and legs flung wide. He, too, wore only a breechclout. She smiled at his innocent posture. He was a miniature Blade, and she wished she could have known the fierce captain when he was a child. At the back of the tipi, Painted Robe lay on his side and snored gently.

The sound of ponies stamping and snorting came from outside, and Theodora realized it was that noise that had roused her. The possibility that yet another brave had sent a marriage proposal to the chief brought a sharp feeling of dread. She rose reluctantly. Without making a sound she tiptoed to the opening of the lodge and crept out.

The worst had happened.

There, in the grassy meadow beside the tipi, was a herd of horses, ground-tethered. By her rough estimation, there were over sixty. Not wild mustangs, but Indian ponies painted and decorated with feathers.

She whirled at a slight movement behind her. Standing in front of Snow Owl's lodge was Blade.

"I didn't smile at *anyone* while you were gone," she blurted out. What she couldn't bring herself to tell him was that no one, outside of his own family, had smiled at her either. On the contrary, she'd been treated by the other women of the tribe as a pariah. Instead of their earlier friendliness, the Indian girls had avoided meeting her eyes. And then yesterday afternoon the medicine man had come and spoken to Painted Robe. By his condemning looks at her while they talked, she'd been certain Short Eared Rabbit was reviling her to the chief. Blade's grandfather had said little. He'd just glanced at her every once in a while and nodded as he listened. But what he did say seemed to placate the shaman, who eventually left in apparent satisfaction.

Seeing the scowl of confusion on Blade's forehead, she stepped toward him. She lifted one hand, her palm facing him, as though swearing an oath. "Honest, I didn't so much as look one man in the eyes."

His slow smile gradually creased his bronzed face. "You must have given *someone* a little encouragement." With his thumbs hooked in the rawhide band of his breechclout, he moved closer to her. "How many horses are there?"

"At least sixty," she gulped. "Painted Robe isn't going to like sending that many back."

"Actually, there's seventy head. But this time he won't have to return them."

"Oh, he has to!" she squealed in horror. "If he keeps them, it means he's accepting the brave's offer."

Blade slid an arm around her waist. "The offer has already been accepted, little bluenose. My grandfather settled it early this morning while you slept. You're going to be married today."

"No, I'm not!" But the confidence of his words left her no room for doubt. "To whom?"

Blade Stalker brought her closer to him. Her emerald eyes were enormous. He leaned down and gently brushed his lips against hers, inhaling the scent of wildflowers that rose from her hair. "To me."

She pushed her elbows against his chest as she leveraged for room to look up at him. "Blade, be serious. We can't get married."

He buried his hand in her brilliant curls. "Why not?"

"Well, for one thing, people don't get married just because they're expected to. What kind of a marriage would that be, anyway? Life together has to be based on mutual respect, common interests, similar backgrounds. All of which doesn't come close to applying in our case. But it does for me and Martin Van Vliet." She lowered her eyes to hide her thoughts, for marriage with the publisher was no longer even an issue. Blade had swept away all her shallow, tepid feelings about her fiancé, leaving her certain of only one thing—no matter what she felt about the handsome captain, she had never really loved Martin.

Her answer stunned Blade, for he'd completely dismissed the differences in their backgrounds as unimportant. Her so-called fiancé counted even less. He slid both hands to her shoulders. In his annoyance he could barely refrain from shaking her. "You don't want to marry Van Vliet," he growled. "You want to marry me. You're just too mule-headed to admit it." He bent his head to kiss her again.

She turned her face, avoiding his lips. Her stubborn little chin went up. "It's common for a man to court a woman first and then *ask* her if she wants to marry him."

"All right, Theodora." He tried to keep his amusement from his voice. "Will you marry me?"

She shot him a look of disappointment and chagrin. "That's your proposal? That's all the courting I'm going to get?"

272 KATHLEEN HARRINGTON

"Just what do you think I've been doing for the last five days?"

Her head jerked up and her brows lifted with self-righteous accusation. "Trying to seduce me."

He grinned. "What difference does it make what we call it? I want you." He pulled her slim body against his aching frame, until her soft hips rested snugly against his tightened thighs. He bent and trailed his mouth across her cheek to murmur softly in her ear. "You want me."

A rosy tint stained her cheekbones, and her eyes were dark with apprehension. "Maybe I do, Blade. Right now, I'm not sure what I want. But I'm not going to let you stampede me into something we'll both regret."

"Theodora, we don't have time to wait while you mull over the idea. We have to get married now. Today."

"Why?" She stared at him in disbelief.

"Because your flirtatious behavior has just about every member of this tribe upset in one way or another. A few of the more cantankerous old crones want to run you out of the village. Three young bucks have challenged one another for you. And probably more than a couple of men are planning your abduction right now."

With an overbright smile pinned to her face, she shrugged in feigned unconcern. "Well, if they feel that way about me, we'll just leave. You were well enough to ride out of here and get seventy horses." She stopped and looked out over the herd once again. "How *did* you get seventy Indian ponies?"

"I stole them."

"I don't believe you! From whom?"

"Those happen to be Crow horses. I took them from a camp on the other side of the river."

"You're offering Chief Painted Robe stolen horses for me?"

He laughed at her look of indignation. "That's the way it's usually done, princess. As a matter of fact, offering horses just taken from an enemy is the highest compliment I can pay you." He sobered and shook his head. "We're not going to leave the tribe and strike out on our own, Theodora. My people will travel with us to the rendezvous at South Pass. Snow Owl is going to meet her husband there. We're leaving with them the day after tomorrow. There's no point in exposing you to need-ess risks by going alone when we can move in perfect safety with my family.''

''And I must pay the price for that safety by traveling as your wife?''

''Correct. The women, not to mention the medicine man, are adamant that you be taken off the market immediately. From now on you're going to be a dutiful, docile, well-behaved wife.''

''Very well.'' She stepped back at his sudden grin and shook her finger under his nose. ''I'll go along with this charade. I'll keep my eyes down and follow five steps behind you. And I won't smile at any man except you. But that's as far as this so-called marriage goes.''

Blade Stalker swung her up in his arms. ''We'll go through the ceremony for the sake of peace in the tribe. Then we'll let the rest take care of itself.''

He had to smother the laugh of anticipation that threatened to betray his true feelings. If she wanted to pretend there'd be nothing between them, he wasn't going to shake her convictions prematurely. When he had her alone that night in their own lodge, he'd make love to her with such passion she'd forget all her worries over their supposed incompatibility. And Martin Van Vliet and his written betrothal contract could go to hell.

The sincere joy expressed by Blade Stalker's family and tribe nearly dumbfounded Theodora. By mid-morning it seemed as though half the village had visited Snow Owl's lodge, and she translated their wishes for the couple's happiness. Over and over they praised Blade Stalker for his bravery and skill in raiding the Crow camp. The fact that he'd stolen seventy horses for her raised her status to a new high. Now, instead of accusing looks, the other single women smiled at her in unconcealed admiration. Gray Fawn, Bald Face Buffalo's pregnant young wife, came to visit Theodora for the first time since Blade had been mauled by the grizzly bear. Her older sister, Deer Walking Fast, brought food to prepare for the meal that evening. By noon, however, all the visitors had left to allow the bride time to prepare for the wedding ceremony.

In the privacy of the empty lodge Snow Owl assisted Theodora into a white doeskin dress. It was as soft and supple as crushed velvet. The fringed skirt fell just below her knees and the bottom was trimmed with tiny bells that tinkled as she moved. A leather belt, decorated with blue and red beads, cinched her waist. On the front of the cape that formed the dress's sleeves was a rosette of colored quillwork. Along the cape's fringed edge, bits of ermine and split quills were sewn in an intricate geometric pattern. The garment had been packed in dried wildflowers and sweet grass, and its perfume drifted up to tickle her nose.

Earlier, Theodora had bathed and washed her hair. Now Snow Owl parted her golden tresses in the middle and braided two thin side braids in front of each ear. She tied them with white rabbit fur and placed a white beaded headband across Theodora's forehead. The rest of her long hair was left unbound to stream down her back, with tiny silver hair ornaments scattered here and there in the curls.

"The dress is beautiful," Theodora told her, stroking the soft fringe that hung from the caped sleeves.

Snow Owl beamed with pleasure at the compliment. "It is the dress I was married in. I am glad you like it. Now wrap this white blanket around you, Little Blue Nose, and we will go. The others are waiting for us. You will ride the pony my grandfather gave you."

Spitfire, perfumed and painted with symbols, was tethered just outside. Feathers had been braided into her black mane and tail. Even the saddle, with its high pommels front and back, was ornamented with leather fringes, beads, and quillwork. Theodora had seen Painted Robe working with the filly in the last few days, and when Snow Owl helped her mount, the pony was gentle and calm, as though she'd been ridden many times before. Then Snow Owl took the reins and led the decorated pony toward the river.

During the afternoon many of the tribe had worked together to build a large open shelter of cottonwood saplings, then covered it with branches and marsh grass. Most of the village was gathered near the arbor now, waiting for the bride-to-be. Under the thatched roof, Chief Painted Robe stood solemnly with folded arms.

When the two women reached the crowd, it parted for them, and Snow Owl led the pony down the aisle. As they stopped before Blade's grandfather, she turned to help Theodora down, then guided her under the roof of the open shelter.

Painted Robe waited until the two women stood directly in front of him. He removed the blanket from Theodora's shoulders and spoke to her. Snow Owl translated. "My grandfather asks if it is your wish to have Blade Stalker as your husband."

Theodora looked around at the waiting, expectant faces. Unable to find Blade in their midst, Theodora looked back at the chief. "Tell your grandfather that I will accept Blade Stalker as my husband," she told Snow Owl, her voice faint and shaky.

Snow Owl had no sooner repeated her words than Blade Stalker came from the outskirts of the crowd. Wrapped in a deerskin blanket of white, he wore a white headband and two eagle feathers in his thick black hair. He strode up to the chief, and the deer-toe necklaces he wore jangled as he moved. Theodora nearly gasped at his confident stride and the look of possessiveness he flashed at her. Without hesitation he placed his strong hand in his grandfather's. Painted Robe took her trembling one and laid it in Blade's steady, open palm. Then he spoke to them, giving advice and counsel for the many years ahead. No one translated for Theodora, but she could tell from the solemnity of the words that Painted Robe was exhorting them to love and care for each other. She peeked at Blade from under her lashes to find him watching her with such tenderness that tears sprang to her eyes. Then the chief replaced the robe on Theodora's shoulders, and Snow Owl led her back to Spitfire.

From her saddle she bent over and whispered to her new cousin, "Am I married now?"

"Not yet, Little Blue Nose. This is not the wedding. But now you have the chief's consent."

They returned to Snow Owl's lodge, where the women prepared the evening meal. "This is not the marriage feast," Snow Owl explained as they set out the food. "We will have that tomorrow."

All of Blade Stalker's family joined them. The tipi was filled with laughter and joking. She sensed that much of what was said between the men was never translated because it was too earthy and ribald. In the midst of the good-natured teasing, Theodora caught Blade watching her with a look of total ownership and felt the heat of a blush on her cheeks.

"It is time for the wedding now," Snow Owl told her when everyone had finished eating.

With a start Theodora sat up straighter. "What do I do?" She tried to breathe deeply to calm her racing heart.

"We will take you to your lodge now. It belongs to Two Moons Rising. She and Weasel Tail are giving it up for you while you remain with us. They will come and stay here with my grandfather and me. They do this to thank you for saving little Potbelly from the bear."

"They don't have to do that!" Theodora blurted out. "They don't have to give up their home for us. I assumed that Blade Stalker and I would remain here in this lodge with you and his grandfather."

Snow Owl stared, her eyes enormous with surprise. "We would not intrude on your wedding night, Little Blue Nose. That would not be a thoughtful way to behave."

Across the tipi Blade's shoulders shook with silent laughter. When Theodora tried to stare him into proper respect, a gaze of such promise shone from his eyes that she looked away. Then the men rose and left the lodge.

After only a short time Snow Owl led Theodora from the tipi. In the sun's last rays, the afternoon was golden. The grassy meadow that ran down to the river rippled slightly in the warm breeze. She mounted Spitfire at Snow Owl's direction. Deer Walking Fast, as the eldest female in the family, took the pony's reins and led her through the village while the tribe came out to watch. At the far side of the camp they came to a small tipi. Just before they reached it, Painted Robe and Blade's two cousins, Bald Face Buffalo and Weasel Tail, came out carrying a white robe, which they laid on the ground. Broken Jaw lifted Theodora off the pony and set her down in the middle of the deerskin blanket. In silence the men lifted it by the corners and carried her into the lodge. Carefully, they placed the blanket on the floor.

Blade Stalker sat cross-legged in the middle of a fur-covered bed in the place of honor at the back of the tipi.

The lodge was crowded now, for the women and children had followed them in. They stood about, their happy faces telling her far more than words that they had completely accepted her as a member of their family.

Still no one spoke.

"Tell everyone they're welcome to stay for a while," Theodora told Snow Owl in a high-pitched, nervous voice.

But her new Cheyenne cousin gave no response except for a warm, encouraging smile. In moments everyone had gone, leaving Little Blue Nose alone with her husband.

She looked across the silent lodge. Blade was magnificent, dressed in a finely crafted white doeskin shirt and leggings, their long fringe spreading across the black bearskin robe he sat on. The necklace of bear claws contrasted vividly against his bronzed neck. The golden hoop of his earring glittered against his skin, turned even darker now by the long summer days in the sun. He sat with his arms folded across his powerful chest, watching her as though he couldn't get enough of her. His jet eyes glowed with unconcealed hunger. Then he placed his hands on his knees and rose with the grace of a lynx.

"It was a lovely day," Theodora blurted out, her voice too loud in the quiet tipi.

Blade crouched down beside her on one knee. A tender smile played on his firm lips. His deep voice was husky with suppressed need. "It was." He lifted one of her long side braids and laced it through his fingers. Tugging gently, he pulled her closer.

She gazed into eyes smoldering with passion. "The whole village turned out in their most beautiful clothes, didn't they?"

With his other hand he touched her cheek, stroking it with the tips of his callused fingers. He bent his head until their lips were only inches apart. "They did."

"Everyone seemed very happy that we were getting m-married." She gulped, determined to keep him talking.

"Everyone." He cupped her cheek with his long fingers and closed the short distance between them. His lips were soft and warm and gentle as he kissed her.

A sigh caught in the back of Theodora's throat and she leaned forward. She slipped her hands around his neck and pressed against his firm chest, returning his kiss with a now familiar longing. Absently, she wondered if he could feel the slamming of her heart against her rib cage. He was the strongest, most courageous man she'd ever known. He was also irresistibly attractive. She could barely keep her hands from moving over his lean, hard body. But yielding to the tremendous physical attraction between them would only cause grief and heartache in the future. That was the whole problem—they had no future. Not together. When this expedition was over, he would be sent on another exploring mission, just as dangerous, while she would return to Cambridge and its safe, orderly world of books and research.

Blade slid his muscular arms under her and lifted her off the blanket, his lips still pressed to hers. He carried her to the bed and placed her in the middle of the deep fur robe, then sat down beside her.

"Have I ever told you how beautiful you are?" The deep resonance of his voice was the sound of seduction itself. With one hand resting beside her head, he lifted the curls that spread across the perfumed pillow with the other. The look of longing in his ebony eyes was hypnotic as he bent over her. "Your hair is like silken sunlight."

Theodora touched his face with trembling fingers. She traced his eyebrows, then followed the high cheekbones down to the strong chin. Her fingers splayed across his cheeks, and she felt the finely molded lips with her thumbs. She studied every feature separately, as if seeing them for the first time.

The touch of her delicate hands sent a surge of raw lust through Blade Stalker. He caressed the pads of her thumbs with his lips. He turned his mouth into the palm of her hand and stroked it with his tongue. He would go very, very slowly. With the patience of a trained hunter, he would wait for his timid bride to come to him. He didn't want her frightened and tense when he entered her. All his years of training as a young Cheyenne male had prepared him to keep his own needs tightly leashed. His satisfaction would come later, after his innocent wife had learned the ecstasy that only he could bring her.

When his tongue touched her small palm, she moaned softly as though an ache of desire had spread through her. He smiled with the knowledge that she was beginning to want him, even if she didn't as yet comprehend what was happening inside her body.

She met his gaze with confusion in her marvelous grass-green eyes. "Blade, we can't..." she whispered.

"Oh yes, we can, my love."

Chapter 21

Blade Stalker captured her face in his hands and kissed her with an open mouth, his tongue demanding entrance. At her surrender he invaded her warm sweetness and savored the taste of her. She smelled of wild roses, and the perfumed scent of her filled his nostrils. He wanted to know every inch of her exquisite body. He planned to spend the rest of his life learning the feel of her silken skin beneath his hands, his mouth, his tongue.

Continuing the kiss, he lay down beside her and pulled her into his arms. His hands roved over her enticing curves. He slid them down her tiny waist and back up to cup her breasts. They grew firm and full in his palms. He could feel the taut nipples through the softness of her white wedding dress. Boldly, his tongue plunged in and out of her mouth, teaching her the rhythm of his mating dance.

As he caressed the globes of her breasts, he could feel her begin to respond. She arched against him, lifting herself higher for his touch. Desire hardening every muscle in his ravenous body, he slid his hand down to cup her rounded buttocks and pull her firmly against him. He lifted one slender leg and raised it over his own heavy thigh, bringing her ever closer to his rampaging need.

He trailed kisses down her neck and covered the peaks of her breasts with his mouth, nipping her softly through the dress.

"You're so sweet, so incredibly sweet," he told her, reminding himself to speak in English this time, so she would understand what he was saying and not become frightened.

Her only answer was a low whimper as her hands caressed the back of his neck and shoulders.

He lifted the cape that was her sleeves and pulled it gently over her arms and head. Her eyes were half closed, and she gazed at him as though consumed with passion. Tenderly, he kissed each lid shut, then returned to explore her mouth once again. He took his time, bringing her with him as he moved his hands over her inexperienced body. Unhurried, he used all his skill to arouse her, and when she timidly touched his lips with her tongue, he invited her in to learn the feel of him.

Slowly and deliberately, his hand slid down her hip and under the fringed hem of her dress. As he moved his questing fingers up her silken thigh, he skidded to a halt. She was wearing the protective string. He'd known that his cousin had shown her how to wear the *nihpihist*; they'd discussed the necessity for it between themselves after her near abduction. Foolishly, he'd taken for granted that she'd been advised to remove it for her wedding night.

"Take the rope off, Theodora," he told her, his mouth pressed against her lips, his voice raw with intense, driving emotion.

"I can't," she whispered.

He moved his mouth to the pink shell of her ear and murmured quietly, coaxingly. "You have to, *nameo*, my lover."

"I can't, Blade." She shook her head and the golden curls danced on the embroidered pillow.

He laughed softly in frustration, trying to make her understand. He could no more violate the protective string than he could manhandle a small child or pistol-whip his grandmother. He nuzzled the curve of her neck with his nose and lips. "You must, love. I can't take it off you."

"I know."

At her words he jerked back to look into her eyes. Too soon the realization of her meaning penetrated his passion-drugged mind. His breath came harsh and heavy between them. "You mean you won't."

When he moved away from her, Theodora felt as cold and abandoned as an orphan lamb lost in a New England snowstorm. She wanted desperately to give in to his demands. The need for his strong arms around her was overwhelming, and the sudden feeling of emptiness he'd left her with was torture. Defensive, she sat up and squared her shoulders.

"I warned you this wouldn't be a real marriage, Blade. I went through that ceremony today only because there was no other alternative than to pretend to be your wife. But there are too many reasons why matrimony would never work for us. Can't you see that? Don't you see how incompatible our lives would be? When this expedition is over I'll return to Cambridge to continue my botanical research with my father's help. That's always been my dream. And you'll be crossing the plains again and again in your topographical work. It wouldn't be wedlock, it'd be a long-term correspondence." Seeing the look of cold fury on his face as he stood up, she couldn't finish what she'd been about to say— that she wanted him more than anything she'd ever wanted in her life, but until she sorted out her confused emotions, she couldn't make a commitment to him.

Walking across the lodge, Blade bent and picked up the white blanket on which she'd been carried such a short time before. He wadded it up and tossed it across the space between them. It fell with a soft plop on the bed in front of her. "Whether you want to admit it or not, we are married, Theodora. Your place is beside me. Not with your father, and not in some musty library in Massachusetts. I am your husband. The only husband you'll ever have. And I intend to be a husband in every way."

He turned, strode to the doorway, and bent to leave.

"Blade, where are you going?" In panic she climbed to her hands and knees in the middle of the bed.

"I'm going to do what every other rejected husband does," he growled over his shoulder, and left the tipi.

The thought that he'd gone to another woman filled Theodora with despair. She lay on the bed in torment. Why couldn't she make him understand her misgivings? She had always dreamed of sharing her life with a well-bred, cultivated gentleman. Someone like her own tenderhearted father. Cosmopolitan. A scholar, perhaps. Not a fierce, sometimes frightening, half-

Cheyenne warrior who could strangle the life from a man with his bare hands and then toss the corpse aside without a twinge of conscience.

But Blade wasn't always so ferocious, she admitted. Her mouth turned up in a wry smile. He could also be very sweet-tempered. She remembered the thoughtful way he'd checked her sunburn, the tenderness he'd shown when he examined the cuts on her legs, and the concern in his eyes after he'd saved her from the Gros Ventre. He was a man of contrasts. A man she hadn't even come close to understanding. She doubted she ever would.

She was wide awake, staring at the smoke hole in the roof, when Blade came back into the lodge in less than an hour. It had grown dark by then, and all that was visible was his solid outline against the open doorway. Quietly, he closed the flap and inserted the lodge pins. She sat up, wishing she could see his eyes in order to read the guilt in their ebony depths.

"You came back," she said, trying unsuccessfully to keep the relief from her voice.

"Of course." His voice revealed his surprise at her statement. As he moved to stand beside the bed, she scooted over for him. She heard the soft sounds of his breechclout being removed, then felt the mattress sink as he climbed onto the furs beside her.

Wordlessly, he reached over and lifted her into his arms. With rapid movements, he pulled her dress up and over her shoulders and head. The musical tinkle of the tiny bells sewn on its hem filled the quiet tipi, bringing an image of a Turkish harem with all its forbidden delights.

"What are you doing?" she asked in astonishment.

"Getting you ready for bed." His tone was matter-of-fact. "From now on, in the privacy of our own lodge, neither one of us will sleep with our clothes on."

All she wore now was the protective string. Theodora gasped as he enfolded her in his arms once again. Her naked breasts were pressed against his wet chest. She could feel his strong, bare legs entangling with hers. His whole body was cold and damp, and water dripped from his hair onto her arm. "You've been swimming!" she cried in amazement.

He chuckled at her surprise. "What did you think I was doing?" he teased, as he nibbled her earlobe. He pushed her against the pillow and leaned over her. His voice was gruff with concern. "You've been crying."

Humiliated at his discovery, but thrilled at her own, Theodora slid her hands up his arms. She drew small circles around his shoulders, unwilling to tell him what she'd been crying about.

He bent and gently kissed both tear-stained cheeks. "I went for a cold plunge in the river, that's all. I'm not going to hurt you, *zeheszheemetovaz*. I'm not going to ravish you against your will. And I'm not going to betray you with another woman."

"I'm sorry. About everything." She pressed her lips against his cold, moist chest, the springy hair tickling her nose. She kissed the scars on his shoulder. "What did you just call me?"

"You who are my woman." Blade Stalker turned her around and brought her bottom into wanton contact with his thighs, teaching her the feel of his rigid arousal pressed against her soft little butt. He folded his arms under her breasts and buried his face in her sweet-smelling hair. "Do you know why it's our custom to allow a shy young bride to wear the protective string with her new husband if she wishes?"

Theodora shook her head.

"It allows the newly married couple time to get used to each other. To the feel of undressing and sleeping together. It's a wise custom, for it gives the young maiden a chance to relax in her bridegroom's arms and learn the security and protection his love will surround her with, before he takes her virginity. The new groom respects the string for ten or fifteen days— but no longer than that." He kissed her ear and spoke in a low rumble. "Even a very shy young girl needs to learn her husband's desires."

"What do they do for those fifteen days?"

He chuckled. "To be specific, it's usually less than ten." He pulled her closer to him. "They get to know each other. Sometimes they lie awake talking all night long." He rested his chin on the top of her head. "What do you want to talk about, little bluenose?"

For Theodora, the feel of his arms around her was heaven. She leaned her head back on his shoulder, enjoying the fresh, clean smell of him, the firm contours against her softness. "Tell me about your childhood. How did you get your Indian name?"

Idly, he caressed the smooth silk of her breasts, stroking the soft nipples until they were tightened peaks. Blade Stalker smiled to himself when she gasped at the touch of his hands upon her. Her chest rose and fell as she dragged air into her lungs; her heart thudded beneath his roving fingers.

"That was the spring of my twelfth year," he said, using his iron will to keep the raging desire from his voice. He continued as though it were the most common thing in the world for her to be lying naked in his arms, his hands caressing her. "I had already been on my first buffalo hunt and had killed a young bull. But I was large for my age, more mature than my childhood companions, and anxious to count my first coup."

"What was your name at that time?" The huskiness of her voice betrayed the wave after wave of pure, carnal pleasure she was experiencing for the first time in her life.

"Tall Boy. Just like Snow Owl's son. Often names are repeated in my people's families."

"And so, did you count coup when you were only twelve?"

He chuckled at the disbelief in her voice. "My grandfather was leading a horse-raiding party that spring. I followed them secretly, making myself known only after they'd made camp at nightfall. Painted Robe was very proud of me, and all the older warriors treated me with respect and consideration. And when the time came to fight, I was given the same opportunity to distinguish myself as the other young braves."

Theodora's green eyes were wide with astonishment. "You were still a child!"

"You'd never have convinced me of that, *vehona*. A Cheyenne youth's greatest ambition is to be brave and fight well. Since I was riding one of the fastest horses, I was chosen to be part of the party that charged the enemy's camp. During the hand-to-hand combat, I was attacked by a Crow brave and counted my first coup."

"You touched the other warrior?"

"No, I slit his throat."

Blade Stalker waited while she digested this information. He didn't want her to be afraid of him, but she needed to understand his heritage. And realize that he was capable of protecting his woman from anyone who might try to harm her. He kissed the top of her head. "What else do you want to know?" As he waited patiently while she searched for another topic, he continued his rhythmic ministrations.

"Tell me more about your childhood," she finally said, her soft, languorous voice heavy with passion. She looked over her shoulder at him. "Unless you're too tired and would rather go to sleep."

He nuzzled her neck and shoulder, then lightly bit the creamy flesh. "There's no hurry. We have all night, *nameo*. You'll find that, like all my people, I am a great storyteller."

Visitors came early the next morning. When Snow Owl and Deer Walking Fast entered the lodge, Theodora rose up sleepily on one elbow. She'd been covered by the white doeskin blanket sometime during the late hours. Blade was nowhere in sight.

"Wake up, sleepy bride," Snow Owl called to her from the doorway. She smiled in understanding at Theodora's wide yawn. "It's time to get up. We brought you some wedding gifts."

In their arms the women carried presents for the newlyweds. "Deer Walking Fast is a member of the *Meenoistst*, the quillers' society. She has learned the sacred art of decorating robes for medicine men and warriors and has quilled some clothes for you and my cousin."

"They're beautiful," Theodora told Snow Owl. She stroked the soft deerskin of Blade's shirt and smiled at the thin, tall woman. "You must have spent many hours quilling."

Deer Walking Fast beamed when Snow Owl translated the compliment. Together they examined the superbly fashioned outfits, which included leggings and moccasins, as well as a breechclout and shirt for Blade Stalker, and the dress for Theodora.

She laid the clothes on her bed. "Have you seen Blade Stalker?"

"He is hunting with his cousins, Bald Face Buffalo and Weasel Tail," Snow Owl said. "They will bring back meat for today's celebration. Now come; we want you to join us for the wedding feast preparations."

The camp was bustling with activity when Theodora emerged from her lodge. Under the shelter built the day before, colorfully painted deerskins were spread on the grass. The women placed baskets of fresh wild plums, chokecherries, and dried Juneberries on the blankets. Large pottery jars were filled with steaming stews made of buffalo meat, sweet potatoes, and wild red turnips. All morning long the women worked, chattering among themselves. They smiled at Theodora and insisted she sit under the open shelter with them, but she was not allowed to help them.

Later that morning she and Snow Owl went down to the river to bathe, then she dressed in her new finery.

When the men returned from the hunt that afternoon, they brought packhorses laden with antelope and deer. The meat was soon roasting on open campfires while the men retired to the river to swim and change into their best garments.

All that day Theodora hadn't seen her husband, except briefly when he rode in with the hunting party. Now he stood beside her, clothed in the soft deerskin shirt, breechclout, and leggings that Deer Walking Fast had given him, and she flushed, too embarrassed to speak. She remembered how they'd lain together, talking into the late hours of the night, until she'd finally drifted to sleep in his arms. She was totally, agonizingly aware of every movement he made.

"Did you get enough sleep, princess?" His eyes twinkled with mischief. "My cousin told me she finally had to enter our lodge and wake you up before you slept the day away."

He looked completely rested, not the least bit tired from the day hunting game, or the long night spent trying to seduce his wife. When she met his coal-black eyes, the open hunger in them brought a flush to her cheeks. She dropped her gaze to his mouth, and the memory of the pleasure of his lips sent desire surging through her. Nervously, she wet her lips with her tongue. Her voice sounded dry and cracked when she spoke. "No one would let me lift a finger with the preparations, so I took a little nap this afternoon."

"Good. I don't want you overtired for the party." He took her hand. The sight of her own small fingers in his strong bronze ones brought back the memory of his hands on her bare, white breasts. The unfulfilled longing he'd aroused in her the previous evening came crashing back.

She nodded, unable to answer him. Call it courtship, call it seduction, call it enticement or beguilement, he was building within her a need for him so great that it threatened to override all her firm resolve. She knew that if she allowed him to make love to her, she might confess just how much she did want him. Armed with that knowledge, he would never let her go.

"Snow Owl told me we'd be at the rendezvous in about ten days," she told him, as though he'd just asked for the information.

He didn't question her meaning. "Come on. Let's sit down in the place of honor so the feast can begin." He led her to one side of the shelter and they sat on a deerskin blanket together.

Everyone in the village wore their most festive clothing. The women's antelope-skin dresses were decorated with discs made from deer toes, tufts of rabbit fur, bits of down feathers. Both sexes had painted stripes or checks on their cheeks and foreheads; some had even painted their hair part. Their braids were decorated with feathers and furs.

After everyone had eaten, the food and dishes were cleared away. One by one, Blade's family brought them gifts. Deer Walking Fast and her mother gave Blade a buffalo robe, marvelously quilled and ornamented with bear claws. Gray Fawn presented Theodora with winter moccasins made from buffalo hide, with its long, shaggy hair inside to keep her warm in the snow. Tall Boy gave her a collection of porcupine quills, and his mother presented her with a brush cleverly made from a porcupine tail.

Their generosity overwhelmed Theodora, and she blinked back tears. Then Chief Painted Robe gave his grandson the peace pipe he'd been working on since they'd arrived. The look of love between the two men as he laid it in Blade's hand brought the tears, valiantly held in check until then, streaming down Theodora's cheeks. How could she have ever called these people monsters? It had been she, the ignorant stranger, who'd shocked them with her uncivilized behavior. The deep family ties that bound them together would transcend time and space.

The afternoon was waning as the tom-toms appeared. The children, who'd been racing around with their dogs and playing all afternoon, returned to the shelter. They were given a treat of sap candy as they sat down on the edge of the blankets, curious to watch their parents, uncles, and aunts. The braves lined up on one side of the shelter, some beating the tom-toms in a steady rhythm. Then the women took the floor. They danced to the beat of the drums and the shake of the rattles, never moving their feet, but twisting and turning their arms and bodies in a slow, mystical weaving.

Then the braves ran onto the floor. They started slowly, increasing the tempo, faster and faster, until the speed of their dancing reached a frenzied tempo. They yelled and shook rattles and tomahawks over their heads. Some had streamers of feathers that whirled about them like tails. It was bedlam. In her fear Theodora reached over for her husband's hand.

Immediately he covered her shaking fingers with his strong ones. "Don't be frightened, *nazheem*, my woman. They're just wishing us a long and fertile marriage."

When the dancing ended, Chief Painted Robe stood alone in the middle of the shelter and spoke to the wedding couple.

"My grandfather says you have a brave heart, little wife," Blade Stalker told her. "He is proud that you are now his granddaughter. And he wants you to have this eagle feather as a sign that you risked your life to save the tribe's youngest child. This is a high honor, for usually only the bravest warriors are entitled to wear an eagle's feather."

Painted Robe walked over to her and Theodora stood. He placed the feather in her hair, pointing it down as a sign of peace.

Blade rose and stood beside her, his eyes glowing with love and pride.

"Tell *namsem* I am proud to be his granddaughter," Theodora said.

* * *

By the time Theodora and Blade returned to their lodge that evening she was relaxed and happy. But at the sight of the empty tipi, with its bed made of two mattresses pushed together and covered with large, thick robes, her nervousness returned. She stood at one side of the lodge and slowly removed the eagle's feather from her hair. From the corner of her eye she saw Blade take off his deerskin shirt. He folded it in half, laid it over a backrest, and sat down on the bed to take off his moccasins. Then he stood and pulled down his leggings. Knowing he now was dressed only in a breechclout, she turned and crossed her arms around her waist, hugging herself in near panic.

He had said they would not wear clothes to bed. Just the thought of lying naked in his arms brought a surge of longing. The *nihpihist* shielded her from her husband's lustful desires, but what about her own? It was her own self-control that would be tested that night.

"I thought we'd take a swim before going to bed," he said.

She whirled around, thankful for the unexpected reprieve. "I'd love that!"

His lips twitched in a playful smile. "It'll be a little cool, but it should feel good after the heat of the day." He led her outside, mounted War Shield, and reached down to pull her up in front of him.

"We'll go a little ways upriver so we can have some privacy."

Theodora sat up straight to avoid touching him. Perhaps this wasn't such a good idea, she told herself. But the thought of returning to the empty lodge didn't seem any better a solution. "I hope the water's not too cold," she said, building an alibi for changing her mind if it became necessary.

"You'll get used to it." He pulled her back, the muscular arm around her waist pinning her to him. Her buttocks were wedged between his massive thighs.

Her emotions were a turmoil of confusion and contradiction. She wanted to swim with him, to lie with him, to press closer and ever closer to him. But she was afraid she wouldn't be satisfied with just that. She shouldn't continue, but she couldn't stop.

He dismounted and lifted her down. He'd found a small, still inlet protected on three sides by a thick stand of cottonwoods and berry bushes. The last rays of dusk had faded and moonlight lit the water.

Blade dropped his breechclout and splashed quickly into the river. He dove under and came up, then tossed his thick hair. The droplets of water sprayed out around him like diamonds. He tread water and grinned at her. "Come on, little bluenose. Let's see if you remember what I taught you."

Uncertain if he was referring to the past swimming lesson or the recent instruction in lovemaking, Theodora watched him cautiously. She'd never wanted anything more than she wanted to join him now. She pulled her dress over her head and stepped into the water. He was right. It was cold!

She let out a yelp of protest. Before she could turn and retrace her steps, he splashed up beside her and grabbed her hand.

"Keep moving," he ordered, the laughter in his voice enticing her further. "You'll be fine in a few minutes."

"You mean I'll be too numb to feel anything," she protested. But she followed him out until they were both treading water.

The feel and smell of being outdoors in the moonlight was captivating. The river was black, except for the silvery reflection of its lapping waves. Overhead, the night sky was filled with stars. The only sound was the splash of the water and their voices as they talked softly. Following his lead, Theodora swam beside him. When he dove, she dove. When he surfaced, she came up right behind him. It was a thrill to find that she hadn't forgotten what he'd taught her. With him, she had no fear of the water. She laughed out loud from the sheer joy of it.

He tread water next to her. "You're a quick learner, princess."

"Why do you call me that?" she demanded in mock irritation. "I understand the so-called humor in 'little bluenose,' but I can't for the life of me see the relevancy of 'princess.' Or do you do it just to annoy me?"

He placed his hand on her waist and pulled her to him. Amusement flickered over his rugged features. "The first time

I laid eyes on you, I thought you looked like a princess from a fairy tale.''

At her astonished look he smiled lopsidedly. ''My grandmother in New Orleans insisted on teaching me to read. At thirteen, under her supervision, I read all the French children's tales I'd never heard before.''

She tapped one finger on his furry chest with every word she spoke. ''You told me I looked like a prudish New England spinster whose only knowledge of life came from books.'' She stuck her lower lip out in a pout.

His unrepentant reply was immediate. ''I lied.''

Chapter 22

The silver flecks in Blade Stalker's black eyes glittered in the moonlight. He grinned at her with such wicked glee that Theodora had to retaliate. She placed her hands against his broad shoulders and pushed with all her strength in a mighty attempt to dunk him under the water. Remorseless, he tipped his head back and laughed at her futile efforts. Determined to make him suffer, she wrapped both arms around his neck and hung on, forcing her body to go limp against him in the hope she'd pull him under. She was as successful as a butterfly trying to wrestle a buffalo to the ground. His arms moved in and out with powerful strokes as he tread the water. The fact that he enjoyed her impotent struggles became obvious when he chuckled, bent his head, and nibbled on her earlobe.

She realized she was making no headway, released him, and moved back. Valiantly, she tried to keep the laughter from her voice. "All right. You asked for it." Pounding both hands against the surface, she sent geysers of water spraying over his head and shoulders. Her sudden change of tactics caught him off guard, and before he could grab her, she screamed in mock terror, dove under the water, and headed toward shore.

In two strokes he caught up with her. He caught her waist and pulled her to him. Even under the dark water, his mouth found hers, and he kissed her roughly, passionately, possessively. As they came up for air, he clasped her tightly to him, and she felt his rigid shaft pressing against her thigh. When they went under again, his hands were all over her body, gliding across her bare buttocks and hips, her stomach and breasts.

Resurfacing in his embrace, she shook her head to let him know she had to stay up. She clung to him as she drew in great gasps of air.

"I yield!" she cried in a hoarse, exhausted voice. She tried not to laugh for fear she'd swallow more water.

At her words his expression of playfulness changed. With one strong hand, he held her above the surface. The hoarseness in his voice was not exhaustion, but desire. "Then surrender to me, Theodora. Let me show you the pleasures I can bring. What you felt last night was only the beginning. Take off the string, love."

She looked at his hawkish features, softened in the moonlight. No matter what happened in the years ahead, she'd never meet a man she would want as much as him. He was entirely unsuitable. And she was completely and irresistibly in love with him. Her efforts to follow the dictates of her scholar's reasoning rather than her woman's heart had failed abysmally. From some corner of her mind a small voice chided: Why not? Why not have the memories of these next few days to treasure? If their lives must go in opposite directions, couldn't she have, at least, these rare golden moments when she could demonstrate in actions the love she could never put into words?

The confusion, the turmoil of her warring emotions must have been written on her lifted face, for he smiled tenderly in understanding. "Let's go in now, *zehemehotaz*."

They returned to their lodge in silence, mounted on War Shield. As she leaned against his solid chest, Blade's arms surrounded her. She'd pulled her dress on over her wet skin and it clung to her, revealing the mounds of her breasts; her puckered nipples were clearly outlined beneath the soft antelope skin. He had replaced only his breechclout, and his cold thighs were sheened with water.

When they entered the tipi, he stirred the smoldering embers of the cooking fire to provide a flickering light, then moved to the mattress and removed his last garment.

Immobile, Theodora watched him. Would she ever cease to be amazed at his magnificent physical stature, at the vitality that emanated from him like a living force? He must have felt her steady gaze, for his eyes sought hers in wordless communion. Without a sound she lifted her dress over her head, folded it, and laid it aside. She bent over her bare thigh, her wet hair falling about her face like a golden screen, and began to untie the *nihpihist*. The rawhide was tight from her swim, and she had to struggle to release her bonds. Finally, the string came loose, and she turned to the binding on her other leg. Her cold fingers trembled as she worked, impeding her progress. But at last that knot, too, was free.

Theodora caught the cord before it fell away and curled it in the palm of her hand. Looking up, she met the passion blazing in his dark eyes.

Blade took one step toward her and stopped. His need for her was rampantly apparent. His thin nostrils flared, the only sign on his hawklike features of the sexual tension that swirled about them like an invisible mist. Without taking her eyes from his face, she moved across the lodge floor until they were only inches apart. She thrust her cupped hands toward him, and for one seemingly endless moment, he stood motionless. To Theodora, it was as though his questioning eyes delved into the far reaches of her mind, searching for the true reason for her surrender.

Then he held out one large hand, palm up, and she placed the rope in his keeping. Whatever he'd read in her eyes, he didn't hesitate once the rawhide was in his control. With a low growl of passion, he hurled it across the lodge and pulled her to him. He lifted her in his arms, his mouth seeking and finding hers. He kissed her passionately, his lips slashing across her own. Effortlessly, he lifted her higher, until her breasts were beneath his mouth, and his tongue kindled burning, licking flames of excitement that spread through her body. When she moaned deep in her throat, he lowered her, letting her legs slide down the rippling muscles of his belly and thighs. She felt his hot, rigid arousal pressing against her moist, cool skin.

His hands moved over her, exploring, and she quivered reflexively as his thumbs brushed back and forth across the tightened peaks of her breasts.

"You talked in your sleep last night, *vehona*," he told her. He stepped backward toward the mattress, taking her with him. "You called my name."

"Which one?" She stared into his eyes, mesmerized by the promise in their dark depths.

"Blade Stalker."

"Did I say anything else?" She held her breath as she waited for his answer.

"Please."

At his whispered reply she expelled the air in her lungs, trying in vain to calm the wild hammering of her heart.

His soft, coaxing tone enticed her. "Touch me, *nazheem*."

Timidly, she slid one hand up his arm, feeling the bulging muscles on his biceps and shoulders. She ran her hand across his shoulder blade and down the bumps of his spine to the lower curve of his back, where her palm cupped his lean, hard buttock. Trembling with desire, she slid her fingertips across his massive thigh, grazed the flat plane of his stomach with her nails, and buried them in the black hair that covered the firm pectorals of his chest.

His shudder seared her very soul. "Touch me, Theodora." The thickness of his deep, throaty voice left no doubt of his meaning.

Her hand lay frozen on his broad chest. She looked up into eyes as black as the river they'd swam in. In their depths she saw once again the image of him running into the water. She'd never seen another adult male naked. His manhood had looked engorged and hardened, yet somehow sensitive and vulnerable as well. Could she hurt him in her ignorance? Suddenly she felt as clumsy and awkward as a schoolgirl. "I don't know how," she confessed in a shy whisper. "Show me."

He took her small hand in his strong one and slid it down past the tapering hair on his stomach. To her inexperienced fingers, he was warm, firm velvet. Hard and silken at the same time. At her first hesitant touch, she heard the sharp intake of his breath as he sucked the air between his clenched teeth.

She watched his face, darkened with passion, become taut and furrows appear between his raven brows. His heavy lids almost covered his eyes; his thick lashes shadowed his bronzed cheeks. "Am I hurting you?" she whispered, worried at his sudden stillness.

His answer was a low groan. "No."

"It pleasures you, then?"

His ebony eyes flew open, and he smiled with incredible tenderness. "Yes, *nameo*, my lover, it pleasures me."

Releasing her hand, he slid his own up to cup her breast. He kissed her, drawing her tongue into his mouth, then returning to hers with his own. He teased her with light kisses across her cheekbones and traced the delicate lines of her ear with his warm tongue. He took both her hands and brought them to his lips, kissing the tip of each finger. Then he slid one arm behind her back, the other under her knees. Lifting her up, he turned and laid her gently on the fur-covered bed. "And now, sweet princess, I will pleasure you."

For Blade Stalker the wait for her to come to him had seemed endless. But the thrill of knowing she came willingly surpassed all expectation. She was his woman. By all the traditions of his Cheyenne upbringing, she belonged to him now. His wife. His lover. And one day, the mother of his children. His and his alone.

Unrestrained at last, he explored her silken skin with his mouth and tongue, suckling the rosy crests of her ivory breasts. His yearning hands roved at will over her hips and stomach and thighs as he learned the feel of every luscious curve and hollow. With iron control he ignored his own rampaging desire and forced himself to slow down. Bending over her, he taught her the feel of his bronze hands on her pale body, encouraging her to respond without shame. He talked to her in three languages as he told her how much he wanted her, how much she wanted him, and even when he spoke in Cheyenne, she seemed to understand.

His strong fingers glided possessively across her satiny whiteness, luring and coaxing and teasing from her an uninhibited avowal of her need for him. He refused to be satisfied with anything less than her complete surrender. When he slid his fingertips across her soft, curly mound, he could feel her sudden tension as she reflexively clamped her thighs together. With a smothered chuckle deep in his throat, he bent and kissed her stomach, laving her navel with his tongue. "Relax, little wife," he crooned. "You belong to me. I want to love every inch of your exquisite body."

He nudged her thighs apart with his knee, caressing the soft warmth of her with his fingers until she gasped with pleasure.

To his delight, she was moist and swollen with passion. With seductive expertise, he slipped his finger inside her to prepare the way for his invasion. The tightness of her virginal passage surprised him. He had hoped to break her maidenhead as painlessly as possible, but realized now there would be no way to avoid hurting her. With dread at the pain he was about to cause, he looked up at her face, and she read the concern in his eyes.

"Is there something wrong with me?" she asked in a voice filled with worry and fear.

"No, darling," he soothed with a deep rumble of laughter at her naïveté. "You're just incredibly small." He kissed her slowly, lingeringly as he moved his lips across her stomach and thighs.

When she realized his goal, she tried to push him away with an embarrassed cry. "Blade, you mustn't!"

Relentlessly, he caught her small hands in his own and imprisoned them against her hips. He lifted her to his mouth, teaching his bride the unbelievable heights of pure physical pleasure he could awaken within her. The moment he touched her with his tongue, she arched against him, and a long, low moan of erotic fulfillment rose from deep inside her as she felt the release of her yearning.

At her cry of all-consuming pleasure, he positioned himself between her slim thighs and immediately entered her, burying himself inside her with one swift thrust.

The incredible sweetness of her soft warmth sheathed him, building within Blade Stalker a throbbing, driving excitement that only the strength of his will kept from exploding inside her. With his weight braced on his elbows, he lay still above her, wanting her to become used to the tumescent feel of him inside her, waiting for the turmoil of the penetration to subside. Gently, gently, he kissed away the tears at the corners of her eyes. "It only hurts like that the first time, *nameo*. Now the pain is over with." He smiled down at his darling bride with all the tenderness he possessed. "It's just that you're so damn little."

"Or you're so big," she responded.

He laughed in complete and utter joy at her innocence. "God, how I've wanted you." Covering her mouth with his own, he thrust in and out with his tongue in a rhythm his body began to repeat. Under his skilled tutorship, she responded with a vibrant, natural eroticism, as she arched against his straining loins and moved her hips in time with his. At last she turned her head from his kiss, struggling for air, and he heard her quick, breathless panting in his ear. "Come with me, little wife," he encouraged, his voice rasping and hoarse with emotion. "You can have it all again. Just think about the pleasure while I love you."

A low, sweet cry of ecstasy sounded in his ear. Increasing his swift, strong strokes in faster rhythm, he found the release he sought in an explosion of sensation and spilled his life and his love deep inside her.

Theodora drifted in a mist of mindless enchantment. She was barely conscious of the weight of Blade Stalker's body pinning her to the bed, and the deep groan that shuddered through him came as only a faint sound in her ear. Wave after wave of shimmering ecstasy started from the spot where their bodies were so intimately coupled and moved out across her hips, thighs, and stomach. Her breasts were hard and full, and her nipples tightened as the shock waves of pleasure rippled through her.

In a daze she felt him lift her in his strong arms and turn them so they lay side by side, still joined together. She took a deep breath, wondering with an unknown tranquillity just when she had forgotten to breathe. Slowly, her heart ceased its pounding race, and she became aware that she was caressing the bunched muscles of her husband's back and shoulders and chest. Languorously, she moved her hands across his coppery skin, trailing her fingers over the scarred ridges left by the grizzly, burying her nails in the thick hair on his chest, and tracing the flat nipples with her fingertips. She slid one hand to his nape and gently kissed the hollow at the base of his neck. She tasted the taut skin across his collarbone with her tongue and breathed in the wonderful male smell of him, then buried her mouth and nose in the black, springy hair of his chest.

Fully conscious at last, she leaned her head back and looked into his eyes. "I didn't know," she confessed, as she touched her fingertips to his cheek.

He watched her with unutterable tenderness. "I know, sweetheart."

He kissed her. It was a kiss filled with the promise of complete possession. "You're my only love, Theodora. There'll never be another woman in my life or in my bed. The name given to you at birth is true. *Maheo* knew I would need a woman who could be both strong and tender. One with wisdom and insight. One who could help me bridge the two cultures I must live in. You are a gift to me from the Wise One Above. And I shall never let you go."

She knew what he wanted to hear her say. She loved him with a love that would last her lifetime, to death and beyond. An impossible, hopeless, endless love. Wanting desperately to tell him, still she held back. To go forward would be to hurl herself into a world of binding promises, ones she wasn't yet ready even to consider. Her throat ached with the pain of her strangled words. Her lips trembled as she forced herself to smile and adopt a light, bantering tone. "You promised to share your knowledge with me, Blade, but I had no idea you'd be such a marvelous instructor. You should have told me, for I'd never have waited so long."

His disappointment at her teasing reply touched her soul. Still buried within her, he rolled her on top of him, lifted her hips, and impaled her more firmly. He slid his hands up her ribs and cupped her breasts. Casually, he flicked her nipples until they were tight, pink buds, and the flame of desire ignited within her once again. He slid his fingers between their bodies, touching the folds of her swollen womanhood. She gasped at the wonderful, incredible feeling and arched her back, bracing her hands on his muscular thighs. As he watched her succumb to the surging, sensual need he aroused so easily within her, he answered her. His voice was rough-edged with irony. "How could I have suspected the prudish little spinster would be such a prize pupil?"

That morning everyone in the tribe took down their lodges and began the journey to the trappers' rendezvous at South Pass. Two Moons Rising and Snow Owl showed Theodora how to dismantle the tipi. They taught her to form a travois with the lodge poles, and then load the covering and furnishings on it. Theodora helped Two Moons Rising pack the sacks of pounded meat, dried roots, and berries she had stored to be used during the winter. Dried meat was wrapped and placed in parfleches, as were the lodge's household utensils.

Blade Stalker joined Bald Face Buffalo and Weasel Tail in the hunting and scouting party. During the day they would choose the evening's campsite and provide meat for the family. Theodora watched her husband ride out on War Shield with a feeling of longing. As they rode by, he looked over at her. She blushed and lowered her lashes, then looked back up to gaze at his broad back until he'd disappeared. The wonder of his lovemaking was vivid in her mind, and she had to force herself to attend to the rest of the packing.

Two days later they reached the bank of the North Platte, only a few miles above the Deer Creek crossing. They'd had blistering hot weather and traveled over rough terrain that had grown increasingly arid. Each evening, after the meal shared in Snow Owl's tent, Theodora and Blade Stalker had gone for a swim, then returned to their own tipi to make love.

The third morning Theodora awoke in her husband's arms. She snuggled against his hard frame, putting off the time of rising. She loved the marvelous feeling of lying beside him, the sensuous luxury of entwining her bare legs with his. Outside, the village was quiet, and she decided it wasn't as late as she'd thought. She peeked up at Blade to find he was also awake. "We'd better get up," she mumbled lazily against his furred chest.

"Mmm, later," he murmured into her hair. "There's no hurry. We're not traveling today. There's a storm coming."

She leaned up and propped her elbow on his ribs. "A storm? You must be joking. It hasn't rained for weeks in this rock garden. Probably not for months."

"Well, it's going to rain this afternoon." He yawned sleepily and slid his hand over her bottom in a gesture of self-satisfied ownership.

She shook her head in disbelief. "There wasn't a cloud in the sky yesterday. It must have been over one hundred degrees."

With an exaggerated sigh he lifted her on top of him. "Are you arguing with me, woman? Don't you know a Cheyenne

wife listens to her husband? This calls for serious punishment."
He bared his teeth in a snarl and growled like a bear. "How'd
you like me to bite off your nose?"

Theodora squealed with laughter. She'd heard of the horrible
custom, though she hadn't seen any proof of it. She pushed
against him in a vain attempt to rise. Her giggles filled the
tipi.

With a mock roar he turned her over and pinned her to the
fur robe. He placed his teeth on the bridge of her nose and
gently nipped. "Mmm," he teased as he licked his lips with
relish. "Your freckles taste like cinnamon." He rose up and
slid his hand to her breast, rolling the pliant pink crest between
his thumb and forefinger. "Now let's see if you have any more
I can taste."

She burst out laughing. "I don't have any freckles, and you
know it!"

One black eyebrow quirked in inquiry. "Want to bet?"

"Are you serious?" She stared at him in shock. At his
teasing look she pushed against his arms and sat up, in earnest
now. "Let me see." When he loosened his hold, she leapt up
and ran across the lodge to his saddlebags. Taking out the small
mirror he used whenever he shaved, she peered solemnly at
her reflection. Sure enough, across the bridge of her nose
marched a sprinkling of freckles!

"Oh, no!" she cried in horror. "I'm spotted!" Frantically,
she searched her shoulders, arms, and legs. Her fair skin had
at last turned a light golden brown from her exposure to the
sun, but there were no spots. She tried to check her back, to
no avail. The fact that her husband was howling with laughter
only made the search more frantic. "What about the back of
my neck and shoulders?" she asked him.

He sat crossed-legged on the bed. "Come here," he told
her, "and I'll look."

Obediently, she crossed the lodge to stand beside the fur-
covered mattress. She turned her back to him.

"Now let me see," Blade Stalker said with an air of complete seriousness. He reached up and explored her shoulder
blades with his work-hardened fingertips. "Looks okay here,"
he told her. He traced his strong hands across the small of her
back and waist with the thoroughness of a doctor examining

his patient. "This is all right too." Suddenly he cupped her buttocks in both large palms. "Wait," he called. "What's this?" He smacked one cheek with a noisy kiss. "Aha," he cried triumphantly. "More cinnamon."

"You scoundrel!" she exclaimed over her shoulder, laughter bubbling within her. "That's a mole, and you know it!"

She turned and fell on him, pummeling him with her fists, while he roared with delight at her futile attempt to punish him.

Effortlessly he rolled her on her back and bent over her. He imprisoned her wrists, pinning them against the fur on either side of her head. When he bent to kiss her, she turned her face to avoid him, and her lips formed a petulant moue.

"You wouldn't want to kiss a woman who's all spotted," she told him.

He grabbed her chin and turned her face to his. He kissed her with thorough, ruthless, and total possession. "You're wrong," he informed her, his eyes twinkling. "I happen to love the taste of cinnamon."

"You kiss me again and I'll bite your tongue." She knew the laughter in her voice belied the sincerity of her warning, but she tried anyway. "We'll see how well you like the taste of your own blood."

"Oh ho!" he exclaimed. "A rebellious, hot-tempered wife. Maybe I should turn you over my knee right now." He lowered his hips and pressed seductively against her. "But I can think of something else I'd rather do instead."

"You wouldn't take advantage of my inferior strength, would you?" she taunted him.

A wicked, devastating grin swept across his bronzed features. "The hell I wouldn't." He nibbled her neck. "I'll tell you what. I was going to suggest a horseback ride this morning. Now you've got my mind on other things. Since you're feeling so feisty, I'll let you choose. We can stay in bed and make wild, passionate love, or go for a ride before the storm comes in."

"We'll go for a ride," she said with all the aloofness she could muster. She wasn't about to admit what she'd *rather* do, after he'd just laughed at her freckles and then threatened to spank her.

"Let's go," he said. He stood and offered his hand to pull her up. "The sooner we start, the sooner we'll be back. We can make love this afternoon while it's raining."

She couldn't help giggling at the leer he turned on her. "Leave it to you to get everything your own way in the end," she scolded him in mock severity.

They were dressed and tearing across the plains in minutes. Astride Spitfire, Theodora raced after her husband on his powerful stallion. Her unbound hair blew in the wind, the side braids with their rabbit fur ties slapping against her shoulders. The antelope-skin dress she wore was soft and pliable, perfect for riding, and her moccasins were like down on her feet. She rode without a saddle. Blade Stalker had taught her how to use her legs and feet to control the pony. The freedom she felt was like nothing she'd known before. She knew he was right. She would never be the same again. The joy of living so unfettered was remarkable. To be able to gallop across the plains astride an Indian pony, to swim naked with her husband under the stars, to learn under his guidance the incredible pleasure of their marriage bed in the peaceful solitude of their lodge—all these enjoyable things must be given up once the expedition was over.

The thought of going home to her sedate life in Cambridge, where she would be expected to follow the rigid conventions of white society, was unsettling. Ruthlessly she squelched the tiny doubt that the first priority in her life would be to return to Massachusetts and her work. She had commitments to keep, despite her personal feelings. Her father was waiting to collaborate with her on the journal that Martin was to publish. With her grandmother's influence, she had been hired by the Linnean Society to lecture on her discoveries at Mount Holyoke the first winter after her return. And with the wealth of botanical specimens she'd collected, it was possible she would even be asked to share her research with the naturalists on the Harvard faculty. How could she possibly tell her family that she no longer wanted to pursue a career as a botanist? That she'd met and fallen in love with a cavalry officer who was half Cheyenne? Good Lord, that she felt part Cheyenne herself! She wouldn't give up her dream, and she couldn't take Blade back with her to the quiet, sedate world of the scholar. He'd be as out of place in Cambridge as a pious monk in a brothel.

Blade Stalker and Theodora splashed across a creekbed and rode up the bluffs that followed the river. They dismounted and gazed westward toward the mountains.

"How far to South Pass?" she asked as she slipped her arm around his waist and leaned her head on his shoulder.

"At least a week. Maybe ten days. It'll depend on the weather."

"We're running very late, aren't we?"

He looked down at her, and she could see the worry in his eyes. "We're a little behind. We'll make up for it when we leave the rendezvous."

He wouldn't say it, but she knew it was all her fault. He'd been swept off course while saving her from the stampede that had cost Baptiste Lejeunesse his life. They'd lost more precious days when he'd been mauled by the grizzly bear. Now, if it weren't for her, he'd be traveling alone, halving the time it would take to reach the expedition.

"I'm sorry I've made such a mess of things. If it weren't for me, you'd be in South Pass with the rest of them and right on schedule."

He slammed her up against him. Bending, he kissed her roughly. "I wouldn't give up this past week for anything in the world, Theodora. I don't want to hear you talking like that again. Understand?"

She nodded happily and slipped her arms around his neck. She laid her head against his chest. "Yes, dear," she said in her most submissive voice.

With a laugh he lifted her in his arms and carried her toward Spitfire. "Come on, dutiful, docile, and well-behaved wife. Let's go back to the lodge."

By midday the storm rolled in with black clouds, thunder, and lightning, just as Blade Stalker had predicted. But inside the lodge it was cozy and warm. They lunched on pemmican and fresh berries. Theodora made a hot tea from herbs, and they sipped it as they listened to the rain pounding on the tipi. She expected company during the day, but he assured her that no one would think of visiting newlyweds without an invitation.

Blade Stalker sat on the bed, propped against a comfortable

backrest. He watched her clean and stack the bowls of pottery they'd used. At a gigantic crash of thunder, she jumped nervously and nearly dropped them.

"Come here and relax, *vehona*," he called softly to her.

With a tender smile she came immediately.

Pulling her slowly on top of him, he spread her legs apart so she sat astride him.

She stretched forward and rested her chin on the top of his head. "I like being taller than you," she teased, leaning back to look at him.

"It can have its benefits," he quipped. "Did you enjoy the ride?" He slid his hands under the fringe of her hem and caressed her thighs.

"It was delightful." She looked at him questioningly, as though trying to understand where he was leading. "Spitfire is so well trained, I hardly need to guide her. And she follows after War Shield like a puppy."

With deliberate movements he slid his hands under her dress and lifted it up over her head. He spread her tousled curls about her shoulders, letting them drift through his fingers. He brushed her bare breasts with the backs of his hands, then spoke to her, low and beguiling. "I thought you might want to go for another ride this afternoon."

Comprehension dawned on her. "But it's raining out," she told him primly, trying not to smile.

"You'll find me very well trained. You'll hardly need to guide me." He lifted her up with ease, and she realized he'd already removed his breechclout. Slowly, surely, seductively, he guided her back down on his rigid shaft.

His throbbing entry brought a cry of delight to Theodora's lips. He leaned forward and suckled her breast, and she buried her fingers in his thick hair and held him to her. With a deep sigh, she closed her eyes and circled her hips against his loins, enjoying the exquisite sensations.

He tipped his head back. "Open your eyes, *nameo*, my lover, and look at me." When she gazed into his passion-filled eyes, he continued in a thick, husky voice. "Look at me, Theodora, and know that I belong to you. Just as I am inside you now, you are inside me. You have walked in my soul, little white woman. We are one."

Drowning in wave after wave of pleasure, she rested her hands on his solid shoulders. "Blade Stalker . . . I . . ."

He moved only slightly, heightening her pleasure.

Whimpering with desire, she never took her eyes from his. "I . . ."

"Say it, *nazheem*, my wife. Tell me what you feel for me."

With trembling fingers she took his handsome face in her hands, awed by the overwhelming emotions he could ignite within her. "I love you, *nahyam*, my husband," she said, wonder and happiness in her voice.

His heavy-lidded eyes flashed with joy and triumph. "I love you, too, princess."

Chapter 23

Eight days later, on the eighth of August, Blade Stalker's tribe reached South Pass, located at the southern end of the Wind River Range, where the trail crossed the Continental Divide. To Theodora's fellow nomads, the pass was scarcely momentous. To her it was a fundamental watershed. Somewhere in that twelve-mile stretch of mesquite plains, she left the United States and entered Oregon Territory.

Blade seemed to understand her excitement, but Theodora hoped that he remained unaware of her growing nervousness. She was encountering vistas seen by no other white woman, except perhaps the two missionary wives who were reported to be traveling ahead of them. And she was seeing it through the eyes of a trained naturalist.

Yet the thrill of each day's discovery was edged with growing confusion. With every mile they drew closer to the rendezvous and the time when she must tell Blade that, although she loved him, she couldn't possibly marry him. She deeply regretted the words of love she'd confessed that stormy afternoon, for since that moment he had demonstrated in every way that he hadn't been speaking figuratively when he told her she belonged to him, that they were one. And that realization filled her with fear for the future, when their paths must diverge.

Bit by bit, she had come to realize that he'd meant every word in its most literal sense: *She belonged to him.* Not in the way he owned his horse or his gun, but rather as though she were actually a part of him. His care of her was natural and effortless. Instinctively, she knew he would no more hurt her,

311

or allow her to come to harm, than he would cut off his own hand. With a growing sense of panic she recalled the words he'd spoken when he'd first made love to her: *I will never let you go*.

Yet when the expedition was over, he *must* let her go. She must return to her family and the course in life she'd already chosen.

At last the trail left the Sweetwater and they camped at Pacific Spring. That evening, after sharing a meal with Chief Painted Robe and Snow Owl, instead of walking her to their lodge, Blade led Theodora down to the creek. He sat on a boulder and pulled her to him. Holding her thighs securely between his knees, he captured her hips with his hands. "Now suppose you tell me what's been bothering you for the last two days."

She looked down at him, then glanced away. She'd been dreading this conversation, hoping to put it off until they arrived at Horse Creek. But apparently he wasn't about to let her keep her thoughts, or her worries, to herself.

"Come on, out with it," he insisted. "You haven't said three words to me this evening. Something has you tied up in knots."

Forcing herself to meet his determined gaze, she ran her fingertips up his arms and rested them on his wide shoulders. She bent her head and stared at the dark hair at the base of his neck. "It's just that I'm starting to regret every mile that brings us closer to the expedition. Our time together has been so wonderful."

His forehead creased in a brief frown. "When we join the others, we'll be very busy, but it doesn't mean we won't have some moments to ourselves, Theodora." He flashed her a teasing smile. "We'll still have our nights together."

She squared her shoulders and cleared her throat nervously. "No, we won't, Blade. When we reach the rest of the party, I'll be sleeping in my own tent. Alone."

"The hell you will," he snarled. He rose and towered over her, his hands capturing her waist in a fierce grip.

She shook her head in frustration at his unwillingness to listen to her explanation. "These last few days have been more than wonderful. They've been a blissful idyl, a romantic daydream that I'll treasure all my life. But when we reach the rendezvous, we return to the real world and the dream will be over. Once again I'll be the expedition's naturalist—its spinster naturalist.''

His rugged features turned to granite. His strong chin jutted out ominously. ''So that's all this has been for you. A romantic interlude. And when you said you loved me? Was that just a fantasy too?''

A flush crept up her neck and suffused her cheeks at the lie she was about to tell. It would be better to let him believe she didn't love him. He'd be so angry that he'd refuse to have anything to do with her. She lowered her lids, unable to meet his irate gaze. ''Sometimes, in the throes of passion, people say things they later regret.''

''Well, I'm sorry to disillusion you, princess, but it's been a helluva lot more to me than just a brief affair.'' He slid his hands possessively up her waist to hold her under her arms, where his thumbs pinioned the sides of her breasts. ''Theodora, I'm going to say this once and I'm not going to say it again. You are my wife. *Nihehtametove*: I am your husband. We are married.''

She pushed against his solid chest. ''Maybe to you we're married. To your grandfather and your cousins and all your tribe, we're married. But not in the white world to which we return. And if you recall, I never agreed to a real marriage. I went along with the Cheyenne wedding because I had to. But I spoke no vows. I made no promises. And until we do have a clergyman and a written document, we're not really married.''

''Bullshit.'' A muscle leapt in his taut jaw. Turning her around, he grabbed her elbow and started toward camp.

She pulled frantically against him. ''Wait a minute! We need to talk about this reasonably.''

He skidded to a halt. Jerking her off her feet, he held her up so they looked eye to eye. He was furious. ''Do you think my mother wasn't married to my father? Or Two Moons Rising isn't married to Weasel Tail? Theodora, there are millions of people in the world who don't have a Protestant minister lead them in their vows. And they're still married. But if we find those ministers at the rendezvous, we're going to go through two ceremonies, just to nail it down." He set her back on the ground.

She jerked her chin up. "You can't dictate what I will or won't do, Blade. And you can't force me to be your wife against my wishes."

His voice was a low roar as he grabbed the back of her neck and roughly jerked her to him. "By God, I don't know whether to throttle the daylights out of you or blister your little backside." He shook his head in exasperation. At her unblinking stare he drew a long, harsh breath and expelled it slowly. His words were low and crisp. "Listen, wife. Even though we're already married, I intend to go through every ceremony available until I get it through your stubborn head that you belong to me. Permanently. If we meet a Buddhist monk on the way to Horse Creek, he's going to preside at a wedding and recite verses from the *Dhammapada*. If we happen to run across a Hindu priest out here, he'll write the vows down in Sanskrit, and you'll sign them. If we discover a Muslim mullah packing a load of beaver pelts, he's going to pray over us from the *Koran*. And when we get back east, I'm going to dress up in a cutaway suit and walk you down the longest aisle in the biggest cathedral in New Orleans." Increasing the pressure on her neck, he bent his head and drew her even closer until they were nose to nose. "But in the meantime just remember, princess, that *I am your husband*."

Without waiting for her reply, he swooped her up, threw her over his shoulder, and carried her to their lodge. Inside, he tossed her on the furry bed and made love to her, roughly and possessively, approaching a savagery he'd never shown her before. He stilled her protests with his mouth and worked his magic with his hands until she was writhing beneath him in mindless passion, all thoughts of a calm, rational discussion soaring to the roof hole of their tipi with her spiraling climax.

There was no white blood in him that night. He was all Indian. Silent and ferocious and dominating. Again and again, through the long, quiet hours, he took her until she was spent and exhausted and moved beneath his hands like a limp, sated doll. At last she fell asleep, sprawled atop him and still impaled on his rigid manhood.

* * *

The tribe rode for two days through sun and wind toward the great river that the trappers called the Siskadee. The sterility of the sagebrush flat was horrible. Every puff of the hot wind blew a whitish, caustic dust on the travelers, and Theodora wondered absently if she could ever repair her dry, cracked skin. The alkaline springs they passed were poisonous to animals, and the horses could not be allowed to graze near them or drink the water. Still silent and angry, Blade spent most of the second day at her side as they passed through this wasteland, while Bald Face Buffalo and Weasel Tail rode ahead to tell the expedition of their arrival.

By mid-afternoon the two Cheyenne braves returned. Riding with them at a furious pace came Zeke Conyers and Louis Chardonnais. They shouted and fired their guns as they approached. Chardonnais had tied a piece of white shirting to his rifle and waved it like a flag. Across the distance came the piercing cry of a war whoop, then another. Behind them, but coming up fast at a dead gallop, was Sergeant O'Fallon and a small detachment of dragoons.

Like an Indian war party the advance group raced in zigzag fashion right up to the column, firing volley after volley over their heads, jumping their mounts over clumps of sagebrush, and whooping in glee. When they reached Blade and Theodora, they skidded to a halt and leaped from their saddles, while their horses bucked and curveted in the excitement.

Zeke was the first one to reach them. "Well, I'll be!" he shouted at Blade, who'd already dismounted and helped Theodora down. "Tarnation, you old hoss, yore a sight for sore eyes." He pounded Blade's shoulder with one fist while he clasped his hand with the other. Then he gripped him in a fierce hug. He turned to Theodora, his arm still around Blade's shoulder. "By gor, lookee hyar! A yellow-headed In'jun gal!"

Theodora broke into a wide smile at his open display of joy. "Oh, Zeke," she exclaimed. "It's so good to see you again." Impulsively, she threw her arms around his thin shoulders, then placed a smack on the coarse gray beard that covered his cheek.

Clearly flustered by her open display of affection, he returned her embrace. "By the eternal, if this don't beat all," he said.

Then Chardonnais stood beside them, and the whole scene

was repeated in French. By the time Theodora had welcomed him, Sergeant O'Fallon and five dragoons had arrived.

"Sure and it's our little *mavourneen*," he shouted from his saddle, his gravelly voice filled with happiness. He dismounted and took her small hand in his big one. "Why, miss," he boomed, "Why, miss, I could just hug you me ownself."

She opened her arms wide. "Then come get your hug, Michael O'Fallon."

They arrived at the rendezvous site in the valley of the Green River, the very heart of the mountain fur trade, in a procession of triumph. Escorted by Conyers and Chardonnais on either side, Theodora rode next to Blade. The French trapper and the Kentuckian seemed to know immediately what her new status was, and Louis even addressed her once as Madame Roberts. But she could tell by the inquisitive looks on the dragoons' faces that they were mystified by her costume.

As they drew near, Theodora saw a scene that was a combined country fair and harvest festival. Along the Green and its creeks, tents and lodges spread for over two miles. There was a mixture of whites, mostly free trappers, and Indians from nearly every tribe in the Rocky Mountains. Squaws moved among them, curing robes, decorating lodge skins, mending clothes and gear, putting up pemmican, and butchering and preparing the meat that the men brought into camp. Some of the men were seated on blankets and robes, gambling at cards. Others were catching up on the winter's news, reading faded newspapers and renewing old friendships. A horse race was being held in a nearby meadow, with the usual betting and hollering. Not far away a target shoot was in progress.

From in front of their row of military tents, the members of the expedition stood and watched Blade and Theodora ride in. As they drew closer, Theodora could see Peter Haintzelman standing beside Wesley Fletcher.

"Blade!" A tall trapper, dressed in buckskins and with a long, thick black beard sprinted toward them just before they reached the tents. He was an enormous man. Jumping up, he grabbed Blade and pulled him down off War Shield in one fell swoop. With a wild hunting cry he wrestled Blade to the ground. Together they rolled in the dust. Then the man lifted

Blade and pounded him on the back. "Blade!" he roared again. He grabbed the captain by the sides of his head, his fingers locked in his thick hair, and bussed him loudly on the lips.

Theodora watched in astonishment, for Blade was actually laughing out loud.

"*Mon père*," Blade admonished through his deep chuckles, "you'll frighten my bride."

"Your bride!" the man shouted. "Let me look at her!" He turned and sprinted over to Spitfire. Without warning he reached up, lifted Theodora off the pony's back, and held her high in the air over his head. In his enormous hands, three feet off the ground, she felt as small as a five-year-old. "*Mon Dieu*, look at the size of her!" With surprising gentleness for his huge frame, he set her down. His booming voice was filled with reproach. "Son, you should have waited for her to grow up."

Blade grinned and shook his head. "She's fully grown, *mon père*. That's the biggest she's ever going to get." His eyes twinkled with hilarity as he turned to Theodora. "As you've probably already guessed, sweetheart, this old mountain reprobate is my father, Jacques Roberts."

Theodora gazed up in awe at her father-in-law. She thought by now she'd become used to big men. After all, her husband was well over six feet. But Jacques Roberts was a giant. Close to seven feet tall, he towered above her. His darkly tanned face was weatherbeaten, with deep furrows around the eyes that had been chiseled by the sun and wind. When he spoke, his roar seemed to shake the ground.

"I'm happy to meet you, Mr. Roberts," she said, and extended her hand in a polite greeting. "But, though we were forced by circumstances to go through a wedding ceremony in the Cheyenne village, Blade and I are not actually married." She refused to meet Blade's gaze, knowing the anger she would see there.

"Are the missionaries still here, *mon père*?" interjected Blade, the steel in his voice giving Theodora no doubt as to his intent.

"The missionaries?" Jacques yelled back and she cringed. Did the man never speak in a normal voice? "Why, they've been gone for over two weeks now." He turned and thumped his son on the back. "Congratulations, Blade. Maybe I'll live to see some grandchildren yet."

The mention of children was all she needed to destroy her composure. She realized there was a possibility that she had conceived a child, but his putting the thought into words brought stark terror to her heart. If she were pregnant with Blade's child, she would be bound to him irrevocably.

Someone cleared his throat behind her, and Theodora turned to find Lieutenant Haintzelman. "Peter," she exclaimed, and hugged him warmly. In a way he had taken Tom's place during that awful time after her brother's death, when she hadn't cared whether she lived or died. With sincere affection, she pressed her head against his shoulder.

"Teddy, we were afraid we'd never see you again. Either of you." Behind his glasses, there were tears in his sincere blue eyes. Releasing her, he reached out and clasped Blade's hand. "Welcome back, sir."

"It's good to be back, Lieutenant." Blade had stepped closer to take Peter's hand. He slipped his arm possessively around Theodora's waist and looked behind the young man. "Lieutenant Fletcher, I trust everything has gone smoothly?"

If the others had been amazed to see them alive, Wesley Fletcher was incredulous. For a moment he seemed too dazed to answer. With an obvious effort he saluted formally. "Y'll find everythin' in order, Captain. I was just overseein' the preparations for tomorrow's departure. We were leavin' for the East in the mornin'." Though he spoke to Blade, he stared at Theodora, taking in the fringed dress with its beads and quilling, the moccasins, and the side braids with their rabbit fur trim. Clearly appalled, he watched her with eyes that seemed to condemn her outright.

"You were going to do what, Lieutenant?" Blade snapped, his voice cold and hard. He released his wife and moved to within inches of him.

In a reflex action Fletcher stepped back. "With you and Miz Gordon lost, I could see no point in continuin', sir, since the purpose of the journey was t'map the mountain pass through the Sierras, if there is one. Without either cartographer, it would've been senseless t' go on. I just finished conferrin' with Captain Bonniville, and he agreed."

"Bonniville is here, then?"

Peter spoke up. "Yes, sir. He's in your tent right now."

The captain moved to go and Theodora caught his arm. "Blade, I need to speak to you for a moment."

"It'll have to wait, *vehona*," he replied as he took her hand and squeezed it. "I need to talk to Bonniville immediately." He glanced at Peter. "See that my wife has what she needs. She'll want to clean up and rest for a while. And have my personal belongings moved to her tent." He nodded to his brother. "I'll see you at dinner."

"We'll have a celebration," Jacques shouted. "Where's Chief Painted Robe? I think I'll make a call on my father-in-law."

Before she could say another word, Blade was gone, Lieutenant Fletcher and Zeke Conyers hurrying after him.

Although many of the trappers and Indians had already left Horse Creek, a considerable number remained at the rendezvous site. Over a thousand Indians of various tribes were camped up and down the Green River in a temporary truce. Many of them swarmed about the traders' liquor tents and low counters. They chattered and swore as they attempted to barter the skins and robes prepared by their women, the horses they'd stolen or trained, and sometimes even the women themselves. Red and white, the men boasted and haggled as they attempted to reprovision their outfits for the coming winter.

In the captain's tent six men sat around the collapsible map table. At one end was Blade, at the other Benjamin Bonniville, while Zeke Conyers and Louis Chardonnais sat across from Lieutenant Fletcher and Sergeant O'Fallon. Blade questioned each of his men one by one, in rapid-fire order. No detail of their trip from Fort Laramie was left undiscussed. Satisfied at last, Blade turned to look at the thickset man at the far end of the table.

Still addressed as captain, although he was actually on leave from the army, Bonniville was the owner of a nearby fort. He'd been in the mountains for the last five years, attempting to build up a profitable business in the fur trade. But he'd come late to the trade, when the beaver had been nearly played out. Each year the profits were smaller and the hazards greater as the trappers were forced to probe farther and farther into the land of the Blackfoot. Still, that didn't seem to bother Bonniville, who appeared totally involved in reading the sheaf of papers Blade had handed him.

Finished, he looked up. "Now that you're here, Captain, we can forget about the expedition leaving tomorrow. And you won't be returning east as Lieutenant Fletcher planned." Bonniville spread his pudgy fingers across the map and tapped it restlessly.

"We'll leave the day after tomorrow," Blade told him. He leaned back and drew on his cheroot with satisfaction. "And we'll be going west."

"You can leave so soon?"

"We have to. We've lost almost two weeks as it is. I want to get these men moving before the dragoons start to get cold feet from sitting around with nothing to do but think. The fainthearted are going to be mighty disappointed when we tell them tonight that they're not heading for home in the morning. Besides, winter comes early in the Sierras."

"I reckon we can stop in B'ar Valley to ready our outfittin's," Zeke interjected. "We'll pick up more horses and meat thar."

"*Oui*," Chardonnais agreed. "Many of the trappers have already left the rendezvous. Watching them go was hard on the ones left behind. The sooner we move out, the better all the men will feel."

"Is this really the best plan, gentlemen?" Fletcher cautioned. "The soldiers have been waiting here for over a week with the expectation that they'd soon be returning to Fort Leavenworth. Can you really tell them now that the dangerous part of the journey is only beginning?"

"The dragoons will take orders, just like every man here, Lieutenant," Blade said preemptively. He ignored Fletcher's sudden stiffening and turned to Conyers. "Now, let's take a look at that map, Zeke, and see what the best route is going to be. Then I want orders issued for every man to recheck his gear. We'll be provisioning from Bonniville's stores." He turned to Bonniville. "I assume you brought supplies from your fort?"

At his nod Blade continued. "Good. Zeke, you and Char-

onnais go over the list with the sergeant. I want everyone to
ave a full pack and a working rifle. And lots of ammunition.
Ve have to move fast and we can't leave anything to chance.
Iow, what do you think of this route, Zeke?" He pointed to
ae map and the two bent over it.

Suddenly the men at the table fell silent. Blade looked up
o find Theodora standing just inside the tent. She had changed
nto her yellow cotton dress. The wide skirt, with its yards of
abric, fell in graceful folds to her dainty feet, which were now
ncased in proper shoes. Her brilliant curls were bound on top
f her head with a yellow ribbon.

"Blade, I have to talk to you," she said as she twisted her
aands nervously in front of her.

He spoke to her softly, trying to hide his impatience. "Theo-
lora, we're very busy. It'll have to wait till later."

"It can't wait, Blade. I must talk to you now." Her green
eyes were huge with concern.

He set his cheroot on the edge of the table and nodded to
he men. "Continue working on the route, Zeke. I'll be right
back."

Taking his wife's elbow, he led her out of the tent. As they
bent and went through the open flap, it seemed to Blade that
she pulled her skirts carefully away from him, fearful that she'd
brush against him and get her clothes dirty. He was still dressed
in the dusty, fringed deerskin shirt, breechclout, and leggings
he'd arrived in. So the honeymoon was over, he thought. He
stood next to her and inhaled the sweet scent of wildflowers
wafting up from her freshly washed hair. He knew he smelled
of sweat and leather and horses.

"What's so important?" He didn't need to be so curt with
her, but the fact that she'd pulled away so fastidiously made
him want to pick her up and shake her. Then slam her up
against himself, dirt and all, and kiss her until she forgot what
it was she'd come to talk about in the first place.

"They've moved your things into my tent, Blade. This just
isn't going to work. I need some time to think the whole thing
through. I've spent years studying to achieve my status as a
scientist. Years spent dreaming of being able to contribute to
the knowledge of the flora and fauna of this country. I'm not
ready to throw it all away—"

"On some Cheyenne half-breed," he finished for her.

"That's not what I was going to say."

"No, you'd never put it in such plain language, but it's wha
you meant." He folded his arms to keep his hands off her.

"The fact that you're part Indian has nothing to do with it,
Blade, and you know it. It's our whole future that's the problem. My life is going in one direction, yours in another. You'll
spend the next ten years mapping the wilderness. You said it
once yourself—I don't belong out here."

He expelled a harsh breath and shook his head. "I couldn't
have been more wrong, Theodora, and I admit it. Look at you.
You're not only surviving on the plains, you're thriving.
You're more vibrant, more alive, more filled with a sense of
purpose than any woman I've ever known. You belong out
here with me, Theodora, not in some stuffy college lecture
hall, and not in some cramped, confined research library. Don't
just talk about life. Live it, *vehoka*! And live it with me."

"I can't. Not yet, anyway. When I'm with you, Blade, you
destroy all my attempts to make calm, rational decisions. You
turn my firm resolutions into indecisiveness. I refuse to be
controlled by my emotions, especially when they're in such a
constant state of turmoil. And until I have time to think it
through, I cannot agree to our getting married."

"Goddammit! We *are* married! Theodora, I can't stand here
and argue about this now. There's too much that has to be
done before we pull out." Realizing he was shouting, Blade
looked around in frustration. "Where the hell is Haintzelman?
I told him to look after you."

"He walked me to your tent, Captain Roberts, when I said
I wanted to talk to you. I guess he felt I was safe once I was
there. But then, *he's* a gentleman. He wouldn't understand a
man like you. And there's no need to resort to profanity. Go
back to your business, if it's so important. I'll leave you alone.
Permanently."

"Haintzelman!" Blade bellowed. The lieutenant appeared
on the run. "Take my wife and see if she can help Twiggs
prepare the mess. It'll keep her out of trouble while I'm busy."

"Yes, sir." Peter turned to lead Theodora away.

"Oh, and Lieutenant," he called after them, his voice deceptively calm once more, "stay with her this time or you'll find yourself in charge of the pack mules right alongside Wesley Fletcher."

Chapter 24

Lieutenant Wesley Fletcher crossed the wide meadow beside Horse Creek, heading for the Snake camp. He was in a cold rage. Just when he believed he'd seen the last of Blade Roberts, the bastard showed up with that blond witch beside him. Certain that the two had not survived the buffalo stampede he'd so cleverly started, Fletcher had succeeded during the past week in convincing Benjamin Bonniville that there was no reason to continue the expedition without its topographical engineer or its naturalist. Fletcher's goal—to take Roberts's command back to Fort Leavenworth in such disrepute that the failure would leave a stain on the arrogant captain's military career even after his death—had been just within reach, only to be snatched away once again. And he, Fletcher, who'd been unjustly passed over for promotion time after time, while that half-breed was given medals and commendations, was once more second-in-command to a filthy, no-account Indian.

Even worse, the mission still stood. And, God knows, it hadn't been for his lack of trying to wreck it. He'd split the strap on Theodora Gordon's saddle and, incredibly, Roberts had managed to pull her out of the flood-swollen Big Blue River alive. Against all odds, the cunning breed had killed the rattlesnake planted in her tent at Laramie.

He'd used the arsenic he'd brought along, a poison that he'd discovered produced symptoms similar to cholera, with better results. He'd managed to rid the expedition of Tom Gordon, one of its most important members. But even the loss of the young cartographer hadn't stopped Roberts. Eventually,

Fletcher vowed silently to himself, the old score between them would be settled.

The lieutenant entered a Snake tipi with a blue crescent moon over its door and stared at the huge mountain man sitting on a filthy blanket. As he waited for his eyesight to adjust to the dim shelter, he noticed a young Indian woman who sat quietly in the far corner.

"H'yar, come on an' sit down, sol'jur," the trapper said, his mountain speech distorted by the large wad of chewing tobacco in his mouth. He spit a stream of it on the cook fire and grunted as Fletcher lowered himself to the dirt floor. "Ya got a job fer me?" the man continued.

"It's private," Fletcher snapped, his eyes once more searching out the woman, who was sewing quills on a fringed deerskin shirt.

"Naw, don't pay no mind ta her," his host replied with a wave of his beefy hand. "She cain't speak nary a word of English."

Fletcher raised his brows at the preposterous idea that what the trapper spoke could possibly be labeled English, then shrugged. "I understand you're in need of some ready cash, Shrady. If you're not overly fussy about how y' earn it, we might just work somethin' out."

Shrady grinned, revealing yellowed teeth with a gaping hole in the front. He scratched his shaggy beard. "Ya jest tell me what ya want, sol'jur. Big Joe'll have it done, quicker 'n a cat can lick his whiskers."

"I want a woman killed. Make it look like a simple rape that got a little too rough. Your best bet is t' beat her up some, stick it to her, and then break her neck. I'll pay y' a hundred dollars if it looks as though the death was accidental."

The mountain man whistled under his breath and rubbed his hands like a miser counting his gold. "Gimme the hun'erd up front an' yer on."

Fletcher reached into his tunic and pulled out the bills. "I'll throw in an extra five for the woman over there."

Shrady shrugged, glanced over his shoulder, then back to Fletcher. "Whar's the squaw ya want killed?"

"She's no squaw. It's the white woman who rode int' camp this afternoon."

"Shit!" Big Joe's eyes were wide with alarm. "That's Roberts's woman. Yer crazy, man! I ain't gonna do this for no hun'erd bucks."

Fletcher clenched his teeth to hold back the obscenity that sprang to his lips. "Someone told me you were the toughest man at the rendezvous, Shrady. I guess someone was wrong."

The trapper rose to tower over him. "I didn't say I wouldn't do it, sol'jur. I jest said it was gonna cost ya a sight more'n you'd planned. Make it two hun'erd, and that li'l blonde'll never see mornin'."

Fletcher stood and nodded reluctantly. "Okay, Shrady. I'll give y' the rest when it's done. But do it right." He turned and faced the woman sitting on a fur mattress. Never taking his eyes off her, he added, "Now get out of here."

Shrady shoved the bills into a leather pouch hanging from his neck, slipped the pouch back under his shirt, and left the tent.

"Come here," Fletcher called quietly to the squaw. He remembered it was said that Snake women were the prettiest females in the mountains.

Somewhere in her mid-twenties, this one was slim, with dainty feet and hands, and a smooth, clear complexion decorated with an intricate pattern of scarlet paint. She rose with a questioning smile and spoke to him in the Snake dialect as he approached her.

With a feeling of satisfaction, Fletcher smashed his fist into her mouth, knocking her flat on the dirt floor. After slowly removing his belt, he unbuttoned his pants and yanked them off. "I don't need t' hear that damn gibberish when I'm takin' y'," he warned her, though she'd probably understood his first message clear enough. "I don't need t' be reminded that you're nothin' but a filthy squaw."

She rose, a trickle of blood oozing from one corner of her mouth. Her small knife flashed in the dim tent.

"Why, y' little whore," he breathed. She sprang at him. He caught her wrist and twisted the weapon from her slim fingers. Then he shoved her down on the mattress, scooped up the knife, and split her dress down the front in one neat slice. Hurling the blade across the tipi, he fell on top of her.

As he rode her, hard and mean, he closed his eyes and imagined that it was a head of golden curls that lay beneath him on the bearskin robe. Then he slowly strangled the life out of her while he climaxed.

Neither Blade nor his staff or guest joined the others for mess late that afternoon. Even the chastised Lieutenant Haintzelman, who was replaced by Basil Guion as Theodora's watchdog, ate with his commanding officer in the captain's tent.

Twiggs had been overjoyed to see Theodora. He took her hands in his gnarled brown ones and held her in front of him. "Miss Theo fine sight. Never been so worried. Knew Captain was with you. Still worried."

She threw her arms around his waist and hugged him. "Thank you, Julius. But your worries were all for nothing, as you can see."

He grinned in sincere thankfulness, his cocoa-colored eyes bright with joy. "Only Captain save you."

Abashed, Theodora looked down at the tips of her shoes. Twiggs was right. Only Blade could have rescued her.

She helped Twiggs and Private Belknap prepare the roasted buffalo ribs. There was also the meat of antelope and red deer, which abounded in the mountains. The two cooks carried the tin dishes into the captain's tent, while Theodora dished out the food to the other members of the expedition. She avoided Blade, for she'd no intention of facing him in front of the others. When the cleanup was done, she retired to her own tent. She wanted to be by herself to sort out her feelings.

"You don't have to wait around, Basil," she told the French Canadian, who now followed her everywhere she went. "I'm going to retire early."

Guion smiled broadly at her as he rubbed his pudgy hand across his thinning hair. "I'll be right here beside the tent, Madame Roberts."

The title startled her. She spoke to him earnestly in a low voice, conscious of the dragoons who lounged around the campfire nearby. "I'll be using my own tent, Basil, now that we're back with the expedition. And I'd appreciate it if you'd call me 'Miss Gordon.'"

Guion gave a Gallic shrug, clearly unconcerned by her plight. "*Oui*, Madame. Where you sleep is the captain's business, not mine. But I will be right outside your tent, if you need anything."

"Thank you, Basil." Ignoring his phlegmatic statement, Theodora nervously looked around, only to find a burly mountain man standing close by. It was clear he'd been listening to every word.

Inside her tent, Theodora sank down on her bedroll. Peter had seen to it that someone had put up her tent and unpacked her gear before she'd even arrived at camp. As Blade had ordered, his own belongings had been carried in and stacked along one side. One by one, she checked her own packs. With relief, she discovered her specimens were all in order, just as she'd left them. Her journal as well. She put on her long white nightgown. The luxury of sleeping in cotton lace that night would raise her spirits. Nostalgic, she thought of her days in the Cheyenne village and of Snow Owl, whom she hadn't seen since they'd arrived and the Indian woman had been reunited with her trapper husband.

Outside, the bivouac grew noisier with the sounds of gaming, betting, bartering, and even courting. Theodora concentrated on writing in her diary, for she wanted to put down what had happened during her stay in the Indian village, excluding the moments of intimacy between her and Blade.

The light coming through the tent opening gradually faded, and she laid the papers aside. The noise outside continued to rise until, curious, she pulled her robe on over the gown and peeked out the flap.

In front of her shelter Basil Guion sat on a striped Hudson blanket. Parts of his musket were laid out beside him in neat rows. When he turned and saw her, he stood.

"Is there something you need, Madame?" he asked, his brown eyes concerned. He was a stocky man, shorter even than she.

"No, I just wanted to see what all the noise was about."

"The trappers are wild tonight, but don't mind them. They're having their last bit of fun before they start into the mountains. They will be alone all winter, except for their squaws and children."

"Thanks, Basil," she said with a nod of understanding. "I'm going to retire for the night. I won't bother you again."

Just as she moved to lower the flap, she once again saw the trapper who'd been listening to them earlier. His wide shoulders were propped against a nearby tree. He was a large, thickset man in dirty buckskins. His dark brown hair and beard were long and unkempt. When he saw she'd noticed him, he pushed away from the tree and shoved his filthy hat back on his head. His grin was marred by a large gap where he'd lost a front tooth. She shuddered at the leer he gave her before he turned and sauntered away. Drawing back inside, she quickly closed the tent flap.

Theodora spread a bearskin robe across her bedroll; she'd become accustomed to the luxurious feel of the soft fur while she slept. As she smoothed it out, she heard someone enter the tent. Certain it was Blade, she didn't even turn around. "You can just go on back to your own tent, Captain Roberts," she snapped. "I'll be perfectly comfortable here. I wouldn't want to take up any more of your precious time."

"H'yar now, little girlie. Shrady can give ya all the time ya need."

She whirled to find the mountain man who'd been watching her earlier. He had just dropped the tent flap. As she rose, he moved over to her and clasped her elbow. "Get out of here," she ordered in a loud voice, certain that Guion would rush in when he heard her.

Shrady lifted a dirty hand and grabbed her hair. "Since ya don't want the captain no more, I'm gonna claim ya for m'self. I liked ya even better dressed like a little Shian gal, but you'll do all right this'a way."

She could smell the liquor on his fetid breath and turned her head as she willed herself not to gag. When she tried to scream, he clamped his greasy fingers across her mouth to muffle the sound. Where was Guion? she wondered frantically.

The man held one huge hand over her lips and yanked on her hair with the other, jerking her down on the soft bearskin. "Be quiet," he snarled, "or I'll have ta get rough." He pinned her to the bed with his knee.

She stared up into his bloodshot eyes in horror and realized he was stone, cold sober. He might have had a cup of whiskey earlier that evening, but he was in complete control of his senses now.

"Yer goin' ta like this," he promised with an obscene leer. As he released her hair, he grabbed her breast and squeezed painfully. Theodora bit the hand that covered her mouth. He pulled it back to hit her, and she screamed before his palm struck her face. Despite the stars that danced in front of her eyes, she screamed again.

The sound of her cries brought Blade running. He dashed past the inert body of Basil Guion, who lay crumpled beside his rifle on the blanket, and raced into his wife's tent. A trapper knelt over her prone figure, unbuckling his belt. With a roar of rage Blade pulled the intruder off and flung him to the ground. He lifted him into the air and hurled him out of the tent, which collapsed about them as the man's flying legs caught against the shelter's taut ropes. Blade flung the canvas aside and strode forward.

Blade Stalker had been angry all afternoon. He'd rejoined the expedition and assumed command only to find that Fletcher had ordered the soldiers to be ready to move east in the morning. Then the information that the missionaries had left two weeks previous had made it impossible to marry Theodora in a white man's ceremony. Her capricious treatment of him that afternoon, coupled with her remark about leaving him permanently, had festered like a wound from a poisoned arrow. And his renewed fears for her safety, now that they were once again within striking distance of whoever had tried to kill her earlier on the trip, had heightened his anxiety.

Now this filthy scum had dared to touch his beautiful wife.

Shaking his head to clear it, Shrady struggled to his feet. He flashed a smirking grin as he advanced in a crouch, a hunting knife in his hand. "I'm gonna rip yore guts out, Roberts." He flung himself forward.

Blade twisted, striking the man's sternum with the full force of his cocked elbow, and the knife flew from his hand. The trapper fell with a crash, grabbing Blade's shirt on the way down. They collapsed together and rolled in the dirt. As he scrambled to his feet, Shrady smashed Blade's head with one ham-sized fist.

Blade tossed his hair from his eyes and smiled. He was going to enjoy beating the sonofabitch to a pulp. Light-footed, he circled his opponent. He knew the man. Big Joe Shrady was a bully. It was lucky they were so close in size, for it wouldn't be nearly as much fun to wallop a smaller man. And Blade was itching for a fight.

As Shrady swung again, Blade dodged, feinted, and landed a blow to the midsection that rocked the trapper on his heels. Shrady doubled up with a grunt. Without hesitating, Blade followed up with his other fist in his opponent's face, and the feel of cartilage crunching beneath his knuckles was as satisfying as Shrady's outraged howl of pain. Blood spurted from the broken nose and rained across the mountain man's greasy buckskin shirt.

By now they were ringed by a crowd of men. Trappers, soldiers, half-breeds, and Indians circled them, shouting out bets and encouragement. From the corner of his eye, Blade saw Theodora leaning on Haintzelman's arm. She held her torn nightgown pressed tightly against her breasts, and the sight of the tattered white lace fluttering over her dainty hand enraged him further. By God, he'd kill the bastard!

The two men slowly circled each other and searched for an opening. Holding his injured nose with a beefy hand, Shrady suddenly lashed out with one foot, using all of his massive weight to propel himself toward his opponent's groin. In one fluid motion Blade feinted and sidestepped. Shrady fell with a crash. Blade pulled him up by the front of his filthy shirt. Viciously, he smashed his fist into the homely, bearded face again and again. A gash split one bristly eyebrow and blood streamed down from Big Joe's nose. With the strength of a giant, Shrady broke his captor's hold and rolled free. He lunged for Blade's shins and brought the captain to the ground on top of him.

They rose slowly, locked in deadly embrace. Shrady held Blade in a bear hug, squeezing the breath from his lungs like a blacksmith's bellows. The veins in the mountain man's neck stood out like thick ropes with the awful exertion. The superhuman pressure against his newly healed ribs brought a jolt of excruciating pain to Blade. Desperately, he pushed up with the palms of both hands against Shrady's jaw, but the brute continued to squeeze. At last Blade grew limp against his captor, and Big Joe grinned and relaxed. He lowered Blade slightly. In lightning motion, the captain thrust one leg between Shrady's two massive thighs, diverted his own weight, and toppled the trapper to the ground. The force of their fall knocked them apart. Blade somersaulted, recovered, and turned. Never losing the force of his momentum, he jumped on Shrady feet first. There was the cracking sound of bone sundering from bone. As Blade pulled him to a sitting position, Shrady's right arm hung uselessly at his side. Holding him up and hitting him over and over, Blade pounded the thick features with his fist till the unconscious man's head flopped back and forth with each savage blow.

Through a haze of total, blinding rage, Blade heard someone shouting at him. "That's enough, Blade. He's had enough!"

Blade felt his arms being imprisoned from both sides. He was unceremoniously dragged from the trapper's crumpled form by Zeke and his father, who held him in a relentless grip. Even as they pulled him across the grass, Blade continued to struggle, trying to get back to the man lying motionless on the ground.

"It's okay, Blade," Zeke shouted in his ear. "He cain't feel nothin' nohow. Might as well wait till he's healed, and ya can whop him ag'in, if ya want ta."

"Let go. I'm all right." Blade shook off their arms and steadied himself. Panting, he looked around at the crowd, now silent with awestruck admiration. His voice was hoarse and rasping when he spoke, but loud enough to be heard by his entire audience. "If any man here so much as touches my wife, I swear to God, I'll kill him."

He turned and walked toward her. She stood beside Peter, watching his unsteady approach, her green eyes enormous in her pale, terrified face.

Theodora looked up at her battered husband. He was bleeding from a cut on his cheekbone; one eye was already starting to swell. Splotches of blood and dirt were liberally spattered across his deerskin shirt and leggings. His knuckles were raw and split. The sight and sound of the two big men fighting with such terrible violence had shaken her deeply. Her heart thumped against her ribs as she took a step toward him and lifted her hand to his face. "Blade, you're h—"

He jerked his head back to avoid her touch. His eyes glittered with a rage born of fear for her. Grabbing her upper arm, he pulled her roughly along with him. When he reached his empty tent, he shoved her through the open doorway. "Get the hell in there and stay in there," he shouted in fury as he entered behind her.

Theodora stiffened at his words. Head high, she stared at him in indignation. "How dare you speak to me like that!"

He met her challenge head-on. "I'm sleeping in your tent with you, Theodora, whether you like it or not. By God, it's no wonder you were attacked! You can't set up in a separate tent! Every man in camp saw you ride in beside me. They know damn well what happened while we were gone. If you're not considered my woman, under my protection, every horny male in camp will be after you. You can't possibly believe you can come back after all those days and pretend nothing's changed. Even you can't be that naive."

She felt the blood drain from her face. She tried to speak and almost choked on her fury. Hauling air into her suddenly empty lungs, she straightened to her full height. "Very well, Captain Roberts. You can stay in my tent, giving me the benefit of your *generous* protection. Though after what just happened I can't really believe anyone would be crazy enough to try such a thing again. You may be able to intimidate every man in this camp, but you're not running my life and you're not making my decisions for me. From here on out, you'll sleep in your own bedroll and I'll sleep in mine." She turned to face the wall of the tent and then swung back. Her lower lip trembled when she recalled the fact that he'd just prevented her from being brutally raped. Her voice softened. "And thank you for saving me. That much I do appreciate."

A muscle jumped in his cheek as he clenched his jaw in an apparent effort to regain control of his temper. His voice was low and terrible, and he spoke through gritted teeth. "Sit down, Theodora. And don't say another word."

He strode to the tent opening and stood just outside. "O'Fallon," he bellowed. When the sergeant raced up to him, he spoke more calmly, though his clipped words were still raw with anger. "Raise my wife's tent again."

* * *

In Captain Blade Roberts's tent the next morning the collapsible table was covered with papers and maps. Camp chairs were scattered across the grassy floor, attesting to the meeting of the expedition's commander and his staff that had just broken up. Now only two men, Bonniville and Blade, remained seated at the table.

"How's the beaver trade going?" Blade asked as he puffed with enjoyment on his cheroot.

His guest shrugged in resignation. "For two years now the Saint Louis prices have remained too low to pay a profit." He smiled suddenly. "But you and I both know that wasn't why I came to these mountains in the first place."

"I take it you've been able to gather the information the War Department sent you out here to get?"

"Not quite all of it, but enough to have made this venture well worthwhile. The site of my fort was carefully chosen. It's in the strategic center of the mountain area. Any expedition into British territory would start from right here."

Blade flicked the ash from his cigar and leaned forward, resting his elbows on the table. "And you'd be directly in the path of any campaign moving out of the Columbia region toward the Americans' trapping grounds. Your fort can hold the western approach to South Pass and cover all the routes to Pierre's Hole, the Snake River, and the Great Salt Lake. Not to mention the route to California."

Blade stood and wandered around the table to peer down at a large map. "The War Department has no information whatever about a pass through the Sierras. Our knowledge stops at the Great Salt Lake. The Secretary of War has ordered me to discover if such a route even exists."

Bonniville looked up at Blade. "I'll be sending a communiqué back to General Macomb at the War Department. One of my men, George Warfield, will hand carry it all the way to Washington. You can send your report to the Bureau of Topographical Engineers with him." He rubbed his short, stubby hands across his knees. "Everything go all right on the way here?"

"Not quite." Blade leaned over the table and rested his hands on the map. "As you know, we lost our cartographer less than four weeks after leaving Leavenworth. He died of cholera—I think.''

''What makes you question it?''

Blade scowled. ''It's not common for only one man in camp to come down with cholera, even though we were extremely careful. Gordon drank from a buffalo wallow while he was lost on the prairie. It's possible he was the only one exposed to tainted water. If it weren't for the mysterious accidents, I wouldn't have questioned it.''

''Accidents?'' Bonniville's brow furrowed in a deep frown.

The captain stood back from the table, picked up a wooden ruler, and tapped it thoughtfully against the map. ''Yes, to my wife. A cut saddle strap while she was crossing the Big Blue, a rattlesnake on her bedroll at Fort Laramie, and a buffalo stampede on the Laramie Plains caused by a sudden, unexplained noise. Even the attack on her by Shrady could have been a setup. I was so damn mad yesterday, it didn't even occur to me until I'd almost killed the sonofabitch that someone could have paid him to rape and murder her. He's under guard right now. Unfortunately, he hasn't regained consciousness since the fight. As soon as he does, I'll find out whether or not he was a hired assassin.''

''Jesus!'' Bonniville stood up. His chair teetered back and forth behind him. ''Why would anyone want to kill Theodora Gordon?''

''Roberts.''

At the blank look of confusion on Benjamin's face, the captain added, ''Her name is Roberts now. We were married in my village.''

''Yes, of course. I heard. Congratulations.'' The stocky man paced across the tent floor, then turned. ''Do you want to send her back? I have a pack train of furs leaving for Saint Louis tomorrow morning.''

Blade came around the table and sank into a chair. Holding the butt of the cigar in his fingers, he rubbed his eyes with the palms of both hands. ''I don't know. I suspect the bastard is a soldier from a heel mark we found at Laramie. But I can't be sure. It'd be possible for one of the rear guard to sneak back and get to her once the pack train leaves, though not likely. I feel most comfortable when she's within eyesight, but I can't watch her twenty-four hours a day.''

''Why not let her decide?''

''She doesn't know about my suspicions. As far as she's concerned, they were just unlucky accidents. I don't want her living in fear.''

''I see.'' Bonniville sat down beside him. ''Why not just give her the option of returning with the fur train? Then make sure that after it leaves tomorrow, every man in your expedition checks in every four hours for the next two days.''

''You may be right. I hate like hell to think of sending her back, but if I were certain it was for her own safety, I wouldn't hesitate to do it.''

Benjamin clapped the captain's shoulder. ''Let's hope Shrady regains consciousness. And if he does, that he's willing to talk.''

''He'll talk.''

Bonniville met Blade's cold, hard eyes and shuddered.

As wide as seventy miles across in some spots, the valley of the Green River was a sagebrush plain, treeless except for the cottonwoods that lined the riverbanks. Now, on the twelfth day of August, though many of the trappers had already departed, enough remained to continue to give the rendezvous site the appearance of a shivaree.

Because of this rowdy atmosphere, Theodora was confined to her quarters, except for breakfast mess, unless accompanied by Peter Haintzelman. Blade had been busy all that morning with the job of reprovisioning the expedition. Following his work on the maps with Zeke and his father the night before, he'd come into her tent after she'd fallen asleep. He hadn't disturbed her and was gone when she woke. After the midday meal, a second meeting with his staff, in which Peter was to be included, was scheduled. It was expected to stretch well into the afternoon. But Theodora's father-in-law offered to take her on a plant-collecting excursion. Jacques Roberts seemed to delight in the idea of spending time with her and sharing her interest in the flora and fauna of the valley.

''Call me 'Father' or '*nihoe*' or '*mon père*,'' he told Theodora in his booming baritone as they rode out of camp together.

"Use whatever language you want. I'll answer to any of them."

As they rode, he was full of questions about her. How she had come to be part of a scientific expedition, where she was raised, who her parents were. Every answer she gave seemed to please him. "Well, if you aren't just about perfect, *ma fille*, I don't know who is," he shouted at her from his mount, riding beside her. The fact that she and his son weren't speaking to each other didn't seem to bother him in the least.

He led her up the sheltering slopes of the Wind River Range foothills, past scrub oak, piñon, and juniper trees to groves of small ponderosa pines. Jacques Roberts showed the same love of the land as his son. He pointed out a young kit fox, its fur still reddish in the late-afternoon sun, and a prairie falcon, its spotted plumage almost unnoticeable as it sat on a high rock and watched for its prey.

They rode higher, through the needle and buffalo grass into stands of white fir and blue spruce. Far off, they saw a small herd of mule deer at the edge of an aspen grove. "The grass between the large trees offers the mule deer the best forage," he explained to her. "Then, when enemies come near, they can bound off into the shadows of the forest. In another hour or so they'll come out and feed on the meadow clover."

He helped Theodora gather juniper berries and wild rose hips, alum root and kinnikinnic for her collection. She plied him with questions, committing everything he told her to memory so she could write it down in her journal.

Coming back from the ride elated with her new treasures, Theodora saw Whirlwind Woman riding through camp beside a trapper. The young woman was mounted on a spirited black-and-white pony, with a high pommeled saddle decorated with beading, fringe, and rows of brass tacks.

"I know that girl," Theodora said softly to her companion. "She's married to a brave from Blade's village."

"Not anymore," Jacques replied in his loud voice. "Andy Pickens bought her last night from a nasty young buck called Black Wolf. Paid four horses, a pack mule, two rifles, and a fine hunting knife for her."

Theodora stared in shock as the couple drew near. Whirlwind Woman sat straight and tall, her beautiful pitch-black hair flowing down her back, her dark eyes flashing with pride and happiness. The young, sandy-haired mountain man beside her watched her with unconcealed lust. He had dressed her in a blouse and skirt made of imported St. Louis broadcloth, for which he must have paid an exorbitant price. She was covered with necklaces of elk teeth, and her accessories included scarlet leggings, new moccasins with intricate beading, and even a silk handkerchief tied loosely around her neck.

"That trapper bought Whirlwind Woman?" She couldn't keep the astonishment from her voice.

Pickens and his new bride were right in front of them by now. "How can she look so happy after her husband has just sold her to another man? When her family finds out about this, they'll be humiliated."

"Not likely," Jacques replied, as he scratched under his long black beard. "Her status with her people is higher than ever now. She'll be treated well by Pickens, and I got the feeling Black Wolf wasn't too good to her. Divorce is accepted by the Cheyenne. Since a man can beat his wife to discipline her, divorce allows the woman a way out of an abusive situation. If she finds a man who'll treat her better, she can leave and go with him. Seems only fair to me."

"What about Mr. Pickens? Will he treat her well?"

"Oh, Andy'll treat her like the queen of England. He's only been out here a year. This'll be his second winter. In the months to come she'll help him repair his traps, show him where to place them, clean and tan his hides, cook his meals, and sew his clothes. During the long winter nights, when they're snowbound in her lodge, she'll keep him company. She'll probably teach him a little Cheyenne and he'll teach her English." Jacques's voice held the mellow sound of sweet reminiscence.

"That's what it was like with you and Blade's mother, wasn't it?"

He smiled at her perceptiveness. "His mother was the prettiest girl I've ever seen. She had hair the color of midnight that hung down past her waist. Tiny feet and hands. And bright black eyes."

"What was her name?"

"Morning Sun Comes Softly. I just called her 'Morning.'" His hearty laugh burst out suddenly. "When we got out of bed, I'd say 'Morning, Morning.'" Then his smile was gone, and a faraway look came over his strongly chiseled features. "But mostly I'd talk to her in my own language. When Blade was young, he'd speak French during the winter in our lodge and Cheyenne in the summertime, when his mother would take him to visit her family. She died when he was twelve. That's when I took him back to New Orleans." Jacques gave a deep sigh.

"You loved her very much, didn't you?"

"She was the only woman in my life, *mignonne*. The only one I ever wanted. Even now, I miss her. Her high spirits, her chattering, her singing, her warmth filled my winter lodge. Yes, I loved her dearly."

Jacques dismounted and lifted Theodora down. He walked beside her toward the tent she shared with his son. "It'll be the same for Blade," he continued with a tender smile. "You'll be the only woman in his life, though I never dreamt he'd fall for a bluestocking from Massachusetts. But when I saw you together the first time, I knew you were meant for each other."

"Does it seem that way to you?" she asked in disbelief. "We really have very little in common. He's a professional soldier, with a life of exploring the wilderness ahead of him, and the product of a warrior culture. I've seen him kill a man with his bare hands." She shook her head at the memory. "I was raised in a family that abhorred physical violence for any reason. Even self-defense. And I'm a scientist, a scholar who'll go back to her library and her research when this journey is over."

"Look around you, Theodora. You're standing in the world's largest classroom." Jacques threw his arms wide, gesturing to the magnificent vista of mountains that surrounded them. "Where could you find a better place to do your research than right here beside my son?"

She put her hand on his buckskin sleeve in a plea for understanding. "But Blade and I are so different," she said. "Sometimes he even frightens me."

"Well, *ma fille*, as your Quaker grandmother surely told you, you must follow your inner voice. But I sincerely doubt you will ever meet another man who'll love you more than my son does." He grinned suddenly. "Besides, if I know Blade,

I don't think he has any intention of letting you get away from him. For pure strength of will, a Cheyenne warrior's hard to beat.''

Theodora was silent for a moment, following another train of thought. ''You said Whirlwind Woman could have left her abusive husband. When I was in Blade's village, no one mentioned that divorce was acceptable. How does a Cheyenne wife go about leaving her spouse?''

Jacques looked at her with open suspicion for a long minute, but he finally answered her. ''An unhappy woman can just pile the man's belongings outside her tipi. Since the lodge and its furnishings all belong to her, the brave must find another place to live.''

''That's all there is to it?'' Theodora was incredulous. ''Of course,'' she added thoughtfully, ignoring his skeptical regard, ''if there's no written marriage document, it stands to reason that the divorce would be just as simple as the wedding.''

That evening Snow Owl and her husband, Pierre du Lac, were to join the members of the campaign for supper. Delighted with the prospect of her company, Theodora felt her spirits rise. She'd learned from Jacques during their excursion that Snow Owl and Tall Boy would soon be returning to the mountains with Pierre for the winter trapping.

Theodora wanted to give Snow Owl a gift to show how grateful she was for all her kindness. She searched through her few meager belongings for an appropriate present. The idea of giving Snow Owl any of her clothing seemed ludicrous. The Indian woman's dress of antelope skin was far more suitable for the wilderness than any of Theodora's dresses. As she refolded her clothes, the reflection of light from her hand mirror caught her eye. It was made of carved ivory, with a cameo on the back. She picked it up and looked at herself in the glass. Here was a gift only she could give Snow Owl!

After tying three bands of colored hair ribbons in a big bow on the handle, she wrapped the mirror in a fringed blue shawl. She'd miss both the shawl and the mirror, but she wanted to give Snow Owl something really special. As she placed the gift on her opened bedroll to be ready for that evening, Blade entered their tent.

He stood quietly, the worry on his battered, bruised face clearly evident. They hadn't spoken to each other since the evening before.

The wounds on his face from the beating he'd taken were stark evidence of his intention to keep her with him. "Theodora," he said in a cool, emotionless tone, "I need to talk to you."

She looked away, certain that if she met his gaze she wouldn't be able to maintain her outward calm or her sense of purpose. After her talk with Blade's father, she was more confused than ever. Could Jacques Roberts be right? Did she and Blade actually have a great deal in common, including a future that would mesh both their lives? She fought to keep her voice calm. "Yes, well, here I am. What is it you wish to say?"

Blade hooked his thumbs in his belt and watched his wife in silence. He wondered if this would be their last night together, for if she chose to leave with the pack train heading for St. Louis in the morning, they might never see each other again. He ached to enfold her in his arms, to kiss her and demand that she stay with him. But he had to give her the choice to return home safely, without influence from him. Was he wrong in not telling her that he suspected someone was trying to kill her?

"Bonniville is sending a caravan of beaver plews back to St. Louis. It's leaving in the morning. One of his assistants, George Warfield, will be carrying papers all the way to Washington."

Theodora looked up at him, as if to question why he was telling her this.

"If you choose, you may return home with Warfield."

His words stunned her. She could only stare at him. "Is that what you wish, then?" she asked, and the steadiness of her voice astounded her. Jacques had certainly been wrong about his son's intention of keeping her beside him. What else had he been wrong about?

"What I wish isn't important, Theodora. The choice is entirely up to you. If you continue with us, you'll be facing incredible dangers. I can't emphasize that enough. What you've been through is only a taste of what lies ahead. We have a desert to cross, and after that the Sierra Nevada Mountains. And we'll be going without charts or maps to guide us. If you're wise, you'll turn back now.''

''And if I choose to continue?'' She walked to the far side of the tent and faced the canvas wall. She looked down at her hands and blinked; her knuckles were white as she clasped them tightly together.

His words were precise, detached. ''If you decide to stay with the expedition, Theodora, I must continue to sleep in your tent for your own safety. And I'll appreciate all the help you can give me on the cartography. Other than that, I'll make no demands of you.''

Whirling to face him, she met his aloof gaze. His complete turnabout astounded her. The marks on his face belied his words, but his stoic expression gave no hint of his inner feelings. Damn him! When he turned Cheyenne warrior on her, he was impossible to read. Yet he understood her thoughts as though he saw into her very soul.

In spite of his previous avowals to keep her as his wife, he was setting her free. But at what a price. If she didn't continue with the expedition, her plans to dedicate the map work in Tom's name would be irrevocably lost. She had only one chance to complete the cartography as though Tom had done it himself. And that meant continuing on this campaign.

''I'll need some time to think,'' she whispered. ''When must you have my answer?''

''You don't have to let me know till tomorrow morning. We'll be pulling out then, too. Until it's time to join one of the columns, you can put off the final decision. In the meantime I'll leave you alone to think.'' He turned to leave, then hesitated. ''I know you believe that you hate the wilderness, that you can't survive out here. But when you were with my people, Theodora, it was as though you'd been born on the plains. You were the happiest I'd ever seen you.''

She stared in astonished silence, for that was exactly what she had thought about him.

Then he bent and left the tent.

Chapter 25

Theodora crossed the noisy campsite, lit only by scattered fires, toward the herd of horses grazing in the clearing. A wild celebration was in full swing, as each man tried to make the most of his last evening at the rendezvous. For the trappers, tomorrow would start a fall and winter of loneliness, hardship, and possibly even death. For the soldiers, daylight would mark the beginning of the last and most dangerous leg of their historic journey. All around her, groups of men drank, sang, whooped and hollered, and drank some more.

After the evening meal, which she and Snow Owl had helped Julius Twiggs prepare and serve, she'd given the young woman the hand mirror and shawl. Now Snow Owl sat beside her husband and Peter near a campfire, listening to Zeke and Jacques trade tall tales. Theodora knew she wasn't supposed to leave the bivouac area, but she was consumed with restless energy. Everyone was so engrossed in Zeke's yarn that they didn't even notice her slip away.

As she moved through the clusters of mountain men and dragoons, she searched unsuccessfully for Blade. She knew he'd left after supper to say farewell to his grandfather. No doubt Painted Robe and her husband would talk far into the night.

She left the noise of the revelry behind her and walked into the quiet, moonlit meadow. Halting when she saw a soldier on duty, she realized as he turned toward her that it was Wesley Fletcher. She hadn't seen him since the day before, when they'd ridden in. She assumed her husband had kept the lieutenant away from her on purpose. Since the first day at Fort Leavenworth, Blade had seemed annoyed whenever Fletcher came near her. But unlike the blond lieutenant, Blade had never repeated vicious innuendos about his rival.

Sergeant O'Fallon had told her that the animosity between the two officers went all the way back to West Point, and she wondered what could have happened to cause them to hate each other. She'd never seen Fletcher do anything that wasn't strictly according to military protocol, yet none of the dragoons appeared to respect him. While her husband's mere glance could straighten up a private's slouch, more than once she'd seen a soldier smirk and mimic the Georgian behind his back.

"Lieutenant Fletcher," she called in greeting.

"Miz Gordon." Fletcher tipped his cap and moved to her side. "I've been in charge of the animals since the captain's return. I was just checkin' on the pickets." He made no attempt to hide his bitterness. "I understand that Benjamin Bonniville is sendin' a pack train of furs back t' Saint Louis in the mornin'. I hope y' have considered goin' back with them."

"Yes, I'm thinking about doing just that, Lieutenant."

"That's exactly what we should all be doin'. If Roberts hadn't shown up when he did, the entire expedition would be goin' back home. The men were extremely disappointed when he informed them we'd be headin' west int' God knows what kind of wilderness." As he bent over her his tone grew softer. "May I take this opportunity t' say how glad I am that you've returned safely?"

In the moonlight she tried to search his face for a clue to his real feelings. All she could see clearly in the shadows were his tawny mustache and the glitter of his pale eyes. " I . . . I appreciate your kind thought, Lieutenant."

"Miz Gordon," he said, as he took her elbow, "stay for a few minutes. I'd like to talk to y', and we might not get another chance t' be alone."

"Very well, Lieutenant." Theodora followed his lead and walked beside him through the buffalo grass, away from the camp.

"I wanted to tell y' that I understand what happened in the Indian camp with that half-breed. I wanted to be sure y' didn't blame yourself."

Wondering where his conversation was leading, Theodora said nothing until, at last, his silence became annoying. "I take full responsibility for my own actions, Lieutenant."

He leaned his carbine against a large boulder and swung around to face her. As though afraid she'd run away, he gripped her wrists in a painful hold. He spoke earnestly. "But that's just the point, Miz Gordon. Y' weren't responsible. Roberts is an accomplished womanizer. Y' wouldn't have had a chance t' withstand his smooth, practiced lies. My only worry is that y' may still believe him."

"Just what are you talking about, Fletcher?"

"I'm talkin' about the well-known prowess of Captain Blade Roberts. He sees any good-lookin' female as a possible conquest. He counts his seductions like the savages count coups. Why, he was almost dismissed from the Point because of a woman. Ask him and see if he denies it!"

Fletcher's accusations astounded Theodora. Whatever else Blade's faults might be, insincerity had never been one of them. "The captain's past is not up for discussion, Lieutenant. I haven't the least—"

"Teddy!" Peter's worried voice carried on the evening breeze. "Teddy, where are you?"

"I'm over here," she called, and gratefully turned to meet him. "Thank you for your concern, Lieutenant Fletcher," she said as she moved away.

Fletcher watched her go with a scowl of disgust. He reached down, picked up his carbine, and silently followed them.

As Theodora walked back into the campground with her escort, a bullet whizzed past her ear and struck the cottonwood tree beside her. Reacting instantly, Peter shoved her to the ground, and another ball zinged across the clearing over their heads, the blast barely noticed in the wild clamor of the campsite.

Lying on her stomach beneath Peter, her cheek pressed into the trampled grass, she caught her breath and squirmed uncomfortably.

"Hold still, Teddy," he said in her ear, his apprehension evident. "Cripes, I can't even return his fire. If I move, you're liable to be hit."

Suddenly Blade was crawling across the ground beside them,

his rifle cradled on his forearms. "Stay where you are, Hain-zelman. Theodora, don't move." He scanned the moonl clearing and waited for another explosion with its accompa nying flash of light.

Two shots came one right after the other, followed by th answering blast of Blade's carbine. A man screamed in th dark, and at last the campsite grew quiet.

"I've got him, Captain," Lieutenant Fletcher called fror the meadow. "It's safe now."

Blade raced across the tall buffalo grass in a low crouch reloading his carbine as he ran. There were no more shots, an when the sound of the two officers' voices carried into th bivouac, Peter helped Theodora to her feet. From the campfire others raced over to see what had happened, and together th crowd hurried to where Blade and Fletcher stood over a crum pled heap of buckskin.

Fletcher rolled the corpse over with the toe of his cavalr boot. The dead trapper had been hit right between the eyes.

Zeke pushed through the onlookers to stand beside Blade "That thar's Bushwhacker Willie, Shrady's pardner," he said

Blade turned to Theodora, grasped her hands, and pulle her to him. "Are you all right?" His gaze roved over her dusty form.

The front of her dress was covered with dirt, and she coul feel a smudge of grit on her cheek. Her heart was slowly returning to its normal rhythm. "Yes, I'm fine. Peter save my life."

Blade turned to the lieutenant. "What were you two doing way out here, anyway?" he asked with a scowl.

Ignoring Blade's thunderous look, Theodora answered fo her friend. "Peter was escorting me back from the meadow I had gone for a walk."

"*By yourself?*" Blade's roar was so loud she jumped. "Je-sus!" He turned back to Peter, his rage crackling like lightning on a stormy night. "What the *hell* are you thinking of, Haintzel-man, letting her wander around alone?"

Peter's face was set in grim humiliation. Behind his wire spectacles, which had been knocked askew and sat at a crazy angle on the end of his nose, his blue eyes blinked with painful self-accusation. It was clear that he was prepared to take full blame for the close call to the captain's wife. But before he could speak, Theodora interrupted. "I wasn't alone, Blade. I was talking with Lieutenant Fletcher."

The absolute fury in his deep voice told her there wasn't anything worse she could have said. "My orders were for you to be guarded by Lieutenant Haintzelman," he shouted, "and I expected them to be obeyed to the letter."

"I'm not one of your soldiers, Captain Roberts," she snapped back. "I don't follow orders without a reasonable explanation. And I won't be hollered at."

He lifted her completely off the ground as he yanked her to him. Holding her up by both elbows, he said angrily, "You'll follow my orders, Theodora, or you'll feel the palm of my hand across your backside."

Not one person in the crowd around them moved so much as a muscle. It was clear to Theodora that they were waiting for her answer with morbid curiosity. She also came to the sickening realization that, if Blade turned her over his knee and spanked her right then and there, not one man would lift a finger to help her. As far as they were concerned, he had every right to discipline a disobedient, uppity wife.

She met his angry eyes with obstinate resolution, fighting to maintain her outward calm. "I suggest we continue this discussion in the privacy of my tent, Captain."

Heedless of the disappointment among their captivated audience, Blade set her on her feet and strode beside her to the shelter.

As soon as she was inside, she picked up one of his packs. Staggering under its weight, and without even glancing in his direction, she carried it through the doorway and dumped it on the grass. She returned, only to snatch up a strap on one of his saddlebags and drag it across the tent floor. By then, the exit was blocked with his towering frame.

"What the hell are you doing?" It was clear he'd expected her to scream and rail at him, not ignore him with exasperating calm.

She tilted her head and smiled pompously at him, like a tutor with a particularly large, dull-witted pupil. "Can't you tell?" she asked him with false sweetness. "I'm divorcing you."

"You're what?" His thundering roar shook the canvas walls.

"You heard correctly, Blade. I'm divorcing you. A Cheyenne wife has the right to protect herself from an abusive spouse. That's exactly what I'm doing. From this moment on you can consider yourself my *former* husband. Now if you'll please get out of my way, I'll finish stacking your belongings outside my tent."

Blade shook his head, a crooked grin of reluctant admiration slowly spreading across his face. "You little she-devil," he said softly. "If you honestly think I'm going to let you divorce me, that sharp-witted brain of yours has gone begging."

"You can't stop me." She lifted her chin. "I know my rights. We had a Cheyenne wedding, and now we're having a Cheyenne divorce."

"You're not even Cheyenne, *vehoka*," he scoffed, emphasizing the word that meant "little white woman" and refusing to budge from the doorway.

"Oh, but I certainly am," she replied in triumph, for she'd known he would bring up that point. "I'm the adopted granddaughter of a chief. Painted Robe would be the first one to tell you that I can have a divorce if I want one."

Blade crossed his arms over his chest and stood with feet apart in a stance of mule-headed determination. "Well, I'm only half Cheyenne, Theodora. And the white half of me doesn't believe in it."

She looked at him, nonplussed. That was one argument she hadn't expected. "You can't do that, Blade," she protested. "You can't play by one set of rules getting married and another set getting divorced."

He gave her a wolfish smile. "Who's going to stop me? Besides," he added, leaning slightly toward her, "so far tonight I haven't even laid a finger on you."

Theodora released her grip on the saddlebag strap and sighed in resignation. As long as he stood in front of the doorway, there was absolutely nothing she could do. "Why were you so angry with me, anyway?" she asked. "All I did was go for a little walk. Who could have predicted that some crazy, drunken trapper would go on a rampage and start shooting at the campsite?"

Blade hesitated, wondering once again if he should tell her

that it hadn't been an accident. That someone was actually trying to kill her. But no doubt she'd be safely on her way back east in the morning, and there wasn't any reason to frighten her tonight, now that she was in her tent for the evening. With the five soldiers stationed around it to guard her through the night, there was no need to alarm her.

"I just want to be sure you're safe, *vehona*. That's all." He waited for her reply, and when there was none, he continued. "I can't stay and argue with you any longer, Theodora. I have to meet my father and Zeke to go over the route we're taking to the Great Salt Lake. When I come back, I expect my things to be right where they are now." Hating to leave her standing there, flushed and angry, her stubborn chin jutting in the air, he looked at her for a long minute, then quietly stepped from the tent.

That night Theodora lay on her bedroll and stared at the roof. She went over and over in her mind all the reasons why she should return to St. Louis. First of all, there was her so-called marriage to Blade Roberts. It would never work. If anything proved they were incompatible, the events of that very evening did. From the first moment they'd met, they'd scrapped with each other like fighting cocks at every turn. How could she even consider spending a lifetime with him?

That afternoon he'd caught her by complete surprise when he'd suggested she return with the pack train. He'd offered her no clear reason why he'd changed his mind so unpredictably, and even though he seemed to think it was the wisest choice, still he insisted that they remain married. For it was clear that he believed the marriage was binding, and the longer she stayed with the expedition, the more firmly she would be tied to him. If she truly wanted the freedom to choose a more suitable mate, she should go now, while she had the chance.

The image of Martin Van Vliet rose to her mind. Before she'd met pig-headed, cantankerous Blade Roberts, she had thought the middle-aged publisher was the perfect choice for a husband. Quiet, urbane, learned, he was the epitome of the sophisticated New Yorker. In all the years she'd known him, he'd never even raised an eyebrow at her in anger, let alone his voice. True, he wasn't nearly as handsome as Blade, but then few men were. She had to ruthlessly discount the scintillating magnetism that drew her to the captain. She was much too intelligent to believe that physical attraction was a sound basis for choosing a lifetime partner.

Despite the fact that she didn't love Martin, they had much in common. Theirs would have been a marriage of two perfectly matched workhorses pulling a single plow. Safe. Secure. Dull. Restlessly, she smoothed the covers beneath her hands and pushed that disquieting thought aside.

The second reason for returning east was her family. She knew her father was anxiously waiting for her to arrive with the botanical specimens she'd collected. She now had enough new flora to fill her journal; there was no need to continue on for more. As it was, it would take them months to categorize and catalogue her new discoveries. And there would be the excitement of seeing her journal published. How proud her father and grandmother would be. Perhaps, in some little way, it would soften the tragic grief of Tom's death.

The third reason to turn back was the danger of the journey itself. Blade had warned her that the worst was yet to come. She knew they would have to cross an uncharted desert only to enter a formidable barrier of mountains through which no pass had ever been charted. Could she survive the trip? Blade had told her that he'd changed his mind—that he now believed she could thrive on the frontier. She'd seen the Cheyenne people living as one with the land, the very land that had claimed Tom's life.

And what about Tom? Standing on the cliff at Scott's Bluff, she'd promised her brother to continue his work, so that his death would not be wasted. She longed to see his dream fulfilled and his name on the maps that would be printed. Men and women would safely cross the wilderness in the years to come because of them. She wiped tears from her cheeks, rolled onto her side, and prayed for the answer. Drifting to sleep at last, she heard once again the words her brother had spoken: *Go now, Teddy. Cherish our dream. Do everything we came out here to do. Don't let my death be in vain.*

In her sleep she smiled. She had her answer.

*   *   *

Blade entered their tent carrying the pack Theodora had dumped outside on the grass. He noted with satisfaction that the rest of his things had remained untouched. Exhausted and disappointed to find her sound asleep, he pulled off his buckskin shirt and his boots in the soft glow of the lantern. Knowing this was their last night together, he wanted to talk to her, to reassure her just how much he did care about her, even when he ranted and raved like a wild man. He'd learned only a few minutes earlier that Big Joe Shrady had died, never having regained consciousness. The body of a young Snake woman had been discovered in her lodge just that afternoon; she'd been sexually used and then cold-bloodedly strangled to death. An investigation had revealed that she'd been bartered by her family for a pack of beaver plews to Bushwhacker Willie. More than ever, Blade was certain that both Shrady and his partner could have provided the name of Theodora's stalker. Now both were dead.

Blade walked quietly over to his sleeping wife. She lay on her side, a smile curving her delectable mouth. What had she found to smile about? he wondered. He crouched on his haunches and gazed at her. Oh, *vehona*, will you leave me in the morning? Must I stand by and watch you go, knowing that it's for your own protection?

Blade reached down and lifted a blond curl. He rubbed the silken lock between his thumb and forefinger. Desire for his beautiful bride flamed up inside of him. He wanted to lift her in his arms and carry her to his bedroll, where he'd waken her with his hands and mouth. She'd fight him at first, but he could easily subdue her. Yet he knew that even if he stirred in her the same passion that now pounded through his veins, she'd never forgive him. She'd leave here in the morning hating him. And he didn't want her to return home that way. When his mission was over, he'd go to Massachusetts and get her.

Bending over, Blade brushed his lips softly against hers. "You stubborn little bluenose," he whispered. "I love you so."

Chapter 26

The next morning Blade was already gone when Theodora awoke. All of his personal belongings had been taken from the shelter while she slept. Most of her own packing had been done the night before, and her baggage, too, had been quietly removed. She quickly dressed in her buckskin skirt and cotton blouse, and with Calvin Belknap's help, took down her tent. She was soon ready to join the others. How would Blade feel, she wondered, when she told him that she was going to continue with the expedition?

But she was unable even to get near him. He was closeted inside his quarters, having a last-minute meeting with Conyers, Chardonnais, and his father, as well as the junior officers. Disappointed yet oddly relieved, she grabbed a quick breakfast from Julius and saddled Athena, knowing Spitfire would be brought along in the herd of extra mounts. With her heart pounding in her chest, she led her mare to the group of dragoons, who sat on the crushed buffalo grass waiting for the signal to mount up and pull out.

When Blade emerged from his tent with his staff, he sought her out immediately, as though drawn by some mysterious force. Seeing her waiting beside the soldiers, he quickly ordered O'Fallon to move her supplies, which had already been loaded on the pack mules. A private whistled and drove the animals into position in front of the large herd of horses. As Blade's tent was hurriedly dismantled, he said good-bye to his father and moved off to confer with Benjamin Bonneville.

The fur caravan, heading for St. Louis, left first. Amidst the noise and confusion, Jacques came over to Theodora, and together they watched it pull out.

"Well, *ma fille*, I see that perhaps our little talk has changed your mind about that reprobate son of mine," Jacques roared happily. He lifted her high over his head, then smothered her in a ferocious hug. "I'll see you on your way back through South Pass next summer. Maybe by then I'll have a little grandson on the way."

His smile was so wide, so loving, she didn't have the heart to disabuse him of the assumption that she'd decided to remain in the expedition as Blade's wife. "Good-bye, *mon père*," she said, kissing his bearded cheek. "Till we meet again."

After giving his huge hand a final squeeze, Theodora mounted and took her place beside Peter in the column that quickly formed.

Blade rode up and reined War Shield to a halt in front of her. He lifted his slouch hat politely. "I take it you're coming to California with us, Mrs. Roberts." He didn't smile, and Theodora found it impossible to read his guarded expression.

"I'm going to finish what I came out here to do, Captain. We have an agreement about the cartography, and I intend to live up to it. I want those maps published in my brother's memory. And I would appreciate it if you'd address me as 'Miss Gordon,' since it is my *legal* name."

Blade flashed a grin. "The maps will be printed with Tom's name on them. When I make a promise, I keep it." He wheeled his stallion around. "And I prefer to call you 'Mrs. Roberts,' since you are my wife—legally or otherwise."

He rode off before she had a chance to reply.

Four days after leaving the trappers' rendezvous, the United States Scientific Exploring Expedition reached the headwaters of Bear River, at the western edge of the buffalo range. Here Captain Roberts halted to prepare for the dangerous desert crossing.

The dragoons had been issued buckskin outfits provided by Benjamin Bonneville; their uniforms, as well as the Yankee spring wagon, had been left at his fort. Seventy-six days on the trail had turned them into hardened veterans. Now dressed in the standard attire of the mountain men, all traces of the greenness they'd shown at Fort Leavenworth had disappeared. They looked exactly like what they were posing as: a brigade of free trappers in search of beaver.

The soldiers, as well as the French Canadian voyageurs, now knew their final destination. The first night out of Horse Creek Blade had read aloud the secret orders from the War Department, directing them to discover a passage through the formidable Sierra Nevada range.

When they pulled into the grassy valley of Bear River to make camp that afternoon, it was hot and windy. Theodora had ridden beside Blade all day. She'd spoken to him only when necessary since they'd left the rendezvous. Dismounting before he could help her down, she hurried away to see to the raising of her tent. She'd have time to collect some plants before assisting him with the map work.

During the next few days, everyone in camp helped Julius Twiggs prepare the carcasses brought in by the hunters. The buffalo meat was cut into strips approximately an inch thick and scored crisscross. It was then spread out on racks of cottonwood poles, high enough to keep it safe from wolves, rodents, and other scavengers, where the wind and smoke from the hot coals beneath dried it into jerky.

Some of the jerky they pounded into a pulp. This they mixed with the melted buffalo fat stored in rawhide bags. Sometimes they threw in dried berries. Julius even added maple sugar to one sack.

The pemmican was stored in ninety-pound bags. By the end of the week they had prepared enough nourishing food that would keep fresh over the days ahead for the entire expedition.

On the last evening at Bear River Blade stood outside the tent that served as his office and gazed westward. Each man had been provided with four horses, a stack of blankets, buffalo robes, and every article needed to make the journey safely. Each soldier had a new carbine and plenty of ammunition. There was sixty pounds of substantial meat per man. He'd consulted with the nearby Bannock Indians, reviewed once more the sketches his father had drawn of the area around the Great Salt Lake, and had had last-minute discussions with Conyers and Chardonnais. The explorers were going into country that few men, white or Indian, had ever seen. Beyond that, they would enter a land that no human eyes had ever witnessed. They were as prepared as he knew how to get them.

Only one thing had been left unsettled. He had still not made peace with Theodora. Since leaving the rendezvous, she'd successfully avoided him. The few times he'd caught her watching him, she'd looked confused and wary. She always managed to be sound asleep by the time he could at last leave his work and turn in. He'd known that hers was a sleep of exhaustion, for she'd been working as hard as any man for the last few days.

Blade puffed on his cheroot and turned to look at his sleeping quarters, where he knew Theodora was preparing for bed.

When he'd realized back at Horse Creek that she was going to continue with the expedition rather than return to St. Louis, he'd been elated. He wanted Theodora beside him. He was confident that no one could look out for her safety better than he. There would be plenty of time in the days ahead to overcome her doubts. He was certain he could bring her around. But he had to admit, in the last days he hadn't made much headway. Still, she was in her tent, and the sight of her in her lacy nightgown, sound asleep on her bedding, was a heck of a lot better than having her miles away in the care of some stranger. He smiled to himself. Like the memory of her surrender in the Cheyenne lodge, the image of her cool, ivory limbs beneath his hot hands was even better.

The trailblazers headed toward the Great Salt Lake the next morning, their faces turned into the west wind. They crossed a land of contrasts. Ponderosa pine and spruce forests rose above a desert floor inhabited by lizards and kangaroo rats. Gradually, it became a horizontal land of sagebrush and salt flat, and Theodora could see the signs of the animals most adapted for survival: coyotes, mule deer, and jackrabbits.

She rode beside Blade, who continued to treat her with complete dispassion. Though unfailingly polite, he seemed to be perfectly satisfied with their present estrangement. Yet, he still took time to tell her about the plants and animals they saw.

"It looks as though nothing could survive out here," she said in wonder. "Yet it teems with life."

He smiled at her amazement. "It's quiet now. But at night around the water holes or streams, there'll be a frenzy of activity. Night is when the animals venture out to replace the water they've lost during the day. The watering spots are dangerous places, and those who can drink the fastest or need the least water have chance on their side."

As they crossed a vast high desert and approached the lake, plants and bushes became encrusted with crystallized salt, sometimes an inch thick. In the lake itself, though sparkling clear and sky-blue, nothing lived. There was no marine life of any species.

For six days they searched the western margin of the lake, looking for the outlet of a large river that was marked on an old map Bonniville had given Blade. For years there had been rumors of a river named the Buenaventura, which flowed from the Great Salt Lake directly into the Pacific Ocean. Finding no trace of that mythical river, they turned west and headed onto a barren plain that was almost without game. The sun beat down on them, and they rode in silence except for an occasional whistle or call by a herder trying to hustle up a straggler.

On the third of September Zeke Conyers rode back to the plodding column of men. "Met some friendly Bann'cks camped on a spring up ahead thar, Blade. Way they tell it, we can jest foller the trails they've laid down from one waterin' hole t'other. The old chief said that, by travelin' southwest, we'll come to a mountain covered with snow the whole y'ar round and a large river that eventually sinks right into the ground and plumb disappears. But thar ain't no game ahead. Only a tribe of miserable, no-count In'juns. Beyond 'em is an even bigger snowy mountain, which the chief claims ain't never been crossed."

Blade and Zeke looked at each other in silent exultation. That snow-topped mountain peak was their goal.

"Take Chardonnais and our best horses and go on ahead with a pack mule of supplies. And take enough water to make it back if you can't find a hole. If you do find water, light a signal fire. We'll rest here till nightfall and then follow you."

Sitting astride Athena, Theodora stared after the departing men until she could no longer make out their shapes. "They could be ambushed by those Indians," she said nervously to Blade, who sat on his stallion beside her. "We might never see them again."

"If anyone can survive out there, Zeke can," he reassured her. He dismounted and lifted her down, then pulled his canteen from the saddle pommel. "Right now, I want you to have a long drink of water and then get under the shade of our tent and rest. We'll be traveling all night." He lifted his canteen to her lips and held it while she drank. When she pushed it away after a quick gulp, he raised it to her mouth again. "Take all you want, Theodora," he urged in a deep, coaxing voice. "Just because the men are being rationed doesn't mean you need to go without. You're half the size of the smallest man here. You'll dehydrate in half the time as well."

She started to protest, but her thirst had become overpowering. "I'll have a little more, then," she said, and her voice cracked in her dry throat. She took the canteen and gulped the water, warm from the metal container, careful not to spill a single drop of the precious liquid.

Blade watched her, his midnight eyes telling her without words that he was remembering the first time she drank from his canteen. Every detail rose in her own memory, as though it'd been only days ago instead of weeks. Unconsciously, she lowered the container, as she had that first time, and held it close to her breast. The fire in his gaze was hypnotic. Mesmerized, she reached up to touch his cheek and stopped when her fingertips were only a fraction of an inch from his face. His rugged features were partially hidden by a full beard now, for he hadn't shaved since the rendezvous, and she longed to feel it. How many days had it been since she'd touched him? From deep inside she felt the anguished cry of her achingly lonely spirit. How could she continue to love him so much, when she knew there was no future for them at the journey's end?

When she started to draw her hand away, he grabbed it and pulled it to his face. He kissed her fingers, letting her feel the softness of his thick black whiskers.

"Miz Gordon's tent is ready for her," Wesley Fletcher announced in a caustic voice. They turned to find him right beside them.

Theodora snatched her hand away and shoved the canteen at Blade. "Thank you, Captain," she mumbled, and hurried away.

As they rode in the darkness that night, the desert was ghostlike and nearly soundless. The air was surprisingly cool. Beneath them the ground was a mixture of gravel and sand on which only woody, prickly shrubs existed. All Theodora could hear was the cracking of the salt crust under Spitfire's hooves. After ninety-five days on the trail, Athena was tiring easily, and Theodora only rode her every fourth day in the hope the spirited chestnut would recover her stamina.

On the starlit flat the glint of salt crystals gave the feeling of another world, eerie and supernatural. Against the night sky they could see the dark outline of the high mountain the Bannock chief had told them about. As the dawn light broke, the desert breeze became very cold, and Theodora rode huddled under a buffalo robe.

They stopped to rest while Julius prepared the morning mess of jerky and pemmican. Coffee was being rationed like rare wine. The men sipped it slowly from their tin cups, trying to make it last as long as possible. Too tired to move, Theodora watched a private gather dry thorny shrubs, which burned quickly. Fires were lit to mark their location in the hopes that Conyers and Chardonnais would see them.

Then through the silence of the desert morning came the sound of hooves beating on the sand. With a flourish Chardonnais pulled into camp. "There's water ahead, *bourgeois*," he shouted. "And grass. It will take most of the day, but we'll be out of this god-forbidden desert by nightfall."

Chapter 27

They rode west reaching, at last, the river spoken of by the Bannocks. They followed the alkali river for two weeks and then turned in a southwesterly direction for three more. They skirted a series of lakes with meadow grass, sweet water, and groves of tall cottonwoods. On the last day of September they had their first view of the eastern wall of the Sierra Nevada. They camped beside a river for a day while scouting parties searched for a pass and for game. By this time provisions were low. The dried buffalo meat prepared in Bear Valley was nearly gone. One by one the hunters returned that evening empty-handed. No one had found a pass. No one had seen any sign of game.

Early the next morning they followed an Indian path that Blade discovered, which he hoped would lead them through the mountains. The trail was difficult, and they were slowed by rocks and steep escarpments. When they camped the second evening, there was nothing for the horses to eat, since the ground was covered with snow, and only berries to eat for the exhausted travelers. Everyone felt the bitter cold after the warmth of the desert. They'd made poor speed, but little by little they'd reached an elevation high enough to look out onto the plains they'd just crossed. The view to the east was magnificent.

After the skimpy meal Theodora walked with Blade to the cliff edge and looked out over the desert beneath them, stretching unbroken for as far as they could see. Rivers wound across it like ribbons of silver. The very rivers they had recently

363

followed. From their lofty vantage, they could see the lakes they'd camped beside, with the meager stands of cottonwoods.

Before leaving camp Blade had quietly come up behind her, lifted off her wool shawl, and slipped a coat fashioned from a buffalo robe over her shoulders. It was cozy and warm, with the thick fur on the inside.

"Where did you get this coat?" she asked as they stood gazing at the vista beneath them. She looked up at him over her shoulder in delight. "It's beautiful!"

His pleasure at her surprise lit his eyes. "I bought this for you at Horse Creek. I wanted to be sure you'd keep warm crossing these damnable mountains."

"But you didn't even know if I was coming with you then."

"No, but I hoped you would." He smiled and slipped his arms around her, pressing her against his hard frame. He spoke in her ear. "I see you're wearing the moccasins Two Moons Rising gave you."

With a chuckle Theodora looked down at her toes. She stuck out one foot and admired the intricate beading. "Yes. The fur lining keeps my feet cozy."

"We're going to have some rough traveling in the next few days, Theodora. I want you to take it as easy as possible. We'll keep changing your mount so you'll always have a fresh one. With your light weight, you won't break an animal down like the rest of us." His voice betrayed his anxiety as he lowered his head and softly kissed her temple. "Sometimes I'll have to go ahead with Zeke and the scouting party. When I do, I want you to stay close to Julius. And I want you to carry your carbine with you at all times."

Theodora turned in his arms and placed her hands on his elbows. She searched his rugged features, partially hidden now under the heavy black beard. During the desert crossing he had resumed the daily target practices with her. "I have the feeling you're guarding me, Blade. But from what—or whom—I can't imagine."

Thrilling to the feel of her slim form in his arms, Blade pressed her against his hungry body. He touched a curl the wind had blown against her cheek. It was the first time she'd willingly accepted his embrace since the rendezvous. He'd waited patiently for her to realize they were meant for each other, that she belonged to him. "I just want to be sure you're safe," he murmured, gazing at her soft, beckoning lips.

"I feel very safe right now," she admitted as she looked up at him.

He bent and kissed her gently, holding down with a tight rein the carnal need that reared up inside him like a rutting stallion. "I'd never hurt you, *vehona*," he whispered achingly. "All I ever want to do is love you."

A shudder went through him as Theodora slid her hands over his biceps and across his shoulders, her grass-green eyes searching his face for reassurance. Shyly, tentatively, she caressed his neck and jaw. She took his face, covered with its thick whiskers, in her dainty fingers. "I like your beard," she admitted, a blush tinting her smooth cheeks. "It feels softer than I thought it would."

Blade's heart kicked against his ribs like the recoil of a Kentucky rifle. "It won't scratch you," he promised, his voice low and hoarse. "Not even your silken thighs."

At his words Theodora felt raw, wanton desire spread through her limbs. Her breath caught deep in her chest as he pulled her against the rigid proof of his need. Ignoring the warning voice in her head that chided her foolish behavior, she lifted her lips for his kiss.

This time he wasn't gentle. His full, sensuous mouth covered hers. Insistently, his tongue slid across her lips until she allowed him to enter. Beneath her open fur coat his strong hands moved over her buttocks as he rocked her enticingly, beguilingly against his lean, hard thighs. Fully aroused, she breathed deeply, trying to slow her racing pulse. She pulled back against his tight hold and shook her head. Her voice was quavery and uneven. "This won't change anything, Blade. We still have no future together. After the expedition is over, I'm returning to Cambridge—to my family and my studies."

He released a long, harsh sigh of impatience. "How much longer do you think we can go on like this, Theodora? Not touching each other? Not loving each other?"

"As long as it takes to get to California," she answered.

With one hand cupped behind her skull he pulled her lips toward his. "You're wrong," he whispered roughly, his other hand moving beneath her furry coat. "And I'll prove it."

He kissed her passionately, lifting her off the ground and against his rock-hard body. He held her bottom in one strong hand, and the bulge of his firm arousal pressing against her brought a longing so familiar she trembled. Before they had made love, it had been only a vague, undetermined ache for something she couldn't even define. Now it was a driving need that threatened to overwhelm the carefully constructed barrier she'd built between them. She wanted to remove his clothing piece by piece and then her own, until they were naked in each other's arms and standing on the edge of a precipice that overlooked the entire world.

She tore her lips from his. She knew that if she allowed him to continue nothing would be solved, and she would regret her surrender in the morning.

"Let me go, Blade," she said, and her determination must have communicated itself to him, for he released her.

Even the heavy beard couldn't hide the tautness of his clenched jaw. "I've tried to be patient, princess, but I'm coming to the end of my rope. I'll give you a little more time, but what's going to happen between us is inevitable."

The pass Blade had hoped to find didn't appear. Instead, they began to encounter masses of snow in the hollows, and the animals were swamped, unable to break a trail. While the snow had been only two feet deep, the horses had walked through without much difficulty, throwing aside the snow and opening a track. Now they waded in the drifts with exertion, struggling until their strength gave out. They grew stiff and slow to manage, and the crust on the surface cut their legs so badly that a few refused to continue.

"By gar, must be four foot deep," Conyers reported to the captain when he returned from a fruitless hunting trip. None of the advance party had found game, and it had been four days since they'd had food.

Blade turned to his second-in-command. "I want all the animals taken to the back of the column, Lieutenant Fletcher. And bring every available man up front. Give the lead men forty-minute intervals, then allow them to wait at the side of the track while the others pass."

"How long can they keep this up, Captain?" Fletcher sneered.

"As long as I tell them to, Lieutenant," Blade snapped. "Now carry out your orders."

They camped late that afternoon in near silence. When Blade entered their tent, Theodora was huddled for warmth on her bedroll. He opened his pack and withdrew a handful of pemmican.

"Here's your supper," he told her quietly. He'd given her the same meal for the last four evenings.

Theodora took the food from his outstretched hand and looked up at him, her eyes huge with worry. "Fletcher told me today that the men haven't eaten since we found those berries when we first entered the mountains. He says the soldiers are slowly starving to death."

Blade clenched his fists in disgust. "Someday I'm going to cut Fletcher's tongue out."

"How can I eat this when I know what's happening to them?" she asked in an appalled whisper. "I thought they were eating pemmican in their own shelters."

Blade knelt on one knee in front of her. "Theodora, not one man out there would begrudge you this food. No one would take it from you, if you offered it to him."

"And that's why you've given it to me every night in the secrecy of our tent?" she accused, her face white with apprehension.

"Not secrecy. Privacy. I knew you wouldn't want to eat it in front of the others, especially if you thought no one else had food." He braced an elbow on his knee and rubbed his forehead. "You can't weigh much over a hundred, little girl. Those men out there can afford to shed some pounds. You can't."

Tears blurred her emerald eyes. "I could share it with someone."

"Who?" Blade's sharp reply betrayed his irritation. "Which man, out of the entire thirty-eight, would you like to give it to?"

Motionless, she stared at him. Her lips trembled. "You."

Startled, he looked at her anguished features and read the love there. Touched to the depth of his soul, he kissed her on the tip of her nose with all the tenderness he felt for her. "Thank you, *nazheem*. But your husband happens to be a Cheyenne warrior. Going without food for a few days is considered no more than a minor inconvenience." He placed his hands on her hips and squeezed gently. "I don't want you getting too skinny. I like your luscious curves just the way they are."

A voice called loudly from just outside their closed tent. "Captain Roberts, we'd like to talk to you."

Blade rose and held the tent flap open. Wesley Fletcher stood in the doorway in front of a small group of soldiers.

"Come in, Lieutenant. Men." Blade moved back and allowed the soldiers to enter.

Fletcher stepped into the shelter, followed by Corporal Overbury and three privates. "Miz Gordon, I hope y'll excuse our intrusion," Fletcher drawled as he touched his hand to his cap.

"What is it, Fletcher?" Blade snapped. "State your business."

A mocking smile played on the lieutenant's pale features. "I'm speaking for these men, as well as myself, Captain. We want t' turn around and go back. The idea of crossin' these mountains is insane. We don't have a snowball's chance in hell of making it."

"You're the one who's crazy, Lieutenant. The only hope we have to stay alive is to keep going."

"We want to go back, sir," Overbury piped up. "Even the horses can't make it. What good will we be on foot?"

Blade looked at the men. Then he raised the tent flap once more. "Tell Sergeant O'Fallon to assemble every man in camp," he told the private guarding the front of the tent. "That includes the French Canadians. I want this whole thing settled once and for all."

Chapter 28

In response to Michael O'Fallon's shouts the entire brigade gathered in the snow-packed center of camp.

"I understand that a few of you want to go back," Blade said in a voice that carried through the crowd.

Chardonnais and Guion exchanged surprised glances. *"C'est de la folie,"* Chardonnais called out. "That is foolish talk. We'd never make it to the first lake."

"Even if'n we did," Conyers added, " 'twouldn't do no good. There's no game for thirty days' ride, 'cept'n a few mangy jackrabbits."

"We'll all perish if we continue as we are!" Fletcher shouted. "We haven't eaten in days. The horses are foundering. There's no sign of a pass through these mountains, and the snow gets deeper every day. I say, let's go back."

"Sure and you're barmy, Fletcher," O'Fallon proclaimed, his Irish accent more pronounced in his agitation. The burly sergeant looked at the other four soldiers standing beside the sneering lieutenant. "The man's a fool. If you want him to lead you across that desert, you're as crazy as he is. I'm staying with the captain."

A rumble of agreement spread through the ranks, but the group of dissenters hadn't been swayed. "We just don't think we can make it through the Sierras," Corporal Overbury complained. "I haven't had anything to eat but a handful of berries since we left the desert. I can't go on much longer without food."

"Don't be a fool," Calvin Belknap said. "You'll starve for sure if you go back."

Blade held up his hand for silence. "All right, men. I'm going to give you a choice. If any of you want to go back with Lieutenant Fletcher, you're free to do so. But no one's taking any horses or equipment with them. Those supplies belong to this expedition, and we're keeping them. We'll need everything we have in the next few weeks, and that includes our ammunition. If you go, you'll leave with the clothes on your back, your rifle, and the powder you have now. Nothing more."

One by one, the dragoons moved away from Fletcher to stand beside Chardonnais and Guion. Overbury looked at the lieutenant and then back at his comrades. "Well, shoot," he said sheepishly. "I guess I can last for a few more days." He walked over to the others, refusing to meet Fletcher's irate gaze.

Alone on his patch of snow, Fletcher clenched and unclenched his fists. "Very well," he said at last. "I can't go alone. But I'm tellin' y' now, I warned y'. We're never goin' t' make it t' California alive."

Blade ignored his bitter words. He turned to Julius, who stood beside Theodora, watching. "Twiggs, take these four men," he said, nodding toward the would-be deserters, "and see that they slaughter the two weakest horses."

Julius flashed his generous smile and nodded his grizzled white head. "You bet, Captain. Old Twiggs cook horse just right. Eat fine tonight."

"I'll help you with the mess, Julius," Theodora offered. The thought of eating horse meat appalled her, but then, she wasn't nearly as hungry as the men.

Not ten minutes later she rushed into her tent. "Blade, you've got to stop them," she pleaded.

He looked up from his bedroll, where he sat cleaning his carbine. "What's wrong?"

"It's Athena," she cried, twisting her hands in agitation. "They're going to butcher her!"

He hurried with her from the tent. Together they raced across the bivouac. They barely arrived in time. Overbury was just about to lead Athena to the small spot among the pines where they'd already slaughtered the first horse. "Hold on, Corporal Overbury," Blade called as they approached. "Pick another horse."

"The mare's hardly able to walk, Captain," Overbury said with surprise. "She probably won't last more than another day or two anyway."

"Nevertheless, choose another horse."

As Blade walked away, Theodora clutched his sleeve with her mittened hand. "Thank you."

He turned, his angular profile softened by his deep concern for her. "Theodora, if Athena collapses, we'll have to butcher her. We can't leave the meat to be eaten by wolves when it can be used to keep us all alive. I'm sorry, *vehona*. If it weren't a matter of life and death, I'd never even consider it."

"I understand." Unable to control the shakiness in her voice, she clasped her hands to her breast in an attempt to ease her pain. "But make them wait until she falters. She could rally, you know. I never ride her anymore and no one puts a pack on her." Realizing that she'd just described Athena's present worthlessness, she stopped short.

"I know, princess." With a tortured sigh, he reached over and tucked an errant lock of hair under her furry hat.

She caught his hand and held it to her lips in gratitude. Without a word, she pressed a kiss against his fingers, then left to find Julius.

Alongside Overbury and Belknap, she helped Twiggs roast the horse flesh on skewers made of branches placed over the open fires.

"Out of salt, Miss Theo," Julius told her. "Sprinkle gunpowder, instead."

Soon the aroma of cooking meat permeated the campsite, and the men drifted closer. When the mess was served, they tore into it.

As she sat on a buffalo hide placed on a snowbank, Theodora stared with revulsion at the meal in her dish.

Blade sat down beside her. "I want you to eat all of your portion, Theodora," he ordered. "You'll need the nourishment. Just think of it as a beef steak."

"I'd never have believed we could sink so low," she said, wrinkling her nose in distaste.

"My people eat horses and puppies, too, *vehoka*, when they're starving. Zeke told me about the time he was so hungry he boiled his moccasins and ate them."

Conyers, who'd joined them on the blanket, nodded his agreement. "Yep, 'n that ain't the wust I've eaten, neither. Onc't I was trappin' near the Great Salt Lake with the cap'n's pappy, we were so hungry, we baked up a bunch of them black crickets the Diggers eat. They were real crunchy."

"Please, Zeke!" Theodora begged, and burst out laughing. "It's bad enough trying to eat this stuff." But she took a breath and bit into the charred black meat. It was tough and lean, and she had to wash it down with a swallow of the melted ice water from the steam.

Blade watched her with circumspection. She knew he'd wait until he was certain she'd finished the entire portion in her dish. Thank goodness Athena was still alive, she told herself. God willing, her beautiful mare would make it through the next day, too.

The snow increased to five feet, then six. It was dry and powdery, and the lead men sank up to their armpits. It soon became impossible for them to walk erect, and the first two or three men had to crawl on their hands and knees, with their followers carefully placing their feet in the same holes. After the thirty-plus men had packed the snow down, it was firm enough to support the animals, who soon learned to place their hooves in the indentations made by the men. If they missed a spot, the horses fell into the loose snow up to their bellies and the men had to pull them out.

Every man took his stint leading the way. Even Blade. When it was his turn, he would make four times the distance of any other man, and Theodora marveled that through it all he remained cheerful, confident that they'd make it. He never seemed tired or discouraged, and his example raised the spirits of all the men. They openly strove to earn his respect, pushing themselves beyond human endurance.

Slowly, laboriously, they inched their way into the mountains. They made only two or three miles a day, and sometimes could see the black rings of their old campfires from their new bivouac. The travel-weary column moved gradually upward, finding less and less timber. There were small lakes, with pine, cedar, and redwood, but it was scrubby and meager. Each morning the hunting party, led by Conyers, rode out to search for game; each evening they returned empty-handed. They slaughtered three more horses.

They reached what some thought was the summit, only to travel five more days surrounded by snow and rugged peaks. Everyone was near exhaustion, and the animals were now more of a burden than a help. It appeared that Fletcher's warning would soon come true.

At night they no longer slept in tents. Instead, the men, in sets of threes and fours, dug holes eight feet square down through the snow to the frozen ground. There they placed soft pine twigs, over which they spread their blankets. Two forked sticks were set upright in the snow to the windward of center, and across them the men laid horizontal poles. Over these they piled thick coverings of pine branches to block out the wind. Fires were lit in the bottom of the pits, providing a livable environment, even on the coldest nights.

They suffered more from the frigid temperatures during the daytime. While marching, two men froze their feet. Like Theodora, the invalids now rode on the tired horses. Even in her warm coat, mittens, and moccasins she began to feel the numbing cold. She knew she'd lost weight, despite Blade's insistence that she eat full portions. Everyone else had been on half rations since they first began slaughtering the horses, and she purposely held back at suppertime.

One night after mess she crawled into their shelter early, in search of some protection from the icy wind. As she huddled beside the fire, she shivered uncontrollably, unable to get warm.

Blade came in, replacing the thick roof of pine boughs overhead. A fine sheen of frost covered his beard. Taking off his hat, gloves, and heavy coat, he dropped them on his bedroll. He tossed more wood on the fire, then came over and pulled the buffalo skin tighter around her shoulders.

He drew his black, straight brows together in an anxious frown. "You're still cold, aren't you?" His words were harsh with worry.

"I . . . I can't seem to warm up tonight," she confessed. "I can't stop shaking."

As he hunkered down in front of her, he put out an open palm. "Let me see your feet, love." He lifted one foot and braced it on his heavy thigh. After slipping off her moccasin and wool sock, he felt her toes. "Your feet are like ice, Theodora. You could be suffering from frostbite." His mouth drew into a tight, thin line. "Give me your other foot," he ordered. He stripped off the second moccasin and sock and placed both of her bare feet inside his buckskin shirt. He eased her toes up under his armpits.

The warmth of his body at last penetrated her frozen feet. Leaning back on her elbows, she sighed. "Mmmm. You're as cozy as a steaming teakettle." With a laugh she wiggled her toes. "But the hair under your arms tickles."

A low chuckle rumbled in his chest, and she felt his ribs vibrate against her ankles. "Romantic, isn't it?" he quipped with a wolfish grin. "At least you're not suffering from frostbite, or you wouldn't feel anything. How about your fingers?"

"They're still cold," she admitted. "I should feel better in a minute." But a shiver spread through her and she shook convulsively despite his ministrations.

With a fierce scowl Blade withdrew her bare feet from his shirt and slipped her moccasins back on. He rose and sat crossed-legged beside her on the mattress of sweet-smelling pine boughs. "I'll warm you up, *vehona*," he promised her as he thrust his strong hands beneath the buffalo robe.

Taken by surprise, she tried to pull back, but he impatiently jerked her toward him and the robe fell away. In an instant she was cradled between his muscular thighs. "This is no time to cite your worries about our incompatibility, Theodora," he said brusquely. "I'm going to light a fire inside you that'll burn all night. I'll be damned if I'm going to sit back and watch you lose your fingers and toes."

He pulled the tails of her blouse free of her leather skirt and quickly unfastened the buttons. Pushing the blouse aside, he cupped her breasts. The feel of his strong fingers, as they brushed across her nipples beneath the cotton camisole, brought a whimper of pleasure to her throat. It had been so long since he'd touched her. Boldly, he pushed the sleeves of her blouse down her arms, imprisoning them. Then the straps of her camisole and chemise were ruthlessly shoved aside, and her bare breasts were exposed to his lips.

He suckled and licked her, rumbling low in his throat, and when she tried to move away, he fell back on the blankets, taking her with him. He threw one heavy leg across her, to entrap her body under his, and unfastened the waistband of her buckskin skirt. Freeing her from the weight of his heavy frame, he pulled the riding skirt down her legs and slid it over her moccasined feet. Without pause, he bent over her and kissed the very core of her femininity beneath the thin material of her pantaloons. As he'd promised, fire coursed through her veins, and she writhed beneath him.

"Blade, wait." She gasped, trying to gather her thoughts and repel the siege he'd launched so swiftly against her.

Wait, hell, Blade thought, and softly nuzzled the curly mound through the cotton. He fondled her, his fingers searching. He smiled to himself when her soft, low moan told him he'd found her. Still stroking her, he moved up to cover her lips with his own once more. He thrust his tongue in and out of her mouth, building a rhythm that would remind her of all the times before when he'd loved her. He wanted her to remember how wonderful it had been. Leaving her mouth, he trailed kisses down her neck. He touched the hollow of her throat with a flick of his tongue, then moved on to circle the rosy crest of her breast.

Her hips rose to meet his caresses, and he rubbed his hand between her thighs, stoking the blaze he'd lit inside her like a furnace. When she began to respond in rhythm to his strokes, he pulled back, kicked off his moccasins, and stripped away his buckskins and the breechclout beneath.

"We need to talk, Blade," she said the moment she felt his hands leave her.

"We'll talk later, *nazheem*. You're starting to feel warmer already." He untied the tapes of her pantaloons and pushed them down her slim, graceful legs. When they bunched against her moccasins, he pulled everything off together. "Ah, princess," he murmured, as he spread her ivory thighs apart with his knee and slid his bronzed hands over her creamy skin. "You're as beautiful as I remember."

He entered her with one swift stroke. Despite her earlier protests, she was warm and moist and ready for him. He braced his forearms on either side of her head and covered her lips with his own. He coaxed her to enter his mouth and groaned with delight as he felt her tongue explore him. He moved in her slowly, insistently, bringing her back up with him. He could hear her inhaling drafts of air through her dainty nose, and he lifted his mouth. Soon she was panting in short, heavy gasps in his ear. He pushed back on his elbows and lifted up inside her, increasing her pleasure.

He crooned to her in a mixture of French and Cheyenne, encouraging her to yield to him completely, to think of nothing but the pleasure he was bringing her. At her low, sweet purr of ecstasy, he increased his rhythm, building it until he exploded inside her, while the blood rushed through his veins and his heart pounded against his chest. He braced himself on his forearms and removed his heavy weight while remaining within her. "Now what is it you wanted to talk about, *nameo*, my lover?"

She looked up at him through passion-drugged eyes. Confused, she seemed to search languorously for what she had wanted to say. Then her full lips, bruised from his passionate kisses, formed a petulant moue in feigned disapproval. "I was going to ask permission to remove my blouse, husband. But you never gave me the chance."

He burst out laughing. Her arms were still imprisoned where he'd pushed her sleeves and straps over her shoulders. Above the rumpled camisole and chemise, her pale breasts rose impudently, their pink crests bright and swollen from his suckling. "Are you joking, princess? I should leave you tied up like this all night. It's the only way I've been able to teach you the correct way to address me." For the term she'd used had sent a wave of joy through him.

Despite his threat, Blade gently eased away and sat up. Stripping off his own shirt, he threw it aside and reached for her. With a contented sigh, she allowed him to remove the rest of her garments. Together they slipped under the thick blankets, and he pulled the discarded buffalo robe on top of them. Then he stretched out, yawned contentedly, and brought his exquisite wife up tight against him.

She snuggled close, her head on his shoulder, and wove her fingers into the mat of hair on his chest. "You're better than a hot brick," she told him with impertinence. "I feel toasty all over."

"Just stay right here beside me, little white woman." He ran his hardened fingers over her smooth, tantalizing derrière. "I'll keep you warm all night."

Two weeks after entering the Sierra Nevada range, the expedition continued to travel on top of the mountain, obstructed by snow-filled crevasses, icy rock walls, and sharp drop-offs down which they lowered the packs, horses, and each other. The possibility of avalanches and rock slides haunted them. Despite the piercing winds of the high altitudes, the men struggled to keep moving, yet occasionally they would pause to view the spectacular vista that spread out in front of them. Other than themselves and their animals, they hadn't seen a single living creature for days. They survived on a diet of horse flesh. There was absolutely nothing else to eat. Daily, they faced numbing cold, exhaustion, and the possibility of starvation. Each day they pitted their cunning, strength, and courage against the greatest challenge that any of them had ever known.

There wasn't the slightest sign of a trail or path to guide them. A vast expanse of snow stretched ahead as far as the eye could see. The mountains rose up, peak after snow-capped peak, until it seemed they were wandering in the clouds.

Theodora took on the responsibility of helping the injured and those suffering from frostbite. She rode at the back of the column, where the men too weary to forge into the deepening drifts came to gather their strength during a brief reprieve. One cold, gray afternoon the word came down the line of weary soldiers. The lady's chestnut mare had collapsed.

Leaving Julius to finish tending a man whose hands were bleeding from lacerations caused by falling against sharp rocks, Theodora hurried forward.

Athena lay in a snowbank, her eyes bulging with fear and exhaustion. A small group of dragoons circled the fallen horse, watching in silence as O'Fallon tugged on her reins.

"Come on, lass," he urged the mare, "up on your feet, now."

Several men shook their heads, obviously certain the chestnut would never gather the strength to rise.

Kneeling beside her in the trampled snow, Theodora lifted the beloved mare's head and cradled it in her lap. "It's no use, Sergeant," she said as she took the reins from his hand. "She'll only collapse again."

Theodora stroked the velvety nose and whispered softly to the valiant animal. "You can go to sleep now, Athena. The journey is over for you. No Thoroughbred could have tried harder. Now it's time to rest."

She laid her cold cheek against the mare's head and stroked the long, reddish brown neck one last time. Then she eased out from under the suffering animal and stood beside her. She turned to face the men, unashamed of the tears that streamed down her cheeks. "Sergeant," she said, her voice calm and certain, "may I borrow your rifle?"

O'Fallon's blue eyes glistened. He took a step toward her. "Faith, *mavourneen*, I can take care of it for you."

"No, she's my horse, Sergeant. I'll do what has to be done."

Without another word he handed her the fine percussion carbine he and Blade had taught her how to use their first day on the trail. Theodora slipped her mittens off and brushed the tears from her eyes. She lifted the weapon, aimed, and pulled the trigger, releasing Athena from her horrible suffering.

At the sound of the blast, Blade came hurrying back from his stint at clearing a path in the drifts. He slowed to a walk when he saw his wife standing over her dead mare, the smoking carbine still clutched in her rigid, icy fingers. Only a few feet away, he stopped and waited, wondering if she would break down and fling herself into his arms. But she straightened her shoulders and handed the rifle back to O'Fallon.

"See that she's butchered this afternoon, Sergeant," she said without a tremor in her voice as she slowly pulled on her mittens. "I'll help Julius prepare the meat for the evening mess."

She looked up and met Blade's gaze with tormented eyes. But there were no more tears. "Go back to the front where you're needed, *nahyam*," she urged. "I'll talk to you later.

Private Belknap needs bandages on his cut hands." She turned and walked toward the rear, her spine ramrod straight.

Blade looked at the watching men, their eyes filled with admiration. He'd never been so proud of his wife. He nodded to them in silent acknowledgment of their regard for her. "Carry on with your work, men. Let's keep this company moving."

On the twentieth of October, in a maze of cols, peaks, and boulder fields, they began to encounter small streams that would shoot out from under the high snowbanks, run for short distances in deep chasms, and fall from one escarpment to another until they fell like sheets of rain across the face of the gorge beneath. The trekkers came to the edge of a precipice and stared awestruck into a valley over a mile below them.

Theodora stood beside Blade and peered at the scene of grandeur. Through aeons of time, a gigantic canyon had been carved into solid granite by the elements. Steep cascades and free-leaping waterfalls fell from the cliffs of hanging valleys on either side of the gorge. Across from the amazed travelers, a mountain peak had been sheared in half, its smooth granite face dropping straight down to the floor below. All about them, rounded domes stood against the sky in majestic splendor.

"My God," she whispered in awe as she reached for Blade's hand. "This must be the most wondrous place on the face of the earth."

The men crowded to the edge of the cliff to stand and gaze in rapture. A valley more than seven miles long and of unprecedented beauty spread beneath them. Locked in snow, it lay in pristine loveliness between two sheer granite walls. It was studded with monoliths. Like bridal veils, cataracts fell fifteen hundred feet down its rocky sides.

"Look at that dome over there," she said, pointing to the other side. "How in the world could it have ever been formed?"

"Mebbe by an earthquake," Zeke conjectured. "I heard tell Californee has big'uns. By gor, mebbe one was so big, the front half of the mountain jest fell down."

"More than likely this entire canyon, including that half dome over there, was formed over countless years by glaciers,"

Blade replied. "Look at the scars across the face of the rocks. Like they've been gouged out by the hands of giants."

"Look over there to the west, chérie," Chardonnais said, standing beside Theodora.

She gazed in the direction of Louis's pointing finger. A great waterfall streamed directly out of the winter mist of cloud topping a snow-covered peak.

"Have you ever seen anything more beautiful?" Her voice was filled with wonder.

"There can't be anything on earth prettier than this, Madame Roberts. Ask the *capitaine*. I will bet he has never even read of anything that beats this, and he has studied the whole world in those books of his."

But Blade was already busy making plans with Conyers, who'd just returned from another unsuccessful attempt to find a route down the western face of the mountains.

"We'll follow the ridge westward," Blade explained. "Looks like we're caught between two chasms. We'll keep moving along the top till we find a spot where we can start to work our way to the valley below."

Blade turned back to Theodora. "How are your eyes?" he questioned, tender regard for her softening his proud, chiseled features.

Blade had been covering her cheeks with ashes from their fire each morning to relieve the dazzling reflection of the sun's rays against the snow. The afternoons were bright, and the sun had shone with enough warmth to slightly melt the top of the snow. Each night, the snow would freeze into a firm sheet on top, and the glare in daylight was nearly intolerable.

"I can see fine, but one of the troopers is almost blind," she said, leaning against Blade's secure bulk and placing her mittened hand on his wide chest. She tried to keep the fear from her voice. Since he'd first made love to her that bitterly cold evening, she had clung to him every night, drawing her own strength from his limitless courage. As he'd kept her warm through the long winter nights, so he'd protected her in the days of arduous travel. And his unceasing care had bound her to him even more deeply than his passionate lovemaking. Without words, he had shown her that she could meet the challenge of the mountains. She strove daily to prove his faith in her was not mistaken, matching his iron will with her own firm resolve to best the elements, to survive. She knew now that what he said was true. They belonged together.

"I talked to the soldier earlier." Blade slipped his arm around her. "He'll ride today. Someone can lead him. Just be sure you keep that charcoal on," he warned her.

She looked up into his jet eyes and laughed. "You have this strange penchant for blackening my face."

His eyes crinkled as his devastating grin split his dark beard. "How you can be as pale as you are and still survive amazes me." He shook his head in mock reproach. "Little white woman big trouble. But worth it."

Careful to avoid the charcoal, he kissed the tip of her nose. "Did you talk to Haintzelman?"

She nodded, thinking of the lieutenant's face and hands, blistered as if burned by a fire. His eyes were swollen shut and his lips cracked and bleeding. "I made up more of my infamous salve for him. You should have heard him complain about the smell when I smeared it all over his burns."

Blade chuckled softly. "Having once been a recipient of your evil-smelling remedies, I can appreciate his complaints. I'm only sorry you have to consume your precious samples for medicine instead of saving them for your journal. Does it bother you?"

For the past two weeks, Theodora had used her knowledge of herbs and plants to concoct salves, ointments, syrups, and teas to ease the suffering of the trailblazers. The men had started calling her "Doc Roberts," and Blade had complained with a wry grin that his shelter smelled more like a pharmacy than a honeymooners' boudoir.

She shook her head at him. "You know me better than that. No botanical specimen is more important than a man's health and well-being. Besides, you can take me back to your village next summer so Picking Bones Woman can help me find some more."

Blade lifted the edge of the woolen shawl that was wrapped like a scarf around Theodora's neck and chin. He pulled it higher and tucked it tight. "You can plan on it, princess."

Out of habit he reached inside his heavy coat, then patted his empty shirt pocket. "This has to be the greatest deprivation of all," he complained with a rueful grin. "Giving up food isn't too bad, but going without my seegars is really annoying."

"Why don't you borrow some of Zeke's tobacco?" she suggested.

"He's been out of it since before we reached the summit. There isn't a man in the party who wouldn't trade his evening portion of horse meat for something to smoke or chew."

She clucked her tongue in admonition. "It isn't good for you anyway, *nahyam*. Didn't anyone ever tell you it would stunt your growth?"

He looked down at her from his great height, the delight he felt at her calling him "husband" glowing in his midnight eyes. "My grandmother claimed it was why I never grew to be as tall as my father. But I know that's a lie."

"Why?" she asked in disbelief. "Jacques is almost seven feet tall."

He grinned like a mischievous boy. "Yes, but my father told me once that he'd been smoking since he was eight years old."

She shook her head, trying without success to keep from laughing. "But think how tall the two of you would be if you'd never begun."

From his spot at the front of the column, Wesley Fletcher watched the couple as they stood in each other's arms and laughed like schoolchildren. The sight of them together sickened him. He'd hated Blade Roberts from the moment he'd learned the half-breed had bested him in their rankings at the academy their first year. He'd been certain the only way a stupid, lazy Indian could outscore him was by cheating, but he'd found no way to prove it.

The breed had dogged his career ever since. Their first campaign with Colonel Dodge had been a fiasco for everyone but Roberts, who knew about the danger of tainted water on the plains and tried to warn the others. Roberts had received a commendation when they'd returned, while he'd suffered a black mark on his record.

Then there'd been the skirmish with the Comanches a year later, when Roberts had ridden into the midst of a battle and saved a wounded man that he himself had left to the mercy of

he savages. Fletcher ground his teeth in fury, remembering
the way the half-dead private had stared at him with accusing
eyes as he rode into Fort Gibson behind Roberts. It'd taken a
mouthful of lies to convince his superiors that he'd truly believed the man dead before he left him alone and surrounded
by hostiles. He'd narrowly missed a court-martial that time.

But nothing had been as bad as watching the half-breed
seduce and win that blond witch after he'd tried so hard himself
to impress her with his phony Southern gentleman behavior.
Christ, he'd bent over backwards treating her like royalty, when
all he'd really wanted to do was throw her down and ram it
in her.

His patience was running low, Fletcher admitted to himself,
blowing on his icy fingers before replacing his buffalo-hide
mittens. The mountain men he'd hired back at Horse Creek
had been worthless fools. If Big Joe Shrady hadn't died of
injuries from his fight with Roberts, he'd have murdered the
idiot himself. The same as he'd killed his partner. That stupid
fool had gotten so liquored up he couldn't even shoot an un-
armed woman.

Fletcher cursed softly to himself. Since his unsuccessful
attempt to turn the expedition back after they'd first entered
the Sierras, he'd had to wait and bide his time. He couldn't
afford to do anything more until they found their way through
these blasted mountains. Like all the others, he needed Roberts
to survive. But as soon as they discovered the pass, he'd make
his move. This time he wouldn't leave it in the hands of incompetent hirelings. And this time he wouldn't fail.

Chapter 29

"*Capitaine! Capitaine!* I've found a pass!" Louis Chardonnais came into view on the crest of a rise. He held his hands to his mouth and hollered at the top of his lungs. "I've found a way down!"

Shouts of excitement rose from the exhausted travelers as the joyful news was passed down the line.

Blade stood beside Conyers, who had just arrived to report that he'd once again come back empty-handed. "Wait there, Louis," Blade called, and turned to the others. "O'Fallon, get Guion. I sent him to the back of the column to let Twiggs and Theodora take a look at the cuts on his hands. Zeke and I will go on ahead with Chardonnais. You two join us on the double."

Trudging as fast as he could through the snowbanks, Blade reached Chardonnais, breathless in the high altitude. Louis had dropped down on his butt in a drift and, with his arms propped across his bent knees, rested his head on them. The deep creases on his weathered face were now concealed by a dark, shaggy beard, and the once well-trimmed mustache reminded Blade of the frost-covered tusks of a walrus hanging down on each side of his mouth. But his deep brown eyes retained their twinkle.

"I found it!" he exulted. "It's steep and it won't be easy, but I think we can make it, *bourgeois*."

Blade clapped the winded man on his back. "Good work, Louis. Catch your breath, and then you can take us there."

Chardonnais scrambled to his feet on wobbly legs. Two pairs of fur-lined moccasins had cracked and split over the weeks

385

in which he'd scouted ahead, and there were now pieces o green horsehide tied around his feet with twine. But because of his natural strength and resilience, he was in better shape than most of the dragoons, some of whom had been forced to wrap their feet in pieces of blankets and even the tails of thei buckskin shirts. "Let's go," he panted. "The sooner we ge there, the sooner we'll be out of these devil mountains."

Blade and Zeke followed Chardonnais's lead. They walke in his footprints, trying to stay on the trail he'd already blazed

For the five days since they'd first looked down on the magnificent canyon, they had followed its northern ridge, con tinually seeking a passage to the floor a mile below. The way had been rough and wearisome. One after another they'd con quered hills of drifted snow and ledges of sheer rock. Each morning Blade had sent out small parties of scouts, who'd returned in the evening tired and discouraged. The steady up ward climb, the freezing cold, the blizzards, the half rations— just the very effort it took to move forward each day—had taken a terrible toll on his men. Many of them suffered from snow blindness, their vision so poor that, time and again, they'd fall and roll in the snow, cutting themselves on rocks and brush Some were so discouraged that they pleaded to be allowed to lie in the snow, where they'd fallen, and drift into a sleep from which they'd never wake. They had reached a point of des peration. Blade knew that their situation would be hopeless unless they discovered a way out soon.

"Here it is, *Capitaine*," Chardonnais said, his shoulders heaving with exertion. He pointed to the west.

"Holy Moses," Zeke exclaimed. "Would ya look at that!"

They had arrived at the brink of the range's westernmost edge. Beneath them they saw an almost perpendicular drop. Taking out his spyglass, Blade gazed at the plain nearly three miles away. It stretched westward to the horizon, and from their great height it looked golden and hazy in the distance.

"There it is, men. California!" Blade grinned with happi ness. "By God, we've made it."

Zeke looked at the straight drop in front of them. "Sure as shootin'. All we gotta do is sprout wings an' fly down."

Guion and O'Fallon joined them, puffing as they came.

"Faith, and it's a sight to behold. Sure and we've come to

the end of the world.'' O'Fallon grabbed Zeke, lifted him up over his head, and twirled him around, ignoring his yells of outrage. With the scout's slight build and his own beefy frame, the sergeant carried him about as easily as a child, despite the long weeks of poor diet.

"Careful, Sergeant." Blade laughed. "We don't want Zeke to reach the floor of the canyon without a rope."

His Irish eyes shining with delight, O'Fallon set the mountain man down and moved toward Chardonnais.

"Sacré bleu," Louis exclaimed. "Take one more step near me and you will be the first one over the cliff."

All five laughed with the heady glee of deliverance.

"We'll camp here for the night, Sergeant," Blade ordered. "Tomorrow we'll begin our descent."

That next morning squads of men were sent out to probe the face of the cliff. Everyone worked in a state of euphoria, despite the fact that they were weak from cold and lack of food and suffered from altitude sickness. In the past weeks they'd faced temperatures that sometimes dipped twenty degrees below zero and had beaten a trail with spades and mauls through snows ranging in depth from six feet in the open to as much as a hundred feet in the sheltered draws. But they had survived.

Julius and Theodora continued to treat the injured and lame while the men searched for the path that would lead them safely down. At midday, Blade came back to walk her into a stand of trees, giving her privacy for her personal needs, though he was never out of earshot. Just as she was about to return to her husband, Theodora saw a sight that stopped her heart: *Antilocapra americana.*

She caught her breath in the frosty air. In the timber on the slope above her, only a short distance away, stood a male pronghorn antelope, his branched horns rising up against the clear, cold sky. He stood absolutely still, upwind and looking away from her. On the far side of a small meadow was the female, waiting for his signal to come across.

Theodora dared not move or call Blade. The slightest sound would send the pronghorns leaping away to safety. Slowly, slowly, she lifted the carbine her husband insisted she carry everywhere she went. Since entering the mountains, she hadn't once practiced shooting, for the fear of avalanche was always present. Could she do it? Trying to remember everything her husband had taught her, she braced the butt against her shoulder, sighted down the barrel, and squeezed the trigger.

The blast of the rifle echoed in the still winter afternoon, and Blade was instantly at her side. Knocked backward by the recoil, she'd fallen into a deep, powdery drift, and she thrashed around, trying to regain her footing. He lifted her out and yanked her behind the nearest tree. His face was ashen as he searched for any sign of blood on her. Holding his carbine ready to fire, he glanced up the snowy slope.

"Well, I'll be damned," he said. He lowered the weapon and came out to stand beside the juniper. "Would you look at that!" He turned and grinned at her, admiration glowing in his eyes. "We've had a veteran scout and two seasoned mountain men out hunting every day for three weeks, and my little New England bluenose shoots the first fresh meat. Why didn't you tell me you'd become a crack shot? I'd have sent you out with Conyers and Chardonnais days ago."

Bursting with pride, she peeked out from behind him. There in the snow was the fallen pronghorn, its horns making a dark crisscross pattern in the powdery whiteness.

"Sometimes I even amaze myself," she confessed.

Together they burst out laughing, then charged up the slope to the fallen antelope.

During the dangerous quest to find a way to the valley below, Corporal Overbury tripped and fell against a pile of jagged boulders. He fractured his arm and was carried back to Julius and Theodora. She gave the injured man some hot tea made from herbs to help lessen the pain, but Overbury still had to bite on a leather belt to keep from screaming in agony. The broken bone had punctured the skin, and after Julius set it, Theodora sewed the torn flesh together, just as she'd seen Snow Owl mend Blade's wounds that summer. Through the surgery, Theodora willed her hands to be steady and her legs to support her. Only after the task had been completed did she allow herself the consolation of plopping down on a buffalo robe spread on the snow. She lowered her head to her knees and fought the faintness that enveloped her. Gradually, she felt the queasiness pass and stood up to resume her work.

Julius had just started to make a sling for the patient when Lieutenant Fletcher came up.

"The captain wants y' to join him right away, Miz Gordon," he told her. "He wants y' to see the scenery from that ridge over there. I'm t' take y' to him."

As Twiggs helped Overbury ease his arm into the brace, Theodora nodded. "I'll be right back, Julius," she called over her shoulder, following the Georgian's footsteps through the snow.

Fletcher led her away from the camp and through a heavy stand of western junipers. "That was very clever of y', Miz Gordon," he said with admiration, "shootin' that antelope like y' did. It was fortunate y' had your gun handy."

She smiled warmly at his praise. Her lucky shot had been just that—lucky. She didn't fool herself that she'd become an expert with the rifle. She realized with a start that this time she'd forgotten to bring it along. The gory task of stitching up the corporal's lacerated flesh had been more unsettling than she'd admitted. But since she'd soon be with Blade, she really didn't need her weapon. And the chance of her shooting another pronghorn was slim, indeed. Besides, Fletcher had his own carbine resting securely across his arm.

They halted at the crest of a ledge to admire the view. A snowy slope dropped from their feet in a gradual slide of about two hundred yards. Then the precipice fell straight down, one mile to the valley below.

"It's truly beautiful, isn't it?" she asked him. She inhaled the clear, wintry air. Although they'd been in the mountains for weeks, she was still awestruck at the wild, untouched magnificence of the terrain.

Unexpectedly, Fletcher caught her elbow and turned her to face him. "How would you know what was beautiful?" he snarled, his handsome face distorted with contempt. "Your taste seems t' run t' dirty half-breeds."

She gazed blankly into his silvery blue eyes, stunned by his words. In her confusion she said the first thing that came to mind. "Where's Blade?"

"Oh, he'll be along in a little while." Fletcher's tone was mocking and sarcastic. "I made no attempt t' cover our tracks.

Once he realizes you're missin', he won't have any trouble findin' us.''

An icy chill ran down Theodora's neck. In a split second she knew why Blade was always guarding her. Why he'd ordered Peter and Julius to watch over her when he wasn't near. Why he insisted she carry her own rifle everywhere she went. But even if he'd warned her that someone was trying to harm her, she'd never have suspected the mild-mannered Southern gentleman in their midst, who'd always treated her with such formal courtesy. It didn't make any sense. There was no reason for him to want to hurt her. But the contemptuous look in his eyes told her he planned to do just that.

"You're going to kill me, aren't you?" she asked him in disbelief. She swallowed convulsively. Her legs wobbled, and she fought to remain standing.

"Not right away," he assured her, his pale eyes glinting with hatred. "First, we're goin' t' wait for the breed. Then you and I are goin' t' have a little fun while he watches."

Bile rose in her throat at the thought of what he planned. "You'll never do it while he's alive, Fletcher."

"Oh, he'll do just as I say when he sees my gun pointed right at your blond head." He grinned evilly. "Why do y' think I brought this rope?"

For the first time she noticed the length of cord he carried slung over his shoulder.

"You've tried to kill me before, haven't you?" she asked in bewilderment.

He jerked her up against him. "Y' never guessed, did y'? Why do y' think y' slid off your horse and nearly drowned in the Big Blue River?"

Frantically, Theodora struggled to pull free of him, but he held her imprisoned in his grip.

He laughed wildly at her futile struggle. "How do y' think that rattler got on your bedroll at Laramie? Did y' really believe it just happened to crawl int' your tent?" With a sudden move he bent and slashed his mouth against hers.

She bit his lip, and he jerked away. His fine features were twisted with loathing. Bit by bit she began to ease away from him. He wiped the blood from his mouth with one hand, lifted his rifle with the other, and pointed it straight at her face.

"Don't move, y' little whore. You're not goin' anywhere. I've been waitin' a long time for this," he sneered. "I'm goin' t' enjoy every minute of it."

He took a step toward her, and Theodora moved back to the edge of the embankment.

"Y' know, Theodora, " he said in a confidential tone, as though sharing a secret with a close friend, "I was truly relieved each time my attempts t' kill y' failed. When I tried t' poison both of you Gordons, and only your brother died, I was glad you hadn't drunk that coffee laced with arsenic. I kept hopin' there was some way I could avoid your death, at least until after I took y'. Y' do remember how often I tried to talk y' into turnin' back, don't y'?"

At his shocking disclosure Theodora's breath caught in her throat. She teetered on the rim of the snowy bank. Her vision blurred, and she fought off the darkness that nearly swallowed her. "You killed Tom?" she cried. She willed herself not to faint. Dry, painful sobs choked her, turning her voice into a high-pitched keen. "You murdered my brother?"

"Don't be afraid," he soothed in an attempt to hush her cries. He glanced cautiously down the slope and then moved slowly toward her.

In panic, Theodora looked back over her shoulder, debating the extent of her slide toward the sheer drop-off should she lose her balance.

"Y' don't want t' do that," he coaxed as he crept nearer. "Y' might misjudge your slide and go right over the edge. A mile down is a long way t' fall. Wait for your Indian lover t' come and rescue y'."

"You lied about Blade all along, didn't you?" she asked, frenziedly stalling for time.

Fletcher stopped and grinned with fiendish delight, the tawny mustache spreading above his straight, even teeth. "Y' believed it all, didn't y'?" He shook his head with consummate pride. "Shit, Theodora, y' were easy t' fool."

She eased her feet along the rocky ledge, hoping for some means to distract him. "Was . . . was he really in trouble at West Point over a woman?"

The complacent smirk on Fletcher's face was terrifying. "Oh, indeed, he was. I bribed a harlot to sneak into his room and blame him when she was caught. If it hadn't been for the fact that Blade was doin' research with a professor all that evenin', my plan would've worked, too. But the slut never confessed who'd helped her get int' his room. She met with an unfortunate accident before they could question her.''

"Why do you hate him so much?"

"Because he's nothin' but a filthy breed,'' he snarled, and took a step closer. "I've been passed over time and again, while he's been given commendations and promotions. He's wealthy, did you know that? And I'm dirt stinkin' poor. That story about my rich family was nothin' but a lie. All my life I've wanted t' make somethin' of myself. And every time I had a chance, that sneakin', lyin' Indian beat me out.'' He shook his head, and the wild look in his pale eyes betrayed the depth of his thirst for vengeance. "But not anymore.''

The glittering reflection of sunlight bouncing off metal dazzled their eyes, and they both turned. Blade was standing in the clearing in front of them, his carbine in his hands. He had come up silently through the timber while they were arguing.

"Thank God,'' Theodora whispered, her knees nearly buckling under her.

In a sudden movement Fletcher grabbed her, and they tottered on the rim of the embankment. Holding her fast, he turned to face the man racing across the meadow toward them. With one hand entwined in her hair, Fletcher held the rifle beneath Theodora's jaw.

Blade skidded to a halt in the snow only yards away.

"That's right, Roberts. I've got her. Come on and see if y' can take her away from me.''

Blade's voice was icy calm. "Let her go, Fletcher. This is between you and me.''

"Not on your life, you dirty scum. Now throw your gun in that snowbank over there. Your knife, too.''

"Shoot him, Blade!'' Theodora screamed. "He poisoned Tom. He'll kill us both anyway.''

"Go ahead, Roberts. Shoot,'' Fletcher taunted. "But I promise y', I'll pull this trigger before I go down. And y' can spend the rest of your life wondering what y' could have done different t' save your woman.''

His face carved in granite and completely devoid of expression, Blade pitched his weapon into the snow. Slowly, he unsheathed his knife and tossed it beside the carbine. He spread his hands in a gesture of placation. "All right, Fletcher, just take it easy."

Fletcher swung his rifle, aiming it directly at Blade's broad chest. As he moved, Theodora reached up and shoved the barrel aside.

In that instant Blade lunged for the Georgian. The three of them crashed over the embankment. Slipping, sliding, rolling, they careened down the slope toward the edge of the precipice in a tangle of arms and legs and snow.

Landing in a drift, Theodora crawled to her hands and knees and watched the two men in horror. Just in front of her lay Fletcher's carbine. She snatched it up, jerked off one mitten with her teeth, and aimed.

The two men were locked together. They rolled over and over on the snowy ground, only inches from the sheer drop-off. Fletcher had managed to pull his knife from his belt, and Blade gripped the Southerner's wrist in a clamp of steel. He applied a relentless pressure, and the weapon slipped from Fletcher's numbed fingers. On top of Fletcher, Blade released his hold on the other man's wrists and reached for his throat, but the lieutenant countered the move, his thumbs seeking Blade's eyes.

Slowly the men rose to their knees, and then to their feet, each straining to improve his hold. Suddenly Blade kicked out with his leg and knocked his opponent off balance. Fletcher wobbled like a drunk. With the chopping edge of his hand, Blade struck him a blow across the windpipe that rocked him, and Fletcher fell backward into the snow. Dazed, he shook his head.

Crouching over his enemy, Blade reached down to pull him up for another blow. Fletcher slammed a rock against Blade's temple, and he pitched forward. Fletcher rolled out from under him. Lifting a boulder over his head, he positioned himself to smash it down on Blade's head.

From her snowdrift Theodora pointed the rifle at Fletcher's back. In her mind, she could hear Blade's words. *You don't have the skill to merely wound or disarm a man. So aim for the trunk of the body, not an arm or a leg. And aim to kill.*

This time she kept her eyes open when she pulled the trigger. But her shot was wild, and the bullet only grazed his hand, merely startling him. He dropped the rock, forgotten at his feet, then turned, leaving an unconscious Blade facedown in the snow, and walked slowly toward her.

Horrified, Theodora rose. Fighting the panic that enveloped her, she turned the weapon end over end in her hands. The pale blue eyes bored into her, a glint of triumph in their silvery depths. As he came near, she swung the carbine at him with all her might. He caught the rifle butt and jerked it from her hands. With a foul obscenity he flung it away and shoved her into the snow.

She fought like a wildcat. Screaming, kicking, clawing, punching, she refused to be taken easily. The sound of his horrible, high-pitched laughter brought sobs to her aching throat.

Suddenly he was lifted off her.

Silhouetted against the blue sky, Blade held Fletcher over his head and walked toward the precipice. Without a pause he reached the edge and threw the Georgian over the cliff. Fletcher's screams of terror echoed back and forth across the valley as he fell to the floor, far below.

Theodora crawled to her knees, gasping for breath, her lungs demanding oxygen in the thin air. Blade hurried to her and knelt in the snow, searching her face.

"I'm fine, I'm fine," she wheezed in answer to his unspoken question. She took his bearded cheeks in her cold, trembling hands, and her voice cracked as she spoke. "I tried to shoot him. I kept my eyes open, and I still missed."

He enfolded her, rocking her back and forth in his powerful arms. He chuckled softly in her ear, and she leaned back in wonder to search his rugged features.

"What?" she said. "What is it?"

He smiled tenderly. Cupping her chin in his strong fingers, he gently brushed her tears away with his thumbs. "I was just thinking, *vehona*. You've earned yourself another eagle's feather. For a little Quaker bluestocking whose only knowledge of life came from books, that's not half bad."

* * *

That evening they feasted on roasted antelope and acorns, while everyone once again heard the story of Fletcher's treachery and deceit. At sunrise, without having discovered any easy passage over the rocks, the party prepared for the descent.

"We can drop down from here, Blade," Zeke said. "This is about as smooth and gradual a drop as I can find."

"Gather up every rope in the party, Lieutenant Haintzelman," Blade ordered. "And check them carefully."

He looked at the men gathered around him. Bearded and gaunt, their long hair hanging around their shoulders, their buckskins in shreds, their vision impaired from the constant glare of the sunlight against the glistening snow, they waited for orders. Since Wesley Fletcher's attempt to turn the party back, not one man had turned craven.

"All right," Blade said. "Who wants to go down first?"

Although many men raised their hands and called out in the affirmative, it was Calvin Belknap's tenor voice that carried above the rest. "Let me, Captain. I'm one of the lightest men here. It'll be that much easier for them to guide me down."

Blade looked at the wiry New Yorker, who'd started the journey as an immature kid and, somewhere on the trail, had become a man. "You're on, Belknap."

His sunburned face protected by a scarf, Peter arrived with a group of dragoons carrying ropes. "Here they are, sir. Every bit of rope we could find."

Chardonnais and Conyers tied a harness around Calvin and the other end of the rope to a pine tree and started to ease him over the side. When only his head was still visible above the rock ledge, he grinned at them.

"Anyone want to bet I won't make it?" he quipped.

"Faith, man," O'Fallon exclaimed. "And who'd be betting against you? 'Tis every man here that's wishing you luck, for he may be the next one down."

Inch by inch, they lowered Belknap over. O'Fallon, as one of the strongest, stood at the edge of the cliff face and guided the rope through his huge hands.

The group of men at the top slowly let out the rope, listening with held breaths to the sergeant's instructions. At last they felt a slack on the rope.

"Bless us and save us, he's reached the ledge," O'Fallon

called out as he peered over the rocky edge. "He's signaling to pull up the rope."

A cheer of wild exultation went up.

One by one, the men went for the dizzying ride down the face of the mountain. Hours passed while the few remaining horses and baggage were laboriously lowered over the rocks. At last it was Theodora's turn.

Blade methodically checked every inch of the rope before he tied it around his waist. He walked to the edge of the precipice. "Come on, princess," he called with a smile of encouragement. "You're going down with me."

He tied her to him around their waists, then lifted her in his arms. "Put your hands around my neck. That's it," he told her. His voice was calm and soothing. "All you have to do is hang on to me and keep your eyes on my face. You've done that before," he whispered in her ear.

Theodora was startled at the double meaning of his words. Surely, no one but her husband would bring up lovemaking at a time like this. As they were lowered off the cliff and out into space, her feet dangling in midair, she clung to him with the tenacity of a frightened kitten. With his muscular arms around her, she squeezed her eyes tightly shut. "There's one thing I've never told you," she said hoarsely.

"What's that?"

"I've always had a fear of falling."

"Don't be frightened, *vehoka*. We're just going for a little ride."

Terrified, she pressed her face into his shoulder. She envisioned herself hurtling through an empty void to smash on the jagged rocks below.

Suddenly they jerked to a stop and dangled like two spiders on a single web. She moaned in horror. "There's something else I want to tell you, in case . . ."

"What's that?"

"I think I've loved you from the first moment I saw you," she blurted out. "It's just that you made me so darn mad most of the time, I couldn't admit it, even to myself."

The rope jerked once more, and slowly they started to move again.

She heard laughter in his deep voice. "If I'd known what

it'd take to get you to confess that, after all those weeks, I'd have tied you to me and thrown us over a cliff on a rope long before now."

Carefully, bit by bit, she pulled her head back and looked into his black eyes. She'd been right. He was laughing. "That's one thing I've learned about you, Blade. If I give you so much as an inch, you take a mile."

He squeezed her even tighter. "I don't want much, *nazheem*. Just all of you for the rest of my life."

At last she felt the solid ground beneath her feet. The ordeal was over, and her husband had given her something else to think about besides her fear of falling. "From now on, if you want any more intimate confessions from me, *nahyam*," she told him with a rueful smile, "I'd like you to try something a little less frightening."

Michael O'Fallon was the last man down. Hand over hand, he lowered himself on the rope, until he stood safely beside them on the rocky ledge.

"Sure and I don't think that's much fun," he told them, and his calm remark brought a roar of laughter from the ecstatic group.

Ledge by ledge, they continued their downward drop. The scouting party set out ahead to search for game. The going was steep and hard, but the main body continued until the light was almost gone. The hunters returned after dark with two large black-tailed deer and a black bear, and Twiggs cooked up a feast. That night they sat around the campfires in the snow and told all the tales they'd ever heard of California.

As the expedition descended the mountain, they encountered less and less snow, and the trail became easier. Groves of green oak bushes, redwood, white cedar, and balsam trees covered the mountainside. By the end of the week, over a month since they'd entered the Sierra Nevadas, they camped at the base of the mountain. Game was plentiful here, and they ate their fill of deer, elk, bear, and antelope. An Indian village was seen from afar, but its residents fled at the sight of them.

The exhausted travelers had a rest day at last, and Theodora spent the afternoon straightening her packs. She unearthed the diary she'd begun at Fort Leavenworth and reread her early entries in which she criticized Blade for his arrogance and overbearing sense of authority. She remembered with poignant nostalgia the time she'd sheltered under his cape, and the morning he'd found her under her petticoat tent. It had been the last day of Tom's life. There in the diary, too, were the scathing passages in which she'd denounced the captain for the inhuman way he'd insisted that she speak and eat and work. She knew now that it had been a calculated campaign to force her to return to the world of the living.

She rose from her bedroll with a deep sigh and walked to the doorway of her shelter. In front of her stretched a valley of incredible beauty. Its meadow was covered with snow, but the soil beneath it was rich and bountiful. There were great granite monoliths, one of which Blade estimated was three thousand feet high. One cataract fell fifteen hundred feet from its massive cliffs, whipping into a feathery mist in the cold air before it fell straight down its sheer walls. All was snow-clad, silent splendor, a white wilderness of untouched beauty.

How Tom would have marveled at it all, she mused. The carnival atmosphere of the rendezvous on Horse Creek. The near-silent journey through the desert. The horrible forcing of the Sierra Nevada. She gazed up into the wintry sky. *Oh, Tom, she called in silent prayer. Are you watching us now and smiling that wide, carefree grin of yours? Do you know that I've tried to keep our dream alive? Your maps will be published, just as we planned. And now I must go on, to build a life of my own with the man I love.*

Theodora dropped her gaze to her husband's form next to War Shield, where he was currying the great stallion's coat. Blade was as strong, as unconquerable, as unchanging as the land. But she no longer feared the land, and she no longer feared the life he represented. She wasn't the narrow-minded scholar he'd met that first day at Fort Leavenworth. With his help she'd survived. No, she wasn't afraid of the wilderness and all its challenges.

She gloried in it.

The thought of returning to Cambridge and a lifetime spent within the confines of a stuffy classroom was as absurd as her foolish idea that Martin Van Vliet was more suited for her as a husband than the man who had not only saved her life but also taught her how to live it to the fullest. She smiled tenderly. When she reached civilization, she would write Martin a letter, telling him of her marriage. She hoped he'd understand. For she'd never give Blade up.

She looked at the tall, dark-haired man who belonged to her now. If she searched the earth's seven continents, from the highest peaks of the Himalayas to the jungles of the Amazon, she would never find another human being so perfectly made for her. At last she understood the meaning of the name he'd given her in the Cheyenne village: *Meatozhessomaheo*. He was truly her gift from God.

She moved her gaze once again to the blue sky that encircled the snowy valley like an azure dome. The peace of the afternoon filled her soul, and suddenly she felt Tom's presence beside her. She could hear his carefree voice. *Be happy, Sis. Live your life to the fullest, and I will live through you and your children.*

That night, as she lay sated in her husband's arms beneath the thick fur robes, Theodora languorously wove her fingertips through the mat of hair on his chest. The glow of their lovemaking still shimmered within her, and her voice was husky with the embers of passion. "I hope you brought some gold with you, *nahyam*," she teased, "for you promised to take me shopping once we reached the Pacific coast."

"I did?" Blade pulled her closer and gently kissed her temple. He chuckled softly as he slid his hand across her stomach and down one thigh. "I don't recall saying anything of the kind."

"Oh, but you did!" she assured him. "Back at Fort Leavenworth you said you'd purchase some new gowns for me when we reached California. And there's one dress in particular that I'm planning to buy."

With the self-satisfaction of a new bridegroom, Blade smiled indulgently, his strong fingers roving over her bare skin. "And what's that, princess? Something in velvet, I hope. Shockingly low and indecently seductive."

"No, the dress I want will be quite proper, actually. It'll be made of the finest Spanish lace, with rows and rows of deep ruffles over a full, hooped skirt. The bodice will be lace over satin, with puffed short sleeves and a scooped neckline trimmed with a wide satin ribbon.'' She sighed dreamily, then continued with added emphasis. "White lace over white satin.''

Blade's fingers stilled. He propped himself up on one elbow and gazed down at her in surprise. "That sounds suspiciously like a wedding dress to me.''

Laughing, Theodora gently traced his raven brows. "Well, you did say we'd have a white man's ceremony as soon as you found a clergyman. Naturally, if I'm going to get married, I want a gown suitable for the occasion.'' Her eyelashes fluttered shyly. "Unless you've changed your mind.''

His answer was the deepest, longest, most passionate kiss Theodora had ever experienced. At last, he pulled back, leaving her breathless, his jet-black eyes glittering with joy and triumph. "What made *you* change your mind?'' he asked, his voice thick with emotion.

"Remember when you told me that I'd walked in your soul? That I belonged to you, just as you belonged to me?'' She slid her hands up his biceps and across his broad shoulders, feeling the muscles ripple in response to her light touch, and met his unwavering gaze. "I didn't understand what you meant at the time, Blade. I do now. All my life I've been searching for something. I used to think that fulfillment would come when I succeeded as a naturalist, but that didn't happen. Then suddenly the answer came in a flash of understanding. All this time I've been looking for my own counterpart, the other half of my female self. It's as though our two spirits have blended into one whole.'' She looked up at him with a rueful half-smile, afraid he wouldn't understand, afraid he'd laugh at her fanciful imagery.

"Theodora, in your roundabout way are you trying to tell me that you love me?''

She burst out laughing. "Yes! I love you, Blade Stalker Roberts. We belong together, for the rest of our lives. Do I sound crazy?''

"As a matter of fact, you sound as though you were raised Cheyenne. I never dreamed a *vehoka* would show such promise as a pupil.'' He bent his head and traced a circle with his tongue around the rosy peak of her breast. "I'll explain my people's spiritual beliefs later,'' he murmured. "Right now I propose to teach you about more earthly delights.''

Theodora arched against him and purred with enchanted pleasure at his sensuous touch. He entered her, and she reached up to frame his face with her hands, her thumbnails brushing the thick mustache, her fingertips buried in the full beard. As their bodies melded together, she felt their very selves commingle. ''I love you, my husband,'' she whispered, fearlessly meeting his possessive gaze. ''And I shall never let you go.''

''How shall I ever describe in my journal all the wonders I've seen?'' Theodora asked her husband. ''So much has been larger than life.''

They stood facing the Pacific Ocean, watching the waves roll in on the shore. Blade held her against him, his arms around her waist. ''And what have you written about me lately in that infamous diary you keep?'' he goaded. ''All our secret conversations in the middle of the night?''

Giggling, she laid her head on his shoulder and looked up at him. ''I'm afraid that wouldn't come under the heading of flora and fauna of the unexplored wilderness. I want to have my work published under the auspices of the Massachusetts Linnean Society, not banned by it.''

Blade laughed and squeezed her against him. ''Don't worry about pleasing that committee of old stick-in-the-muds. You just think about keeping your husband happy.''

''And are you happy, *nahyam*?''

He slid his hands up to cup her breasts, and Theodora felt the longing his touch always brought. ''I've never been so happy.''

A wave rolled near their feet and they both jumped back.

''Let's go barefoot,'' he suggested. He released her and she sat down in the sand.

''I just put these shoes on,'' she complained in mock protest, as she tossed her long braid over her shoulder. ''I haven't worn shoes or a dress in over a month. Now you want to undress me.''

He grinned lecherously as he slipped off one of her shoes and rolled her garter and stocking down her leg. ''Don't worry,'' he said with an overt leer. ''I'll help you put them back on again.'' When he'd finished removing her other shoe and stocking, he kicked off his own moccasins and pulled her to her feet. "Come on, let's see how cold the Pacific is."

Catching her full skirt and petticoat in her hand, Theodora ran beside him to the water's edge. The feel of the cool, wet sand between her toes was wonderful. When the first wave came crashing up, she turned with a shout and raced back to safety. Blade stood his ground and the water splashed against his buckskin trousers.

"Come on. It's not too cold," he called to her as he stripped off his breeches, shirt, and breechclout and tossed them onto the shore. "Take off your dress and petticoat and come back in."

Theodora pulled off her dress and approached hesitantly. Attired in her camisole and pantaloons, she reached out and grabbed Blade's hand. The next wave caught her off guard, soaking her legs. She screamed and laughed. "Let me go! It's freezing!"

Another wave crashed against them. This time she jumped up in a vain attempt to avoid it. Instead, she was knocked to her bottom and the water came up to her shoulders. Sputtering and shivering, she allowed Blade to pull her up.

Her teeth chattered. "I'll be ready for it next time," she promised in delight. The next wave came in high, rolling over itself. They were both immersed in the salty water. The exhilaration of the pounding surf was contagious, and when they looked at each other, soaking wet, they laughed out loud with the sheer joy of it.

As the wave receded, Blade pulled her to him. He kissed her passionately. A wave splashed against their legs and sprayed them with foam. "You're right. It is too cold. Let's get these wet clothes off of you," he said. "We can hang them on the branches of those bushes over there and let them dry in the sun."

"What about the others?" Theodora asked, jumping to avoid the next wave.

"No one will bother us. I left word with Haintzelman that we wanted some privacy for a change."

"Whatever will they think?" she asked, shocked at his openness.

He chuckled. "They'll think you're young and I'm in love."

Another wave rolled in, swamping them up to their shoulders. As it receded, Theodora looked over at the grove of trees near the edge of the sand. The shady bower seemed to beckon her. She gazed into his eyes, glowing with desire. "Well, I really should get out of these wet underclothes and let them dry before we go back to camp."

They stopped to pick up their clothes, then tore across the warm sand together. In the shelter of the oaks, they turned into each other's arms. Theodora cupped his bearded face in her hands. He bent his head and kissed her with lingering deliberation.

"My sweet little wife," he whispered against her lips.

They stood facing each other, only inches apart. He spanned her waist with his hands. She ran her fingertips up his muscled arms and across his powerful shoulders. Leaning back, she looked into his heavy-lidded eyes, burning with passion. "Do you love me, *nahyam*?" she asked, her voice husky in her need for him.

"*Hehe, nazheem. Nimehotaz.*"

"Then show me. Show me how much you love me."

He lifted her in his arms and laid her gently on the bed of soft leaves, where he slowly removed her wet undergarments. With infinite care, he aroused her, bringing her with him to an all-consuming crescendo. She was aware of nothing but his strong, skilled hands upon her. He played her body like a lover's flute, and her responses were the haunting melody she'd heard coming from a clearing beside a Cheyenne village on the warm evening breeze.

Epilogue

September 15, 1837
The White House
Washington, D.C.

Tingling with excitement, Theodora Roberts glanced around the Diplomatic Reception Room, filled with over a hundred guests. The buzz of conversation hummed in the room like a massive hive of bees on a warm autumn evening.

Amid the press of congressmen, cabinet members, and journalists stood the members of the U.S. Army's Exploring Expedition. Haintzelman, O'Fallon, Overbury, and Belknap, dressed in their impeccable cavalry uniforms, visited with the elite of Washington society.

Not to be outdone by the soldiers, Chardonnais and Guion, their dark beards meticulously trimmed and combed, were attired in black tailcoats with silk lapels and trousers decorated with braided side seams. Several buxom matrons who wanted to show off their schoolgirl French had cornered the two voyageurs on a spindly-legged settee and chattered away, barely pausing for breath. Though they were held as virtual hostages, the two Canadians grinned irrepressibly, flattered to be the objects of any female attention.

Theodora's father and Lieutenant Colonel Stephen Watts Kearny stood beside her. Across from them was her husband engaged in polite conversation with Grandmother Hannah, dressed in her somber Quaker garb, and a beautifully gowned Mary Kearny.

Blade was resplendent in full dress uniform, the gold braid, epaulets, and brass buttons a bright slash of color against the deep blue of his tunic. A dress sword hung from his side, belted over the orange, tasseled sash. His straight black hair was now trimmed to above his collar. His beard was gone, but the thick mustache remained. And the gold earring still winked impudently in the candlelight.

As though feeling her eyes upon him, he looked over at Theodora and smiled tenderly. Above the stiff gold collar, his face was deeply bronzed from the sun, and his midnight eyes flashed like black jets in the light of the crystal chandelier. He was breathtakingly handsome. His bold gaze roamed in blatant appreciation over the rose velvet gown he'd chosen for her to wear that night, with its full puffed sleeves and yards of hooped skirt.

As they'd dressed together earlier that evening, he'd assured her that the scooped decolletage wasn't scandalous, for after months of wearing her buckskins, she felt half-naked in the low-cut evening gown. With husbandly attention he had even helped arrange, in the blond curls piled high on her head, the diamond-encrusted combs he'd given her as a wedding gift. Since their arrival in Washington, Blade had showered her with presents. She dropped her eyes briefly to the ring on her finger, sparkling with diamonds and sapphires, only to lift her lids and meet his searing gaze once more.

"I understand your journal will be published sometime next year, Mrs. Roberts," Colonel Kearny said to her, interrupting the couple's frank perusal of each other. "Your family must be very proud of you."

"Indeed, we are, Colonel," Charles Gordon agreed. "My daughter has surpassed all our expectations, and I can assure you, they were high to begin with."

"Oh, Papa." Theodora laughed. "You'll embarrass me with your boasting. Besides, it's your hard work classifying and categorizing the botanical specimens I've brought back that will make the journal possible."

Her father shook his gray head. "But you were the one who found them, Teddy. You just keep sending me your discoveries from the wilderness, and I'll be happy to do the tedious, but safe work of cataloguing them."

Theodora looked with love at the slight, scholarly man, attired in formal evening clothes, who beamed at her so proudly. He'd accepted her marriage to a French-Cheyenne topographical engineer with amazing aplomb. From the minute he'd met Blade he'd treated him as a beloved son, and she suspected that the terrible loss of her twin brother was somehow eased by this new, vibrantly masculine addition to the Gordon family.

Twiggs and Conyers, still attired in the soft, fringed buckskins of the mountain men, joined their group. His cocoa-colored eyes glowing with enjoyment, Julius smiled at her. "One fine day, Miss Theo," he told her fondly. "Old Twiggs mighty proud."

"Tarnation, pun'kin, if'n this ain't the dog-gondest place I've ever seen," Zeke added as he looked up at the ornate ceiling. "Never thought in all my born days I'd be hobnobbin' with the president hisself."

At a signal from the soldier on duty in the hall, the noise faded, and the guests took their places in the chairs that had been arranged in precise rows across the oval carpet. All eyes turned to the doorway through which President Martin Van Buren entered and walked to the podium at the front of the room.

"Ladies and gentlemen," he addressed the audience, "it is with pleasure that we welcome to the Executive Mansion on this delightful September evening the members of the United States Army's Scientific Exploring Expedition. And a special privilege to have the opportunity to honor the expedition's commanding officer, Major Blade Roberts.

"The astounding amount of information this campaign has brought back has truly opened the doors for settlement in the trans-Mississippi west. I believe that our dream that one day this great nation will spread from the rocky shores of the Atlantic to the golden beaches of the Pacific will be a reality, made possible in part by the bravery, the heroism of the soldiers of the First Regiment of Mounted Dragoons and their valiant commander.

"So it is with a great sense of personal humility that I ask Major Roberts to come up and receive this commendation on behalf of all the participants of this extraordinary mission."

At the burst of heartfelt applause, Theodora thought she would never know such joy again. She watched through misty eyes as her husband received the bronze plaque and shook hands with the president. Her heart was bursting with pride for the man who had brought them all safely across countless miles of unmapped prairies, deserts, and mountains.

Van Buren lifted his hand, and everyone in the room quieted once again. "Before I let Major Roberts resume his seat, I want to present another commendation—one that has been kept a secret until this evening. Would you please come up and join your husband, Mrs. Roberts?"

Astounded, Theodora rose and stood before her chair in blank surprise. Her husband's wide, mischievous grin drew her to him, and she moved on shaky legs to the front of the audience, where Blade slipped his hand beneath her elbow, steadying her. She turned to face the crowded room. All of the members of the expedition were beaming at her with unreserved pride.

Van Buren smiled warmly and bowed to her. "It is my great pleasure, Theodora Gordon Roberts, to place in your hands this presidential commendation, awarded to you, and posthumously to your brother, Thomas Algernon Gordon, for the incredible wealth of cartography with which this expedition has returned. Through the service both you and your brother have rendered so courageously to this country—at the cost of his life and very nearly your own—thousands of men and women will emigrate into the wilderness in the years ahead, safer and with a smaller loss of life."

Theodora took the heavy plaque, engraved with the presidential seal, in her trembling hands. She looked out on the shining faces before her, astonished to see the audience rise to its feet, applauding in sincere appreciation for her and Tom, and for the achievement of all they'd set out to do.

Shortly afterwards, Theodora and Blade walked upstairs toward the State Dining Room, where a banquet was to be served in their honor. As they reached the center hall, Blade pulled her apart from the other guests. He slipped his arms around her and gently kissed her forehead.

"I told you I'd get a presidential commendation for carting

you across the plains with that God-awful mud smeared all over you," he teased, his black eyes glowing with laughter.

She pursed her lips, struggling to keep from bursting into unsophisticated giggles. Gaily, she reached up and flicked his barbaric gold earring with one fingernail. "Mary Kearny told me that her husband has already given you our next assignment. Where do we travel from here?"

He grinned at her. "How would you like to explore the Arizona Territory with your half-breed husband and map a southern route into California?"

"I'd love it," she exclaimed, and hugged him in delight. As he moved to escort her into the dining room, she tugged on his elbow. "Wait a minute, *nahyam*, before we go in. Your epaulet is all askew."

While he waited patiently, she straightened the gold fringe with wifely care, then met his smoldering gaze with all the love in her heart. Shaking her head at him, she smothered the smile that tugged at the corners of her mouth. "Big Cheyenne warrior much trouble," she told him solemnly, lowering her voice to imitate his baritone. "But worth it."

*If you enjoyed this book, take advantage
of this special offer. Subscribe now and . . .*

GET A *FREE*
HISTORICAL ROMANCE

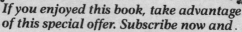

— NO OBLIGATION(a $3.95 value) —

Each month the editors of True Value will select the four best historical romance novels from America's leading publishers. Preview them in your home Free for 10 days. And we'll send you a FREE book as our introductory gift. No obligation. If for any reason you decide not to keep them, just return them and owe nothing. But if you like them you'll pay *just* $3.50 each and save at least $.45 each off the cover price. (Your savings are a minimum of $1.80 a month.) There is no shipping and handling or other hidden charges. There are no minimum number of books to buy and you may cancel at any time.

send in the coupon below